# Legacy of the Pink Victorian

A Pacific Northwest Family Saga

**Peg Lewis**

Cover designed by Best Page Forward

Edited by Amanda K. Lewis



Peg Lewis, author

www.amazon.com/author/peglewis Printed in the United States of America

First Printing: February 2021

San Juan Publishing ISBN-9798796495223

Retitled 12/26/21 from the original: *That Old Pink Victorian On Main Street*

## Contents

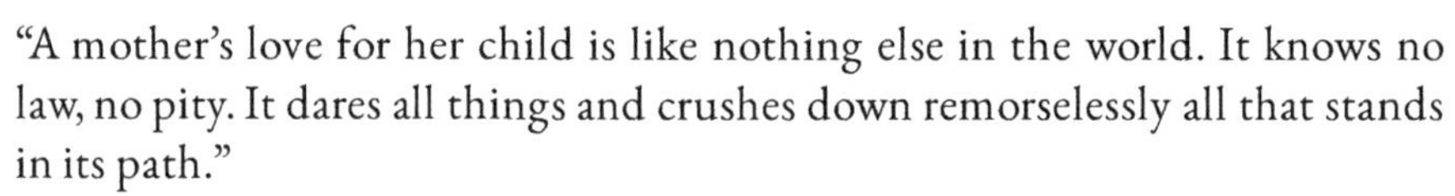

"A mother's love for her child is like nothing else in the world. It knows no law, no pity. It dares all things and crushes down remorselessly all that stands in its path."

—Agatha Christie

This story is dedicated to my mother, Ruth Clark Horan Adams (1911-1999), teacher and librarian.

## LATE SEPTEMBER 1985

IT'S DARK SO EARLY, and the rains won't stop for months. Such a bleak time of year. I can barely remember what it's like not to have it rain every day.

And even with this incessant rain, that pathetic child walks home from school every day. She must be soaked through when she gets home. But then, why doesn't she hurry in? Why does she go to the garden first?

Why doesn't her mother, if that's her mother, greet her at the door?

Well, none of my business. They can't see me here, wouldn't even think to look for me, here in my upstairs window.

And I can barely see the child now. The streetlamps down the block, even the glow from the grocery blocks away, are brighter than their backyard. Our backyard.

You'd think she'd grab a flashlight.

And now the bang of a door. The henhouse, as always. She's put away those few pathetic hens and ... what? In the summer I could see her feeding them with scraps from the garden before locking them in. But that was late in the evening when the summer twilight had finally faded.

Maybe she finds a few scraps even this late in the season. It's too dark for me to tell.

In the summer, she'd be collecting eggs.

She'd wanted more hens but we said no. And we prevented her from ruining our peace and quiet with a rooster. It is hard to forget how disappointed she'd looked when I said no to a rooster. Can you imagine! It's not supposed to be a barnyard, after all.

And then, the impertinent waif had muttered, 'protects the hens' or some such. Sassy brat!

And her mother, busy just inside their open door, said not a single word of rebuke to her.

Well, we have our agreement and they well know that even the chickens are a stretch. They must keep to themselves, to their garden. What a fool of a husband I have who allowed them to continue to live in the caretaker shed, let alone use part of the garden as their own.

He is not happy that he said yes, either, but he didn't stand up to their tale of woe. So what if they'd lived in that shack for years? So what if this house had been in their family in the past? So what if the mother had lived in this house when she was a small child? We paid a good price for this house, this land—too good a price if you ask me, but of course Jack didn't ask me—and we're going to get our value out of it if I have my way.

It was supposed to be a good investment, a worthy fixer upper. It supposedly had 'good bones.' But every contractor Jack brought by made outrageously high bids, and the work that needed to be done was far greater than we'd thought when we bought it. Granted, bought it for a song, but still not something that would pay off. And now we are stuck. I kept telling Jack, we could be comfier in a retirement place and for less per month. But he won't hear of it.

Who cares that this old house was built by the waif's grandfather or great-grandfather? That doesn't make it hers. No more than my father's fishing boat is mine today.

Thank heavens.

And what does she want with any of it, the pathetic child? What does she do out there? When will she go in, so I can stop keeping an eye on her?

That shack must be unbearably dark. It has only that one window, facing the alley, and I have seen only a hint of light coming from it. The story I heard was there was once an old caretaker, years ago. They say this was a lovely estate at one time. Maybe before electricity. Maybe before plumbing, even.

That shed next to the henhouse could have been the caretaker's outhouse back in the day. I'm surprised they have plumbing in the cottage, but they must. They don't use the shed as an outhouse, certainly.

The question is, if it was an outhouse, why is it locked?

Yes, I've walked around out there. When they weren't home, either of them. And that old shed is most interesting. It has four locks, combination locks.

So it's no longer an outhouse. But what's inside it that would need four locks for protection?

Jack says that the shed is part of our property. So I've been keeping my eye on it. If one of them makes a move to open it, I'll be right there, just in case there's something of value inside. Because whatever is in there is ours.

I've lingered here at the window far longer than usual tonight. In the summer it was easy to see what the child was up to, tending vegetables, planting or weeding, digging or whatever. By the hour. Alone now, but until a few years ago with an older woman, maybe her grandmother. Who disappeared, died no doubt.

Today the child has gone to school, come home, dumped her backpack at the door, and gone straight to the garden.

For all the years we've lived here, close to twenty by now, that little girl's grandmother and mother lived in that cottage, the mother going out to work until the baby was born, at least. Where the baby came from, I have no idea. Not that I'd been all that friendly with Isabelle, the grandmother, but we did speak from time to time. Isabelle sometimes wandered around the yard, as well as gardened. I was out looking at the rosebuds, pleased to see that something worthwhile grew in that tangle of a backyard, when I heard some sound or another and looked up, and there she was.

She looked at me with some sober expression, then turned and walked away. I think she thought of the yard as hers, and she certainly didn't ask permission when it came to what she planted and where.

I usually hid myself behind the tall weeds that grew between our house and her garden to avoid saying anything to her, but that day I had somehow not seen her in time.

After a few such encounters, we began to exchange words, and if she was ever disgruntled at having that baby show up, having an extra mouth to feed, she never said so. Nor did she seem to rejoice in it.

What I did know about Isabelle, besides her name, was that she was one to come and go of an evening, often returning late, or perhaps not till morning. While that other one, her daughter, stayed home. Except for work.

So where the baby came from was hard to say. Isabelle was perhaps the more likely mother, other than the fact that by the time we moved in she was perhaps 55 years old and the baby wasn't born for years after that.

I also bumped into the child herself once. She never showed any further interest in me. So she has never even looked this way to see me watching her from my upstairs window.

Tonight, though, I think she might have been peeking at me from time to time as she made her way along the rows in her garden. Finally, she turned toward her little shack, her arms full of vegetables. She dunked them into a waiting bucket—she always did this—and after pulling them out clean and dripping, let herself in the door.

A tiny light received her. So dim it could have been a candle. Then she was gone. I went to make supper.

## THE LAST FRIDAY IN SEPTEMBER 1985

"HI, LILY, WHAT DID you find?"

"Carrots and potatoes," said Lily. "And onions, but they need drying. I'm leaving the beets for the market. They're so pretty."

"It's getting dark so early, I'm surprised you can see enough to tell which ones are ready to pick."

"Oh, I mark them with a stick when I let the chickens out in the morning."

"Smart. OK, get changed into something cozy. I'll add to the fire."

Lily watched Katherine scrub and scrape the vegetables and add them to the pot. The little room had warmed to a coziness but it took Lily several minutes standing in front of the wood stove to get the dampness out of her little being. Then she gathered the veggie scrapings into a pan and set it by the door.

"That lady who lives in your house watches me from the upstairs window, Ma," said Lily.

"You can see her?"

"Depends on the lighting, but I think she does it a lot. She did in the summer."

"Whyever, do you suppose?"

"I don't know. To make sure I put the chickens away?"

"I think she's not too happy we're living back here."

"Why?"

"I don't know, she might think she needs this cottage and the rest of it."

"But look at all the space she has! That house is huge! How many bedrooms does it have?"

"Four, as I recall. It looks like more, but the way the roof bends and slopes, there's no room to stand up for a good part of the upstairs. Anyway, what about homework? What have you got?"

"Nothing. I did it in school. Can we go to the library?"

"What about the books we got on Saturday?"

"I finished them. Did you finish yours?"

"Well, yes, I did."

"So let's go. It's open tonight."

"Right. But only till seven, Friday night."

Lily nodded. She was finishing her stew, wiping the bowl with bread. "I'm warmed up enough, Ma. Let's go."

"OK, but get enough this time."

"It's raining too hard to pull the wagon."

"True. But it's likely to keep raining till next summer, so fill up your backpack. I'll help you carry it if you can't make it home."

The library was beyond the school by several blocks: from their house a short block to the busy street, another long block to the center of town, a few blocks to the right, four more blocks up a small hill and down again, and there the library stood before them, greeting them with bright light streaming through narrow windows. Narrow windows with long stacks visible on each side, extending enticingly deep into the library.

They had been rained on since leaving home. They had shared an umbrella, but they also had their hoods up. The rain was blowing in from the west, so it was right in their faces for most of the walk. Streetlights reflected off puddles, and cars turning at the various side streets had splashed water on them. They had walked speedily along, well-practiced, and Lily had had to shift her backpack full of returns from side to side only a few times to relieve her shoulders. Same with Mom.

"No one's out tonight, Ma. Do people stop reading in the winter just because it's raining?"

"I'd be surprised if we saw many people out walking again till next summer."

And it was true. No one else was out on the streets. They were two shadowy figures, alone on the road aside from the cars. Rush hour was almost over, with its splashes and bright headlights that sometimes caught Lily in the eyes.

And the parking lot at the library had only a single car.

But the library was warm and cheerful. Also empty. They went their separate ways as always. "Meet you back here at 6:45," said Katherine.

Lily knew where the chapter books were in the children's section and picked out the next four in her favorite series, then added a few animal picture books. Her backpack was full, heavy. She dragged it across the floor to the librarian's desk.

Lily didn't have her own library card yet. But at nine she thought she'd try again so she could get books when Mom wasn't with her, such as after school. So when she laid her stack of books on the front desk, she asked.

"I'd like my own library card," she said.

She was familiar with the librarian on duty tonight. She wasn't as stern as some. She smiled. Her name tag said, 'Miss Horan.' After a long moment, she nodded. "As long as you can fill out the form, you can have your own card. Do you think you can do that?"

Lily nodded. She looked at it. Name, address. That was all.

Her name was of course easy, while her address would have been a problem if her mom hadn't come up with a solution: 1 ½ Main Street. No one had questioned them yet.

Grandpa's house, the big house up front, was 1 Main Street. So that made their little cottage in the back 1 ½, Mom had reasoned.

The only problem was that maybe no one was supposed to live there. Katherine had told Lily more than once, "Don't ever tell where we live."

Lily had asked why, and Katherine had just shaken her head. And Lily had known enough not to press her on it. She was nine now, and she knew better than to make her mom upset.

Miss Horan looked at her printing on the card. "Now can you sign it?" she asked.

Lily had to think about what signing it might be. She had written her name. And wasn't that the same as signing it? So she wrote her name all over again on the last line.

Miss Horan looked at it for a bit, then smiled. "That's very nice," she said.

When Mom came up, Lily showed her her new card, then put it on her stack of books, just like Mom did with her card.

The two piles were enormous, too big. There was no way they could carry them all home. Ten books each was about five too many.

Katherine spoke very quietly to Lily: "We're going to have to put some back," she said.

Miss Horan said, "You could put some on hold and pick them up tomorrow."

"I can come after school tomorrow," said Lily. "And maybe I can pick up yours and mine both, if we take the heaviest ones now."

They could hear the rain on the skylight, pouring harder than ever. All three of them looked up as the pounding of the raindrops increased.

"We'll get these backpacks completely under our raincoats," Mom said. They smiled at Miss Horan and headed for the door.

"If you can wait fifteen minutes while I close up," Miss Horan said, "I can give you a ride home." She was looking at the card Lily had filled out. "It's a bit of a long walk."

"No, thank you. We'll be fine," said Mom.

Lily wanted to say that with a ride they could take all the books. She looked at the stack they had left behind. Then she looked at her mother. Her face was shut down. It looked the same as it had on all the occasions when she'd told Lily firmly, strongly, that they didn't need anyone's help.

Lily was hanging back a bit. She wasn't being disobedient, just slow to give up the offer of a ride on a night when there was no way to avoid getting soaked on the way home. But she didn't want to upset Katherine.

"Come, Lily," her mother said sternly.

They stepped out into the deluge. It was only rain, after all, as Mom often said. Mom put up the umbrella, but the wind from the west was strong and threatened to tear it from her hands. She put it down again. Then as they turned eastward toward home, Lily could feel the wind pushing them along from behind, speeding them up. The traffic was almost non-existent, leaving the streets dark, the shadows deep, the puddles invisible.

The runoff was loud, strong, racing downhill to storm drains. In the storm drains Lily could hear the rush of water as pipes carried it away.

"Where is it going?" Lily wondered. "To the sea, I think."

It was impossible to avoid the water coursing down the streets. Their steps made splashes that filled their boots.

"We're invisible," said Katherine.

"What?" Lily wasn't sure she'd heard.

"We're invisible in the dark. Be careful. Of cars."

Lily looked around. The town was shut down. They crossed the business district without seeing a car. They hurried along, caught at times in swirling wind but mostly pushed along by the wind at their backs.

"I love this, Mommy," said Lily.

Katherine turned toward her with a grim look. Lily thought she said, "I don't."

## THE LAST SATURDAY IN SEPTEMBER 1985

BY THE TIME THEY got home, after fifteen minutes or so of being swept along by what was clearly a winter storm, Lily was thinking longingly of getting into her pajamas and huddling in front of the woodstove. And reading. And talking to Katherine.

It wasn't too late.

But then she remembered it was Friday. The next day was farmers market. They would need to be up before dawn to harvest more veggies and collect the eggs. Then they would need to scrub clean every carrot, every beet, every potato.

"Natural is great," Katherine had told her more than once. "But no one wants to buy veggies so natural that they're still covered with dirt."

"And I don't want to give away the dirt from the garden," said Lily. "It's precious."

In the morning it would take them an hour just to get ready for the market, and then there was the setting up and laying it all out so it was attractive. And managing to look neat and tidy themselves. And that was after walking over to the market.

And it might still be raining. And then only a few customers would show up. And if the wind were still blowing, they would have fewer customers and the added challenge of keeping their large umbrella, usually used to keep the sun off their displays, from blowing over or their tablecloth from catching the wind.

Fortunately, the market was only several blocks down toward the old railway depot and the harbor beyond. Grandfather (or was it Great-Grandfather?) had built the depot. It was no longer used for railway passengers, so it had been made over into an art gallery and studio with space for parties and even small productions. No veggies were allowed in the new depot.

But it had a lovely plaza around it, where rail passengers had once collected. Later the plaza had been adapted for use as a farmers market for local farmers and their customers, such as townspeople, tourists, or even sailors in port for the day. In the summer.

But fall was progressing, the veggies were abundant and ready for harvest, famous for their flavor because of the maritime climate and long season where they were grown. The frost would come soon enough, in another month or maybe two, and put an end to it all. The ever-popular eggs from grass-and-veggie fed chickens had already dwindled to nearly zero, though, as the hens responded to the much shorter days. Lily could have sold dozens of her super-fresh, golden-yolked eggs, but this time of year she had only one precious dozen left to sell.

Eggs were tricky. They were hard to carry over to the market, however close it was, unless she could use her little red wagon. And that depended on whether there was so much rain that it would fill up the wagon and ruin the egg boxes.

These were Lily's thoughts as they walked the remaining blocks from the library. No reading tonight. It was harvest time. Either now or in the morning, before the sun was up.

So as they walked in the door, Lily and Katherine looked at each other and said, "Farmers market!"

"Let's do it now. We can leave them out to keep cool and hydrated."

Mom agreed. Lily was glad for Mom's help, even though Mom didn't like to get dirty in the garden. Lily knew the story: Grandma Isabelle had given up on getting her daughter, young Katherine, involved in growing their own food, but Katherine's baby Lily had loved it all and had worked at Grandma Isabelle's side from babyhood. And then she had continued to grow their favorites even after Grandma Isabelle died, when Lily was six.

After the harvest and all the other preparation, they would go straight to bed. No reading the precious new books. Just finding their outfits that made them look like well-scrubbed farmer-girls and making sure they were ironed. Laying out the backpacks to be filled with produce in the morning. And tonight bringing in the little red wagon so it would be dry in the morning and could be loaded with more clean veggies.

Her grandmother had told her the real way to say the word was vegetables. But she liked to say 'veggies.' It made people at the farmers market laugh. And now, a few years later, she heard other people say 'veggies' when they meant vegetables. Maybe she had invented a new word!

Anyway, Lily thought, there would be enough veggies to fill her toy wagon to overflowing. But this might be the last time the harvest would be that robust.

But what if in the morning it was still raining? That would mean perhaps not as many people at the market, and a diminished number of visitors meant to Lily that perhaps she should harvest fewer vegetables. Once pulled, they would lose their freshness quickly and then would not be available next week if the sun should be shining again.

And if it turned out she took fewer and then didn't have enough, if the veggies sold quickly, she could leave Mom at the market to keep selling them and hurry home and harvest more.

Better not to waste the veggies. So Lily harvested half the usual number. If bright sunshine awakened her in the morning, she would get up and harvest more. Better that than to waste them. They had a long winter to get through, and it was always a question of whether to sell or to eat. Waste had no role in their way of life.

Soon, when the rains came reliably every day, there would be no market at all, and no income. Unless she could figure out some other way to contribute cash to their little family of two.

This thought was so new, so astounding, that she stopped pulling carrots and looked off into space. Why hadn't she thought of it before, that she could earn in some other way?

Simple. She was nine years old. There was nothing else she could do.

Just the farmers market.

Just veggies. Just a few eggs. And no more eggs than those three hens could lay, because the lady in the big house had said no. No to eggs, to all eggs, but Mom had told Lily that they had always had chickens and to tell the woman they were grandfathered at three hens.

Lily had never heard of something being grandfathered, but she figured it meant that something was true when her grandfather was alive.

Lily knew how hard it was for her mom to speak up like that herself, but she enjoyed explaining such things to the disagreeable woman.

And when she did it, that woman had turned, stalked away, and never mentioned it again.

Lily had room for more layers in the henhouse, but she wasn't allowed to have them. And that was that. Though she didn't understand why the woman from the big house could tell her what she could and couldn't have in her henhouse. She understood about the rooster. Not everyone wants to wake up as early in the morning as a rooster does. But hens? They were busy laying their eggs at that hour and were no bother at all.

Lily guessed the hen house had once held a dozen hens. And how many eggs might that be?

So while eggs would be easy to sell and could bring in a little cash even over the winter, they were off the list.

And as winter approached and the farmers market was ending, her list was growing emptier. She'd still have veggies, but no one wanted to shop outdoors, such as at the farmers market, in the rain.

And that sad fact left her searching for how she might make some money.

These thoughts had left her restless in the night, and now, waking to the sound of rain on the roof and heavy gray clouds overhead, she was glad she had not harvested more beets and carrots. They bundled up in sweaters and raincoats and headed out.

They set up their booth in the usual spot under the huge umbrella they stored at the depot. The day had partially cleared, with rays of liquid sun, the kind that has no strength. Lily could see customers who typically lingered every Saturday and socialized and listened to the music, and even had lunch at the picnic tables, now hurry past each booth, and then, huddled against the persistent wind, dash to their cars. It would be a day of not many sales, and chances were, the managers of the market would close it down for the season at day's end.

What would be the point of keeping it open if the season wasn't going to cooperate?

Still, their regular customers did come by. They didn't stay to chat, but they did buy all the veggies. Lily and Mom decided not to harvest more. The storm was picking up and they didn't feel they could hope for more customers in the blustery wind and intermittent rain. By midday they had only scraps of greens to sweep up, the tablecloth to put away, and the parts of the booth to fold and furl and store away. Lily and Katherine did an extra-careful job of tidying up, as if it were the final Saturday of the season.

When they were done, they bought a little wheel of cheese from the cheese ladies and shared it. And they bought a loaf of homemade bread, their weekly treat. There might not be more until Spring.

Then came heavier rain. The morning drizzle, fine, not bothersome, now turning to real rain, drove them briefly into the depot. There were the usual pieces of fine art by local artists or local amateurs from any of a dozen surrounding towns. And colorful knit pieces and embroidery were displayed on set-up tables.

Lily had once fallen in love with a set of towels with horses hand-embroidered on them. But Katherine had showed her how carelessly they'd been stitched. From then on Lily checked front and back of each piece. And she soon realized these were not the sort of thing she could make and sell for money. However sloppy her mother thought these were, her own efforts would be worse. By the time they left the depot, Lily had decided that she could not do anything but raise veggies and eggs, and not nearly enough eggs to make a difference. It would take her too long to learn the necessary skills. And then each design would take a long time to stitch. She needed something like carrots that grew themselves, or eggs that showed up each morning. Or maybe a railroad where people bought tickets to go places and ... well, how did a railroad work? She didn't know. But her grandfather John S. Steele had known. And maybe there was a book in the library about how a railroad made money.

## THE FIRST WEEK IN OCTOBER 1985

KATHERINE WORKED AT THE nursing home eight blocks south. She could walk there in ten minutes. She put her hair in a net and rubber gloves on her hands and cleaned bathrooms all day. "It suits me, Lily," she said. "No one thinks to talk to me."

Lily loved to watch the pile of paper money, tens and twenties, grow in their breadbox. Katherine had devised the hiding place back when they settled, after Isabelle's death, into their own lifestyle in the cottage. Katherine got a job, something her mother, Isabelle, had frowned on, as soon as her mother died. When she brought home her first paycheck from the nursing home, she walked to the bank, converting the check to bills of various denominations and some odd change. Since that time Lily and Katherine both had added to the pile of money, and they rarely took anything to spend, except for food. The pile grew and they kept track and rejoiced together in its growth.

The cottage had one room with a bathroom built into one corner, an apparent addition to the original cottage. They had running water and electricity. Katherine had spent a quarter inch of bills to buy them a new mattress and bed frame. She also bought a sheet, a couple of blankets, and some kitchen things. Their clothes came from the various thrift stores. Katherine was determined to make the stack of money grow. It was not that they were poor. Lily had no idea how much money was in the breadbox, she just knew that there was nothing worth buying with it compared with the value of watching it grow taller.

And Lily wanted it to grow taller faster.

Sometimes her mother was gone for hours and came home with a thick stack of bills.

And that's what she wanted to do, find a way to bring home stacks of bills.

When Lily questioned her about how she'd gotten them, she'd say, "It's just something someone owed me," and that's all.

All night after the farmers market, Lily tossed and turned trying to work out what she could do to bring home such stacks. Or any-sized stacks. But every idea in the end came down to growing and selling veggies.

And when you put it like that, the answer was obvious.

By morning she knew: She would continue selling veggies even though the market was closing. And since it was closing, she would do it door to door.

Starting, she thought, with the lady in the big house. Or maybe Miss Horan at the library. And Miss Clark, her teacher at school. Probably these busy people wouldn't have time to grow their own.

So she told her mother.

Who said, absolutely not. "Absolutely not, Lily," she said. "You don't want to be out in public selling stuff. It's ... " she said, but she didn't seem to be able to think of the word for it.

"It's unseemly," she finally said.

But Lily didn't know what unseemly meant.

"We have enough money," her mother said. "Especially if I keep my job. I just have to work a little harder and faster than everyone else so I can keep it."

"And now that you're older and can take care of yourself, I can get more hours at the nursing home," she said. "That will make the pile grow faster."

Lily was thinking that if her mother was gone more, what difference would it make if she herself was home or not? It wouldn't be any fun to be at home when Mom wasn't there. Maybe she could get a janitor job at school so she was gone the whole time Mom was gone.

"I don't want you to be gone," she said.

"But now that you're in school, I might as well work. And build our pile of money."

"What's it for?"

"Just in case."

"I don't care about just in case. I care about being with you."

"We'll still be together at home," said Katherine.

"Home can be anywhere at all, as long as we're together," said Lily. "I don't even like being here unless you're here too."

"So you're happy going to school? Because I'm going to go take you out if you're not. I don't like them telling me you have to go."

"I really like it. I learn a lot."

"Yeah, but what do you learn?"

"Math. Science."

"Reading? Writing?"

"I already know those."

"Right. Which is why I think if you want to stay home, you should. Even if I'm not here. Because of work."

"I want to go, Ma," said Lily. "Please don't take me out. I just learned everyone's name. And Miss Clark is really nice."

"Well, we got lucky then."

"Didn't you have any good teachers?"

"I don't remember."

Lily had a pile of old seed packets from Grandma Isabelle. She was sorting through them, reading them all and taking out the ones that said they could be started in the fall. Several of these had names she didn't recognize, including the label, "oriental greens." She could plant the fall seeds now, and maybe Mom would change her mind about her selling them. She couldn't very well start them later if she did change her mind. In fact, it was late already. Only some greens would grow for certain. As certain as a garden ever was. Others should have been planted back in August.

It was a lot of work to get more space in the garden in good enough shape to plant. She had to pull out the debris from whatever planting had been in that part of the garden in the summer, such as vines from squash, or potato greens now withered. But despite all the rain and the resulting mud, she managed to plant several varieties of greens, little rows and patches of them. And then she was done and just needed to wait for them to grow. If she hadn't been too late getting them started.

At least she didn't need to worry about watering them.

And then there was nothing to do. Katherine would be gone till suppertime and beyond. Lily began cooking what she could, boiling carrots, boiling potatoes, baking squash.

She didn't know what to do about meat. So she took a few bills from the ever-growing stack and bought some bones at the store, as Mom had done, and added them to the pot.

Out came overcooked veggies with a tiny bit of meat flavor and a few nibbles of actual meat from the bones. The meat was delicious.

She'd have to see about getting some real meat. Eat as she would, she never felt full.

These days Mom ate at work. After she fed the patients. It was a new job and it paid more.

Lily started staying late at school. She asked Miss Clark, the teacher, if she needed help. She didn't so Lily went home.

The next day she bought some hamburger on the way home.

Mom brought home a nice stack of bills.

Lily had to go to bed only a short time after Mom got home.

Lily liked the paper money pile getting bigger. Mom made a ceremony of it the first time she came home with a big pile of cash from work.

Lily didn't dare tell her about the garden. Some seedlings were now up. They seemed to be growing as fast as lettuce did in the spring.

Maybe if she could sell them, when they were grown enough, Mom wouldn't have to stay so late at the nursing home.

Then Mom had a day off. "What would you like to do after school today?" she asked Lily. "I'm going shopping in the morning, so the afternoon is free."

"I want to stay home and have some cocoa—can you buy some cocoa and milk?—and then you can tell me about when you were my age?"

"There's not much to tell."

"Well, tell me something about when you were nine and went to school. I know you lived in the big house."

"I moved from there when I was seven."

"You did? Why?"

"There's no time now. You need to go to bed. But yes, I'll buy some cocoa and milk and we can talk about when I was your age."

## EARLY OCTOBER 1985

IT WAS RAINING. LILY ran home from school. Mom was just coming back from the grocery store, pulling the bags of groceries in the red wagon. She had them covered with an old blanket. Even so, the paper bags were soaked and had to be thrown out. She pulled the wagon right into the cottage and they hurried to dry everything and stack it all up at the far end of the table up against the wall. Lily put the box of cocoa and quart of milk on the counter next to the stove.

"Let's get changed," said Mom. "I don't think we have to go back out today."

"I hope not," said Lily. She assumed Mom meant they wouldn't have to do some expedition to town. Of course Lily would have to go out and put the chickens away before the hour when foxes might sneak up and eat them. Or raccoons. Or coyotes or stray dogs.

The garden, though, could wait until tomorrow.

So they put on their sweatshirts and old jeans and Mom made cocoa. What a treat! If only they had popcorn. And then Lily saw that Mom had gotten popcorn too.

While it was popping, Lily reminded her. "Mom, about when you were nine, or you can start when you were seven."

"About when I was seven. Well. That was actually a difficult year."

"Why?"

"Just let me think for a few minutes. I'm not sure where to start."

So they had their cocoa and popcorn.

"You know about your Grandmother Isabelle."

"Yes. She taught me how to garden."

"Yes, right. She was my mother. You were six when she died. That wasn't that long ago."

"Didn't she live here with us? I not sure if I remember."

"Yes, most of the time."

"Where did she sleep?"

"You really don't remember, do you. She slept in the bed with me."

"Then where did I sleep?"

"On a little pile of blankets on the floor. At the end of the bed."

"What about your dad?"

Lily knew then that she had made a mistake. Katherine was looking out the window, their one window, and not saying anything.

"I don't know."

Lily knew this was a time to keep her mouth shut. But she was also curious, very very curious, because she also wanted to know about her own dad, and she thought if she could find out about Mom's dad, she might find out about her own.

So she said what she wanted to say.

"You never met him?"

"Not that I remember."

"What about your mom? Didn't she ever tell you about him? Or have him over to your house? Didn't he ever live with you?"

And all the while these were really questions she had about her own dad.

Which Katherine seemed to understand. So instead of answering those questions the way Lily had asked them, she responded as if they were about Lily. And her dad.

"Your dad loves you, Lily."

This was shocking news to Lily. She didn't know her dad knew her. Was he nearby, then? Had she met him?

And then Katherine said, "I'm sure he does."

And Lily let all the air out of her lungs and sank down in her chair and felt some tears start to build. Which she didn't want Mom to see. She tucked her head down, then rotated on her chair so she was turned away and her face was in the dark.

"I know, Lily," said Mom.

Lily didn't know what Mom knew.

Lily found herself being filled with anger.

"Did your dad love you, then?" asked Lily. And regretted letting herself ask that poisonous question. Because she was sure that Katherine didn't know that about her dad.

But Katherine said quietly, "My mom said he did. But I never found out for sure."

Lily was sad. It didn't seem reasonable. Here mom was, getting old, and she hadn't found her dad or learned anything about him.

Or did she know anything?

"Mom. Mom, listen. Do you know anything about your dad?"

"No."

"Your mom never told you who he was, why he wasn't at your house, anything?"

Katherine thought for a while. "Maybe he was a fisherman," she said.

"Is that what your mom told you?"

"I can't remember. I may have made it up. I used to tell myself stories about him. That he was coming. Coming for Christmas. Coming for dinner. Coming to get us to live with him after we had to move out of the big house."

"You had to move out of the big house?"

"Yes. When I was seven. You know that."

"I knew you moved out but maybe I didn't know someone made you move out."

"Yes, someone did. All of a sudden, with no warning. One day we were living there happily enough, me, my Aunt Agnes, and my mom. Then suddenly we were grabbing what we could and moving into the cottage here. Later my mother told me investors bought the house. I think the idea was that they would fix it up and resell it for a profit. That was in 1950. And then that woman in the window and her husband bought it about fifteen years later. In between it was empty. For years, for the rest of my childhood, I remember it being empty.

"Well, the investors never fixed it up. And I didn't understand as a child why if it was empty we couldn't keep living in it. But no one would tell me. And then when the new people bought it, they tried to kick us out. That was in 1965 when Aunt Agnes was very old. But she stopped them even so."

"And then the woman let you stay here?"

"She didn't want us to. Her husband agreed that we could."

"Why?" asked Lily.

"Why did he agree? I don't know. Just that Aunt Agnes made it happen. We got this end of the property and they got the yard and house and so on.

"Hold on. I have to put the chickens in for the night."

So Lily went out to collect the chickens. She had peelings from supper prep with her and an armful of garden waste. The hens were in the hen house, settling in on their roosts for the night. It was already dark and they had put themselves to bed.

Except that the open door was an invitation to night critters and if she'd forgotten to close it, she might find in the morning that they'd been dragged away overnight.

She lay out the food scraps, which would keep them happy in the morning, then returned to the cottage.

Her thoughts were on her father. Why had Mom not told her who he was?

"Mom, tell me about my dad."

"No, Lily, I can't."

"Why? You want to know about your dad. And I want to know about mine."

"I just can't. You wouldn't understand."

"Why wouldn't I?"

Katherine didn't say anything. She had cleared the table and set down a pot of stew and spoons and bowls.

"Come on, Mom," said Lily. "Was he some awful criminal? Was he a bad guy?"

"No, he's smart and good looking."

"Does he know about me?"

"I told you he loves you."

"How can he love me if he doesn't even know me?"

Katherine put down the serving spoon and stood staring at Lily with a hand on her hip. Then she turned back to the task of serving their supper.

"He does know you," she said very quietly, then covered her face with both hands. Lily couldn't tell if she was crying.

Lily was in fact in shock. Her dad knew her. How could that be? Had she ever met him? Didn't he love Katherine? Were they divorced a long time ago?

Katherine wouldn't say anything more. Not a word. Lily asked and asked, but Katherine just shook her head. Lily kept asking until finally Katherine got up from the table and returned with a book for each of them. "Read," she said, and opened her book.

Lily got up and cleared the table and wiped the pot clean with their last piece of bread and drained the last drops out of both cocoa cups, changed into her pajamas, and lay on her side of the bed with her book.

She'd find out about her dad. Or find out why she couldn't find out.

She looked across the room at the lonely figure of her mother at the table. Her book was lying shut on the table beside her. She had covered her face with her hands again, and this time Lily knew she was crying.

Lily called across the room, "Sorry, Mom." And then she added, "I just really want to know. Don't you?"

## AN EARLY OCTOBER SATURDAY 1985

IT WAS SATURDAY. MOM was at work by the time Lily woke up, later than usual. The farmers market had been canceled for the rest of the year. Lily was not sure what she would do, but the idea of a whole day ahead of her was lovely. And ironically, it wasn't even raining. The market would have been fine.

She thought she might try the idea of selling veggies door-to-door. Maybe just a few to start with. Maybe just to the lady at the big house.

That lady hadn't ever really talked to her, except to say no to a rooster, and that was last year.

Lily pulled some carrots. They were long and almost a glowing orange once she got the soil off. How many should she take to the lady? Maybe just two, for her and her husband. These were huge carrots. And then a few potatoes. And an onion. That would be enough to make a meal out of.

She put them all in a basket. If she didn't want them all, she could pick the ones she wanted from the basket. Twenty-five cents each, a dollar for the whole basketful. A real bargain.

She thought about putting in one of her precious eggs, but the lady didn't like the chickens, so she probably wouldn't appreciate the eggs. And maybe she had plenty from the grocery store.

The basket looked pretty. The veggies were lovely in the sunlight. If she was lucky, she wouldn't have anything left to sell after she went to the big house and showed what she had to the lady. And she would come home with $1 to add to the pile.

But how to go there? No one had ever used the back door, the one that faced their cottage.

So there was an unused nearby door, but she might as well go to the front door as anyone wanting to drop something off for the lady of the house would do.

Also there was a gate between the front and back yards of the big house on the left, and a garage on the right, not quite attached, but to get to the opening to the driveway she would have to walk right across the lady's mowed lawn. And maybe the lady wouldn't like that.

She would have to walk around the block instead.

She would go out behind their cottage to the alley she took to school, the one she and Mom took to town, a public place but not paved like a road, just grass with tire tracks in it. If they had a car, this is the way they would come in. Parking it would be tricky because the cottage backed right up to the alley, and if you turned in beside the cottage, the chicken house and the little shed were in the way. But they didn't have a car, and any visitors they had parked out on the street, not in the alley.

So she walked out past the shed—which they called the treasure house, for reasons she didn't know—and past the hen house, then out to the alley. Then right so she could follow the alley to the street, right on the street till she got to the corner of Main Street, then right and past a couple of other old houses until she came to the big pink house. Her mom's big house.

They were all big houses, but only one was Mom's. And hers, Lily's, she supposed, though she had never even stepped in it.

In the front, the house had a chain-link fence across its front yard, with a gate that opened to a concrete path that led to the front steps and the huge front porch. The kind of porch people used to sit on to catch the afternoon breeze in summer and greet their neighbors, as Mom had pointed out to her when they were out walking one summer day.

There was also a gate to the driveway, closed. And at the back end of the driveway, beyond the house, the garage, also closed. Its doors looked as though they could swing to the sides. But these too were closed.

The car was sitting in the driveway.

Lily knew all this because she had just walked past the house several times. She was excited. Or maybe nervous.

She knew well where she was. If she turned left at the end of the street, and then right, she'd be at the depot. It was that close. Main Street wasn't much of a main street despite the name, but tucked at the end of a block that went nowhere. Mom had said her grandfather had built it with the intention that that would be the edge of downtown, but downtown had grown up several blocks away.

And now, these days, the big house was at the edge of everything but not really anywhere. Just beyond the house, where the street turned left, was a mini-forest of old cedars. Maybe they were part of the property owned by the big house. Lovely, she thought.

The front yard had still-blooming rose bushes, bright and pretty. And chrysanthemums, fall flowers, gloomy and too dark to be pretty, Lily thought.

As she walked past, as if she had no interest in doing business there but just happened to be walking past—even though she had already walked past several times—Lily tried to figure out how to open the gate. This time as she went past she saw that she might lift that, and the next time she went past she saw she might swing it this way, and she didn't stop her pacing until she was sure she could open the odd-looking clasp.

And by the time she stood in front of it ready to open it, the front door had opened and that lady was standing in the opening with her hands on her hips and an entirely sour look on her face.

Lily had rehearsed what to say. "I thought you'd like some nice fresh vegetables today, now that the market is closed."

While she said this, she held the basket out and tipped it toward the lady so she could see into it. The carrots glowed, the potatoes were clean and rosy, the onion huge and shiny. At the last minute Lily had snipped off some fennel and had laid its wispy stem of delicate leaves just under the potatoes.

The lady said nothing, but she did take a step forward and another, walked down the stairs, approached the gate. Then she reached out and took the basket. Turned her back, and walking into the house, shut the door, having said nothing.

Lily stood looking at the closed door. Should she just go home? Should she knock on the door and ask for her basket back, her carrots and potatoes? Tell the woman the price?

Her mom would just go home. Lily had seen it many times: Mom liked to avoid awkward situations. Lily wasn't sure if that's what people were supposed to do. Or whether that's what she should do now.

So she stood outside the gate and looked at the house while she waited and thought about it.

If she opened the gate and went up to the door, she might be trespassing. Katherine had said many times not to trespass into their yard, their part of the garden, anywhere beyond the line drawn by other people at other times that kept them away from the house that Katherine, and probably Isabelle before her, had called home. Their house, their home.

Then Lily thought she saw some movement inside the house, inside those big, beautiful windows at the front of the house that looked out on the porch, the front yard, and the street beyond.

And there it was again. Someone noticing she was still there, someone keeping an eye on her.

So she stood there, not doing anything, not touching anything.

At first she thought that maybe the lady had gone for some money. But no, it was obvious she wasn't going to come out, that she had perhaps thought the basket was a gift. Or maybe she had some sort of rights to it.

Why?

Lily, still standing at the gate, looked through the nearest window, not that she could see well. Inside the big windows was a room lined with shelves, a sunnier room beyond. Some plates or something on the near shelves, a table beyond.

No one was in sight.

She sighed.

She didn't want to go home. She wanted her basket. She wanted her vegetables to sell. Or she would like to be paid.

## AN EARLY OCTOBER SATURDAY AFTERNOON 1985

SHE LOOKED AROUND. THIS little corner of town, so close to downtown but tucked away as it was, was nearly as familiar to her as her little garden. She had wandered around exploring since she was little.

The woods often drew her in, and she knew it well. A gravel path led to a little brook that ran full and swift when it rained and probably carried rainwater down to the harbor. An old plank bridge crossed the brook. Beyond the bridge was more path, no longer leading anywhere. It had grass growing through the gravel and slender trees poking up. She would dabble in the brook without reservation until Mom told her not to come home muddy again.

As a tiny girl she had puzzled about that. Not to go home? OH, not to be muddy when she went home. In between the two thoughts, she had wondered where she should go if she did get muddy.

But she had been little then, maybe three or four.

And now, tired of waiting for the lady and the basket, she had wandered toward the woods, had scooched down at the edge of the brook so she could see if there were tadpoles, maybe salamanders. She jumped over the little brook with only the heel of one sneaker landing in the water. No mud. And then she sat on the bridge and dangled her feet over the water.

Beyond the little brook and the path that seemed to lead only to thick, uninviting woods, sapling trees, berries, and darkness she could see such brightness that surely the woods must end there. She knew that beyond these dense woods were the railroad tracks that ran past the depot north toward town and the harbor beyond. She decided to follow them. She had done that before but that was a long time ago. She couldn't remember where they went.

She had to go back out of the woods the way she had entered them, by the big pink house, then turn up the street that went to the depot and around until she encountered the tracks. Then instead of turning north to follow the tracks toward the harbor, she turned south back toward the depot.

The tracks had weeds poking through the wood ties, and in some places the ties seemed to be missing. She tried walking on the metal tracks themselves, but they were narrow and it took her a while to get the hang of it. The edge of the plaza was just in sight, still a few hundred feet away and partly blocked by the woods. The depot was just beyond, but it wasn't yet in sight.

Of course the plaza would be abandoned today. No farmers market. But maybe the depot would be open.

She could see, as she got closer, how the tracks ran alongside the depot for its whole length, then continued alongside the docks where visitors could tie up their boats and wander around town. She wasn't sure where they went next. Or where it went in the other direction, the way she'd first been following it. Toward town.

The plaza next to the depot wasn't as empty as she'd guessed. None of the vendors were out, but several people were leaning against the fence, looking at the busy harbor and watching the boats arrive and depart just beyond.

She tried the door of the depot. It was closed and locked. No more art gallery. And no more bathroom. The bathroom was inside the depot.

And Lily needed to use a bathroom. Which meant going home.

If she went through the woods, she would be home fast, and good thing. She could stay in the woods until she got to her garden. She just had to be careful not to leave the woods too soon or she would come out in the lady's backyard instead of her own.

Feeling some urgency, she ran across the tracks and into the woods. The trees were thicker here than where she'd been earlier, and the ground under them was rough and covered with debris, fallen branches, toadstools, pricker bushes with some blackberries still on them, and in one place, gravel piled up for some reason. Maybe to build a better path. Where she was walking there was none.

It became nearly impossible to walk through these woods. She could give up on her shortcut and go back to the plaza and home the long way or continue and take a chance that she would come out into her yard.

And what if the lady was out there? She almost never was, not that Lily had seen, so it was unlikely.

OR what if the lady *was* out there? Maybe she could get her basket and veggies back. So that would be good.

And if she did get her veggies back, maybe she could take them to the plaza and offer them to the people enjoying the view of the harbor. For sale. After she went to the bathroom.

She pressed deeper into the woods. She could see a patch of the faded pink color of the big house just beyond the few large trees that were still in her way. It looked as though she would come out in front of their garage. She was not far enough along yet to come out in her own yard.

Just as she expected to emerge from the protection of the woods, she came up against a wire fence. She had been going faster, and then the fence had stopped her dead. She hadn't known about the fence. It looked old. It was rusty. It was also tall, well over Lily's head.

She couldn't go that way.

And how far toward her own yard did that fence go?

She walked along it in the general direction of home. The going was rough because of the shrubs and saplings, and her trip to the bathroom became more urgent. She found a smooth spot, mossy with no pricker bushes nearby, and squatted down and peed.

From that new angle she could see a bit of an old footpath, a somewhat washed-out gravel path, very welcome. It was faint, as if it had not been used very much. Or at least recently. The path took her to a section of woods that was much less dense, with no tall trees. It had lots of pricker bushes, though, and more sunlight. She scanned to the right and the left, but saw no sign of any path here. She turned toward what she hoped was her garden, or second choice, the lady's yard.

When she got on the other side of a tangle of shrubs, the fence was still blocking her way, though it looked much newer than that earlier fence.

She followed along inside it, squeezing past the massive pricker bushes. The ground was squishy, muddy. Then a huge bush, with blackberries still attached—moldy ones—hanging from several of the canes, barred her way. She snagged her jacket on the stickers again and again, and got her hair caught in them. She covered her eyes and pushed on.

With her eyes covered, thinking she would come out of the fenced area once she got on the other side of the giant blackberry, she ran into another barrier, and the unexpected impact nearly dumped her on the ground. It was another fence, or the same fence but now turned at a right angle so that it was blocking her way again. What was this? On the other side of it, straight ahead, was the overgrown extension of the grassy alley that ran past their little cottage. She could make out an occasional glint of railroad tracks far to her left, and could hear the brook, more of a stream now, nearer to her to the left. And a clear view of her cottage over to the right.

Both this unused section of alley straight ahead and her cottage to the right were completely unreachable. The fence was ahead of her and beside her, between her and the alley, between her and her house. What she didn't know was whether the fence wrapped around yet again toward the tracks and along the tracks and maybe all the way back to the depot.

What options did she have? Should she push past the blackberries toward the tracks and maybe find an opening where she could just run down the alley toward home, or should she go back the way she had come, pushing through the edge of the massive blackberry bush and all the other bushes, with their near-lethal stickers?

She looked longingly toward home.

Whose fence was this, anyway? Where had it come from and when? Why hadn't she encountered it before? And where did it go?

She was in the corner where the fence that went past the big house turned the corner to go along the unused section of alley. The blackberry that had entangled her filled the space around her except for that one corner. She could stand there and not be torn to shreds. But she couldn't go anywhere without plowing through it at her peril.

Where was Mom? At work of course. On which schedule, Lily couldn't remember. Saturday could be a long day for her. Or a half-day, in which case she'd be home soon. Maybe she was already home.

Standing there with no ability to go anywhere, Lily could hear the brook. It was running faster than what she'd seen earlier, and maybe that made sense, since her yard and the lady's yard would drain into it down at this end, the woods would drain into it maybe, and for all she knew the plaza and depot would drain into it.

The brook sounded nearby. Closer than she would have guessed. Had she ever explored this part of it?

The berry bush was a tangle of canes, with all sorts of birds coming and going at the top, way up above her reach, and from which vantage she was probably invisible to them. A safe place, if you were a little bird. And probably full of berries that no one but those with wings could reach.

And down at ground level, those canes that spread out in such a broad tangle came from a narrow area, from a single root maybe. She looked at it more carefully. That taper might give her crawl space. She might be able to wiggle out by creeping on the ground until she was past the bush because there were no canes that far from the root. Maybe that might even mean she'd end up past the fence. Without having to go through the prickly canes again.

It would work, she was sure. Unless there was a fence on the far side too.

So she lowered herself, not without pokes and scratches, down through those long canes until she was sitting on the ground, then eased onto her belly and began to creep along.

Debris from the canes needed to be pushed aside, and her hands were bleeding from the prickers. Her shirt caught at times on the lowest canes. But she was making progress, finding easier passage than what she had had getting herself into this pickle in the first place, when she had just plowed through.

She found out quickly that she had to keep her head down, her face turned away from the canes and toward the fence.

Then the canes were no longer scratching her. She cautiously raised her head. Straight ahead of her she could see the fence had turned again and was directly ahead of her, maybe ten feet away. And beyond the fence, the tracks. And on this side of the fence, the rapidly running brook.

The ground was becoming ever damper, muddier. Bird footprints were visible even several feet from the brook. But no more pricker bushes.

She pushed herself to standing when she found there were no more canes overhead. She looked around. The fence between her and the depot was in front of her, and the other section, between her and the grassy extension of the alley, was beside her. There was no way out of the fenced area except to go back the way she had come, or maybe to walk upstream in the brook where there might be no significant barriers.

There were no barriers that she could see in the brook from where she stood. But it was a long way back and the brook was cold, and the rocks that filled it were probably slippery.

Toward the alley, the brook went under the fence and across the alley through an eroded channel.

Where she was standing, the brook was running rather fast.

That eroded channel on the other side of the fence was only what? Fifty feet from the cottage?

The brook had piled up a large mound of debris, leaves and small branches and scraps of paper on this side, against the fence. And water ran freely out from under it into the alley. But the mound blocked Lily's way.

She was stuck. She looked back up the brook. It looked easier to go that way, though it would be far longer. She would go that way.

The first few steps were cold, burning cold. She slid along on the rocks, hoping to find an opening on one side or the other where she could get out of the brook and walk on dry ground, or even mud. And then soon she should be at the little bridge and just opposite that, the front of the pink house.

So she was surprised when another fence crossed the brook right in her path. It couldn't have been attached to the other parts of the fence or she would have encountered it. Robust berry bushes filled the space beyond the new fence. What could its purpose be, or maybe have been in the past?

On the right this fence that crossed her path was attached to the fence that ran along between the brook and the tracks. On the left the fence ran through the berry bushes and she couldn't see where it ended up.

But by backing up, Lily was able to find an area clear of berry bushes. She left the brook and squeezed between a pair of slender saplings. Other saplings beyond threatened to bar her way, but she managed to move ahead a few feet. Looking over toward the fence that had just stopped her, she could see just beyond the berry bush.

A manmade object of some sort, a piece of machinery, partly covered in canvas tied on with rope, a chain wrapped here and there around it secured with a lock, sat in a wet depression. It was sunk up to its axles in mud and water. The wheels, rusty, were railway wheels, like those on a train. But she didn't see any tracks.

A good part of the view of the vehicle was blocked by vegetation, and it was out of reach due to the crosswise fence. Lily wondered if there might be a gate into the area that held the odd vehicle, but she didn't have time to explore. Her way along the fence was blocked by one kind of vegetation or another. And her feet were burning with cold. She needed to get home, and the only way she knew was to run back down the brook and crawl under the fence where the brook had eroded the soil. After she removed the pile of debris. If she could move it.

But if she could move it, she would crawl under the fence where the brook ran through it, and then she would be free.

The thought of getting in that icy brook made her think again about going back through the berry bushes, but when she looked back over her path and saw how dense the vegetation was, she set to work cleaning debris from the brook.

It took her a half hour or more to move the debris. The sun was getting low in the sky. Her hands were wet, nearly unbearably cold. She could hear her mother come home, bang the door to the cottage. Come out and call her name. Lily called back but her mother didn't hear her.

She was nearly done removing the debris and could see the bottom of the fence as it crossed the brook. She was confident she would fit.

Scooping aside the last of the debris, her hands red and sore, her feet aching from being in the cold water for so long, she found her way blocked by a horizontal bar that ran across the bottom of the fence. She would have to bury herself deep into the stream bed if she was to get underneath.

She sat only long enough to peel off her jacket. She pushed it under the fence, then flattened herself on her belly and used her knees, feet, hands, whatever she could think to do, to push herself under the fence.

She kept her face to the side, but even so her nose was in the water. She took big gulps of air, holding her breath in between and pushing with her feet. She made little progress, and her ear rubbed painfully against the gravel-and-mud channel bottom. She'd have to go headfirst, face in the water.

She scooped out the rocks and gravel again from beneath the crossbar. Her hands were too painful to make it deep enough, so she tried using her feet. Her boot-covered heels worked well. It was difficult to clear the rocks and stream pebbles far enough beyond the fence to make her feel she could get all the way out and not get stuck with her face in the water. But she had to give it a try.

She was soaked already and it would be worse before she was free. She flopped down into the stream and pushed with her feet. She wanted to protect her face with her hands, but she could see tall grasses to the sides of the stream ahead so she thrust her arms forward and grabbed for them. Then she pulled with her arms and pushed with her knees and feet, took a breath and put her head under the crossbar.

She felt frantic with her head under water. She pushed harder with her toes and grabbed new tufts of tall grass and pulled, and suddenly her head was beyond the crossbar and she could breathe again. The water had penetrated through all the layers of clothing, and she shivered violently.

Then her progress was jerked to a stop. She was stuck at her waist by something snagging her jeans, maybe a belt-loop. She tried backing up but couldn't free herself.

She realized she could die there and no one would know where to look for her. She couldn't move forward or backward. She had to get rid of her jeans. She rotated a bit and got a hand on her snap. Her fingers were frozen, too frozen to open it. She tried again, and it gave way. She tried pushing with her toes again and she jerked forward. Her jeans were still stuck but she was able to turn and free them.

She clawed her way forward until she could get up on her knees, then crawled the rest of the way, her jeans down past her knees now. She stood, awkwardly turning to free them from where they'd caught on the fencing, then pulled them back up. She grabbed her jacket and ran the fifty feet or so home.

## AN EARLY OCTOBER SATURDAY EVENING 1985

KATHERINE PUT LILY INTO the shower, mentioning mud and bad choices. Lily had to agree.

They decided on an early supper. Neither had had lunch. And both were tired. Katherine opened a couple of cans and they ate the hot food while they sat in silence, Lily still chilled and wrapped in a blanket as well as her bathrobe.

Lily was tired, yes, and at the same time excited by her adventure. The thought of her loss of her basket had faded. And Mom didn't know anything about it, and maybe Lily could get it back before she noticed the basket was missing. It was for their bread, and at the moment they had run out of bread—because of no farmers market—so she still had time to get it back.

But what was really on her mind was the fence. Had her grandfather or great grandfather built it? And why?

"Mom, who built that fence over there?" she asked. She'd been thinking about it and now she had just blurted out the result of her thoughts and of course her mother had no idea what she was talking about.

"What fence?"

"In the woods, over there," said Lily, pointing.

"Probably something John Steele put up."

"Who's John Steele?"

"Your great-grandfather. Great-great or something like that. He built everything around here."

"But there's new fencing in there."

"I have no idea."

"So was John Steele your ... grandfather?"

"No, his son William was."

"So William and his wife had Isabelle and then Isabelle had you?"

"Yes. That's what my mom always told me."

"So you didn't meet William?"

"No, he died young. When Isabelle—when my mom—was seven. He had the Spanish flu."

"What's that?"

"A bad sickness."

"How old was he?"

"Younger than I am now. Under forty."

Lily thought about that. What if her dad had died when she was younger than she was now, even this age? She had no idea. She had never had a dad.

"So you didn't ever meet your grandfather?"

"No, just his sister, Aunt Agnes."

"Aunt Agnes? I don't remember her. Is she still alive?"

"Oh, no, she died a long time ago. She was the person who kept her eye on our house and made sure we understood the importance of keeping it in the family."

"What is the importance of keeping the house in the family?"

"You'll see. We'll talk about it."

"So your whole family died?"

"Well, yes. And today my favorite patient died."

"Oh. So she was old?"

"Yes. She was old. And she had been in the nursing home for years. And she couldn't do a thing for herself anymore. It was very sad."

"Is your father dead?"

"I don't know. I don't know who he was. Or is."

"Is my father dead?"

Mom paused, and Lily noticed that. Then Mom said, "I don't know."

"You don't?"

"Well, he might as well be."

There was a lot of silence then. But Lily didn't mind. She was tired, ready for bed, even though there was still some light in the sky.

She stood in front of the little window that gave her a view of the alley behind the house. Now she knew it only appeared to stop just beyond their house to the left. Beyond that was tall grass, but just beyond that was the stream she had crawled in, and beyond that the tracks and then the harbor, boats, the bay, mountains, who knew what else. From here, though, all she could see was the grass behind their house that had been driven on by anyone who might need to come to their house, and beyond that, out of sight beyond the cottage, inhospitable and hidden, a pathway to a new world that her great-great-grandfather had once carved out.

"Ready for bed?" asked Katherine. "I have to go back to work."

"Back to work? Why?"

"They need me. And you'll be asleep. I should have a day off tomorrow. Want to go to the library?"

"Sure."

Lily wasn't awake long enough to mind about Mom leaving again. But as she went to sleep she had the thought that maybe she was going to go on a date with her dad. It was Saturday night, after all. She called after Katherine. "Have a good time," she said with a smile.

"Thanks, Sweetie," she said. She had pulled the cotton curtains over the window, making sure they overlapped. She looked around the tiny space. All was well. Lily was already deeply asleep, she thought. "Good night, my little love," she whispered.

## AN EARLY OCTOBER SATURDAY NIGHT AND SUNDAY MORNING 1985

KATHERINE HAD LIED TO her daughter, but it was a forgivable lie. And now as she approached the nursing home where she worked, just a few blocks down a side street, she realized how cold it had become, how early the sun now set. She was just in time to meet Gloria, her nurse friend and nursing home mentor, when she got off at 7:00 p.m. Their plan was to have a meal together. It was Gloria's supper break. But of course Katherine had already eaten, with Lily, and she would be able to avoid spending any of her precious dollars.

She hoped Gloria wouldn't mind. She barely knew her. She oozed authority, Gloria did, and made a great boss and mentor. And Katherine was about to ask her a favor, maybe too big a favor, but she had nowhere else to turn.

It had started up again last weekend, though the first inklings went back years. And how many years had it been? Back when Lily was what? About six? So three years. And yes, that was right, because it was just before Isabelle died. Isabelle, her mom, who would be no help with this at all. Isabelle whose last sickness had wiped out every dollar they had accumulated. Isabelle who went to a doctor at every opportunity. Quite the opposite of being a help. So maybe she had kept quiet about it even when Isabelle was still alive.

It had begun to cause her true worry recently, though, about mid-week. And by tonight she was scared.

But probably Gloria would tell her how silly she was, how she didn't need to worry. And then she would sigh with relief and enjoy the company for an hour. Lily would be fine.

She wasn't sure what Lily had discovered over in the woods today. But given the adventure she'd had, she would no doubt sleep deeply all night. Katherine didn't know there was a fence there. Maybe her aunt had had animals, but not that she could remember.

Gloria walked toward her. They met up on the sidewalk that could take them directly to town, to shops, restaurants, and then eventually to the high school, the community pool, and beyond, wherever they might want to go. Gloria told her right away how sorry she was that her patient had died and gave her a hug. Katherine was embarrassed, but smiled a stiff smile.

And now it was Katherine's turn. And she didn't think she could do it. She tried out asking one way and then another, and was so obsessed with getting it right that she forgot to walk. Gloria turned around when she noticed she was walking alone.

"What is it?" she asked Katherine.

Katherine looked up. The kindness of Gloria's voice disarmed her and she felt tears erupting. "I have a lump," she blurted out.

"Oh," said Gloria. "My poor girl, let's go back to the nursing home and take a look."

"Oh, dear. I don't know. I thought I could just tell you about it."

"None of that. If you don't want to go back to work, we'll have to go to your place. It's not far, right?"

"No."

"No what?"

"No, let's go back to the nursing home."

So they backtracked.

Gloria found a free room. Katherine endured with great embarrassment the necessary observation and gentle probing that resulted in Gloria telling her that her observations had been perceptive and perhaps lifesaving.

The kind words were terrifying.

Katherine felt she had to gasp for air, but she didn't want to draw attention to her panic. She needed to look as though she was going to handle this calmly, like every other woman residing in her imagination. All those competent women, ones with husbands, ones with husbands and several beautiful children, ones with careers that didn't include bathroom-cleaning. Those other women.

And then she gasped and gasped again and Gloria hugged her.

She didn't realize she had brushed Gloria off but very soon she found she was halfway home. Had she even said goodbye to Gloria? What about thanks?

Gloria had said, you need to see a doctor. But in all but the words she spoke, Gloria had said, "You have cancer."

She had no doubt about it.

Cancer, and a nine-year-old daughter.

"I will die, and they will take Lily and put her in a home. And that must not happen."

She was walking home rapidly, but when she got there she headed out again. She wasn't ready to face ... anyone. Certainly not Lily.

Gradually her thoughts, tornadoes of them, calmed. She walked and walked. She went all the way to the shipyards. And all the way to the football fields across from the high school. And even out to the ferry terminal. She walked fast. And as she walked and her thoughts began to calm, all the words settled down to just a dozen or so:

"I will die. I must hide Lily. I must save the big house."

Sunday dawned rainy and chilly. Lily was up early. Katherine saw her making oatmeal but pretended to be asleep. Lily would go out and fuss in the garden, sweet little worker that she was. The rain wouldn't stop her. When Katherine was out there with her, Lily was always singing, humming, moving confidently despite her floppy rubber boots. So she would be OK. And Katherine needed time to think, maybe even to mourn.

To feel sorry for herself, in other words.

But not just sorry for herself. Sorry, too, for Lily.

Bad things happened to seven-year-old girls in their family. First Isabelle. Then Katherine herself. And now Lily.

Maybe Aunt Agnes, too, though she had never said. Never would say such a thing, she from the perfect family.

Granted Lily was no longer seven, but she had been nearly seven when Katherine first suspected the lump. More than three years ago.

It was an odd sort of curse.

Or, if Katherine was smart, maybe not quite the curse for Lily. If she could keep her safe. Big if. However would she do that?

So she lay in bed and cried while Lily gardened.

She probably drifted off, because only sleep would have left her as dim-witted and incompetent as she felt when a loud noise woke her.

It was a banging on the door but not with a hand. With a stick, maybe. Or a couple of sticks.

"Little girl! Open this door. Come out of there. Do you hear me?

The voice was deep, gruff, male.

Katherine had a choice. Should she let him know she was inside? Would he break down the door if she didn't? What would he think if it wasn't a little girl?

Katherine said, "Who is it?" while she wrapped her blanket around herself.

She wasn't going to open the door, but then again Lily was out there.

Lily! Where was Lily?

"Who is it?" she asked again, louder. Intending to be heard.

"Police. Open up."

"What do you want?"

"Open up."

Katherine, wondering where Lily was, hoping Lily was nowhere to be seen, opened the door. But only a crack.

The heavy-handed cop was a middle-aged rather paunchy fellow she thought she might recognize from back in high school.

He was clearly startled. "Who are you?"

"Who are you looking for?" Katherine asked. After she said it, she thought it was the best thing she could have asked.

He beat his palm with his stick. It struck her that he was acting like a cop, almost like a cartoon cop.

"Who are you looking for?" she asked again.

He hesitated. Did he even know?

Finally he said, "A little girl."

Katherine realized she could blurt out, "Oh, my daughter Lily." But she felt cautious, even suspicious. Why, after all, was he here? Why did he want to know about a little girl?

"Was there a complaint, officer?"

"Someone reported a child vandalizing their garden shed."

"No vandalism here. It must be some other garden shed."

He looked around. Meanwhile she was making up her mind not to let him see inside. He didn't need to know they lived here. Though the fact that she was wrapped in a blanket might suggest that she did.

Or even if he figured out she lived here, he didn't need to know a little girl did.

But why the complaint?

"Who complained?"

"I don't think you need to know that at the moment. So there's no child here?"

Katherine didn't want to lie. And of course Lily could come prancing up any moment in that full-of-life way she had, and that would be awkward if Katherine had just denied her existence.

So she said, "You can come inside if you want to see for yourself." Then she made to open the door wider but didn't move it more than an inch.

"No, that's all right. Sorry to bother you."

He walked away. His partner had long since disappeared around the corner of the cottage, and after the cop was gone, Katherine stood in the partly open door, either looking for Lily or waiting for Lily, she wasn't sure.

She had a clear view of the upstairs window of the big house and happened to look that way just in time to see the woman turn away.

"Hmm," she mumbled to herself.

In a vague way, she was waiting for Lily, in case she had been hiding from the cops. Or maybe she was off exploring. Or who knew what. Katherine once again felt how much she wished she had been that confident a child. How she wished she were that confident an adult.

And all the while she was fingering the lump in her breast.

It was a habit by now, she supposed. Why else would she do it? In the vague hope that one day it would be gone? But it wasn't gone. It was bigger. Clearly bigger. In the beginning, three years ago, it had been barely detectable. But last night Gloria had had no trouble locating it.

And had had no hesitation in telling her to get to a doctor right away. Not a recommendation, more like a direct order.

And what about that? Even if she felt good about spending the money on a doctor—and of course it wouldn't be just one visit—there were issues.

Namely Lily.

What would happen to Lily?

Lily, who was happy as long as they were together.

Lily, who had suddenly appeared from nowhere and was now hugging her around the hips.

## EARLY OCTOBER SUNDAY 1985

KATHERINE GAVE LILY A kiss, shucked off the blanket, got dressed, and got them breakfast. Then, while Lily was eating, as calmly as she could, Katherine asked her where she'd been.

"Hiding from the cops, Mom. What did they want?"

"Why were you hiding from the cops?"

"I don't know."

"Did you do something?"

Lily stared at her, and she immediately regretted asking her. It made her, Katherine, Lily's mother, sound suspicious. And she wasn't. As far as she could tell, nothing at all had happened.

"I'm sorry, Lily. They said they'd gotten a report that a child was vandalizing someone's tool shed."

Lily, not happy, said, "What's vandalizing?"

"Damaging it, destroying it, he didn't say. He was trying to find out if there was a child inside. He seemed surprised to find me here instead."

"I'm glad I hid."

"I'm glad you hid, too. I don't like the whole thing. But tell me, do you know what this is all about? Did anything happen?"

"I don't think so."

"OK. And I guess I should tell you I saw that woman who lives in our house—in the big house—was standing in the window."

Lily nodded slowly.

"Do you know why?"

"No. She does that a lot. When I'm in the garden."

"Does she ever come out and talk to you?"

"No ... "

"But?"

Lily sighed.

"What? Tell me."

"I ... I took some veggies to her yesterday. To her front door. Well, not all the way to her front door."

"Lily. I told you never to talk to her."

Lily looked down. "I wanted to sell her some veggies."

"What did she say?"

"Nothing."

"Not anything? Like 'go away'?"

"Nothing. She just came out. I was standing outside the gate. And she took my basket with the veggies in it and went inside and didn't come out again. I waited but she never came out."

Katherine shook her head.

"I'm sorry, Mom."

"You didn't do anything wrong."

"I just want to sell veggies. Now that the farmers market is closed." She was quiet for a moment, then added, "Mom, you should see all the people in the plaza! The market is closed but there are a lot of people there anyway. Maybe they would like some fresh carrots. I have plenty."

Katherine smiled. What a smart, confident daughter. She fingered her chest. Maybe she would be all right if Katherine were laid up for a while. Maybe she could find a doctor. Maybe she could have a quick removal of the tumor and be home in a couple of days. Maybe.

Because the first step would be going to the doctor. And once she did that, she would have decisions to make. Treatments to agree to. Like surgery, or even chemo.

She shuddered. Could Lily take care of herself? For how long?

Because if she couldn't, she would probably end up in a foster home.

She shuddered again. NO. It was not worth the risk. A simple trip to the doctor to find out what was what, and the outcome could be—almost certainly would be—that her daughter would end up in foster care.

And who knows where that would be?

And NO. Katherine's thinking slammed shut at that point.

Lily was looking at her. "What's the matter, Mom?"

"Nothing. Nothing at all. Let's go to the library."

So they got ready. Lily was muddy again. Katherine was of two minds: Find out where she had been hiding, or remain ignorant of that detail, in case she should be asked and blurt it out. Maybe getting muddy wasn't the worst thing Lily could do. Maybe some of her Mommy rules were fine for earlier days, but not now. Maybe she shouldn't put restrictions on Lily such as not selling her veggies. Let her make some decisions on her own. Maybe she'd have to. In what might be her best possible future world, she'd have to. For a while anyway. In case Katherine ended up in the hospital.

Lily didn't have to grow up as Katherine had, taking orders from her mother. Of course. And her mother's aunt, Aunt Agnes, the bossiest of them all, the cranky old woman who had never stopped talking about the beautiful pink house her father had built.

And that would always be theirs, no matter what.

Katherine wished her mother was still around because the whole business about the house didn't make sense to her. How could it be theirs when it clearly wasn't?

And yet she had already impressed on Lily that she must always keep an eye on it, because in the end it was theirs.

Here it was, 1985, and the house had been lost from the family for the past 35 years. So how could it possibly be theirs again?

Isabelle had said it had needed paint and a new roof and other things so someone in the family had decided to sell it. Maybe they couldn't afford to keep it up.

Then what about the treasure in the shed? Why hadn't they just used that? Surely losing the house had been an emergency.

So, she was supposed to keep an eye on it, just in case. And then do what?

And what if she wasn't able to come home to the little cottage for a while? Should she prepare Lily to be ready to take over?

Katherine thought the whole idea of reclaiming the pink house someday was crazy, the thoughts of an old woman who never stopped talking about it. But at the same time she didn't want to leave Lily unprepared.

And now Lily was pulling on her sleeve. "Come on, Mom. Let's go."

And Katherine really did want to go. Maybe she could find a book or magazine article on breast cancer. Maybe if she read about it she would find a way to avoid going to the doctor, and none of the challenges, the decisions that were driving surges of adrenaline into her bloodstream, would be necessary.

The day was sunny, breezy, chilly. They hurried along, the wind in their faces. The library had shorter hours on Sunday. The parking lot was almost empty. Often on Sundays they spent the whole afternoon there, browsing, sometimes sharing some new knowledge, mostly relaxing in the easy chairs in the various nooks.

And then the question popped into Katherine's mind, what would Lily do if Katherine weren't there to go to the library?

'She'd do fine here by herself,' said the inner Katherine.

'True, but how would she get here?'

'She'd walk. Just like today.'

'But would she be safe? There's a busy road out there.'

'Teach her.'

Teach her. But would Lily be able to do it? Of course she would. She already ran ahead and punched the button that caused the light to turn green for pedestrians. She had been doing that since she was a toddler, just about.

And, Katherine mused, she herself had been the slow one, the one who had insisted on holding her hand when she had never run into a street, whether a major thoroughfare or a neighborhood two-laner.

And Isabelle had also held Katherine's hand. For years and years.

So, teach her. Teach her what she would need to know in case Katherine decided to go to the hospital for a day or two. She'd make a list of things she would need to know, and leave notes for her at the cottage.

And then if she had questions, she could ... what? Come to the hospital to ask her, during visiting hours?

Were visiting hours during school hours?

What if she had an urgent question?

Katherine realized then that her list would need to be very thorough. Because Lily might not always be able to come ask her how to do something.

Not that Katherine intended to go to the doctor. Unless she read something that gave her confidence that that would be the right choice.

So she looked for books that might tell her more. There were some, all several years old. So she switched to magazines. She found articles that told her how to prevent cancer, and some stories about movie stars and TV personalities who had experienced cancer, some of it breast cancer.

Basically none of it was helpful, though some did quote doctors.

She sighed, walked up the long flight of stairs, picked out several mysteries, and went to find Lily.

She was running out of the library's collection of mysteries to read. Some she had read several times.

Lily was nowhere to be seen, not in her usual place curled up in a chair in the far corner, or elsewhere in the children's room. Katherine was early, but still, where could she be?

Sometimes she would find a friend and go out to the little playground outside, but she knew she was supposed to tell Mom before she went out.

Katherine was still searching when Lily came up.

"Miss Clark is here!"

"Your teacher?"

"Yes. She's nice. I was talking to her. Out on the steps so we wouldn't bother anyone."

It was all so reasonable. She could see her nine-year-old self being caught up in the excitement of seeing her teacher, and getting to talk to her. And that was the reserved young Katherine. Lily was much more of a chatterbox.

"And how is Miss Clark?"

"Fine. She's nice. She lives with Miss Horan."

"Miss Horan, the librarian?"

"Yes, she's nice too. And guess what? They both have the same first name! It's Ruth. Ruth Clark and Ruth Horan."

"How unusual! How did you find that out?"

"Someone called one of them by name and they both answered, so I asked them and they laughed and said yes, they were both Ruth."

"And do they call each other Ruth?" She didn't expect Lily to know, of course.

"They call each other Clark and Horan." Lily giggled. "Maybe I should call myself Steele!"

"Just be sure you call them MISS Clark and MISS Horan."

"I will."

"So you didn't get any books, it looks like."

"I did. They're up at the desk. I forgot my library card. Can I put them on yours?"

"Sure. And I have a game for us to play on the way home. I want you to walk ahead of me and pretend you're going by yourself."

"OK," said Lily.

But Katherine could see she was more excited about her books than the game. "No reading on the way home, though, Missy," she said. "That's one of the rules of the game. Pay attention. There's not much traffic on Sundays, but you still need to be careful."

"OK."

## LATE OCTOBER 1985

AS THE DAYS WENT by, Katherine thought of several other games for Lily to play. Lily seemed to love them. She could already make cocoa and heat up cans of soup, but what about other meals? And what about laundry? That was trickier, but Lily enjoyed running the wringer on the old tub. But getting the clothes rinsed well enough was proving a challenge.

Katherine surprised herself by wondering how much a modern washing machine would cost. In case she couldn't manage the wringing and even the hanging on the wood rack for a while. Well, they'd still need to hang them.

Meanwhile, the lump seemed to be growing. She'd need to find out about doctors, just in case. Maybe she'd ask Miss Clark. Or Miss Horan. The Ruths. One or the other: She didn't want to alarm anyone, or even call attention to herself as having a problem. Maybe she could ask 'for a friend.'

So, a new washing machine? Maybe. She might ask Miss Clark what a good brand might be.

Lily also needed a new coat. Katherine was a little late thinking about that, given how Lily was growing. They might all be gone at the various local thrift shops. They'd need to go on her next day off.

And then a thought came to her that took her entirely by surprise: Maybe Lily could go by herself after school one day and find one and ask them to hold it for her.

Or maybe she could even just go ahead and buy it.

Katherine thought about it a while longer, and it seemed worth trying. Which led to another decision. As soon as Lily came in, she told her she could sell veggies. They both agreed that she wouldn't go back to the big house. The loss of the basket still made Lily mad, but Mom said never mind, it was only an old breadbasket.

So Lily went to various thrift stores and in the end found a fur-lined, fancy coat that was unlike anything she had ever owned. And which she loved more than anything else she had ever owned. And she found a nice woven basket for 25 cents.

And meanwhile, Lily saw her mother touching her chest again and again, and finally asked her why, and Mom said it was a bug bite.

But Mom didn't seem quite right. Sometimes Lily found Mom crying quietly when Lily came bounding in from the garden. Or even during dinner.

One late afternoon Lily came in full of excitement. Her new basket was empty. She had sold all her carrots and potatoes at nearby houses, and one lady had told her to come back next week. She reached into her pocket and took out 3 one-dollar bills, held them up in the air with a flourish, and put them on top of the stack in the breadbox.

Mom had jumped up when she came in, and now gave her a hug. But Lily broke free and ran back out the door. The chickens needed to be closed in. Lily returned with two eggs in her jacket pocket.

"I wish we could still get the farmers market bread, Lily," she said. "I'm not surprised people want your veggies. That was a great idea."

"That lady told me to come in and get a cookie," Lily said.

Mom sucked in her breath. Lily had said something wrong.

And when they sat down to eat, eggs and carrots and potatoes, Mom looked rather serious. Lily was sure Mom was going to give her a lecture, but what had she done wrong?

Mom was silent, but her face was full of distress. Again she took a deep breath, then grabbed Lily by the arm and squeezed tight, too tight. "Lily! You must never go into anyone's house. Never."

"Mom, she's nice. You know her from the market. She sells hazelnuts."

"Oh, well, yes I do know her. And she's probably safe. But the rule stands. You must never go into anyone's house. Or no more selling veggies."

"Why, Mom?"

Lily could tell Mom didn't want to say. But then she did say. "Sometimes people hurt children, Lily."

"Like beat them up? Spank them?"

"Things like that."

"OK," said Lily.

"I mean it, Lily. You can't trust anybody."

"Not even cops?"

Mom was silent. Then she whispered, "Sometimes cops, Lily. But ... maybe only at the police station?"

After a long silence, Mom said, "I can't make rules for everything, Lily. There will always be situations you can't make rules for. Surprises happen."

"Then what do I do?"

Mom looked at Lily, pulled her long bangs out of her eyes, rubbed a smudge of mud from her arm, reached over and kissed her. "Lily, you have to listen to your feelings. If you don't feel good about something, don't do it. And if you do feel good about it, check your feelings inside too. And never go into anyone's house. Ever."

"OK, Mom." Lily was perplexed, surprised. What Mom had just told her seemed so strange. She lay awake thinking about it. She could, of course, sell her veggies standing outside on someone's porch, but even though she hadn't told Mom, other people had invited her in and given her a cookie, a glass of milk. Sometimes they had asked her questions about her garden, about school, about Mom. It was fun to sit and have a conversation.

In the morning, Lily needed to get herself ready for school because Mom was still asleep. With no bread she would need to make oatmeal again. The blackberries were gone, so it would be plain. She should pick up some apples on the way to school. No, on the way home. Chopped apples made oatmeal delicious.

And then she had the thought that she could perhaps gather a lot of apples, and sell them, too.

The apple tree where they'd always gotten apples was huge, and many of the apples were now on the ground. It must have been a family's apple tree sometime in the past. It was near downtown outside a house that was now a little bookstore. No one paid any attention to that tree, and long ago Lily and her mother had asked the store clerk if they could have some of the apples that were lying on the ground and the woman had said, "Of course."

So today on the way home from school she stuffed her pockets, but that was only four apples. Mom was at work when she got home, so she made the decision to use her little red wagon to get a full load of apples.

She counted the apples in the wagon: thirty. She had trouble getting them down off the sidewalk to the street and up again. It took her much longer than usual to get home. All along the way she wondered if she could make them a pie. They had flour, she was sure of that. But maybe not butter. She'd have to ask Mom if she needed anything else for an apple pie. And oh yes, they might be out of sugar.

Mom was home when she got there. She ran to her when she opened the door.

"What's the matter, Mom?"

"Where were you?"

"Getting apples." She explained, and then asked Mom about how to make apple pie, and in the end they walked together to the grocery and used some of their dollar bills to get what they needed for pies for now and in the future. Mom said something that Lily thought was weird but really nice: "I want you to be able to make apple pie any time you want it." So they got two of everything, and a new little can of cinnamon.

Mom went to bed right after supper, right after taking the pie from the oven. Lily had to eat her pie alone. She got a book and ate and read and stayed up too late, but Mom didn't wake up. So Lily brushed her teeth without being told and went to bed.

## EARLY NOVEMBER 1985

KATHERINE QUIT HER JOB. Gloria was asking too many questions, and they all pointed to the necessity of Katherine getting herself to a doctor. Plus, Katherine was tired.

And she didn't want Lily to know she was now unemployed. Lily was always asking questions, maybe worrying. Worrying about money for sure, a trait that made Katherine sad. From a young age, maybe from the time she was four, Lily had kept an eye on the pile of cash in the breadbox and had taken obvious delight when the pile grew.

So much so that one day—it must have been four years ago when Lily was five—when she'd noticed the pile of small denomination cash had mounted up, Katherine had decided to take them to the bank and get all twenties. She had enough for thirty or forty twenties, all in singles, fives, and tens. So the stack had been huge. She had stuffed her purse with them, and then Lily asked: "Can I carry the rest?"

So they had gotten Lily's backpack and Lily had proudly carried the remaining cash to the bank.

At the bank, they were taken to a small, glassed-in room. Lily added her stack to Mom's, and the banker began to count. One hundred, two hundred ... eight hundred, nine hundred. Then he replaced all the singles, fives, and tens with the proper number of twenties. The pile was much shorter.

Then he gave the pile to Mom, who counted it again. She gave a few twenties to Lily to carry and put the rest in her purse.

"Where's all our money, Mom?" Lily had asked, upset.

"Right here, Sweetheart," said Mom.

"No, the rest of it."

"I'll tell you at home. Let's go. Someone's waiting to see Mr. Kelly."

She had taken Lily by the hand. But Lily wouldn't move. "Let's talk outside," said Mom, so Lily went outside with her. But when Mom started walking toward home, she threw herself down right in front of the bank's front door and refused to move or get up. Instead, she screamed, "Give me back my money!" Katherine had to carry her, squirming and screaming, the four blocks to the cottage.

And even at home, she tried to run back toward town. She refused to go into the cottage but braced her arms against the door frame.

It was only when she had thrown herself on the ground and begun to yawn that Katherine was able to move her into the house. Exhausted and embarrassed, Katherine dumped her child on the bed, offered her a snack, and covered her, hoping she would sleep.

But she would not. Sniffing and wiping snot from her face, Lily once again said, "I want my money."

How do you explain that one twenty equals a ten plus a five plus five ones? One bill instead of seven? For example. Well, she would have to try.

"Sit down, Lily. At the table. I want to show you something."

"And then will you go get our money?"

"I already have our money, Lily. Watch."

So Katherine showed Lily different ways to make piles worth twenty dollars. She had to use paper because all her small bills, except a few, were already traded in. It took an hour. Lily was fascinated. They ate their bowls of soup and kept talking about the way money worked. They covered making change. They covered coins.

Then Lily said, "And when we spend a $20 and get change back, it's less money but more pieces of money. I get it."

By the time Lily was six, Katherine was letting Lily carry the cash to the store, pay the cashier, check the change, and make a few decisions about what they would buy for supper. It was Katherine's tendency to buy the smallest, oldest, cheapest, but when Lily asked for a head of broccoli from the regular display, not the day-old collection, Katherine had begun to say yes.

Lily could almost have done all the shopping. Almost. But there was no need for that.

Though if Katherine did go to the hospital or find herself laid up in bed for a couple of days, Lily could do the shopping. With a list of course.

And now Katherine had to come to grips with not having any salary coming in. She'd have to find a different job, something that was not at the nursing home.

And where would that be?

She'd thought about waitressing. But all those people to deal with for several hours a day? The very thought was exhausting.

Or maybe she could clean houses.

Then, contrary to her deepest convictions she had the idea, quite unbidden, that perhaps she could clean the big house.

Ridiculous!

But oh, how great it would be to be inside her house again, her home! She had lived there for her first seven years and within sight of it for all the other years of her life. She knew the floor plan, remembered the steep stairs to her bedroom—to her beautiful pink and white bedroom. She remembered the upstairs bathroom on one side, and a window straight ahead of the stairwell.

That would be the window the woman who lived there must use to keep an eye on Lily.

Because she was definitely keeping an eye on Lily, and was therefore likely the person who had called the cops on her.

Thoughts of the cops banging on their door still brought Katherine a surge of adrenaline. What had that been about?

Katherine turned her thoughts back to the house, to the lovely front sitting room, lined with books, old books. Nothing like the books they had in school, bright and colorful as they had been. These were forbidding brown books, whether due to their age or their content she didn't know. Forbidding because they looked uninteresting, difficult, grown-up. And Katherine had been only seven. Not forbidden, though. Aunt Agnes was always encouraging her to take them down and explore what was inside.

She couldn't think of a single other kind word her old Aunt Agnes had ever said to her.

There was one book in particular Aunt Agnes had tried to interest her in. She had sat Katherine down and put it in front of her. It was huge, thick. It would fit only on the bottom shelf. Or the top shelf that was so far above Aunt Agnes's head that she would not have been able to access it or anything stored up there.

This huge book had printing as books do, and handwriting in black ink in some places, blue in a few other places. Katherine had been surprised, shocked, to see the ink in that book, on many pages of that book: She had been warned from the time she was a little girl that she must never write in a book.

Aunt Agnes had put the big book on Katherine's lap and then sat next to her. The book was heavy, too heavy, and Aunt Agnes had said over and over, "Sit still."

And then Agnes had pointed to names: "This is my father. This is my grandfather, my father's father. This is my great-great-grandfather. He was born in England. He was born in 1790." Or some such year, something long ago.

Katherine remembered being overwhelmed. And Aunt Agnes had done this many times. Katherine was not certain she remembered any of it.

Except Agnes's father's name. It was John Steele. That was easy, because she was Katherine Steele.

But it was confusing. Why did she have his name? Why didn't she have her own father's name?

John Steele had built this house. That she remembered. And he had built the whole town, Aunt Agnes said. Katherine wasn't sure what that meant.

Aunt Agnes had said, "It's all yours, this house. It's your mother's and yours and so on. Make sure you don't lose it. My father built it strong and solid so his progeny could enjoy it."

Katherine had decided not to ask Aunt Agnes what progeny was.

So if she got a job cleaning the house, she would be able to see it all again. Would the books still be on the shelves in the front room? Would her bedroom still be pink?

Would the basement still be scary?

And what about the attic? She could remember being in the attic. But she couldn't remember how to get up there. Were there stairs? She didn't remember stairs.

But that woman who lived there now, who stood watching Lily, didn't seem like the kind of woman who would tolerate a stranger in her home. Katherine thought about what she might say to gain entry, and finally had one idea: Knock on the door and offer her services but not let on that she was from the cottage out back. Because she rarely lingered in their little yard and certainly she spent no time in the garden.

"I was younger than Lily is now when we moved," she said out loud.

And then another thought: 'Lily would like that book with all the family names in it.'

And where was that book?

And what secrets did it hold, maybe ones Katherine had not been old enough to understand?

When Lily came in from school, she ate a banana and went to work in the garden. Mom was home. Day off, maybe. Lily was almost out the door when Mom called her back.

"Lily, sit a moment. I was thinking of cleaning that lady's house. There's a book I want to find from when I was your age, and she probably has it on her shelf. It's all about our family. If she knew that, she wouldn't want it. And I want to show it to you."

"There are no books on her shelf. If you mean the living room shelves. They have plates on them, and photos."

"However do you know that?"

"Because when I was waiting for her to bring my basket back, I looked in the windows to see if she was on her way."

"You went up on the porch and peered in the windows?" Mom sounded shocked.

"No, Mom, I just looked from outside the gate."

"And you could see all the bookshelves and there were no books?"

"I don't think I could see all the shelves. But the ones I could see didn't have books."

"I wonder where that book is then. Thrown out, I suppose."

"What book is it, Mom? Can we get it at the library?"

"No, it's a book about our history. Our family history. Our ancestors, like my grandfather and great-grandfather and so on."

"What about your dad?"

"It didn't go that far. Isabelle—my mom—was the most recent, I think. And it just had her name and her birthdate."

"I want to see it. I know Isabelle is your mom. And her mom was ... I don't remember."

"Her mom was Millie."

"I never heard of Millie. Did she live in the big house?"

"Well, for a while. Mom and I did live there with Grandmother Millie and her husband."

"So your mom's dad?"

"No, he died when Isabelle was seven."

"So who was her husband?"

"I don't remember. She had a couple of them after William died."

Lily was anxious to get outside. A drizzle had begun. The ground was already muddy from earlier rainy days. And she had some veggies to harvest. The squash was now ready, huge green-and-orange globes that she could barely lift.

So she put on her raincoat with its hood, then her boots. It was all part of her routine. Before she came in again, she'd close in the chickens. With the sun setting so early, with the shortest day of the year coming up—something Miss Clark had told the class just today—she would be in again in less than an hour.

Once she was outside, she realized the rain had picked up. She wouldn't linger. She'd brought out a knife. She would just cut the stems of the three squash, rinse them off in the rainwater bucket, and bring them inside to ripen. She'd read about it and that was the way to do it at this time of year.

The clouds were low and heavy, the wind picking up. It blew her raincoat open, her hood off her head. She hunkered down by the first, the biggest squash, and began to cut. Then to saw. The stem was too hard. It barely yielded to the knife. A saw would work better, but they didn't have one.

The rain was ever heavier. She tossed the knife toward the door and ran to the hen house, hopping over the little fence that kept the hens from wandering away or scratching for bugs or snacks in the garden.

They were already settling down for the night. In the downpour she quickly tossed in the weeds she had plucked. They could have them in the morning if they were too sleepy now. Then she locked the door, top and bottom.

Lost in thought, she almost ran into the Treasury, that little tool shed that was locked and never opened. She never paid attention to it. But it was the obvious place for a saw, and who knew, maybe other tools she could use.

And maybe she could also have more chickens if she had more space to put them in. Winter eggs were always in short supply and now they were getting only about an egg a week, and if they wanted eggs badly enough, they would have to buy them at the grocery.

The Treasury was well sealed with combination locks. That was good. Mom would know the combination and they could open it up and put it to use. And maybe find some tools she could use in the garden.

She burst into the cottage. "Mom! What's in that other shed out there? Do you know the combination? Can we go look in there? I need the tools."

Mom stood looking at her, not saying anything. No response.

At last she said, "You mean the Treasury?"

"Yeah. And why is it called that?"

"We can't touch that, Lily. Not ever. Unless it's an emergency."

"Why? It's a tool shed, isn't it?"

"I guess it was."

"So what is it now? What does Treasury mean?"

"It means where the money is kept. Or other things that are valuable."

"Money? There's money in there?"

"I don't think so. I don't even know if there's anything valuable in there."

"So, let's open it and find out!"

"We can't."

"Why can't we?"

"Aunt Agnes said so."

"That's silly. She's dead. When did she say that?"

"She said it to Isabelle, I guess."

"Did she say it to you, though?"

"No, but my mom did, Isabelle did."

"What did she say exactly?"

"Don't open the Treasury unless it's an emergency."

"Like our house is burning down?"

"I think more like needing money, or maybe hiding from someone bad."

Lily was silent. Hiding from someone bad. That was a lot to think about. She was silent during dinner. And after she crawled into bed she was still trying to figure out what an emergency was.

Just as she was falling asleep, she had a new thought. "Who put the locks on the tool shed, Mom? Most recently?"

Mom was silent for a while. Lily was just about to succumb to sleep when Mom said, "Agnes, my grandmother. After we moved in here."

"Was that an emergency? Moving here?"

"I thought it was. Yes, we all thought it was. We were losing our home. Agnes always resented having to move. My mother, Isabelle, avoided being here in the cottage as much as possible. She is the one who made the garden. She liked to be outside. She also had a job sometimes. And Agnes took care of me."

"And Agnes? Did she have a job too?"

"No, she was too old. I think she was about seventy when we moved here. But she was a powerful woman even when she was old. She was the one who made it possible for us to live in the cottage. She knew it was important to keep an eye on her father's house. She was always scheming about ways to get it back."

"But she never did."

"No, she never did. It's almost like she's still waiting."

"And Isabelle? Did she want to go back to the house?"

"I'm not sure. She talked a lot about buying a house in town where we could all have our own bedrooms."

"That sounds like a good idea."

"But Agnes always said we couldn't afford it. Then Isabelle would say, 'We can use the treasure,' and Agnes always had an answer for that."

"Like what?" asked Lily.

"Like, 'That's not what the treasure is for,' or, 'We can't afford a house.'"

"So it wasn't an emergency?"

"Isabelle thought it was. She spent more and more nights away. Of course she had always done that. That's what Agnes said more than once."

"What did she say?"

"I guess Isabelle had a lot of boyfriends. But never mind that."

"Oh." Lily was confused, trying to understand the different ages of the people who had lived here in the cottage. How small it must have been for three people. How it might have been for a little girl to live with her mother and grandmother in this small space together.

"So Isabelle never married?"

"I wasn't aware of her having a husband while we were in the big house. Not after we moved, certainly."

"So you never had a dad."

"Not that I remember."

## AN EARLY NOVEMBER WEEKDAY 1985

KATHERINE, WALKING TO TOWN to pay her water bill, mulled over that conversation with Lily. Lily was a fresh set of ears, ears that listened without missing a thing, and Katherine had learned to listen to her, to what she said, for several years now. And the big contribution her sweet daughter had made in the past 24 hours was to ask what an emergency was.

Or in other words, what had Agnes meant by an emergency?

Katherine was trying to remember what Agnes had put into the Treasury, 'Or let's just call it a tool shed,' Katherine said to herself. 'If I can remember.'

It could be full of old-fashioned vases and bowls and so on. Things that had been on various shelves in the big house before they moved, for example. And why call it treasure? Perhaps because it could be sold over time?

But what would old pewter pitchers bring? Katherine could easily see them sitting on a shelf in a thrift shop, in other words, donated. And if they were donated they would not bring a cent. Or, given how Agnes had always protected her father's memory, perhaps these old objects were just to remember him by and the 'treasure' was sentimental.

Not much use in an emergency, though.

Katherine didn't remember these sorts of objects from her early childhood. Aunt Agnes had never made a fuss over things like that. Aunt Agnes had been interested in holding onto two things, and neither of them were in the tool shed: Family, as in family pride and family reputation, and the big house itself.

It really all came down to Agnes's father himself and his works.

Because Katherine did remember, now that she thought of it, that Aunt Agnes was always saying, "My father would do it this way."

And then there was the one time when Katherine had asked, "What about your mother?" But she hadn't gotten an answer. Agnes had perhaps turned away.

Agnes had also had a brother, named William, but he and his father—their father—had died only a day apart during the Spanish flu epidemic of 1918. Agnes had been ... here Katherine had to do some calculating. She thought about early 40s, her own age at this moment. And William had been a couple of years younger.

The other date she knew was the year they lost the house, 1950. When she was seven. What she knew is that one day she had lived in her pretty room in the big house and the next she was squeezed into the little caretaker's cottage down in the back, along with Agnes and Isabelle. And while they carried their things to the little hut, as Agnes called it, Agnes was busy directing the caretaker to make a line across the backyard. Her precious garden, both flowers and veggies, were to stay with the cottage.

Some anger had hovered in the air, and Isabelle had hurried Katherine along and closed the door behind her.

No one moved into their house, but they had to move out. Isabelle once said someone was supposed to come fix it up, but Katherine couldn't remember if that had happened.

No one would tell Katherine what was happening. But she never stepped foot in her house again. And in the next few days she moved herself from sleeping with her mother and aunt to sleeping on some bedding on the floor. That was in 1950.

Aunt Agnes had died when Katherine was twenty-four, but until then she had ruled the roost. Some nights it had been just Aunt Agnes and Katherine, Isabelle being one to be away overnight from time to time. After Aunt Agnes died, it was either Katherine and her mom, or just Katherine alone.

She remembered well, with a whole new wave of embarrassment and, yes, excitement, the night she first brought Ben home. Only the essentially non-residential quality of her tiny acreage had allowed her to take him sight-unseen into her home, her little cottage, and sneak him out again before dawn. For his sake. Because he was well-known in town. And yes, for her own sake. Aunt Agnes had never let her forget John Steele's legacy.

Well, yes, she had liked Ben. Still did. His status as a married man and having a highly visible position in town meant that unless his wife went out of town again—that one time had been because of the death of a parent—it would be the only time.

The nights had been glorious. The first night had gotten a slow start, with neither of them expecting to move so quickly to the bed. Except it was the only furniture except the table and straight-backed, rather uncomfortable chairs. The next three nights, before his wife returned, were eagerly awaited by both of them, Katherine was sure. Ben had said so, many times.

Many times during those nights, and even a couple of times since then, though only in code because of his position, they had made sure the other knew of the deep appreciation they held in her memory, in his.

In other words, when she had seen him, the few times she had seen him those following weeks and months, she had noticed, even felt, the warmth he held for her. And she reciprocated.

Even when she'd found she was pregnant. His apologies had been sincere: His career would not allow him to make their liaison known, but he would always support Katherine. She was hugely relieved and told him she understood and would always remain silent about Lily's origins.

So Lily knew nothing about her father. But she would like him, would like to know that he was handsome, witty and smart, a natural leader. Katherine was secretly proud of the time when he had loved her, body and soul. But Lily must never know.

And Lily must not know that it was his payments for her upkeep that made the stack of bills grow as it did.

Whether she sold veggies or not.

Ben had stopped by late one night when Lily was a couple of months old, and had held her and loved her, and then had set her safely on the other side of the bed and had loved Katherine with great passion.

Then and then not again. He was married, and that was that.

As Katherine reminisced about all this, she realized she was missing him, missing him a great deal at this moment. It was having Lily that had kept her from thinking about dating for these nine or so years. But why hadn't she thought of this before? She needn't keep Lily away from Ben. She might need her father someday, and while she would never break her word and tell her that this was her father, they could still have a little visit, an impromptu bumping into each other.

Why not? She knew just where to find Ben, day and night. She would figure out a way to make it reasonable that she and Lily would show up and say hi. And now that she'd thought of it, she could barely remember why she'd been avoiding him.

The day had gotten busy with routine things, and it wasn't until Lily was asleep and Katherine was hoping to go to sleep that she thought again about visiting Ben with Lily. It was an exciting thought, and she slid deeper toward sleep enjoying her visions of such a visit.

And then her brain snapped as if she had been hit in the head with a board. Lights, a loud noise, pain hit her all at once. Her breath left her. Moments before, Ben had been a possibility. But now she realized she wouldn't survive to find a way back into his arms.

Or any arms.

She was going to die. Maybe not for a couple of years, if she was lucky, but it was entirely likely she would then.

And how interesting would a dying woman be?

And Lily, charming daughter at a distance, would ruin his life, his career, if they were seen together. And knowing that because of her very existence she had ruined him, she would lose that charming confidence and independence.

Katherine could not let Lily know he was her father. Her existence was poison to him, and if Lily knew that, to herself also.

And Katherine could not let him know she was dying.

Her grief-wounded head wanted her to scream. Oh Lily, blessed Lily. I will have to leave you. I will have to hide you. I will have to train you to raise yourself. And never to let on you are alone.

She wrapped her arms around her baby girl, now no longer a baby but a half-grown and amazingly competent child, and silently cried herself to sleep.

She woke up an hour later. There had been a knock on the door, a light tapping. Ben! She got up. Crossed the room. Opened the door. There was no one there. She stepped outside. The moon lit the clouds from behind. The air was dry, chilly. She spread her arms, accepted the cold because it showed her she was still alive, searched the sky for stars, dipped her fingers into the rainwater bucket and sprinkled the cold water on her face. Still alive, good to remember. There's still time. Time to make a plan. Maybe a plan where Ben meets Lily.

Reveling in the possibilities, she splashed her face with a double-handful of water, shuddering from so much cold. Maybe a bit too much.

## A NOVEMBER SCHOOL WEEK 1985

LILY CAME RUNNING THROUGH the door from school and tossed her backpack on the bed. She knew better: take out her homework and put it on the table. But she was too excited.

Mom looked up but then back down to a piece of paper she was writing on.

"MOM!" said Lily. "Mom, guess what? Miss Clark sent you a note." She fetched it from her backpack and handed it to Mom. "It's about going to a volleyball game!"

Mom read through it, shaking her head. It looked like 'no' to Lily. She took her backpack off the bed and carefully laid out her homework, then helped herself to an apple.

Mom looked up. "She wants you to go to a volleyball game at the high school with her?"

"And with the new girl, Susan."

"Who's she?"

"She moved here. She came about two weeks ago."

"Is she nice?"

"I guess. I don't know her very well. She doesn't play with anyone. I think she's shy."

"And Miss Clark wants to take just the two of you to a volleyball game? Do you even like volleyball?"

"Sure, it's fun."

"So do you want to go? It says after school on Thursday."

"Sure, it sounds great."

"You'd have to walk home by yourself."

"I think Miss Clark is going to drive us."

"Hmm."

"Please, Mom. I really like talking to my teacher."

"OK, then. We'll try it once."

Lily hugged her and ran out to the garden to tend to things. She had some oriental-veggie seedlings up.

"I'll be right back, Mom."

Katherine said OK as Lily ran back out the door. How unusual that her teacher would take her to a volleyball game. But maybe it was because Lily was a nice girl and the other little girl, Susan, was shy. And new. Oh well, why not.

She went back to her paper. She was still all a-buzz with making the plan that had come to her last night.

Strangely it was all based on the sure knowledge that she was going to die. Well, of course everyone was going to die. But she was going to die maybe next year, maybe the year after. And she had a young child.

Yet she felt the same good way she did when she crossed off the last thing on her to-do list. Or when she finished a good book. She had a sense of accomplishment, and it felt almost like a relief. As if the end of a task were in sight.

Which it was.

She suspected she would feel other emotions before it was over, but right now she was excited—excited that she could figure out how to do this right for Lily.

She didn't know how, but she would figure it out.

So she needed a plan.

And the plan on the paper she had laid in front of her was beginning to take shape.

As she looked back to the paper, she saw the words 'Help Lily connect to the community.'

Wow, Miss Clark's invitation was a tiny beginning of this sort. Someday Lily would be going to the high school. Why not give her a taste of what high school was like?

So Katherine signed the note and tucked it back into Lily's backpack.

She could see through the little window that it was a bright, sunny day. She didn't want to expose her face to the window overlooking the garden in case the woman was watching, so she pulled her rain hat down over her hair. She'd go out and take a look at what Lily was doing, then the two of them could walk into town and maybe to the library or the playground.

She turned the paper over so Lily wouldn't read her notes, few as they were so far.

She opened the door. Lily was hunkered down in the garden at the end of a bright green patch. Katherine looked up toward the window, carefully because she didn't want to be caught looking, and the woman was standing there.

Why?

Why, why, why?

Why would she spend her time watching a little girl working in her garden?

She had a flash that that woman was acting just like Aunt Agnes, who couldn't keep to her own affairs but was always watching, commenting, criticizing, correcting. She had been suspicious of everything. Katherine remembered tiptoeing into a room hoping her slightly deaf aunt would not notice her. And that wasn't only when Katherine was a child.

Maybe that's why she so resented the woman in the window.

She looked up again. The woman wasn't there.

As if she didn't want to be caught looking.

"Mom, look," said Lily.

Katherine was careful to keep to the narrow paths between the wide green patches of whatever veggie Lily had planted.

Lily had slid her hand into a patch of greenery and lifted up the tiny leaves. Katherine didn't know what it was.

"What's that?"

Lily stood, holding several seed packets. The names were unfamiliar to Katherine. "They're oriental greens," said Lily. "I'm going to sell them to the Chinese restaurants. I bet they have to shop a long distance from here so maybe they'll buy mine instead."

Katherine was surprised, impressed.

"How much more time do you want here?" Katherine asked her. "Because we could go to town, maybe get some groceries."

And, Katherine thought to herself, where else should we go? What else does she need to know about? We need to extend our range. Not easy on foot, but possible.

Of course they could take a walk that happened to take them past Ben's house, a bit of a long walk but certainly doable. Then he could see Lily with her, and she wouldn't have to face him or avoid telling Lily that this was her father. That would be up to Ben to do if she ever were to find out. Because Katherine had promised. And he would know what Lily looked like, in case he ever bumped into her. Of course it was a long shot. It depended on his looking out the window just then. And she realized it was a thought left over from when she used to walk by his house just to feel close to him. It wouldn't do.

But it would be fun, even so. As much fun as it used to be, because it meant being close to him.

But sunset was only an hour away. They put off other adventures until the next day, Saturday. They walked the short distance to the grocery store, picked out their groceries, and walked home in the dark. Katherine had bought chicken to go with their rice. It was time for Lily to learn to cook chicken.

As she lay awake late into the night, her mind busy adding to the plan, tweaking the plan, she realized that for all the chicken recipes and trips on the ferry—her idea for tomorrow's excursion—she hadn't addressed the major issue: how to keep Lily safe and free and independent. She fell asleep with no answers.

But then toward dawn she had not only an idea but a powerful understanding of what she needed to bring about. Because it was the only way Lily would be safe.

And of course that would include Lily keeping her eye on the big house and all that might mean to her future.

She mulled the idea over a few times, but it was obviously the only solution.

She would need to prepare Lily in all ways to be able to live on her own. And then she, Katherine, Mom, would need to disappear.

Because what she couldn't afford to do was to die right here in town. Then Lily would be scooped up and put in a foster home regardless of her ability to live on her own.

Nor could she get sick and deteriorate where everyone could see it happen. As soon as her prognosis went public, Lily would be scooped up and put in a foster home.

And she had already figured out that Ben couldn't be part of it. Sure he was her father, but he had a whole separate life, his wife, kids, career.

So she would have to disappear.

Not even Lily could know. Because she would tell someone.

And the nosy woman in the window could not know, even though she would be a daily witness. So she needed to get used to having Lily around but not Katherine. Katherine would need to be out of sight in the near term so that no one expected to see her. Even though she'd be here, probably for the next two or so years.

Maybe longer.

No, don't go there. Don't hedge. Think two years. Period.

Lily would be almost 12 by then, because now she was almost 10.

It would take some cleverness for Katherine not to be a familiar figure. Wouldn't it? So her disappearance would not be noticed?

And how long would that be, when Lily would have to go along living on her own?

Six years? Maybe five if she did well in school and graduated early?

Wow. Could she do that?

Katherine sank in a moment of despair, but revived herself. She can do it, she told herself.

After all, she doesn't need to do it now. We have two years to prepare. Probably.

She didn't know how she'd disappear without leaving a body behind, but there was time to figure that out.

She fell asleep at long last.

## A NOVEMBER SATURDAY JOURNEY 1985

"CAN MISS CLARK COME for dinner, Mom?"

Katherine panicked. She didn't speak right away. Then she asked, "Why?"

"I was thinking if she drove me home after the volleyball game, she could stay for supper."

"Oh, Sweetie, that's a nice thought."

"Well?"

"I'll think about it." But she had thought about it. Instantly. How to tell Lily she didn't want anyone to see their humble circumstances?

They were gathering their things for their adventure on the ferry. It was a short ride, and cost little, and it set sail at a dock not far from the library. People who lived on the little island it serviced often drove their cars to town and beyond, and then back onto the ferry. And off on the other side to take them on the twisting roads to their homes. Katherine had been once with Isabelle and had been scared of being in the boat, being on the water, watching the cars drive on at one end and off at the other.

She would not be scared today because she was grown up, and because she couldn't be afraid in front of Lily.

So they walked to the ferry. The day was breezy, sunny but with a lot of clouds out over the sound. Katherine and Lily, plus a few other folks, were standing in the walk-on line. And several cars were lined up along the street waiting for the ferry to arrive.

The ferry had left the far side and begun its five-minute transit. Lily was surprised at how small it was. Its deck held only a few cars, and a little cabin to one side held the walk-on passengers.

The ferry arrived. The crew tied it to the dock with heavy ropes, and in no time the cars had driven off and the arriving foot passengers, the few that there were, had walked off. And now time for the departing vehicles and walk-ons to take their places.

Lily shuffled onto the ferry, holding the rope railing with one hand and Mom's hand with the other. She wished she'd put her jacket on instead of leaving it in the backpack. The breeze was chilly here at the shore. The ferry swayed and Mom held her hand in a tighter grip.

She had seen the ferry while walking around town and even on her way to school, but had never thought about going on it.

They were already seated when the cars were signaled to drive on. The workers lined them up carefully on the deck so they took as little space as possible. It was interesting to see how tightly they could be fit together. The ferry was moving up and down a little. Not all the cars fit, and Mom said they would have to wait for the next sailing.

Sailing, but no sails. Instead, a rumbling engine that made the whole ferry jiggle.

And then they were underway. Lily stood so she could see more. The ride was over too soon. Well, they'd be going home on the ferry again before it was too dark and she would be able to see more then.

As they approached the shore, Lily could see the pedestrians on the island who would be getting on the ferry for the next trip, and an even longer line-up of cars. Mom said, "It looks like those people are going home after a day on the island."

The ferry slowed, and the foot passengers picked up their bags. Mom had said they had to get off fast as soon as the ferry stopped so the other people could get on and go home.

So Lily was ready to move. There were a couple of foot passengers ahead of her. She was watching keenly as they docked, and when the passengers moved, she began to move. And then their line passed the line of waiting foot passengers. Standing in that line were both Miss Clark and Miss Horan. And also another lady with them.

"Hi, Miss Clark!" she said.

Miss Clark had her arms full of bags of veggies, and so did Miss Horan.

Miss Horan said, "This is our friend Edna."

Mom was pushing Lily along from behind, but Lily asked, "Is there a farmers market here?"

They had already passed by, but Lily could hear Miss Clark say yes. And then she asked, "Is this your mother?" But they were already past.

As soon as Lily was free from the disembarking passengers, she saw the market. It was up a hill across the street. Cars just off the ferry were driving up that hill and stopping. It seemed it was a popular place.

And it hadn't yet been closed down for the winter.

She could bring her remaining veggies here, her great numbers of potatoes, her carrots and beets. As much as she could carry.

"Maybe we can find some bread here," said Mom.

"And eggs. Good eggs," added Lily.

They climbed the hill. The sun was lowering. The air was cooler over here on this island. Mom had taken a schedule from the ferry and was reading it as they walked. From the hillside they could see that their ferry had already arrived back at the dock on the far side, where they'd gotten on. They would never make it back downhill to get on the next one.

"Two more ferries tonight, Lily," Mom said.

"What happens if we miss it?"

Mom laughed. "I guess we have to sleep here on this grassy hill. It looks soft enough."

"Mom!"

"OK, let's hurry to check out the market, then."

By the time they got there they found only about a dozen people still at the few tables that made up the little market. They took the two remaining loaves of bread. And one dozen eggs was all they could get into the backpack with them. The squash were beautiful but too heavy to carry.

Then they turned to see where the ferry was. They had plenty of time.

So they sat on the grassy hill. It looked over the entire harbor and then beyond it they could see their little town. It too was hilly, two side-by-side hills, the one they were sitting on and the one they lived on, divided by a strait of salt water. Salt water that connected way over to the west with the Pacific Ocean, which was much too far away to see, maybe a hundred miles.

On the distant hillside where their town was, they could see the grocery, with its name in lights. And there was the little park across from the library and the back of the library with its lights on. And their own house should be way over to the left, beyond the downtown area.

And there it was, the old pink Victorian on Main Street, its west windows reflecting the setting sun. And of course they lived right behind that.

The depot and the tracks leading to it were hidden by the woods next to the big house. The tiny forest with treacherous sticker bushes and little brook and unexpected fence, none of it visible from here, of course.

And where did the tracks go after they passed the depot? Lily couldn't see them as they wended their way between the huge buildings that filled up the port.

Lily said, "I can see my school," and pointed at it.

Mom said, "There's the high school, where you're going for volleyball."

"And for school when I get older."

"Yes," said Mom. "In four or five more years."

Lily laughed. "That sounds like forever."

Katherine nodded. "It was forever. Once. And now it's forever ago."

Katherine could see Lily thought that was a strange idea.

It was time to go. The ferry was coming, the sun was setting, the lights all over town were coming on. They walked down the hill. They could see the ferry arrive on the far side, and they'd be just in time to get back on when it got back to this side.

"That was cool, seeing the whole town spread out like that. I had no idea it was so big," said Lily.

"I know. I've lived here all my life and I probably haven't seen it all."

Lily was silent for most of the rest of the walk. If Mom hadn't gone anywhere … . She thought she'd tell Mom what she had just figured out. "So my dad is right here in town. Or maybe he used to be. I hope he still is."

Katherine was suddenly on high alert. But by then they were seated on the ferry and it wasn't a good place to talk about things like that. Thank heavens.

## A NOVEMBER WEEKEND 1985

KATHERINE THOUGHT, 'MY SMART daughter!' She had not intended for Lily to conclude her father must have been here.

It had been a close call. If they hadn't been in public, Lily would be pressing her about her father right now. Again.

And what about my own father? Had Isabelle ever left town? She could have. Katherine remembered times when Agnes and she were alone in the cottage, including overnight.

So maybe her father was here, too. But maybe not.

And probably he wouldn't know he had a granddaughter in any case. He might not even be alive.

And that would make a big difference as she created her plan. If he turned out to be interested in his granddaughter.

For that matter if he turned out to be interested in his daughter. Did he know he had a daughter? A daughter Katherine?

Isabelle had told her contradictory things. Katherine's father was a fisherman. He had died in the war. She didn't know where he was. She had loved him. She had not loved him.

That last was most disturbing.

Katherine had long since concluded her mother didn't know who her father was.

But if she did, Katherine had wanted to know all about him. As Lily wanted to know now about her dad.

Well, it was a dead end. She had realized when her mother, Isabelle, died that the knowledge of her father had died with her.

Hadn't it?

Oh, but what about a birth certificate? Katherine had been born here in town. She could go look on Monday. When Lily was in school.

When Lily was in school because if Lily knew such information existed within walking distance, she would be there at the first possible moment. And then the big secret would be out and Ben's entire life would be ruined. Unless she hadn't put his name on the birth certificate. She couldn't remember.

Probably not, though. She had been so embarrassed.

Along with secretly proud that such a fine man was the father of her baby.

But probably not.

The ferry arrived at the terminal. Mother and daughter walked up the hill to the street above and turned toward home. The setting sun was at their backs. Katherine was exhilarated all over again, first about the plan for Lily, but now also the possibility she might find her own father. After all these years. Why hadn't she realized she could do this before?

Probably because Isabelle had told her the information wasn't available.

Hadn't Isabelle missed him? Hadn't she sometimes wished she were in his arms? Or was he so completely gone that she had abandoned such hope?

Perhaps she had known he was dead. Which meant she knew who he was.

Which realization hit Katherine with a stab in her heart. Just like Lily, she wanted to know who her dad was. And on Monday she might find out. The county clerk's office was only a mile away.

## A NOVEMBER MONDAY 1985

SHE AWOKE TO RAIN. No surprise there. She bundled Lily up and sent her off to school with the umbrella. Katherine would head out later, maybe during a lull in the storm. Meanwhile she worked on the plan. The Plan, as she had written on the top of the paper.

But then the rain got heavier, dauntingly heavy. Like a real winter storm driving itself in from Alaska. Not entirely unexpected, perhaps a bit early, uninviting. Katherine hoped it would abate by the time Lily got out of school. Oh well, it was only half a mile, the walk from school home.

But it was so heavy now that she decided not to go to the county clerk's office today. Her disappointment was softened only because she had The Plan to work on.

The paper was still nearly empty. She had written down Lily's idea of selling apples, but really that category was more like 'sell stuff' or 'sell garden stuff.' It would be up to Lily to figure out the details.

And as she had said as Katherine tucked her in last night, "Now I have two markets. Here and on the island." She smiled even as she fell asleep.

So Katherine sat at the table, thinking. What would Lily need to be able to do on her own? Entirely on her own?

Today the thought of Lily on her own, of her own absence, filled Katherine with sadness. She wanted to be there with and for Lily. She felt her breast. The tumor wasn't shrinking, probably growing. She needed to find an article to learn more about what was coming.

She sat back, pondering. No library today.

Even if she had a car, she wouldn't want to venture out in the squall that was now buffeting the little cottage.

She heard a strange noise. Probably just a few little branches hitting the roof. She got up to look out the one little window, but couldn't see anything other than the trees down the street bending in the strong, blustery wind.

And then the sound became louder, and all at once sounded close by, only a few feet away.

Katherine turned. A loud splash, a spray—rain on the table, on her paper—then a constant and loud dripping. Something had happened to the roof. Out the window she could see shingles, two or three, and a wide swatch of tarpaper. From her roof, no doubt about it.

And, she realized, more could tear away in this winter wind.

She would have to go to town, get new roofing materials, repair it before it got worse. Now. In the storm.

She would pay a bit more and ask them to deliver: tarpaper, shingles, nails, a hammer? She'd have to ask to be sure.

The shingles that had just torn away were in tatters, strewn across the alley.

She put a bowl under the stream of drops and covered the table with a towel to catch the splashes. She laid her raincoat across the bottom of the bed to catch any spray.

The Plan was a soggy mess.

And wasn't there a message in this deluge? Hadn't she just wondered what was the worst Lily might need to do all by herself? She hadn't even thought of repairs of this sort.

If she had enough money she would be able to hire someone.

Big if.

Katherine would have to talk to Ben and make sure he kept up child support. These days he sent the money in the mail, all 10s and 20s as she had requested. That needn't change. He needn't know that Katherine was gone.

Lily would have the key to their PO box, so no problem there. He'd just have to understand—she would need to send him a message to this effect—that he couldn't be late, decide to drop it off, stop by ... .

Yes, once or twice he had been late, and on those occasions she had found an envelope with the whole $100 in a single bill in an envelope slid under the door.

And when he'd pushed the $100 under the door, she'd had to go to the bank to change it into twenties. Too bad she couldn't take Lily with her on those occasions. She would have loved to see one bill turn into five! But then she would have asked too many questions about where the money had come from.

Well, this was just one of those things that needed working out, but other than adding it to The Plan, it was not something for right now.

For child support issues, she had time. For the roof, she had no time at all.

The leak was worse, the storm was worse, and she thought she heard more shingles tear away. She hauled an old tarp from deep in their closet to cover the bed, put on her raincoat and boots, and went out into the storm.

The wind caught the door and wrenched it from her hand. She could hear the hinges screeching as they were strained to their limit.

Bent, too, the top one at least, she realized. Something else to repair.

She latched the door behind her. The seal would not be as good until she replaced the bent hinge. But at least the door would keep the storm from inundating the entire cottage and all they owned.

Would Lily be strong enough to close the door in a wind like this? She'd better be. That was just a reality she might face.

A storm like this one didn't happen that often, though. And in saying that to herself, Katherine realized she was trying to make things easy on Lily. Again.

And on herself. On her plan. On the very idea that she could leave Lily entirely on her own.

Well, she'd have to. The alternative was foster care. Possibly years of foster care, possibly several homes until she was tossed out of the system at eighteen because she would be an adult.

An adult with no prospects for education and a limited future.

Isabelle had been a bit of an absentee mother, too, but Katherine had had the firm hand of Agnes in her life until she was solidly an adult. If she'd had only Isabelle, though ... .

Once outside, Katherine ran around to the alley to see the damage up close. At first she thought there was only one largish square of tarpaper and a few shingles, all in fragments and hard to count, strewn over the neighborhood.

But then she turned and saw more roofing blowing away, ripping from the roof, curling and flapping in the wind as it sailed across the alley.

She couldn't see onto the roof. She had no ladder. A newly torn-off piece grazed her face. She ducked and turned away. Her face smarted. She ducked another piece of shingle, then ran for the indoors.

The wind was so strong she could barely make it to the front of the cottage, and she was soaked to the skin when she got there. She inched in the door, holding it tight so it wouldn't blow open, then latched it and locked it.

Poor Lily.

On the other hand, Lily was just as likely to run home from school and burst in the door in great excitement and exhilaration from the storm, soaked, even chilled, but full of joy and eager to share it.

While Katherine huddled in their blanket and sipped hot tea.

Well, good thing Lily saw all of life as an adventure.

And good thing if that were her way of looking at life today, because as soon as she got home, they would need to go to the lumber yard and start the process of fixing the roof. The leak had grown worse, the bowl needed emptying every hour, the towel was soaked and would need wringing out and a day to dry.

But why wait for her to come home? Katherine, though feeling reluctant, realized that she should go meet Lily at school and from there hurry to the lumber yard. That would save Lily half a mile of walking and cut the transit time to the lumber yard in half.

She took up the new paper and wrote The Plan on top and copied what she had written on the sodden one. And with her mind deeply settled into that project, she realized that today she could give Lily an experience that would serve her well when she was alone: to let her negotiate the roof project. The whole thing.

They could talk over the details, the amount they'd need, perhaps the rental of a ladder, even know-how about roofing. Whatever she thought she'd need.

Not that Katherine knew about roofs, but together they could probably figure it out, and then Katherine would hand the whole project over to Lily.

But when she put it that way, it sounded awful to Katherine. What kind of mother was she?

A dying mother. Though she had to remind herself often, that truth never changed: She needed to prepare Lily to live on her own from the time she was twelve, maybe even eleven, and there was no help for it. The alternative was foster care or worse. Lily would need to make a home for herself.

She had once said, "Mom, my home is where you are." And ideally that would be true, Katherine thought. But it was not to be that way, and Lily would need to be able to make herself a home without Katherine. Right here in the cottage. Keeping an eye on the big house. Being ready to take possession of it when the time came. Or if. Avoiding interference because no one would know Mom wasn't at home anymore. Because Mom would vanish. Lily would think Mom had discovered her father somewhere, that Katherine's father had been found, and that she'd gone to bring him back.

Yes, Lily would be OK. She was that tough and strong, and that full of joy in adversity, in life's storms.

So armed with a small stack of 20s tucked deep in her pocket, covered in raincoat and boots, an apple in another pocket for Lily's snack, and with time to spare, Katherine headed to the elementary school on the other side of downtown. The same school Katherine had gone to as a child. A school which she typically avoided out of shyness.

At least now she had seen Miss Clark, just Saturday on the ferry. Miss Clark had looked pleasant, cheerful. Lily adored her.

All the parents would be picking up their kids today, though, and Katherine couldn't figure out how to avoid them. Some she would know from third grade last year.

She pulled her hood down further over her eyes. Maybe they wouldn't notice her.

As soon as she got on the other side of the one major downtown intersection, she could see that school had not gotten out yet. Classroom lights were visible through large windows. And the side street was filled with cars parked in an orderly fashion. She knew the rules: Park the car, come to the classroom, take your child. No kids running, their papers trailing after them, to their cars. It was now more orderly than when she was growing up.

Soon she was climbing up the steps to the building. There were no hallways. Classrooms emptied directly onto the school sidewalks. Remembering which room it was (she hoped), she might succeed in being there before Lily could come out with the walking kids and head for home, when Katherine might conceivably miss her.

No, she was there in time. Moms were waiting outside the fourth-grade classroom door. They nodded, said hi, smiled. Katherine smiled back and looked away each time.

Then the door opened, the moms took charge of their offspring, Lily waved to Katherine from toward the back of the line, then took her hand at the door and waved goodbye to a friend or two, and Katherine guided her to the sidewalk that led south along the edge of town and in the direction of the lumber yard, explaining what had happened.

Lily skipped along happily enough, told Katherine the lights had gone out at school so the teacher Miss Clark had gotten out a flashlight and read them a scary story, and it was so much fun, Mom, too bad you couldn't hear it, and so on, all the way to the lumber yard.

Mom had explained that they were going to make a game of this project and told her all she knew about the roofs. Then she handed the money to Lily and sent her into the huge hardware store part of the lumber yard. Mom had said, "Pretend I'm not here. I trust you."

And then suddenly Lily was entirely on her own.

She had forgotten to ask Mom about the other building, the little Treasury and its locked door. If she had enough money, she would get enough roofing for it, too.

Lily started by finding someone to help her. She told him the whole story, and he said he could help. By the time she was done, she had bought enough roofing for the three buildings, both tarpaper and shingles. He told her how delivery would work and that it was free, and then she asked how to do the shingling.

The conversation went on for a long time. Mom was nowhere to be seen. And then the man asked Lily if she had a ladder.

Buying a ladder would cost too much. Lily counted through the money several times. Maybe she didn't need a ladder. Maybe she could climb up on a chair. But she didn't really think so.

And then the man asked her if she'd like to rent a ladder for a few days. Only $2 a day. Delivered with the roofing materials.

"But how will I get it back to you?"

Lily was feeling as though the whole project was slipping away.

And then she had the thought, what if she did buy the ladder? They would deliver it with the roofing. And then she could use it after she was done with the roofing and earn some money by ... maybe roofing someone else's henhouse? Better than throwing the money away on a rental. Delivered. And the money was sitting in the breadbox at home.

"Could I give you the money for the ladder when it's delivered?" she asked.

She could see the man smiling behind the hand he held up to his face.

"We can arrange that," he said.

And then they talked about roofing nails, and a hammer. She sighed. It had to be done. She nodded. "Yes, please add those."

He wrote it all up and showed her what she owed for the ladder and had her sign the paper.

And right about then Mom was coming back in the door of the store.

Lily shook the man's hand. Turning to Mom, she said, "It's coming tomorrow."

## A BUSY WEEK IN MID- NOVEMBER 1985

AND SO BEGAN THE great project of reroofing the cottage. The truck with all she had bought arrived early the next morning, Tuesday. The day was beautiful, no storm clouds anywhere and just a small, pleasant breeze. She begged Mom to let her stay home from school to get on with the work, and in the end Mom agreed.

She did as the man had told her. It was tiring. As she removed the old roofing, Mom picked up the pieces and stacked them and held them down with a large rock.

And so it went. Lily finished the cottage on Wednesday, including replacing the bent hinge, and then Mom said she needed to go back to school, so she couldn't work on the little buildings until the weekend. Miss Clark inquired about why she'd been absent, and when Lily told her, Miss Clark asked her to tell the whole class during Show and Tell. She also gave Lily a stack of homework she'd missed and told her to bring it back on Monday.

But Lily had said she couldn't do it till she was done with the other two buildings because rain was coming.

Miss Clark nodded and turned her back, and when Lily said, "But I'll do it, Miss Clark," and when Miss Clark turned back, Lily was surprised to see tears in her eyes.

"And don't forget," Miss Clark said. "Today is volleyball. I hope you still want to come."

Lily had forgotten. "Yes! It's Thursday, isn't it. I can come. Mom probably remembers."

"Or we can drive by your house and you can run in and tell her. And did you remember your shorts so you can play during halftime?"

"No, I forgot. OK, if we have time, I can get them really fast. I don't want to miss it."

So that's what they did. Susan and Lily sat in Miss Clark's backseat. They didn't really talk to each other, and then Lily told Miss Clark to stop at the end of the alley out at the road. It took her only a minute each way and then she was back with her change of clothes.

Then pointing at Lily's partly open bag, Susan said, "Let's see your shirt. It looks cute," and Lily showed it to her. It had her name on it in glitter, which Susan traced with her finger. And after that they chattered along and Lily decided she liked Susan very much.

They were at the high school in no time. Miss Clark took Susan and Lily into the girls' locker room so they could change into their play clothes. Then they all went out to the bleachers. One team of girls, in red, was from their high school, and the other team, in yellow, was from a high school in the next town over. All of them were practicing with balls, with each other and alone. The game itself wouldn't start for another half an hour.

High schoolers were coming in, talking, finding seats. Moms and dads, it seemed, were there too, sometimes with younger children. Some others looked like grandparents.

And then there were other teachers. Miss Clark pointed out some she knew. "This one teaches math, that one teaches music, that's the principal, that one is the librarian."

"Like Miss Horan!" Lily said.

"Yes, but she's at the town library. The high school has a whole separate library."

"Really? Wow," said Lily.

"Yes, and the librarian at the high school is a friend of mine. Her name is Miss Finley, Edna Finley. I'll introduce you if we have time."

And then there appeared people in striped uniforms with whistles who were the ones running the game.

The only volleyball Lily had played was where she had tried to hit the ball over the net again and again. She didn't know how it was scored or how the game was played by people who knew the rules. She asked Susan if she knew how to play, mostly because she was enjoying talking to Susan but didn't know anything about her, so she didn't have much to say to her so far.

"I don't know how, do you?" she asked.

"Nope," said Lily. "But we get to play during half-time, Miss Clark said, right?"

While the two girls were chatting, Miss Clark stood up and waved to some adults across the gym who had just come in together and were talking in a group. They were all wearing red sweatshirts. Miss Clark said they were high school teachers, and they would sit together and cheer and the team would know everyone wanted them to win.

"Someone is waving to you, Miss Clark," said Susan.

Miss Clark had sat down, but stood again, then waved. Maybe she was waving to Edna. To Miss Finley. Lily wondered if she'd be sitting over with those teachers if she didn't have two little girls with her. She was even wearing a red sweatshirt.

A whistle blew and the court cleared. Then the game began. Even without knowing how the scoring worked, Lily thought it was exciting. The teachers cheered loudly and the score went up and up. One girl would fly across the court to get her fists under the ball and pop it back up in the air so some other girl could hit it over the net. She couldn't wait until she got to play.

"We're winning!" shouted Miss Clark as she clapped.

"Yay," said Lily. "Yay, yay, yay!"

Next time she'd wear her red shirt!

Then it was half-time. Miss Clark sent the two little girls down onto the court, with a dozen other children. Miss Clark drifted toward the rows of faculty. Lily saw her shaking some hands, and hugging some of the teachers. She thought she saw Miss Clark pointing at her or Susan, probably saying, "Those are my students." Lily was proud to be in her class.

She wondered if she could come to volleyball another time. Even if Miss Clark didn't want to come.

When the half-time play was over, Miss Clark came to get Lily and Susan. She had one of the teachers with her and introduced him to the girls.

He said hi to them, then, "Let's see what it says on your shirt. Ah, Lily! Is that your name?"

"Yes," said Lily.

"It's a pretty name," he said. "Like the flower?"

Lily couldn't believe he'd thought of that. Yes! She was Lily. Some people thought her name was Lillian, but it wasn't, it was Lily like the flower.

"Yes, like the flower." She couldn't have been more delighted.

Then he turned to Susan and talked to her for a bit, while Lily was full of joy that someone understood about her name. So Lily didn't hear what he said to Susan.

Miss Clark was moving them along so they were no longer in the way on the court, and the other teacher came with them until they were all back at their seats.

Lily wondered if the teacher was Miss Clark's boyfriend.

The game was over. Their team won! Everyone was shouting, cheering, celebrating.

"Time to go home," said Miss Clark. "I'll take you home first, Susan, and then you, Lily."

Susan froze. She simply wouldn't move. Then Lily noticed that she had started to cry. She looked like she didn't want to be seen crying, though.

Miss Clark took a tissue from her bag and wiped Susan's face. "Let's go into the locker room and get you cleaned up," she said. "Want to come, Lily?"

Lily didn't want to go. She wanted Susan to have privacy. "I'll just walk home, Miss Clark."

But she didn't know if Miss Clark heard her.

Lily wondered what was wrong with Susan, but she knew how to mind her own business. Mom reminded her about that a lot.

Then the teacher said, "OK," and Lily realized Miss Clark had asked him to wait with Lily, because she and Susan would only be a minute.

So they found a quiet spot out in the lobby. Most of the families, most of the team members, had left.

"So, did you like the game?" he asked.

"I loved it. I want to play again. I wonder if I can come if Miss Clark can't come."

"I bet you could, but you'd need a ride."

"No, I don't. I can walk."

He smiled. "Tell me where you live that's close enough to walk. That will be convenient when you're in high school."

"I live at 1 1/2 Main Street."

"I never heard of an address like that."

"Well, there's a big house, and then Mom and I live in the little house in the back. The big house is 1 Main St, so we are 1 1/2. Mom figured that out. We don't have a house number on our house, though."

"Oh. I see," he said with the kind of frown that showed he was thinking about what she had said. And then a moment later he looked surprised, really surprised, and then Miss Clark and Susan were back.

Lily could tell Susan might be ready to cry again, but of course she didn't say anything about that. Miss Clark said, "Thanks, Ben," and then the two girls went with her to the car.

"I'll drop you off first, Lily. And then I'll take Susan back to where she lives."

Lily thought that was a strange way to say she'd take her home.

After Miss Clark dropped her off, Lily thought she'd have time to do some outdoors things, but the sun had already set. She closed the chickens in as she passed by on her way to the cottage door, and there was Mom, just unlocking the door herself.

They went in together, and as Mom made a quick supper, she listened to Lily talk and talk about the volleyball game and how fun it was to play at half-time, and how nice Miss Clark was.

Katherine put the soup on the table. Lily was giving her a running description of every ball she had hit and every person she had met, but Katherine was only half-listening. Her mind was still on her trip to the county clerk's office.

She'd filled out a form so she could get her own birth certificate. There it was, her name: Katherine Agnes Steele. Mother: Isabelle Steele. Father: (not filled out).

And the same thing for Lily, just the way she had recalled filling it out: No father listed. Except the form had said, 'Father: unknown'.

For whatever reason, she had avoided the complication of acknowledging ... what? That there'd ever been a father? Just as her mother had pretended?

Lily had cleverly deduced that her father was right here in town, as could have been true of her own father. Unless back then Isabelle had traveled. In which case she'd never know who he was.

Well, she'd probably never know in any case.

She'd been hopeful, hopeful enough that she was feeling disappointed now.

She tried to figure back. Yes, her father could have been a serviceman who died in the war. Was there any way to verify that? Had there been deaths among the men who had lived in this small a town, in Steeletown, during World War Two?

Maybe a trip to the library was in order. Because if there had been a casualty, it could have been her dad. Just as her mother had said. Depending on when he was shipped out and when he died.

Lily had wound down about volleyball. Katherine could tell she was tired. Then she perked up again, just as excited as before. "I think Miss Clark has a boyfriend. He's a teacher at the high school and his name is Ben."

"Really," said Katherine.

"That's nice," she added after she caught her breath.

It rained all day Friday, but Saturday dawned with some feeble sunlight, and if the rain stayed away for a few hours, Lily could perhaps do the rest of the roofing. Or some of it.

But Mom wanted to go to the library. "Mom, let me stay home and do this. It's going to start raining every day soon."

Mom left right after breakfast, and Lily was already at the henhouse adding a new layer of tar paper. Before Mom got back, she was done.

Now for the Treasury. It was tall enough to need the ladder again.

And it was a good thing she had thought to do it, Lily could see right away. There were some shingles left but a lot were missing. And she could see a hole in one corner of the roof that went all the way through the wood. It wasn't a large hole, and without a flashlight Lily couldn't see inside. She tried to wiggle her hand into the hole. It was barely big enough for her to get her fingers in, but finally she could reach as far as her wrist.

She encountered something solid and flat, featureless, like a slick plastic or cloth tarp. She had expected lumpy things, vases or lamps. Something protective must have been put over whatever the flat thing was. Reaching as far as she could in every direction, she felt nothing but that smooth plasticky surface. With puddles of water sitting on it here and there. Rain had gotten in.

But maybe it hadn't gotten below the covering to the treasure.

Mom came out of the cottage. "I'm out of flour and a few other things. I'm going to go to the store. Want to come?"

"No, this is going to take me all afternoon and now that I've got the tar paper off I have to finish it before it rains."

"OK. I hope whatever's inside is worth all that effort."

"Me, too," said Lily. "Let's look and see!"

Lily was kidding. She knew Mom had always said no, not unless it was an emergency. Save it for a rainy day. Lily was quite happy to wait for the next rainy day and then open it.

"I barely have enough tar paper for it. It's got a hole in it. I wish I knew that it was worth it. Are you sure we can't open it?"

Mom just shook her head and left for the store, and Lily threw her last piece of tarpaper onto the roof, climbed the ladder with the bag of nails and the hammer, and began to hammer.

"Get down from there."

Lily was startled and felt the ladder wobble.

The voice was loud, harsh.

Lily looked down. On the ground right next to the ladder was the woman from the window. Lily knew her well enough not so much from the window but from losing her basket to her. And here she was, holding onto the ladder.

And now shaking the ladder so much that Lily thought she might fall.

"Stop!" yelled Lily, but when the woman didn't stop, she threw herself across the roof of the shed and hooked her legs around the ladder.

"Get down from there," the woman said again.

"Let go of the ladder and I'll come down," said Lily.

The woman gave the ladder one more good shake, then backed off. She stood only a few feet away with her hands on her hips.

"What are you doing up there?" she yelled.

"I'm shingling the roof."

The woman was silent. Lily could see an odd look on her face. Then she turned and walked straight across the garden and disappeared around the corner of the big pink house.

She hadn't bothered walking on the garden paths but had left deep heelprints in Lily's new beds of oriental greens.

Lily went back up on the roof. The question was how to deal with the hole at the corner, to make sure rain couldn't get in.

As she looked at the hole again, she wondered how it had gotten there. Maybe an animal. If so, it could just bite through the new tarpaper and open it up again. Better to add some shingles, too. She didn't have enough for the whole roof, but she could cover the hole certainly.

It was tricky work. The shingles didn't bend the way she needed them to. In the end she used several scraps of tarpaper to build up the corner.

As the sun set below the rainclouds that hung out on the horizon, over the sea to the west, Mom came back with groceries. Lily put away the ladder and picked up the scraps. And when she glanced up, she could see the woman in the window again.

## A MID-NOVEMBER WEEKEND 1985

THE RAIN OVERNIGHT KEPT Lily and Katherine awake. Lily listened for leaks, but there were none. It was a good thing that she had been able to get the roof fixed in time. This was serious rain.

The next day, Sunday, the rain did not let up, so by mid-morning Katherine made them some popcorn and cocoa, and they talked.

Lily had been out to the garden to check the damage and told Katherine about the sudden appearance of the Woman in the Window, as she had started calling her. The damage to the oriental greens would probably be permanent, but she could plant more, and they would grow slowly throughout the winter. Unless the Woman in the Window came back.

Lily also told Katherine about the hole in the roof, probably due to some animal looking for a winter home, they agreed. After all, the little tool shed that had been turned into the Treasury was really old.

"When did you move out of the house, Mom? Isn't that when the treasure was put into the shed?"

"That was in 1950. Thirty-five years ago. A long time."

"And then the Woman in the Window and her husband and kids moved in?"

"Oh, no, it was empty for years before they moved in. My mom always said the people who bought it were going to fix it up but they never did."

"Why did you move out?"

"It was falling apart. And I think my mother and Aunt Agnes couldn't afford to fix it up themselves. By which I mean they couldn't afford someone to do all those jobs for them."

"What was wrong with it?"

"It had some leaks, which I think the buyers patched right away. The electric was outdated. The plumbing. Everything. When we moved out, the house was almost 50 years old, and after John Steele died, there was no one to take charge and keep it up-to-date, and that was more than thirty years earlier. I suppose he expected his son William would take over, but the only ones left were his wife and Aunt Agnes, or really, Aunt Agnes."

"So the buyers did some work. And then what happened?"

"Nothing. It just sat there empty until I was in my early 20s. So all through my childhood."

"So who moved in next?"

"That woman and her husband."

"And you were living here in the cottage the whole time?"

"Yes."

"Why? It's not very big for you and your mom. I mean, what if you wanted to have your boyfriend over?" she asked, giggling.

"Because we had to keep an eye on the big house. Because Aunt Agnes said if we did, someday it would come back to us. Because it was really ours. And maybe someday we could buy it back."

"But you didn't have enough money."

"Right."

"So how would that work?"

"I don't know. I guess I'm just keeping the hope alive. Or the tradition."

"So do we own the garden and these buildings?"

"I don't know, exactly. It's like a lease or something."

"Would you be sad if I wanted to live someplace else?"

This question hit Katherine in the heart with stab after stab. Would she mind? She'd be dead. Would she mind? Would she want Lily to be trapped as she was? Would she want Lily to bring her boyfriend here? Raise children here, even? Stab stab stab.

"I don't know," she said. "No, that's not right. That's Aunt Agnes speaking. Or her dad, John Steele. If you wanted to move away, I wouldn't object."

And then Katherine said, "Don't forget we have the Treasury for emergencies."

"But what's in there? If it's something that was pretty in 1950, it might not be wanted even at the thrift store now. I think we should open it and find out. And then we could decide to lock it up again for an emergency."

Katherine was shaking her head, but she didn't know why. She was curious, too. But she had been warned so many times not to open it except in an emergency.

"Do you think there's money in there?" Lily asked. "Because that would explain everything. It would be hard to keep it safe once it was unlocked and maybe it would be stolen."

"That would be a lot of money. And I think if we had that money we would have just fixed up the house."

"So, Mom, what if we opened it? And took and hid what's in there someplace else?"

"Where would we do that? If we put it in here, first there's no space, and second it would be easy to break in here and take whatever it is."

Lily was unconvinced. Why not know what they were dealing with? What kind of emergency would match what was inside?

Then she remembered about the sudden appearance of the Woman in the Window earlier when she was dealing with the Treasury roof, and told Mom about it. Katherine agreed it was strange and they sat in silence for a while.

Then Lily blurted out something she had barely had as a thought in her own mind. "I think the Woman in the Window wants to find out what's in the shed. Maybe she thinks she owns it."

Katherine had to think about that. The oddest part was that she had come out at all. Or maybe not. Maybe it was because the woman had known Lily was here alone.

"That makes it even more dangerous for us to open it," she said.

"Unless we can find a place to put it when she's not watching."

"Wherever that might be."

Lily had an idea but she didn't want to talk about it anymore. Not with Mom.

And Mom was ready to change the subject too, it seemed. Anything but the awkward subject of opening the Treasury, including protecting the unknowns inside from the Woman in the Window and the related subject of who owned the shed, anyway.

Katherine had gotten up to pop more popcorn. "Guess what I did today, Lily!" She knew she was sounding fake-cheerful, as if this were just any old subject, and Lily had already said, "Tell me," as in 'Get it over with.'

"It's not bad, Lily," said Katherine. "Not that bad, anyway. I went to the county recorder's office and looked at my birth certificate."

Lily was suddenly on high alert. "And mine?" she said.

"Hold on," said Katherine. "One thing at a time!"

"Well, did you find out anything about your dad on your birth certificate?"

"I looked. There's nothing on it. It's blank."

"That means your mom wasn't married to him," said Lily.

Ah yes, that's what it probably meant.

"I'm trying to find out more at the library. If he was a soldier going to war as Isabelle once told me. Do you want to help with that?"

"What about my birth certificate?"

"What about it?"

"Did you look at it?"

"Yes."

"Did it have my dad's name on it?"

"No."

"So you didn't put it on there when I was born?"

"Right."

"Will you tell me?"

"I can't. I made a promise. I can't break it."

"Mom. I want to know as much as you want to know about your dad. Don't you get mad at your mom when you remember she never told you in time?"

Lily was sad. What would it be like to have a dad? Even if there wasn't much room in the cottage?

Even if it meant they'd move out of the cottage?

Then they would be able to live as a regular family. It would be fun. They could go to volleyball games together like those families at the game on Thursday. They could get a car. And a clothes dryer: She and Mom always had damp laundry draped on the little rack and overflowing onto the furniture.

But it would mean leaving the big pink house behind, and that was theirs. If they could get it. And that would mean lots of rooms! Maybe brothers and sisters! Friends spending the night.

It began to seem that the reason she didn't have a dad was because Katherine wasn't willing to move out of the cottage and leave the big house behind.

But it also sounded like the big house wasn't necessarily a great place to live. Because it was old and falling apart.

"MOM!" she said. "I need to get into the big house and see what it's like. Maybe you don't want it."

Mom looked utterly surprised at this strange turn of conversation. How had Lily gone from not knowing who her dad was to the big house's need for repairs?

"Well," Mom said slowly, "I was thinking of going over there and asking her if she wanted her house cleaned for free. In case she wanted to hire me and was trying me out. And then I could look around. I want to see whether that old family history book is still there somewhere."

"And I want to see if the house is falling apart. Does it have leaks now? It can't be in good shape now if it needed work thirty years ago."

So they put their heads together to make a plan. It sounded silly to begin with, but as they refined it, it seemed to become more practical, Lily suggested getting a wig at the thrift shop and maybe some make-up, and before the afternoon was over they had a plan.

It helped that Katherine really wanted that book, and Lily really wanted to see if the house was worth waiting for.

And when would they do that? As soon as they could get Katherine's outfit together. If it wasn't pouring on Monday after school, they could meet at the thrift shop and see if there was a wig. And if not that shop, another one. There were four or five to try.

Monday was rainy but not stormy. So they met at their favorite thrift store. The only wig was blue. So they went to the next store and found a blonde wig, and after looking in the mirror and with encouragement from Lily, Katherine bought it. As for make-up, she had some at home. She knew she was going to use it someday.

The obvious flaw was that the woman would say no. The only evidence Lily had that it might work was that this woman had already shown that she was willing to take something for free—like Lily's veggies and basket.

Why? Was she hard up? Was the house too expensive for them, too? Did they have upkeep issues? Lily hoped Mom would remember to notice those things.

Because maybe they didn't want the house, the two of them. Or maybe the Woman in the Window didn't want it. Whether she knew that or not, yet.

Meanwhile their errand took them to the library. They had been walking home from the thrift store with the wig, and as if with one mind, they veered from the path home. The library was only a block out of their way. Rush hour traffic reminded them that they'd be delaying their dinner, but Lily was always ready for a library trip and Katherine had barely scratched the surface in her search for World War Two casualties.

Katherine could see no harm in sharing with Lily what she suspected about her father. "I was born in 1943, right in the middle of the war years," she told Lily. "And Isabelle told me many times that he was a serviceman who served his country."

"So she was proud of him?"

"She seemed mildly proud of him. Only mildly. Maybe that's why I'm not sure of the story."

Lily was interested in finding out about whoever this guy was. He was, after all, her grandfather. So she stuck with Katherine at the library. Katherine had discovered a whole section of the shelves dedicated to local information, all about their town, and then another all about their state.

Katherine handed Lily a large photographic history of the town. "Start here. It's excellent. I had only enough time this morning to thumb through it. I'm trying to find out all I can about who lived here in Steeletown and served in World War Two. We can make a list."

The project was fully engaging. The hours went by. They found three names of men who had served and a woman who was enlisted into the U.S. Army as a nurse.

Then Miss Horan came up and told them she was closing for the night. Lily reminded Miss Horan that she was in Miss Clark's class. And Miss Horan said, "Have you met Miss Finley? Edna Finley? She's the high school librarian and lives with Miss Clark and me, and she's come to pick me up. So I must leave."

They said hello to Miss Finley, and Lily remembered not to ask the question she had on her mind, which was: Did they call her Finley? Or Edna? She thought probably Edna.

Edna said nice to meet you and do you want a ride, but of course Mom said no thank you.

Mom surprised Lily by suggesting they pick up some fish sandwiches and french fries on their way home. They never ate out. "And then," said Mom, "we can talk about what we found and make a list of what else we can look for."

The shop that had the wonderful fish sandwiches was several blocks away. The evening was nice enough, just a little drizzle that kept them moving along, deep inside their raincoats.

The shop was crowded, popular. Lily couldn't remember the last time she'd been here. The fish was delicious.

"And tomorrow," said Mom, "I will go see if the Woman in the Window wants a cleaning lady."

"But Mom, I was thinking. How will you get there without her seeing you?"

Mom was silent for a long time. "I have no idea," she said. "Maybe I should just be me."

"Hmm," said Lily.

It was all they could think of. They wouldn't need the wig with this plan.

"Let's sleep on it," said Mom.

Lily yawned. Mom yawned, too. It was a bit of a long walk home.

Katherine was close to sleep as soon as they went to bed, but with her last wisp of consciousness she realized she felt happy. She fingered her breast lump as a reminder of what both she and Lily were facing, but still she felt happy. She had had a wonderful day with Lily, and it felt as if The Plan was going well, too. And maybe she was closer to finding her own father. Her mother's lover. Lily had been a willing ally in finding him.

Too bad she could never reciprocate and tell Lily who her father was.

## A LATE NOVEMBER WEEK BEGINS 1985

KATHERINE PROCRASTINATED GOING TO the big house on her errand as a potential cleaning lady for a few days, while Lily went about the business of being a good student as usual. The only hiccup in the week was when Lily looked up at the roof of the cottage and became upset that it was a sloppy job. Not that she went up on the ladder—Katherine wouldn't let her—but she could see from ground-level the uneven ends of shingles sticking out in a haphazard fashion.

She wanted to fix them, but Katherine pointed out that there had been no leaks during one of the heaviest rainstorms ever, and they would have to do for now.

They had decided over the weekend to meet at the library each afternoon to find out more about local casualties from World War Two, and Lily began a scrapbook with copies of articles about the local soldiers who had gone to war.

She was always moved to tears when a serviceman with one of the names she had found turned up in a following article to have died.

"It could be your dad, Mom," she had said each time.

And the occurrences were mounting up.

Then Lily found a copy of the local newspaper listing 750 names of men and women who had served during the war. It also listed the twenty who had died.

"Mom, look," she said.

Mom turned from the articles she was reading. "It says 750? I'll never find him."

"But your mom said he died in the war, right? So it has to be someone from this list, and there are only twenty here. And one of them is a woman."

"You're right. We can probably eliminate some of these."

"Like if they died before you were born."

"We'll have to do some math and see if we can eliminate any. Like here: This soldier died in Pearl Harbor. That's too early."

Together they figured out that her father couldn't have left earlier than the middle of 1942, and Pearl Harbor had been at least six months before. And once they knew that they were able to cross out two—but only two—soldiers.

"But he could have left after you were born, Mom," said Lily. "Even months after. This is going to be hard."

Looking more closely at dates, they were able to eliminate seven others who had left too early. And after eliminating the one woman, they were down to twelve.

"Mom, this isn't going to work. Not without some clue. Are there any names here that mean anything to you? Like something your mom might have said by mistake?"

So Mom looked over the list. She recognized three names of the twelve as being from local families, names she knew from a store in town, a street name, a friend with the same last name.

The remaining surnames meant nothing to her.

So she turned to the first names. And it was just a list of common first names. Michael. John. Nathaniel. Joseph. Nothing triggered a memory.

Then a name she knew, Benjamin Brown.

Ben, her lover Ben, had lost his father in World War Two? He'd never mentioned it. Not that they had spent much time together.

Meanwhile her finger had lingered on the name, her mind being lost in thought. And Lily noticed.

"What, Mom? Is that him?"

"What? Oh, no. It's just a local name, that's all. This must be his father. The local guy."

"So, well, that's not your dad. How are we going to find your dad? There are so many soldiers here. So many who went, and so many who died."

"I'm beginning to think it truly is hopeless."

"Don't give up, Mom. It's important."

"Is it? Why? It's just a name. In fact that's what my mom said. 'It's just a name.'"

"I don't think it's just a name."

"What do you think it is?"

"Half of who you are," said Lily. "And someday I'm going to find out who my dad is. You won't have to break your promise. I'll find him myself.

Because it's important. He's half of who I am."

"You're John Steele's great-great-granddaughter, that's who you are. You can be proud of the Steele name you carry."

"Mom, he lived a long time ago. I know he built this town and built the big house, but my own dad is doing something right now that's more important to me. Even if he's a bad person, he's my bad person."

"He's not a bad person, Lily. He's a fine person. Doing good work."

"What work is he doing, Mom? I want to know."

"I can't tell you. You know that."

"Well, give me a hint. Just a little hint."

"I can't. You're way too smart. Just like him. You'll figure it out and I will have broken my promise and hurt him."

Lily was smiling. He was smart! That was good to know. She felt closer to him already.

"Let's go, Mom. We have to figure out how to find your dad. And I have to figure out how to find out about mine. I want to meet him. I just have to figure it out for myself. I know you can't tell me."

Lily wanted to go because she had an idea, and it would take Mom getting into the big house. Lily knew about the big book, the heavy book her aunt had put on her lap when she was little, that had the names of family members in it. And what if Isabelle had put Mom's name in it, and her dad's name? Had Mom ever looked? She hadn't seen the book since she was seven years old, and maybe for a time before that.

And quite possibly that book had been thrown out, but it also could be in the big house.

Lily knew it was unlikely that the book would be there. But if it was, it might hold important family information, such as about the building of the town, of the railroad, of the house. All done by John Steele. And she knew John Steele must have been written about in that book.

And why would it be in the big house? First, because once it had been. Mom had seen it. And second, because it was all about the big house. It might even add value to the big house. So just possibly the Woman in the Window had kept it. Just for the sake of making the house more valuable, probably.

So Lily told Mom she had to go look for the book.

"I don't know, Lily. I don't know what to say to her."

"Just show up at her door like you're going door-to-door offering your cleaning services. And if the book is there, we'll figure out how to get it another time."

After a long pause, Mom nodded.

Tomorrow was Wednesday, and that meant that volleyball was coming soon. Lily wanted to go, even if she had to go by herself. So when she got to school, she asked Miss Clark if she was going to volleyball tomorrow, and she said she didn't think she'd be able to.

"OK, I'll go by myself. And I'll ask Susan if she wants to come."

"I wouldn't do that, Lily. She won't be able to go. She gets picked up by her foster mom every day."

"Foster mom?"

"You didn't know she's a foster kid? I thought she told you."

"No. I don't really know what a foster kid is, but I thought she was just a regular kid."

"A foster kid lives with a family that's not hers when her mom and dad can't take care of her."

"Oh, that sounds hard," said Lily.

"I think it must be."

"No wonder she's a sad girl," said Lily. "That's why I wanted her to come to volleyball with me. Plus I like her."

"It's a lovely thought. But it would be too much responsibility for you."

"I wouldn't need to do anything. We're the same age."

"I know. But ... well, she might try to run away. She doesn't like her foster home. That's why she was crying when I said I'd take her home first. She didn't want to go at all."

"OK, I'll go by myself. Mom said it was OK."

"Are you sure? You'll have to walk all that way home when it's already getting dark."

"That's OK."

"Well, you know Mr. Brown. You can always ask him if you need help. He'll be there."

"Who's Mr. Brown?"

"You met him the other day. Ben Brown. Remember him?"

"OH ..." and here she almost said, "... your boyfriend," but she stopped herself at the last moment.

So she said, "Oh, the guy who waited with me. Yes, I'll ask him if I need help."

She liked Ben Brown.

And wasn't that the name Mom found in the World War Two files yesterday? A casualty named Benjamin Brown? She'd ask Ben Brown if she talked to him tomorrow if his father had died in World War Two.

When she got home, Lily found that Mom had decided to go to the big house tomorrow. She'd go as herself, and she'd have her new cleaning bucket with her, and see what happened.

Lily said, "Don't forget to see if the book is there. And if the house is in good shape or falling apart again."

Lily hadn't told Mom her idea that her dad's name might be in the book. She was going to but Mom was so excited about getting into the house that they had ended up talking about whether her doll might still be in the attic. Shirley-Doll had disappeared when they had moved to the cottage, and Mom could picture just where she might be in the attic.

Lily thought that was a long time for a doll to wait, thirty-five years, but maybe Mom would find her beloved Shirley. And if the doll, maybe the book. Maybe no one had gone up into the attic all these thirty-five years. Mom said it was an attic you could barely stand up in, and had roofing nails poking through the roof, and you had to get up there by climbing a ladder. And when she went up there, she was afraid she would stand up in the wrong place and get one of those nails in her head.

Then she told Lily that she had been the only one who would go up there. Isabelle and Agnes had sent her up the ladder to get their Christmas lights, which were all that was stored there. They wouldn't go themselves, or maybe they couldn't, Mom didn't know. She did remember it was hard getting up into the attic from the ladder.

"So maybe no one has been there since we moved out, and maybe Shirley-Doll is up there. Maybe I left her when I was up there one time."

There was long pause.

"Maybe our Christmas lights are still up there, too."

"And the book, Mom," said Lily. "Maybe the book is up there. If it's there, I hope you can bring it."

"I'll bring it if you're interested in it."

"Mom! I forgot! I think your mom might have written your dad's name in it! We need that book!"

Mom stopped what she was doing, heating up soup for supper. "You're right, Lily. How brilliant!"

So they both went to bed excited and were up early.

Katherine waited until Lily was out of sight, on her way to school. Then before she could talk herself out of it, and carrying the bucket of supplies, she walked around the block to the front of the big pink house.

She hadn't been on the front side of the house for who knew how long. It was shabby. The paint was faded to a lavender, you might call it. The white trim, which she remembered as snappy, setting off the pink of the house, was dingy and peeling. A basement window was cracked, not shattered though. One of the steps appeared to be crumbling, with signs of rot, and overall the paint of the steps and porch boards was scuffed. Katherine didn't need to go inside to know the condition of the house. It had not been well cared for.

Was this what it had looked like when they'd been forced out, she and her mother and her aunt?

She took a deep breath and knocked on the front door. The woman would know her by sight, so as an afterthought she stepped away from the door, off to the side, so her face couldn't be seen. She didn't want the woman to know who it was before answering.

Next she tried the bell. She could hear it buzz.

It still took the woman a few minutes to arrive. Katherine took a deep sigh when she realized the moment was upon her.

"Hi," she said. She had decided at the last minute not to identify herself as the woman who lived out back.

"I'm starting a house-cleaning business. And to get the word out I'm cleaning houses for free. Are you interested in having me clean your house for free?"

"For free? The whole thing for free?"

"Yes, or as much of it as you want." Katherine was thinking about how big the house was. It could be a lot of work. Well, it was probably worth it.

"I can't guarantee I'll hire you again."

"That's ... OK. Just tell a friend if you like the job I did."

So the woman let Katherine in. Katherine was surprised, but so far so good.

The woman had appeared not to recognize Katherine.

"I usually start at the top and work down," said Katherine. "Will that be convenient?"

"Well, as long as you get to the kitchen before you quit."

"I'm sure I will. I work fast," said Katherine. And, she reflected, she had indeed learned to clean fast from working at the nursing home.

So the two women went up the stairs. Katherine could see that the bookshelves that lined the whole front room contained no books, not one. As Lily had suspected.

Climbing the stairs, Katherine could see the outline of the attic entry above her, an opening in the ceiling with a board that slid into it to seal it. She remembered being on the top of the tall ladder, having to reach over her head to move that board, that inset, out of the way so she could keep climbing. It had been an A-shaped ladder. It had felt flimsy beneath her and she'd had to step on the next to top rung to be high enough to pull herself into the attic. If she lost her balance, she would fall the several feet she had climbed, or possibly down the big stairwell too, all the way to the first floor.

She hated being the one that had to do it. But who else? Then one year she said she would put the Christmas lights in her closet, and that was that.

And now maybe they were in the shed.

There was no ladder in sight. She couldn't remember where they'd kept that ladder. And meanwhile the woman was directing her to the hall bathroom.

"Start here," she said.

"And where do you want me to go when I'm finished here?" Katherine asked.

The hallway had several closed doors. Katherine was having trouble recalling which was which. She wasn't even sure which had been her bedroom.

"Is there a master bath you want me to clean, also?"

"No, never mind that."

"What about the attic? It's surprising how much dust can accumulate in an attic, and often there's dangerous debris that can start a fire."

Katherine was making this up and laying it on thick. She wanted to get into the attic, though, and it was worth a little drama. "Do you have a ladder? I can get that cleaned out in no time."

"No, no ladder."

"Oh, too bad."

Katherine of course knew where there was a ladder. In fact, she could see it now out the big window at the end of the hall, on its side, leaning against the cottage. This window must be the place where the woman stood by the hour watching Lily. In fact, an armchair faced the window, where she might sit comfortably by the hour. Watching Lily.

How badly did Katherine want to go up into the attic? Should she mention their ladder? She'd leave it alone for now.

So she began by cleaning the hall bathroom.

Which reminded her: Where was the woman's husband?

"Should I do this room now, Miss?" Katherine asked. She thought adding 'miss' made her sound humbler.

"No, no, never go in there. That's my room."

"OK, any of these other rooms?"

"Maybe this one. I don't know how dirty it could be."

"It won't take long, then."

The window from this room overlooked Main Street. The minute Katherine opened the door, she was certain that this was Aunt Agnes's room. It would be just like Aunt Agnes to keep an eye on the comings and goings on Main Street. Back when it was still part of downtown.

The room was dusty, musty. Katherine used her dust rag to clean it while she searched it thoroughly with her eyes. If this were Agnes's room, the big book could be here. One wall had shelves, but again, no books. The bed was high off the floor, just as Aunt Agnes's had been. She said it was warmer up there. And there was a bureau, with an embroidered cloth on the top that was deeply yellowed and seemed viscerally familiar. A tiny box with hand-painting was the only object on the cloth.

Katherine thought she remembered the little box and the embroidered cloth. Could this room still be intact, literally just as Aunt Agnes had left it, after all these years?

It was almost like being in a museum, seeing what a bedroom was like in the old days. Katherine hadn't seen it for thirty-five years, and yet here it was, eerily seeming to be waiting for the day to be over and Agnes to come get herself ready for bed.

And yet so many other things weren't here. There was no lamp, just a little table that could have been used to hold a small lamp. And no books, just bookshelves. She knew there had been books there. Where were they?

And so it went. The next room had no furniture at all. Its single window overlooked the driveway and the woods beyond. Had this been hers? The wallpaper was floral, old-fashioned, more a peach than a pink, again giving the appearance of being like the original room, museum-style.

Katherine was striking out when it came to finding any books, let alone the family history volume, and Lily would be disappointed about that. But her memory was feasting on seeing things half-remembered. Whole scenes from the past were flitting into her mind and out again, mostly too fast to capture.

"I'd like to do the attic before I go downstairs," she said. "I do want to be thorough. I wonder if a tall chair would work?" She knew it wouldn't but maybe the woman would now remember the ladder.

But she was just shaking her head no.

It was awkward carrying the cleaning bucket down the long steep stairwell with its highly polished dark wood stairs. She remembered them as being slippery, though now they were scuffed, not highly polished as she remembered them. She held onto the railing to keep from slipping, then realized she might be doing that because she had done it as a young child.

She followed the woman into the kitchen. It was at the back of the house, dark, set off in the corner that was entered through a serving area that connected it to the dining room, a huge room with large windows facing west. Modern appliances had replaced the white-knobbed gas stove Katherine was remembering, along with the round-topped refrigerator that had needed defrosting every couple of weeks, and the chipped porcelain sink.

Those things were gone, though the replacement appliances were certainly not up to date, nothing like the kind that were featured in ladies' magazines or the front windows of appliance stores these days.

But the table and chairs wedged into the narrow space at the end of the kitchen she knew instantly. They appeared to be the ones they had used back when she was a small child. Three chairs, just like the old days. They'd had one of those old toasters that dinged when it was time to turn the bread to the other side. She remembered opening those little doors that held the toast, being careful not to burn herself. It had resided permanently at the end of the table, but it was gone now. In its place was a stack of newspapers.

She almost expected to see an old calendar hanging above the table.

The chairs were certainly maple, just as hers had been, lovely turned maple. What had her aunt done, sold the house furniture and all?

It seemed possible. Because the little cottage, their destination, had had no room for anything but a bed and a tiny table for cooking as well as eating, and that bed, as Katherine knew well, was just a mattress, first on the floor and later on a frame.

Hmm, this was interesting, a new notion to her. Her seven-year-old self might have known, but her adult self had never suspected that they had just walked away from all they had owned.

And did that include the books?

Katherine had been cleaning for several hours, right through lunch. She had finished the downstairs lavatory, wedged in awkwardly under the stairs. She didn't remember it. Maybe someone had added it. She washed the kitchen floor, even cleaned out the refrigerator. She was aware that the clock was ticking, then remembered that Lily would not be coming home today at the usual time because of the volleyball game.

But the woman didn't know that, and at 2:45, at about the time Lily would appear, she climbed the stairs to sit in armchair and look out over their mutual yard.

Katherine smiled to herself. How disappointed the woman would be today.

Katherine called up to her. "Miss, should I check the basement for leaks? Or will that be it for today?"

"Sure, check the basement. And then you can go. Next time—not saying there will be a next time, mind you—you should do the windows too."

"Yes, Miss," said the subservient-acting Katherine.

She found the basement door, opposite the kitchen. The stairwell was barely visible, the air dank, cold. Her hand happened to hit the light switch or she would have been sabotaged by the dark. As it was, the light, a single bulb over the bottom of the stairs, did little good.

She was afraid to venture too far. She was only looking for the book, and she was convinced that if it had spent even a year of those thirty-five years in this basement, it would have turned to dust. She retraced her steps with haste.

"All right, good-bye now, thank you."

She hurried out the door before the woman could ask her name. She had been willing enough to give it, but having gotten this far without divulging who she was, she felt she had escaped with an important secret intact.

On the other hand, she couldn't very well go straight home or the woman would see her out the window.

What to do? She had her bucket and mop with her. She needed to ditch these things, at least. And once she did, she could go into town for a bit, even meet Lily at the game if she wanted, and not go home till later.

And what was that that Lily had told her about going through the pricker bushes? That she had gone into the woods after the woman had kept her veggies and basket that one time, and had gone home by crawling through the blackberries? Katherine wasn't sure about that, but if there was that sort of thick growth in the woods just beyond the old pink house, Katherine could ditch the cleaning things there and they would not be noticed. And then she could collect them after dark.

It took her only ten minutes to find the right spot. She'd gone into the wooded area, found the fenced area, and left her things behind a blackberry bush there, not twenty feet from her great grandfather's rail line. And then she went back toward town, keenly aware that she had not had lunch.

First stop, the grocery store, where she bought a few small packages of crackers and cheese. Then to the apple tree, where yet more of those apples had fallen. And then where?

It was tempting to go to the high school, but she had no idea when the game was over. And the route home along city streets could result in her missing Lily altogether. And what if Lily got a ride from Miss Clark? And there were other complications at the high school that she didn't dare deal with where Lily might notice things.

Or she could just go home. How long would the woman wait for Lily? Would she still be sitting in the window?

Katherine was tired. She could go a round-about way, but she would still have to use her door, and that would of necessity be in full view of the woman's window. She might as well go straight home. Come what may.

As she approached the alley from the town-side, she wasn't sure if the woman was in the window. By now Lily would be more than an hour later than usual coming home and surely she would have given up by now. She couldn't see her, but she knew it didn't mean much, there being no lights on in the house.

So she decided to take a chance. Maybe the woman hadn't looked closely at her. Maybe she'd seen just the apron and cleaning bucket, now stashed behind a berry bush. So Katherine strode along with all the eagerness of someone who is tired and knows a cup of tea is only a minute away.

The well-trodden path between the cottage and henhouse was muddy from all the rain. It led from the alley, past the two small buildings, and then turned to the right toward the front door, and it was the only way to get to the front door. Katherine was reminding herself that with so much mud, she would need to leave her boots outside.

So she didn't see a figure in her way until she bumped into her. It was the woman from the big house.

The woman gasped, or maybe it had been a quiet scream. A tool of some sort dropped out of her hand. As the woman bent over to pick it up, Katherine stepped on it. She wanted to see what it was.

What on earth had the woman been doing?

It appeared to be a chisel or maybe a paint scraper.

The woman had run off, straight across Lily's garden again.

Katherine looked at the shed, the Treasury. A patch of fresh wood lay exposed next to one of the hinges, and the hinge itself had a scrape across its weathered surface.

She had been trying to break in.

Katherine looked after her, but she had disappeared. Presumably into the big house.

Katherine took the chisel with her into the cottage. Lily would be home soon, but instead of starting supper, Katherine crawled under the covers on her side of the bed. She thought she might take a quick nap and refresh herself, but she found instead that she was angry, too angry to settle down and rest her exhausted body.

At first her anger was on the attempted break-in. Then it turned to the fact that the woman hadn't even thanked her for a full day of cleaning. Then to the mystery of where the husband had been, the possibility that had come to her that maybe he was an invalid. Then to the need to get the cleaning bucket out of the little patch of woods. And then she did fall asleep.

She never heard Lily come in. Lily tried to wake her. She was hungry, so she looked over their stacks of canned foods. She was cold and damp, and wanted something hot, so she chose chili and heated it.

Once again she tried to rouse Mom. Why was she sleeping so long? Lily wanted to tell her about volleyball, and she was curious about the footprints across her garden. There were Mom's muddy boots right outside the door, and those footprints in the garden. It didn't make sense. Mom would never do that.

Certainly it wouldn't be the Woman in the Window again. In fact, the woman hadn't been in the window when she had gotten home.

And what was that chisel on the table, also muddy?

Mom wasn't going to wake up, so Lily found some crackers and served herself half the chili. She had locked the chickens in for the night and she was glad she didn't have to go out again. And with Mom sleeping, there was nothing else to do but read, or do her homework.

Homework first. Then one of the library books from the pile.

She added a small amount of wood to the stove. She could hear rain on the roof, heavier rain than earlier. She decided to get ready for bed before reading, and then read in bed. Mom could eat when she woke up, or maybe she needed to sleep till morning.

Lily finished her book. Mom hadn't stirred. Lily turned off the light, then lay awake for a while. Volleyball had been fun, but not as much fun as when Miss Clark had been there. And of course, Susan. The teacher Ben had said hi, nice to see you again, and then talked to another teacher and walked off. The half-time free play had been fun but most of the kids had been bigger. So after free play she had left. And then decided to go to the library instead of straight home. She'd thought Mom might be at the library, but then she remembered she'd be cleaning the big house if that had worked out. She thought she'd keep looking at the local World War Two materials, and found out about some of the casualties, also local fears about the Japanese attacking the town and some debates the town had about what to do about that.

But she didn't know what might be important and what not, so she decided to go home. And now here she was, in bed much earlier than usual. Because what else could she do, really, on a cold, rainy winter night with no one to talk to?

She awoke early, before dawn. She reached across the bed for Mom, but she wasn't there. Had she heard the door open and close and that's what woke her? Where would Mom go at this early hour?

Lily looked at the clock. Not as early as she had thought. Late fall meant that the sun was barely up before she had to leave for school, and the heavy rain made it darker still. The alarm would go off in five minutes. She got up and started getting ready for school. Made breakfast, made lunch, packed up her backpack, put the homework in its folder and slid it down the side of the pack so it would stay neat.

Then she sat at the table waiting for Mom, hoping she would come home before she needed to leave for school.

Lily hadn't realized how bleak it was without Mom.

For one thing, she had news for her. Susan had left the class. Miss Clark had announced that she had moved, and that was all. Susan hadn't said anything about it the day before when she and Lily were kicking a ball around on the playground. So at lunch Lily had asked Miss Clark what happened to Susan, and Miss Clark had said that she had been too unhappy at her foster home and asked to be moved.

"She didn't ask to go home to her parents?"

"Well, I'm sure she did, Lily," said Miss Clark. "But her parents can't have her right now."

"But why? What did she do?"

"I'm sure she didn't do anything. Maybe one of her parents was mean to her. Or something like that. Or maybe one of them got sick."

"I think my mom's sick," said Lily. Though she hadn't meant to.

"Oh, does she have a cold?" asked Miss Clark.

"No, I don't think so. I think she has something wrong in her chest." Lily had put her hand on the place on her own chest that Mom was always feeling.

"Oh," said Miss Clark. "I hope she gets better soon. Are you going out on the playground now, or do you want to stay in today and draw or read?"

"Maybe I'll stay in."

And thinking back on that, Lily remembered that Susan was gone and was sad about that. Maybe she could find out if she was still in town, just in a different school. And Lily remembered all over again how nice Miss Clark was. No wonder she and Miss Horan were such good friends.

And then she heard a thump at the door. She ran over and unlatched it, and there was Mom with her cleaning things. "Good morning!" she said. "I have to leave these things in here for the time being."

"How did the cleaning go? Did she let you in?"

"That's a long story," said Mom. "I'll tell you the whole thing later. Did you have breakfast?"

"Yes. And I made lunch. I'm all ready to go. Do you want to meet at the library and look at the war files? Or should I come home?"

"Home, unless I meet you at school."

"What's that chisel, Mom?"

"Oh, that. That belongs to the woman in the big house. She was trying to break into the Treasury."

Lily was astonished, ready to listen if Mom had more to tell.

"I caught her at it. Now I think you should go. But Lily, listen. You know all those times she's been watching you? I think she was keeping an eye on the Treasury, making sure you don't get into it and take whatever is in there."

"That's weird. Bye. I miss you, Mom," said Lily as she hugged Mom for a long time.

Katherine had awakened at midnight, chagrined to see the hour, to realize she had slept through Lily's homecoming, not to mention supper and bedtime. She had been thinking about getting the cleaning supplies as she woke up, but did it really need to be at midnight? She had decided not to and went back to bed. Then at 6:00 she had hastened to take care of the errand, wondering if she had slept at all in between.

And then she remembered the incident at the Treasury. It had been odd then and remained odd to her now.

Had she waited for Lily to be away to make her assault on the little building? Had she done that before?

Could she be responsible for the hole Lily had found in the roof and had just a few days ago covered over?

She had, after all, appeared at Lily's side when she was fixing the hole in the roof.

In some twisted way, might she be thinking that Lily was breaking into the Treasury?

Absurd, of course, because it was not that woman's building.

And then there was the question of whether Katherine should confront her about it. Or maybe call the police.

She should talk to Lily about it. She knew what Lily would say: open it and see what's in there.

But wouldn't that expose whatever the treasure was to the woman? Make it easier for her to take whatever it was? Unless of course she didn't like what it was. Ha! This woman seemed to like free things, seemed eager to help herself to what wasn't hers.

She was a real danger. If she could get into the shed. And if there was anything appealing to her in there.

Maybe instead of opening it, she and Lily should find a way to seal it up better. It already had those four combination locks, from back in the day when Aunt Agnes had decided to secure it. She was still little then. She remembered it as being right after they had moved. What more could she and Lily do?

She put the cleaning supplies away and the bucket outside behind the henhouse. The woman would not be able to see it there and put two and two together.

Two and two and two. She hadn't seemed to recognize Katherine as the lady who lived in the little cottage in her backyard, and then after spending the day with her as the cleaning lady, didn't seem to recognize her as the owner of the shed.

Maybe she was blind. Not likely if she sat in a window watching Lily all day, of course.

## A LATE NOVEMBER SCHOOLDAY 1985

THE RAIN CONTINUED, LEAVING Katherine uninspired to do a few things she had had in mind for the day: Go out and see how much damage the woman had done to the shed; go out and see how much damage the woman had done to Lily's garden; go out and spend some time at the library.

It was the 'go out' part she was balking at. So she got out the paper with The Plan written across the top. What more could she add to it?

One big issue was Ben's payments for Lily. He would need to keep sending them in the mail to their PO box, as he'd done—most of the time—these past nearly nine years. Most of the time, but not always, and that was the problem. He'd have to be reliable from now on.

When he was late in the past, he had a way of stopping by at the oddest hours to drop the envelope off in person. When he did that, it always gave Katherine a flurry of feelings she could not manage. He was so handsome, had grown handsomer over the years.

And chatty. But she could hardly let him get started. She knew she'd never want him to stop. And they had decided nine years ago that the whole thing had nowhere to go. Since he was married. With kids.

So why was he tormenting her, being chatty like that? She rebuffed him each time before he got started so she wouldn't have the pains of withdrawal after he left.

But even a small moment with him caused her torment for a few hours. Better that he stay away.

And what would it be like for Lily on her own to have this stranger show up at the door and hand her five $20s? No, she'd have to tell him it had to be sent in the mail, and on time. And if he inquired why, she would have to be most careful not to give him a clue that she would no longer be ... anywhere.

So on the paper she put, 'Write to Ben re $$.'

Nine years, nearly ten! Oh my. Eleven years since .... What-ifs flooded her mind. Never mind that! That was the path to pain.

But nine-plus years! That meant it was almost Lily's birthday. A week before Christmas, just a month away. Katherine would have to ask Lily what she wanted, some small token of the occasion that would be affordable. Maybe a book. Maybe a journal, a place to record her thoughts. Yes, a journal. Though she'd ask Lily in case she had a different idea.

Katherine had wanted a birthday party when she turned ten. Of course they couldn't have one. The cottage was too small, too humble, too embarrassing. She remembered all these reasons for no party, not so much from Isabelle but from Aunt Agnes.

"You can't show anyone how low this family has gotten," she'd said far more than once.

It would be fun to give Lily a party, Katherine thought. Almost as if she herself had had a party at ten. Ten was such a wonderful age, suspended as it was between childhood and womanhood. Yes, a party. If the weather was nice so they could have it outside.

At least she could mention it to Lily. She might not want one, after all. She was such a practical child.

Probably her gift she'd ask for would be for the shed to be opened. Well, once she heard about the woman trying to break in, she would give up on that idea.

Finally Lily was home from school. Katherine hid The Plan, having added only the one item about Ben's payments.

Lily was dripping rain as she removed her raincoat and boots. The winter was upon them. Just like the night she was born. Which reminded Katherine of her birthday.

"Your birthday's coming up in a few weeks. I've been thinking of what present you might like. And also if you would like a party."

"A party, Mom? I would love to have a party. It will be raining so we could have it at the depot. It will be open on Saturdays at Christmastime. They have tables there. We could sit at those tables and have cake and ice cream."

"Who would you have come?"

"All my friends. Miss Clark and Miss Horan. I wish Susan still lived here. And Ben. Mr. Brown. He's the Principal. I wonder if he would come. He's nice."

Katherine had lost her breath entirely so it was several moments before she responded. "No kids?" she asked.

"Maybe," said Lily. "If they want to come. But probably we should have only eight so we can fit around those tables at the depot."

"When were you ever at the depot?"

"All the time. When it's open. In the summer. And I think it opens again next week so people can sell Christmas crafts."

Katherine wondered why Lily, the child, knew these things, but she, the mom, didn't.

Lily had started counting on her fingers: "You, me, Miss C, Miss H, Mr. Brown. And then three friends. I wonder if Miss Clark knows where Susan moved to. She didn't before but she might now."

Then she added, "We could have it on the day before my birthday. That's a Friday. We could have it right after school. The depot is not as crowded then as it is on Saturday. If it's open. I'll check."

Katherine made popcorn and cocoa. Lily didn't have homework because it was Friday, and Katherine wanted to talk about yesterday. About being at the house. About the shed.

So she filled Lily in on things. But Lily had endless questions.

"Was it fun being in your old house, Mom?"

"Is it in good shape?"

"What was the most interesting thing?"

"Did you find the book?"

"Was the woman there the whole time?"

After she was done telling Lily about the house and her discoveries there, the things that seemed to be there still from when she left, the things she couldn't remember, the fact that she hadn't gotten into the attic and that the basement was scary, Lily asked her again if it was in good shape.

And Katherine was caught between the reality of it and the throwback she had experienced while moving around inside it. Until she finally confessed, "No, it was in bad shape. I mean, the house is solid enough, well-built I think. But the paint is bad, things like that."

"But no big book."

"No books of any kind."

"I have an idea, Mom. Are you willing to go to town in this much rain? I want to go to the library. Because if there are no books in the house, then maybe Aunt Agnes donated them to the library."

"Wow, that's a real possibility. She loved those books, and it would be just like her to put them someplace where people could see them."

"Like with her name in them, Donated by Agnes Steele, something like that?"

"Exactly. Yeah, let's go ask them."

"Miss Horan will know."

"I don't think she's old enough to have been there back then, Lily. I think she's more like my age."

"Well, she'll know how to find out."

"If she has time."

So they headed out into the storm, walked briskly to the library, and asked for Miss Horan. She appeared at the main desk in a matter of moments. Lily said, "Miss Horan, could you come to my birthday party? It's in three weeks."

Miss Horan smiled hugely. "I'd love to, Lily. I'll have to look at my calendar."

Then Lily told her their errand. Had her Aunt Agnes Steele ever donated a large number of old books?

Miss Horan said she'd never heard of that, but she'd look into it. And it might take a few days.

So Katherine and Lily went to the World War Two collection to see what they could see in the short time before the onset of the early sunset. And just as they were leaving, Miss Horan came up. "I found a record of donors over the years. It goes back 52 years, and there's nothing there from any of the Steele family."

"No books at all?" asked Lily.

Miss Horan shook her head.

## END-OF-NOVEMBER DISAPPOINTMENT 1985

"I WAS SO SURE," said Lily.

"You didn't know Aunt Agnes," said Katherine.

They were walking through downtown when Lily said, "Look! A second-hand bookstore! That's like a thrift store for books, right? Maybe she sold them there and got money for them."

"But that was thirty-five years ago."

"Well, maybe one of the people who bought them didn't want them anymore. Like the big book with all your family names in it. Like your dad's name. And brought back one of the ones they bought a long time ago. Or their kids did."

So they went into the Great Blue Heron Used Books Bookstore and browsed around. The store was almost empty of shoppers at this hour. There were few truly old books, the dull brown kind that Katherine remembered and had fallen in love with, their outsides anyway. Whenever they saw older ones, they checked to see if Agnes's name was in them. But it never was.

"Did they have dumpsters back then?" Lily asked. It wasn't a real question, just a sign that she had given up.

"I didn't remember this," said Mom, "but we had bookshelves upstairs too. I wonder how many books they had."

They were almost home, just now walking down the alley. The cottage was ahead to the left, just after small side-by-side buildings, the henhouse and then the Treasury. The muddy path where Katherine had literally bumped into the woman was steps away. Katherine was describing it to Lily all over again. Lily could see the bared wood where the woman had tried to pry up the hinge. But in her mind she was trying to figure how much space it would have taken for all those books from all those shelves. At least a dumpster full. It would have been a big job to throw away all those beautiful books.

Lily locked the chickens in, and she and Mom went into the cottage. The woman was not in the window. Lily stood at the door looking at their one room with new eyes. It was such a small space. A bed, a table, a fridge and stove. And a bathroom. It reminded Lily of what Mom had told her of the kitchen in the big house. Without the bed.

No room for books here, except for the current stacks on the floor by their sides of the bed so they could read before falling asleep. Others stacked on the table. A few in the bathroom. Whatever would they have done if they'd had all those books? It was hard enough that three people had to squeeze into the cottage. Including Mom as a small girl. So no books. They had to get rid of them.

Unless.

Lily stopped breathing. She grabbed for Mom, squeezed her by the arm, leaned on her.

"Mom. I know where Agnes put the books."

Katherine was used to Lily. She was often enthusiastic, full of ideas. And here she was again. 'Mom, I know ... .'

What had she said?

"I know where Agnes put the books."

'Well, honey, that was long ago. They're gone.' These are the words Katherine was formulating. She was trying out what words to use to keep from destroying her exuberant daughter.

But before she could do that, Lily blurted out the words she had in mind: "The books are in the Treasury. They are the treasure!"

Katherine didn't understand at first. Yes, the books were a real treasure, beautiful, old, highly desirable. "OH! The books are in the shed? The books are in the shed!"

Lily was trying to get Katherine to dance with her.

"Mom! The book, the big book, with your family information in it! It's in there. I'm sure she would put it in there."

Mom was stirring at the stove. Lily was talking non-stop about the books. The question was, now what? It was just as they had talked about before, once they opened the shed, what would they do with the treasure? Now they knew that the treasure was books, and that they could not put the books in the cottage, not if they intended to live here anymore.

Before the evening was over they had agreed that for the moment the shed needed to stay shut. Katherine was reluctant because of the big book. Her father's name might or might not be there, she knew that. But there would be other family lore that might answer some questions. And Lily wanted to see it all.

"But Mom, in what way is it a treasure? We'd sell them?"

"I think the point is that we could sell them, if we needed to."

"So is that why the Woman in the Window wants them, to sell them?"

"I'm sure she doesn't know what's in there. I think she wants whatever is in there."

"But why does she think she has any right to them? They're ours."

"I don't know. It may have to do with the agreement we have about the land. Maybe she thinks it doesn't have anything to do with the buildings and those buildings are hers. I wish I could remember what Aunt Agnes told me about all that."

"Isn't it written anywhere?"

"It has to be. Maybe at the county offices."

"Let's go then and find out and maybe make a copy for the woman so she knows those are our buildings."

"Good idea. We'll have to wait till Monday, though. They're not open tomorrow. And speaking of tomorrow, what would you like to do?"

"It's going to rain. Maybe we could go over on the ferry and walk around."

"How about if we go to the thrift store and buy you a few new shirts for school. Or for your birthday."

"Sure," said Lily. "Maybe another one with Lily written on it." But she knew that was unlikely. No one else she knew had the name 'Lily.'

"But, Lily, maybe you could get some glue and glitter and put your name on it yourself."

"I could do that?"

"You could learn how. And maybe practice a bit before putting it on the shirt."

"Maybe I could make shirts for girls at school and sell them!"

"You are definitely John Steele's granddaughter. Great-great-granddaughter, but still."

"Speaking of John Steele, now that we know where the book is, how are we going to get it out of the shed?"

"I don't think we can right now, not with that woman determined to get in there."

"Not until we have the paper to show her so she knows she doesn't have any rights."

So they went to the thrift store and found a few shirts that looked like new. Katherine was always amazed at the kinds of clothing, other things too, that people donated to thrift stores. Then they went to the craft store around the corner and with some help found the glue and glitter. And Lily went wild with ideas for things she could make that she could sell.

"And Mom, when the weather gets nice again I can teach classes to girls my age who want to learn how, and they can pay me to teach them. Or maybe they can buy the glitter and stuff from me instead of buying it here and I can make money that way."

It was hard to drag Lily away. Every aisle gave her a new idea. So they added some additional supplies to their shopping basket and decided this would be her birthday gift.

"But I still get to have the party, right?"

"Right. You need to make some invitations to pass out so your friends save the date."

So Lily found some envelopes and pens and added them to the basket. Mom was looking alarmed, so she said, "I'll pay you back for those, after I start my shirt-painting business."

"If we didn't know about John Steele, I'd say 'whose daughter are you'."

Lily looked shocked for a moment, then laughed. Then she sobered up and said, "Yeah, Mom, whose daughter am I? And whose daughter are you? We need to know those things."

## AN EARLY-DECEMBER SATURDAY 1985

WHEN THEY GOT HOME, Lily made the invitations. One for Miss Clark, one for Miss Horan, one for Mr. Brown. It took a long time. Then before she stopped she made three more, simpler ones. She'd add Susan's name to the envelope if it turned out she lived in town. And then she'd think about the other two. She had lots of friends in her class, and only eight places at the table in the depot.

She had used up Saturday without selling any veggies to the tourists on the plaza. Without going to the little island on the ferry. Without figuring out how to get the book out of the shed without causing huge problems.

She and Mom had a simple supper and read themselves to sleep. The rain beat down on the roof. Winter weather had arrived. Lying in bed, waiting for sleep, she remembered she hadn't gone back for the final load of apples. She'd get a load tomorrow and take them and a few carrots to the plaza at the depot and see if any tourists were brave enough to be seeing the sights in this weather.

Lily headed out early as soon as she'd finished her oatmeal. It was easy to pick a whole wagonload of apples off the ground. If she sold these, she might be able to do a second load. She pulled the wagon through town as far as Main Street and turned right, toward the depot. It was three blocks to their big pink house, then a turn left and another turn right and there would be the plaza and the depot. The rain was steady, maybe too much for tourists. But she was enjoying the blasts of rain from the westerly wind, at her back for most of the walk, exhilarating, clean, fresh when she changed directions at the corner and it hit her in the face.

Hit her in the face too hard. She turned so her back was toward it, until the blast of wind passed by.

And so she was facing the big pink house when someone drove up in a car in front of it, took something out of the car, and started hammering. Then drove off.

It was a for-sale sign.

Lily wondered what the woman, or maybe her husband, might be selling.

The sign didn't say. It just gave a phone number.

That made no sense.

She continued on until she reached the plaza. It was empty except for a man walking diagonally across it toward town. Probably from a boat in the harbor, in port for the day or maybe for longer.

She thought maybe she could walk along the docks with her apples, but she couldn't get the wagon down the steep walkways to the docks.

And, she thought, the Christmas boutique in the depot was closed on Sundays. Wasn't it?

She pulled the wagon across the tracks toward the depot itself. The door was open. And then she could see people inside, shoppers. She would just stand at the door for a while and see if anyone going in or out wanted an apple. At twenty-five cents each.

But once people got out into the rain, they dashed toward the parking lot.

Lily was getting chilled just standing there, so she gave up on customers and turned toward home. She could go back the way she had come, or pull the wagon through the tall grass of the alley, the part that hadn't been used in years, outside that fencing that had caught her last summer.

Or, she thought, she could follow the tracks and see where John Steele had laid them, beyond the depot, farther into town. So she turned around and put the wagon between the rails and pulled. It was easy enough. The ties caused only small bumps. She went past the road she had come in on, then into an area with tall grass and broken concrete. An enormous building loomed directly ahead, but she couldn't tell if the tracks went beside it or into it.

She kept walking. The rails split into two pairs, one that went outside the building, and one that went inside. The building was the tallest she had ever seen, much taller than a train. It would have been fun to look inside but its enormous doors were shut. And there were no windows.

She went on bumping along the tracks. A sign said 'Steele Shipyard.'

'Steele Shipyard'? Where were the ships? There were either no ships left, or they were inside. Maybe still being built.

The tracks were covered with debris, paper cups, soda cans, all sorts of scraps of things.

She plodded along. The rails were running diagonally through the north end of town. And she knew that beyond the north end of town was the salt-water sound, the body of water that the little ferry had crossed. And that the island they had visited last week lay just beyond. Soon she would run into the end of town, the end of land, and that's where the tracks would have to stop. Wouldn't they?

What had her great-great-grandfather John Steele had in mind when he had laid these tracks? They looked as though they were going to end up at the ocean.

Meanwhile, the pair of tracks she was on merged again with the tracks from the large building.

She walked on. She began to see the end of downtown ahead of her. She could see the water beyond that, and then the island. It was still a distance off and her arm was getting tired from pulling the wagon of apples.

She came to a street, an actual town street with traffic. The tracks went across it. She looked back. The pink house stood out as it always did. It was blocks and blocks away now.

She crossed the street and continued between the tracks on the other side. She was looking down, being careful not to trip on the ties, which was why she was surprised when a barrier stopped her, the kind that came down and stopped cars when a train was coming. She had seen them in movies, and now here was one, and it was as if she was the train, being in the tracks as she was.

She looked up. On the other side of the barrier was an enormous something-or-other, high up on scaffolding.

It was a ship! It had a name on it, high up. It said, 'Liberty.' And under that it said 'Seattle.' The bottom half of the ship was red, the top white.

It was out of the water.

John Steele had been building a shipyard where ships could be built. Or maybe repaired. The barrier had kept her out of the shipyard, and the sound with its cold water and sea traffic just beyond.

Shipbuilding sounded like an interesting business.

She spent a long time looking at the ship. It was high up on the scaffolding, but below it was the ocean, the sound.

Then as she turned back toward home, she could see that the rails had split again. She had followed this one set that ended in the water, at the ship.

Where did the other one go?

She was tired. She'd find out some other day. Maybe when she didn't have a wagon full of apples. So when she got back to the little street she had crossed, she turned toward home and used the street to get there. In no time she was in downtown. The rain had eased up, so she pulled the wagon under the awning of the used bookstore and stood there. Plenty of people were in the bookstore, and as they came out they looked at her, and she offered them an apple and said, "Twenty-five cents." When she had four dollars she went home.

The road home took her down to her alley. Past the shed and henhouse to the muddy path. And then into her cozy cottage.

Which is why she forgot all about the for-sale sign out in front of the old pink house.

She did notice as she took her boots off before going into the cottage that the woman was not in the window.

"Where have you been?" asked Mom.

"To John Steele's shipyard. Can I have a snack?"

## THE FIRST MONDAY IN DECEMBER 1985

KATHERINE HAD BEEN WORKING on The Plan. And she had reached the conclusion that Monday when Lily was in school, she would need to go to the high school and leave a message for ... for Ben ... about the money. She had started writing it, but hadn't figured out how to explain why she was changing their arrangement without letting on that she was leaving, dying. Dying faster than she'd thought.

And under no circumstances could she let him believe she had divulged to Lily that he was her father.

The errand, needing to happen so soon, had her feeling jumpy, nervous. What would it be like being face-to-face with him in conversation, if it happened that way? When was the last time she'd had a face-to-face conversation?

Well, there was that horrible time last winter. She hadn't seen him for quite a while, maybe two years if that was possible. And she had been thinking fond thoughts of him each night as she lay trying to go to sleep, his sweet warm little daughter lying at her side. Lily had been what? Six? Or seven?

And after several nights of realizing how much she was missing him, of longing for him, of remembering that most of the times they'd been together had been sweet, that perhaps she was wrong that he didn't want her in his life, even entertaining a fantasy that he was no longer married, she had bumped into him.

It had felt like fate at the time.

But she also had been embarrassed. As always. She felt almost as if everyone in the grocery store could see a big letter A on her chest.

So as he looked at her, clearly had been surprised to see her, had turned toward her, had started to walk toward her, ignoring the person he had been talking to, she turned her back to him. She had blushed. She had almost vomited. She had started to shake and had kept on shaking for the whole afternoon.

And so she had not talked to him. When she had gone outside and cooled off a bit and maybe stopped blushing, she had gone back to the door and peeked in and he was finishing at the checkout. She hid, kept an eye on him, and when he was safely driving away, slid back into the store.

And then when she had gotten home, and for weeks after that, she had wondered what would have happened if she hadn't turned away.

Why couldn't she at least have said hi to him?

It took her months to get over that near encounter. And now she was thinking of facing him intentionally. Unless of course he was busy, in which case she would leave the letter.

The letter that she was having so much trouble writing.

The letter Lily must not see under any circumstances, and now here she was, back from some adventure.

So she tucked it away, along with the The Plan.

And meanwhile Lily would be inviting him to her birthday party, and how would that be? She was both exhilarated at the thought of spending those couple of hours with him, and nervous.

Would he think she had put Lily up to it?

Lily came home from school with the good news that Susan was still in town, at a different foster home. This was the first Katherine could remember her mentioning that Susan was a foster child. It would be interesting to meet her. But Lily didn't think she'd be able to come.

"Why?" asked Mom.

"Her other foster mom didn't want her to go anywhere. She thought she would run away."

"So this is a new foster mom?"

"Yes. And she would have to drive Susan. Unless Miss Clark wants to. Maybe I could ask Miss Clark."

Mom didn't think she should ask Miss Clark, but Lily didn't see a problem. She made a plan to ask her when she gave her her invitation.

And then she would go to the high school and give Mr. Brown his.

But when she got to the high school the teachers were all in a meeting. She wrote 'Mr. Brown' on the envelope and left it on the desk outside his office.

When she came out, Mom was just coming in.

"Mom!"

"Lily!"

Then she added, "Wait a minute and we can walk home together." She dashed into Ben's outer office and dropped her envelope on the desk. She could hear the meeting breaking up in his office, so she turned to dash out before she could get caught. Her envelope landed right next to Lily's.

And then Ben came out. Katherine saw him noticing her, shocked to see who it was who was standing before him. And then Lily, standing a bit behind her, well within his view. She could see him take a deep breath. Turn back to the person walking out behind him. "One more thing ..." he was saying, and closed his inner office door behind him again.

## FRIDAY, DECEMBER 17, 1985

THE DAY OF THE party came. Katherine and Lily made two trips each with the wagon. Lily had gone early to the depot to save her table. Susan had said yes, if she could get a ride. And Miss Clark volunteered to do that. The two friends Lily had picked to fill up the table were expected. The only question was Ben. Mr. Brown. The high school principal.

And maybe, thought Lily, Miss Clark's boyfriend.

She told Katherine that for about the third or fourth time, and Katherine finally said, "That's just not true, Lily."

"Why? They like each other. I saw them together at the high school. They're always hanging out together."

"Because he's married," she blurted out.

"He's married? How do you know that?"

"I ... I don't know," Katherine said. She was sure she was sounding as evasive as she felt.

"Well, you'll see. He likes Miss Clark."

"If he comes."

"I hope he comes. I really like him. And I really want to show him my new Lily shirt. He told me he liked my old one."

"When on earth was that?"

"When I went to the volleyball game with Miss Clark."

"He knows your name is Lily?"

"Yes, of course. Miss Clark introduced me and he said, 'Yes, I thought your name was Lily. It's on your shirt.'"

"Oh my," said Mom.

"What, Mom?"

"Nothing."

"Yes, and then he and Miss Clark went off by themselves and talked and talked. It was while I was playing volleyball at half-time."

They were waiting for the guests to arrive. Lily was excited, while Mom was nervous and getting more nervous. She would be face to face with Ben. Unless he didn't come. And she was determined not to run off. She told herself she wanted to spend this precious time with him. And she told herself that again.

And then he and Miss Clark and Miss Horan and a little girl Lily's age—Susan, no doubt—were walking in the door of the depot.

Lily had jumped up and run to the group. She dispensed hugs to Susan and then Miss Clark and then Miss Horan. She held back with Ben, but he reached out for her and she hugged him, too. Then Lily introduced Susan to Mom. Both Miss Clark and Miss Horan greeted her warmly and said, "Call me Ruth," and then everyone laughed. And Ben walked through the little crowd to Mom and gave her a hug and said, "Hello, Kate."

Kate? But Lily was receiving gifts from everyone and while she was doing that her two friends from school had arrived and shyly greeted Susan.

Meanwhile Mom was busy pointing out the buffet already laid out on the table, saying 'do sit down' and 'so glad you could come' and in every way avoiding looking at Ben. Except that Lily could see that she was taking little peeks at him.

And then to Lily's surprise, Ben did not sit down next to Miss Clark but next to Lily's seat of honor.

So Lily had Mr. Brown on one side and Susan on the other, and the three of them talked about Susan's new home, volleyball, school, the rain, the fact that Lily's great-great-grandfather had founded the town, the ferry to the little island, and even about growing carrots. And Miss Clark and Miss Horan talked to the other girls and Mom, but Lily didn't know much about what they said.

And Lily almost forgot that Ben had hugged Mom, and what was that about? But in between things it did make her smile. Maybe he wasn't Miss Clark's boyfriend.

But was Mom right? Was he married?

Married men don't hug unmarried women, do they? Or maybe he was just a friendly man, which Lily liked very much, because she liked his hugs, too, just as Mom obviously did.

In fact, right now, even though she was talking to Miss Horan in a polite way, because she didn't know her well, she was letting smiles wash over her face in between words.

Lily thought she didn't know Mom could be that happy.

The time went by quickly. They were just cutting the cake that Mom had made when Ben stood up and said, "I have to go. Prior commitment. My daughter is here to pick me up."

Daughter?

The cake was delicious. Susan had three pieces. Everyone asked her about her new home, but she didn't really want to talk about it. Just before all the food was gone, Susan said, "Besides, my mother is going to come get me."

"Your real mom, you mean?" asked Lily.

"Lily. That's rude," said Mom in a harsh and audible whisper.

"Yes," said a subdued Susan.

"We'd better go," said one of the Ruths.

And then it was only Mom and Lily and the two classmates, and then it was time for their ride to come, and then Mom and Lily cleaned up and wheeled the residue home.

From their route, Mom could see a line-up of cars in front of the pink house, more cars than ever came on that little section of Main Street. When she pointed them out to Lily, Lily said that that was because the woman was selling something, but she didn't know what. And told Mom about the sign she had seen being pounded into the ground.

"What did it say?" said Mom.

"Just 'for-sale,'" said Lily.

"WHAT?" said Mom.

"For-sale. What's the matter, Mom?"

"Our house is for sale. It's going to be sold. Look at all those buyers. I wonder what's going on?"

"Mom, is that going to make any difference to us? Maybe then we don't have to worry about the Woman in the Window anymore."

"I don't know. It's just a whole new situation all over again. I feel like every time it's sold it gets farther away from being ours."

"Mom, don't let it make you sad."

"But don't you want the house for your very own?"

"Maybe. John Steele built it. So in a way it's my house. But maybe I'd rather have his shipyard."

"Lily! A little girl owning a shipyard? Besides, that was never ours."

"I bet it was. Or at least your mom's."

"Not that anyone ever talked about. And I'm glad I don't have to worry about it."

"Well, pretty soon you won't have to worry about the pink house, either."

"But I promised Aunt Agnes. And Mom, my mother."

"But weren't you only seven?"

"Seven, and many many times after that. And I made you promise to keep an eye on it, too."

"When did you do that?"

"When you were about seven."

"Well, I unpromise."

"You can't. If I can't keep my promise, you have to keep it. To keep the legacy of John Steele alive."

"Just by being alive I keep his legacy alive. And just by having me you kept his legacy alive. So you're done."

"But Agnes made me promise to own the house again."

"And yet she put the treasure of the house in the shed."

"Well, the house is more than a thousand books. It's a roof."

"We have a roof. And I have you and the books. And as long as I have you, I have a home. I don't need a big house, I just need you. And as long as John Steele has me, he has his legacy."

"And as long as Aunt Agnes has kept the books safe, we have her legacy. Or—were they her books or someone else's?"

"They had to be John Steele's. Or his wife's. Those books came from the east coast and Europe and were hauled here I don't know how. By rail? Ship? Why? Why bring hundreds of books all this way?"

"Because if all this went away, Mom, they would be a treasure. Not the books, but the knowledge in the books. Remember, they didn't have a library here yet."

By now they were home. Lily was ten years old, double digits. Old enough to make big decisions, someday soon if a big decision or two needed to be made. And what would they be? More than answering the question, 'What should we have for supper?'

Well, tonight that was easy. Leftovers from lunch. Otherwise they were both full. Lily put the chickens in the henhouse and checked the locks on the shed. All was well there.

The woman wasn't in the window.

The sun had set.

Once inside, she debated about whether to share with Mom an idea that had just come to her. Poor Mom. She was worried about things, things maybe she could help, and things she probably couldn't.

"So that was Susan," Mom was saying.

"Yes, she's nice. But she misses her mother."

"Yes, what happened to her family?"

"I don't know. She hasn't ever said. But she does think her mother is going to pick her up someday soon and take her to her real home. So she probably didn't die or anything."

"Does she like this foster family better?"

"I think so. She said they don't spank her like the other one. Mr. Brown asked her a lot of questions about that. At first he thought she was still getting spanked in the home she's in, but she said it was just in the first one."

"I hope she gets to go home," said Katherine.

While they were talking they were getting ready for bed. Time to read before sleep.

But Lily was thinking about her party. It had been wonderful. She had received two journals, some markers, and twenty dollars inside a card that wasn't signed. But she knew it was from Ben, from Mr. Brown. That was really nice.

"Mom, he called you Kate! Why did he call you Kate?"

"I don't know," said Katherine. But of course she did know. Because when they had awakened at dawn that first night, Ben had said, "Katherine. That's an old-fashioned name for a sprightly girl like you. I'm going to call you Kate, if you don't mind." And he had probably kissed her. 'And why do you think he kissed you then,' she asked herself. Because everything during those precious hours had been reason for a kiss. One or perhaps several.

Oh, Ben. She shuddered, felt the lump in her breast. The day she had looked forward to these few weeks was now in the past, nearly. The birthday party had happened. He had come. And gone. With his daughter.

His daughter, who had been perhaps ten back then. His daughter, who had first seen them together at the park .... There'd been that glorious Friday night spent in each other's arms. Then Saturday, when they'd walked onto the little ferry and strolled around the island it took them to, returning to the cottage after dark to lie together for a second night. And then Sunday, when they'd finally had to take a break from the glorious togetherness she had never expected nor solicited and had gone for a walk in town. Their unplanned path had taken them past the park. And without warning this same daughter had run across the playground calling out 'Daddy,' and he had said "I love you, Kate. That is my daughter. I must go. Forgive me."

So how ironic that this daughter of Ben's had been the one to put an end to Lily's happiness today.

Or was that perhaps overdramatic?

Three months after his daughter's surprise arrival at the park, Katherine had known she was pregnant. And then he had come that one time more, when the baby was three months old, and since then she had been alone.

Alone! Bitterly alone. Except for Lily. What would she ever do without Lily?

"Mom, are you still awake?"
"Yes."
"I think he likes you. I think that's why he called you Kate."
"Good night, Lily."
"Good night."

## SATURDAY, DECEMBER 18, 1985

"MOM, ARE YOU AWAKE?"

It was morning. Lily was stirring something on the stove, maybe scrambled eggs, except she didn't like eggs if they weren't from her hens, and they weren't laying now that it was so late in the season.

"Mom, thanks for the party."

"You're welcome. I had a good time."

"I have an idea."

Katherine had learned to cringe when Lily said she had an idea. "What is it?"

"I know where we can put the books where they'll be safe and a legacy for John Steele and his wife and Aunt Agnes."

"You mean, if they're in the shed?"

"Of course they're in the shed."

"But wait, before you tell me, remember they are there for emergency use —if they're there at all."

"What does that mean?"

"I'm sure it means we can sell them if we need the money."

"Well, this is better. I mean, it's better because it's for a lot of people, not just for us. Because if there's an emergency, it's that these precious old books that John Steele brought all the way from the east with him are in danger."

"Danger? You mean from the Woman in the Window?"

"From her, or from someone else breaking in to see what they could sell. Or from rain. Or from being forgotten."

"OK, I get it. Even if I don't think that's what Agnes meant by an emergency. Though the way she took care of her dad's things, even the house, she could have meant for us to save the books, not for them to save us."

They both thought for a minute. "OK, tell me," said Mom.

"We can donate them to the library!"

Lily was exuberant.

"Whyever for?"

"So they are appreciated. So they get read. And so they are safe from the Woman in the Window or other people who take over the house."

"I wonder if they'd even want them."

"Of course they would. Well, not everyone would. If someone found them, they might just think of them as old and throw them away. But other people would treasure them. Like John Steele did, or he wouldn't have brought them all that way with him.

"Think of it. It could be the Mr. and Mrs. John Steele Collection, donated by Miss Katherine Steele."

"I'll think about it," said Mom. "Right now they're safe where they are, though, right?"

"I hope so."

"I wonder how much we could get for one of them. What do you think they are worth?"

"I have no idea, but did you see all those books at the Great Blue Heron? It was filled with used books. Would someone just dropping in for a few minutes even notice one old treasure of a book?"

"I said I'd think about it. But right now I've got some cleaning and laundry to do."

Lily put a few minutes into collecting her laundry, but then said, "Mom … ."

"What, Lily."

"Do you mind if I ask Miss Horan about book donations? I wouldn't have to say we had books to donate."

"All right. But let's get our chores done. The day isn't getting any younger."

Lily went out to work in the garden. She knew the Woman in the Window had walked across it, and now as she inspected it she saw she had left more than one set of footprints. She could see comings and goings, and more than one of each. In fact it looked as though she had walked through the garden three times each way.

But Lily knew of only two, when she herself had bumped into her, and when Mom had.

It appeared she had visited the shed a third time. Very recently.

Lily looked up into the window. The woman was there.

Lily set about trying to repair the damage from the footprints. One square of oriental greens had been severely damaged, but the others might be salvageable. She pulled the remaining baby greens and set them aside to feed to the chickens, who would love them.

She assessed the three-by-three square that had gotten the most damage. She'd just replant the one square and get it started. The seedlings would fill in the winter garden with a fresh block of green. She used her hand tools to cultivate the soil again where the heavy footprints had ruined the tilth of the soil, and then sprinkled the seed. It took her an hour to be satisfied.

When she looked up into the window again, the woman was there, whether again or still she didn't know.

She counted the carrots, now mature and waiting for harvest, not yet ready to go to seed. Fifty or so left. And beets? Not many, maybe eight or ten. They might as well eat those. And potatoes? The vines were still alive. They had not had a frost yet. Each vine could harbor as many as a dozen potatoes. And Lily counted twenty vines before she stopped counting. Maybe they should save those for themselves, too.

"Must be lunchtime," she thought. She had no idea how long she'd been out in the garden. She never did.

When she went in, Mom had gone back to bed. She let her sleep, made a peanut butter sandwich and ate an apple and thought about the books and what she would say to Miss Horan about donations.

But she had left the garden tools outside and the rain was no longer just a drizzle. She put her raincoat and boots back on. If they could just use the shed, she could put them away there, but as it was she had to clean them in the rain bucket and bring them inside. Oh well.

She closed the door quietly so Mom could sleep. She'd been so tired recently. The seeds were still in the pocket of her raincoat, and she was tempted to prepare another bed, the one where the squash had grown, the squash that were lined up beside the cottage door awaiting their turn at providing dinner for Lily and Mom. Four squash, an adequate harvest from a single plant.

As she turned to admire them, she could see there were only three now, and another set of footprints had come and gone. When had that happened? Just now after she'd gone inside?

The woman was not in the window.

The squash patch would make the perfect place for more oriental greens, and if she could sell those to the Chinese restaurants, it could bring in good cash. But the rain was picking up and she'd need to do a lot of prep work before she could sow any seeds. Better just go in.

And maybe take the squash with her. That was their winter food. She couldn't afford to lose any more. Could the woman actually have taken their squash?

And if not the woman, who?

Maybe Mom. She'd ask when Mom was awake.

But if they had the shed to use, the squash could be locked in there. The tools, too. And the cleaning bucket that was out back against the cottage.

And she could then buy and store chicken feed and keep the hens laying longer.

And she could stop worrying about losing the books. If that woman was a thief, what would stop her from breaking in while Lily was at school and maybe Mom was asleep?

Of course the woman didn't know the shed had books, not the kind of valuables that most people would store away so securely. So she might break in, toss the books out into the mud so she could continue her search for something of real value, and walk away.

Lily was more determined than ever to donate the books to the library. If it weren't Sunday, if she were sure Miss Horan would be there to ask, she would go even now and start the process. Surely the library would want them.

Of course they would not pay for them. So in a way, if they donated the books, they'd be cutting off a source of income. Well, Lily had plenty of ideas for income. And she didn't believe those old books would find a big market in their little town.

Lily carried the squash in. They were huge and awkward, and dirty. She splashed water from the rain bucket over each one, then put them in a row under the end of the bed. There really was nowhere else, and they barely fit. She decided to roast one for dinner.

And then she settled down to practice writing fancy letters that she could use to paint names on tee shirts for kids her age. She'd gotten a book at the library with various scripts to guide her.

Mom slept until dinner time. Lily had roasted the squash and added potatoes to the oven. They had some butter left. It would make a fine meal.

The wind had come up but the rain seemed to be diminishing. The house was cozy from the oven having been on for a couple of hours.

They read while they ate. It was the beginning of a peaceful evening. Except that Lily couldn't stop thinking about the books. While Mom was asleep she should have found the combinations to the locks so she could make sure that was the treasure the shed held.

"Mom, I am going to ask Miss Horan about the books. And I need to make sure the books are there before I do that."

"I thought you were already sure."

"I am. But before I ask ... ."

Mom was weary, even after all that sleep, Lily could see that. And she didn't want to aggravate her. But she could so easily see the woman going to extremes to break into the shed.

"I don't want to think about it now," said Mom.

"OK."

Lily knew not to mention it to Mom again. Maybe if she'd reminded Mom that the big book was probably in there and probably her father's name had been written in it next to her mother's, she'd be more interested. Well, too late. Lily knew she had said as much as she could.

But she hadn't done as much as she could.

They enjoyed the squash and potatoes. The one cooked squash would last them all week.

She hoped the woman, or whoever else had taken the fourth squash, would enjoy it all week, too. Would not take just a few bites and throw the rest away.

## MONDAY, DECEMBER 20, 1985

SUNSHINE! TEMPORARY AS IT no doubt was, Lily enjoyed it on her walk to school. It was low in the sky and had little warmth, but it was cheerful.

And Lily was cheerful. After school she would not go straight home but go talk to Miss Horan about the books.

She was also thinking about the odd thing Mom had said this morning.

"Lily, I want you to go around to the front of the big house and see if that for-sale sign is there. Every day. And if it's not there, let me know."

"Why, Mom?"

"Because if the sign is taken away, that means someone has bought the house."

"That's good, right, Mom? Then the woman won't live there anymore."

"I think she's harmless."

"She's not," said Lily. But she didn't want to bother Mom with her suspicions, so it was more of a mumble than real words, and Mom let it go by.

And now as she approached the school, Lily was thinking Mom had been worried that the big house would sell and she wasn't sure why. Lily would be happy if the Woman in the Window had to move away.

And then Lily arrived at school, and all during school she thought about talking to Miss Horan, and then school was done for the day and she walked to the library. The sun was still shining, the air cool and crisp. It felt like it might snow instead of rain later.

At the library Miss Horan was behind the checkout desk and greeted her by name. Lily got in line behind people with stacks of books, and when it was her turn she asked Miss Horan the question:

"Miss Horan, if someone came with a large number of books, would the library take them as a donation?"

"It would depend what they were," said Miss Horan. "Are you talking about the same donation you were looking for the other day?"

"Well, maybe," Lily said slowly. "But not just any donation? What if they were special books?"

"It still depends. We have plenty of some books and can't take them. They would just go in the trash. If you give me an example of one or two in the collection, I could tell you more."

"I don't know what's in the collection," Lily mumbled as she walked away.

She had been so sure Miss Horan would say yes, and now she was so disappointed that she forgot to say thank you.

Miss Horan was surprised to see Lily upset. She had walked away without saying thank you, not like her at all, such a polite child usually, and now she was leaving the library without picking out any books. Miss Horan felt like running after her, but of course she couldn't. Well, maybe Clark would shed some light on it. Maybe something had gone wrong at school.

So when Horan got home that night, and was seated at a hot meal Clark had concocted, excellent as usual, Horan got right to the point.

"You know your lovely student, Lily. She came by today and seemed strangely upset. Did anything happen in school?"

"She was daydreamy, not entirely focused. But I didn't notice anything else. Why?"

"She just asked me a question. About donating books to the library. And I couldn't tell her the answer. And then she just walked away. I can tell you I've never seen her droopy like that before."

"Was her mother with her? I didn't see her pick her up today."

"You know they don't have a car."

"Right. I've noticed that."

Clark was looking as concerned as Horan was feeling.

"I think we need to keep an eye out in case there's a problem at home. I mean, all seemed fine at the birthday party, and that was only two days ago."

"Well, we've got a short week at school this week because of Christmas. And then she'll be off for a couple of weeks. That's a long time. Things go bad quickly for kids if they're having trouble at home."

"I know," said Horan.

"Why don't we have a little Christmas party? Right here at our house. Invite her and her mother, Ben and his daughter. Maybe that's all. Have a little gift exchange. Or maybe just have gifts for them. I don't know their situation and I wouldn't want them to have to bring something."

"Oh, that would be delightful. The library closes halfway through Friday, Christmas Eve. We could do it that evening."

"Perfect. I'll make some quick invitations."

"Why Ben?" asked Horan.

"He's taken an interest in Lily at volleyball. I'd think he might like a little party himself, now that it's just him and his daughter. Of course she may have plans."

"And so might he. For all we know, he's dating again. Said he never would but who knows."

"Well, he can always say 'no.' He's a good guy. Who else should we invite? You're usually quick with an idea to do some matchmaking. I wonder if Lily's mom is dating. She's single, I'm fairly sure."

"What about that foster kid from your class?" asked Horan.

"She's at a different school now. Lily does enjoy her. Again, no harm in asking. Though I'd probably ask the foster mother, not Susan herself, in case she can't come."

## THURSDAY, DECEMBER 23, 1985 – LAST DAY OF SCHOOL

MISS CLARK CALLED LILY to the front of the room the next day, which was the last day of school, and slipped her the invitation. "This is just for you. Don't show it around, just to your mom," she said, and smiled.

Lily showed Mom, who thought they shouldn't go. "Why not, Mom? I want to."

So Mom said yes, and we need to take some gifts, so Lily started making glittery Christmas cards shaped like tree decorations and Mom made brownies after a quick trip to the store.

## FRIDAY, DECEMBER 24, 1985 – CHRISTMAS EVE

LILY WAS EXCITED TO go to Miss Clark's house, also Miss Horan's. So it would be the four of them and that would be fun.

Miss Clark and Miss Horan lived down by the ferry she and Mom had taken to the little island. They had a small house on the side of a hill, with a giant picture window that looked out over the sound. They could see Christmas lights on the little island across the sound, and then Lily saw a whole procession of boats float past in front of the island. They were all decorated with Christmas lights, and Lily could see the shapes of their masts as well as their whole outlines, depending on how they were decorated.

In the living room, on a table with a window behind it, was a small Christmas tree. With lights. They had seen it from the street.

Miss Clark and Miss Horan were working in the kitchen, a shiny white cheerful kitchen with room for them both. They said they didn't need help.

Then the doorbell rang. Someone else was coming. Miss Clark asked Lily to answer the door. It was Mr. Brown and his daughter.

Mr. Brown gave Lily a hug, and said, "This is my daughter Angie. She's home for Christmas from college."

Lily was still feeling his hug. How sweet it had felt.

Mom was still across the room by the window. Lily knew she was surprised by other people coming. Lily was also wondering if Mr. Brown would call her Kate again. And give her a hug.

But Mom was just standing there staring.

All at once everyone was in motion except Mom. Angie started talking to Lily. Ben crossed the room to look out the picture window but didn't say anything to Mom. Miss Clark came in from the kitchen and gave Ben a kiss. Miss Horan came in from the kitchen and took Miss Clark by the arm.

And then everyone gravitated toward Mom. Miss Horan took Mom by the arm too and took everyone over to the couches and asked them to sit down and then brought in a hot dip that smelled of seafood and onions and cheese.

Mom and Ben ended up sitting next to each other. And Angie and Lily. And Clark and Horan.

The dip was served with chips and crackers and tiny slices of bread, their choice. Lily watched Clark and Horan to see what they did, then copied them. Mom was sitting back, not taking any. But Ben made one for her and she took it. Lily thought Mom didn't look good, but she enjoyed the dip and Ben made her a second without asking.

Then Clark got up and asked Lily to go with her into the kitchen. One whole counter was covered with serving dishes of all sorts. Clark asked Lily to carry them out to the table, the big table, while Clark heated something.

"How are things these days?" Clark asked. "Are you missing school yet?"

"I have a lot to do. Working in the garden, mostly."

"How's your Mom?"

"OK. I guess."

Clark told Lily to sit back down after all the serving dishes were on the table.

Angie, Ben's daughter, was home from college, she said, and then said, "Your name is Lily Steele? Steele is a famous name around here. Are you from that family?"

"I guess so. My great-great-grandfather built the depot and other places like that."

"You must be proud to carry his name."

Lily knew Angie was just being nice, but she couldn't help saying, "I wish I had a different name, though. My father's name."

"Lily!" exclaimed Mom. "Don't talk about family things."

Lily was embarrassed. "Sorry, Mom."

Angie spent the next few minutes talking about college, her challenge in picking a major ... anything to change the subject. Lily knew that's what she was doing. Lily had embarrassed Angie and she was sorry and said, "What's a major?" Lily didn't know. It was a real question.

Ben had gotten up and was looking out the big picture window again. "What a great show this year, don't you think, Lily? Come on over and take a look. You, too, Katherine."

Lily went but Katherine didn't. So Ben turned back toward the sitting area, still standing with Lily by the window, but speaking loud enough so everyone—except the Ruths, who were in the kitchen—could hear him.

"Angie, what do you think? Want to enter our boat in the New Year's Eve boat parade next week?"

Lily was suddenly alert. Did they really have a boat?

Angie said, "Sure, Dad, let's. Maybe you'd like to help, Lily. And you, Katherine. It's fun. A lot of work but then it looks so great."

"And then we could wave as you went by," said Lily.

"Or you could come with us. It's fun. We can see all the other boats because when they get to the end of the sound, they turn around and come back, so we pass each other."

"Oh, Mom, let's!"

"Unless you have other plans," said Ben.

"I have to leave to go back to college the next Sunday," said Angie. "I'd love to do that and take a great memory back with me."

"We'll talk about it, Lily," said Mom.

The Ruths had crossed the room by then, but Horan had missed what they were talking about. Ben filled her in. "Why don't you two come, too, as usual. The more who work on it, the more fun it is. And there's room on board for the six of us."

Horan laughed and said, "Not a chance for me. I don't do water. Even the ferry scares me. But I don't mind helping. I'll stand on the shore and be a cheerleader."

"Same for Lily and me," said Katherine.

"Mom!"

"You can help but ... well, I don't think we should impose."

"Kate, it won't be the same without you. Please."

"I'll help, and Lily will too. That's all I can commit to."

They sat around the dining room table once all the food was laid out. They each had a plate and the serving plates, maybe twenty of them, started to circulate. Angie told Lily to take just a little of each thing until she found out what she really liked.

"And there'll be dessert too. I've been here before. You will be stuffed to the gills before you go home." Then Angie kept Lily informed as the food went around about what it was, with a little help from Clark.

Lily wanted to ask Horan about donating the books, but Mom had told her not to talk about it. It seemed like a waste of time not to find out now about any new information or decisions, but she had promised. She was happy to have Angie there, talking to her as if she were Angie's age, talking about her boyfriend, her choices of major, how much fun living in the dorm was.

But she was distracted by a story Miss Clark was telling. She hadn't heard the beginning. Now she was saying, "... and so we decided it made sense to share a house. We each have an office, and I'm the cook and shopper. Horan is a disaster in the kitchen, and a much better housekeeper than I am. It's been twelve years and it's been great."

"And then we met Edna and asked her to join us," said Horan. "I knew her when I was studying library science and told her about the job at the high school. She's busy writing a book about libraries up in the mountains where no one is going to interrupt her. She's only been here in the house with us for two years. She's a real sweetheart. You'll see."

Lily was surprised a bit when Clark reached across the table and squeezed Horan's hand. They both smiled.

Sweet, thought Lily.

"Has it been that long, twelve years?" asked Ben. "I guess that's right. Angie would have been six. I can remember when we helped you move in. Getting your things off the boat was certainly interesting," he said to Horan.

"You lived on a boat?" asked Lily.

"And Arabelle was two," said Angie at the same time.

"Who's Arabelle?" asked Lily.

"She's my little sister."

"Where is she? Didn't she want to come?"

"Oh, no, she lives in Seattle with our mother. I spent Thanksgiving with them, so I'm spending Christmas and New Year's with Dad. She was supposed to come but this year they are going to Mom's parents' house in California."

"Oh," said Lily. She was thinking that was sad, for the sisters not to be together.

Ben said, "I like it when all my girls are around for Christmas."

Mom was choking on some food she had just put in her mouth, even though it was only asparagus. Ben looked like he was laughing at her, though he had covered his face. Then Mom excused herself, maybe to go to the bathroom. When she got back, she said, "Lily, we need to go."

"Don't go," said everyone. "We're just getting started. We're all lonely folks this time of year. Let's just pretend we're family tonight."

Mom ran back to the bathroom. Miss Clark got up and followed her, then came back without her.

The major Angie said she'd been thinking about was business, but she wasn't sure. Lily didn't know people went to college to study business, but it was something she wanted to know more about. So she told Angie her idea of getting involved in the shipbuilding business. "My great-great-grandfather John Steele was involved in shipbuilding. Also railroad building," she told everyone.

Angie was impressed. "So do you live on Steele Street?"

"No," said Lily. "We live on Main Street. You know that big pink house, the Victorian? Down at the end of the street?"

"Sure. Wow, that's your house? Everyone knows that house!"

"No, not right now, but it used to be, and it's going to be again someday. We live in the back where the gardens are. And our chickens."

"Really!" said Angie. "That sounds interesting."

"Yes, I sell eggs in the summer when we have enough, and veggies at the farmers market and I'm planning on selling some oriental greens to the Chinese restaurants. But the woman who lives in the big house walked through the garden and I had to replant a lot of stuff and it will be a few months before they're big enough."

"Wow, so you have a regular business."

"I'm trying to. I'm trying to find some new markets now that the farmers market is closed for the season. One time we went to the little island on the ferry, and we saw Miss Clark and Miss Horan there, and they had veggies from that market, so after Christmas I'm going to see if it's still open and sell my carrots and maybe my potatoes there."

Mom, who had drifted back to the living room during this conversation, was looking at her lap. Lily couldn't tell if she was sad or embarrassed or laughing or crying or what.

So Lily added, "But Mom doesn't want me to go on the ferry by myself. And that means she'd be stuck over there the whole day, right, Mom? There's no place for her to read or anything there. When the normal farmers market at the depot is open, I can just walk there from the house by myself."

She knew she was talking too much, so she asked Angie what her business was. But Angie didn't have a business yet.

They had finished dinner, and Miss Clark announced there would be a few surprises in the living room while they ate their dessert. In front of the little tree.

"Wait," said Lily, and added their tiny packages to the other gifts under the tree. Two from Mom, two from her, because they didn't know Ben and Angie were coming.

Angie and Lily sat together on the floor, Miss Horan had taken charge of the distribution of packages, and Miss Clark, Ben, and Mom sat on the couch, which had been pulled up close to the tree.

Angie asked Lily if she wanted to play games after.

"Games?" asked Lily, looking around.

"Yes, they'll bring out cards and things. We do this every year. Well, the past three years since Mom and Dad got divorced. He and Clark are best friends."

Lily looked around. Indeed, Ben was holding Miss Clark's hand.

He was also holding Mom's hand. Clark was talking to Ben, Mom was looking at her lap.

Lily thought Ben would make a good boyfriend for Mom, but she had been right before: He was already Clark's boyfriend. And Mom had said he was married, but Angie had said he was divorced. So he probably was Clark's boyfriend.

Horan passed a gift to Lily, as the youngest. It was a book, the history of their town, written a long time ago. Perfect! Horan had probably picked it out for her. Then Lily picked out a gift and it turned out to be for Ben. It was the ornament she had made for Clark or Horan, and then switched to Ben.

He opened the homemade ornament, and before she could sit down again, gave her a kiss on the cheek. "A treasure, Sweet Girl," he said as he showed it around. "It's lovely. Could I put it on this tree for now?"

"Sure!" said Lily.

So Ben got up and hung the ornament and everyone clapped.

So it was Ben's turn. He gave Clark a little package, and everyone tried to guess what it was. A book?

"Yes, it's a tiny book, a handwritten book of poetry by Emily Dickenson, with hand-painted borders on each page, each one different," Clark said as she fingered through it. "Did you make this?" she asked him.

He nodded. "A few years ago. I wanted it to go to someone who would appreciate it."

Lily knew then that Ben really did love Clark. Clark looked happy.

Lily looked at Mom, but Mom was still looking at her lap.

So now it was Clark's turn. She picked out a package for Mom. It was also small. Mom looked it over and said it was from Ben. She gave him a little smile and opened it. Out fell something metal. Mom picked it up and spread it out. It was silver, a bracelet.

"Read what it says," said Ben, clearly eager for her to enjoy it.

"It says ... 'Lily 12-18-75.'"

"How did you know my birthday?" asked Lily.

"A little bird told me," said Ben, and flashed a smile at Mom. So Lily knew that Mom was the little bird.

"Put it on!" said Ben. And he reached over and helped Mom put it on her wrist.

And then he gave her a kiss on the lips. And when Lily looked at Mom again, she had tears in her eyes.

"Thank you," Mom whispered. "Thank you," she said more loudly.

So it was Mom's turn, and she picked out her gift for Clark, the brownies. And then Clark picked out the other package of brownies and gave it to Angie.

Angie gave her gift to Lily. It was a photo album, the kind where you keep photos of your family and friends. And in it was a little stack of photos, one of Mom, one of Ben, one of Angie, and one of the big house.

"Where did you get these photos?" Lily asked as she hugged Angie.

"I took them with my Polaroid. And now I'm going to take your photo so you can put that in the 'my photo' place."

"And see? Here's a place for your mom."

"And here's one for my dad, when I find him."

"Yes," said Angie. "And friends and grandparents and brothers and sisters and so on."

So Angie got out her Polaroid and took everyone's photo and groups of them, too: Clark and Horan together, Mom and Ben together, Lily and Angie together, Lily and Angie and Ben and Mom together, and so on.

"See what I mean?" said Clark. "We're all family."

Clark distributed more little packages, including Christmas cookies for all. Homemade ones with names on them. Then Horan brought out a huge stack of games.

"Oh, no," said Mom. "We should go."

"No, you should not," said Ben. "Lily and Angie are going to play games till midnight and then we'll ring in Christmas together. Remember, we're family."

And then when Katherine didn't respond, he added, "Clark said so."

And Lily could see that Mom nodded a tiny bit, maybe.

So Angie and Lily sat on the floor together and Angie taught Lily a game. The four adults sat in a circle and talked, and after a while Horan said, "Tell me about that house of yours. I know it's been here forever."

"I don't remember much," said Katherine. "I was only seven when we moved."

"Why did you move?"

"For some reason my aunt, my Aunt Agnes, had to sell. I think she ran out of money to keep it up. So my mother and I had to move too."

"Agnes was the daughter of John Steele. He and his son and heir, William Steele, died during the Spanish flu. On his deathbed John Steele made Agnes promise she'd always take care of the house. William was supposed to take care of the shipbuilding company and other things, but he died too, and Agnes said he was a ne'er-do-well.

"So we ran out of money I think, and to keep an eye on the house we moved into the caretaker's cottage in the back. That was in 1950. Much later Agnes died, then I had Lily. And then Isabelle, my mother, died. Lily remembers her, a little. And then since then it's been just the two of us."

"What happened to the house?"

"The new owners supposedly fixed it up, new roof, paint, lots of things inside, I guess. I never went back inside. Until the other day."

"You and the new family are friends, then," said Horan. "How nice."

"No, not at all. I barely know them."

"Mom figured out a way to get in, though," said Lily.

"Yes, I pretended to be a cleaning lady. I wanted to find out if the books I grew up with were still on the shelf. But they weren't. Some of our furniture was there, though. I think Agnes sold it furnished. Or maybe 'as is.'"

Lily said, "I know where the books are."

"Anyway," said Mom, clearly cutting Lily off, "now the lady who is living in it is selling it. There's a for-sale sign up as of last week. And Lily says it's still there."

"Is that a problem?" Ben asked.

"There's always the question of why we're living back there. Every new owner calls it into question."

"Do you have proof that you can be there?" asked Horan.

"Yes. Agnes told me we do. But I've never seen it, I don't think. Maybe when I was seven. I seem to remember she showed me a paper and then put it away someplace for safe keeping. I have no idea where it is."

"But it should be recorded at the county offices," said Ben. "So you should be OK."

As the hour became late, Clark and Horan decided to serve cocoa. It was only an hour to midnight. Ben invited Mom to go out on the little balcony that gave an unobstructed view of the harbor. The decorated boats had disappeared. He held out his hand for her. "Come on," he said. "Just because it's Christmas."

So she got up. She was weaker than she expected and almost fell back onto the couch. He caught her and held her up as they made their way to the door to the balcony.

"Are you OK, Kate?" he asked once they were outside. She was shivering, though the night was no colder than most this time of year. He wrapped her in his arms.

She nodded.

"No, tell me, are you OK? You seem a bit down."

"We're fine," she said.

"Lily is a fine girl," he said.

"I don't know what I'd do without her," said Kate. She hadn't really realized it till she said it, and now she was upset because saying it made her realize how true it was, how much responsibility Lily took.

She turned toward Ben, for the first time in all these years relaxing into his arms. She buried her face in his chest.

"Angie really loves being around Lily. She's really impressed by her."

"Angie's nice," said Katherine.

"Obviously you know they're sisters."

Katherine pulled back. Obviously. Now that he'd mentioned it. She hadn't stopped to think about it, but yes, they were sisters. She turned back toward the living room, watching them through the picture window. The two girls had a certain similarity: the brown curls, the same noses and chins.

All Ben's.

It took Katherine a few moments to compose herself. "Does she know?"

"Yes."

"Is she OK with it?"

"She's curious. And she likes her. Kate. You know I'm divorced."

"I heard that. Tonight. Is it true?"

"It's been true for three years. I tried to tell you."

"When did you do that?"

"So many times. When I saw you. When I came by late at night with the money. At the store."

"I've been trying to make sure no one knew."

"Does Lily know? My guess is, you haven't told her."

"I promised not to tell anyone. You surely remember that. I didn't think you were going to tell anyone, either."

Ben recognized the strident tone in Kate's comment. He didn't realize that she felt she was being held to that ten-year-old promise. So much had changed. Caroline had left him, had custody of Arabella. Of both daughters until Angie had come of age.

"Well, Ben, I guess everyone knows besides the little problem herself. You might as well tell Lily. I'm not going to."

"Why not?"

"It would be hard to explain to her why you haven't been in her life all these years."

"You sound bitter."

"I'm bound by a promise you yourself are not keeping."

"Not everyone knows. Just Angie."

"Not Clark and Horan?"

"No."

"Plus you're in love with Clark."

"No, not in that way. We've been friends for years, that's all. Since college. We did date then, but now we're just best friends."

"Close friends."

"Close friends, it's true, but not lovers. I think Clark is just as close a friend with Horan as with me, and maybe with Edna too.

"Horan's nice, too. I don't really know Edna, though."

"Another roommate, as you heard. She's away at the moment or we'd all be together tonight."

"Well, you sure do seem cozy with Clark."

"Kate, I think maybe Clark and Horan are lovers. If not, they're a special kind of friend. She has no interest in me except, as she says, we're family."

Kate was silent.

"So why, if she doesn't know, did she invite you?"

"We come every year. We have for the past three years. In addition to our early years together, Clark was Angie's teacher, and we all have kept in touch. You're the new folks, you and Lily. I confess when she asked me if I'd mind if she invited you, I was so enthusiastic that she asked me if I had my eyes on you. And you know what I said? Yes, I do. And then I laughed. But guess what? I do have my eyes on you."

Kate was silent for long minutes. Then she said, "You're too late."

"What do you mean?"

Kate just shook her head.

"Maybe Angie would like to invite Lily to spend the night tonight."

"Whatever for?" asked Kate.

"Because then you could invite me to the spend the night with you."

"Out of the question," she snapped, and let herself back into the house. The night air as she left his arms was cold after all.

Ben was dismayed. He so loved Kate, and thought she had loved him, too. But clearly she had fallen out of love with him. No wonder she had continued to rebuff him, every time—the few times—he had seen her. And Lily was such a lovely child. But she seemed to be carrying a weight on her shoulders, too. From Ben's point of view, having the four of them under his roof, or three when Angie was at college, sounded like a perfect arrangement.

Midnight was only ten minutes away. Kate had told Lily they were leaving, but Clark had pointed out how close to the ringing in of Christmas they were, so Katherine had said, "Well, Lily, it will take that long to put away the game and clean up, so we'll stay till then. And really, Clark and Horan, it was great, thank you."

Then Ben had said, "We'll see you next week. On New Year's Eve, during the day so we can get the boat ready."

"Yes!" said Lily.

"No, I don't think so," said Katherine.

"Great, we'll pick everyone up," said Clark.

"I can't wait," said Horan. "Except no boat ride for me, remember?"

"And if you're not going, I'm not going," said Clark. And she gave Horan a hug.

Had she done that before? Katherine hadn't noticed.

Katherine was trying to clean up the little scraps of wrapping paper, but each time she bent over her breast sent out severe stabs of pain that caused her to wince and stand up again.

Then Angie, smiling, gave Lily a hug and said, "Want to spend the night?"

"Oh, can I, Mom? I'll come home in the morning."

"Out of the question."

"Why? Angie is my new best friend."

"I'll make sure they get to bed as soon as they get home," said Ben.

"No," said Mom.

"Please, Mom."

Katherine was by now simply looking forward to sleep. She felt drained. It was late for her, and she was scared to feel this extraordinary fatigue that had come upon her.

So she said, "OK. And I'll probably sleep in. Don't get up too early. You'll be cranky all day."

Lily looked sad. "Sorry, Mom," she said. "I won't be cranky."

"And don't stay up all night talking."

"OK, Mom."

## SATURDAY, DECEMBER 25, 1985 – CHRISTMAS DAY

AND THEN IT WAS midnight. Clark turned up the Christmas music and they all sang carols together. Then came hugs all around, and Ben said, "I'll drop you off, Kate. You can't walk home at this hour."

And Kate was so tired she accepted.

The four said goodnight and thank you to Clark and Horan, who stood with their arms around each other in the big front door. Then they walked the short distance to Ben's car. The girls got in the back, Kate in the front. Ben lived up the main road the ferry was on, a block over from Clark and Horan, just ten blocks away, and not far from the high school, as Lily pointed out.

He dropped the girls off, and then drove Kate to the east part of town where the big house made a dark silhouette on the skyline.

"It looks gigantic from here, doesn't it," said Ben.

"You can't come in."

"I'm coming in."

"I'm tired."

"I know you are. And I don't know why. What's going on?"

"Nothing. What do you mean?"

"You don't seem yourself."

"Lily is growing up."

"Is that it? They all grow up. Wait till she goes to college."

"I ... I can't imagine that happening."

"Well, start preparing because it happens fast."

"Hard to picture," Kate said.

"I know," said Ben

"No, you don't. But that's that."

So that was the end of the conversation, and Katherine saw how close they were to home, and Ben was going to be coming in, and that was a dream come true. And what if Angie in the quiet intimacy of a sleepover told Lily the truth? Lily, Katherine knew, would be happy, ecstatic. She really liked Ben.

So why was she so nervous, Katherine asked herself? Not nervous, but reluctant. Was it simply fatigue? Or was it because she had resented Ben for so long, because he could go on with life and ... ? Well, because she had Lily to care for, but then suddenly it was more like Lily had her to care for. Though Lily never seemed to notice that gradually, she was doing more and more.

And there was the alley, and now the short walk into the house and what if Ben wanted to spend the night and all that implied? She couldn't let him. He would discover her ... her affliction. And then that would be the end of Ben. Because as she had figured out before, he wouldn't want to stick around a dying woman.

And she and Lily would be fine without him. Right here where they could keep an eye on the big house.

The dark and imposing big house, with no signs of life. Had the woman and her husband already left, or were they just asleep already?

As long as they didn't see her bring Ben home. Ben, whose reputation was at stake. Ben, a well-known figure, coming home with her, Katherine Steele, a remnant of a grander time. A dying breed.

He was parking the car at the verge of the alley. He opened the door and the light came on. He held out his hand. "Keys, please," he said. She fished them out of her purse and handed them to him.

He was taking charge and she was glad for it. She was unbearably tired.

Is this how she was with Lily these days, too? The poor child, as uncomplaining as she was.

Ben shut his door and came around to hers. He helped her out, supported her as she walked along, unlocked the door of the cottage, flipped the light switch, took her coat. Took off his jacket. Heated water, made tea. Sat her on the bed and took off her shoes. She let herself fall to the side and lie there on the bed, still dressed, in a state of exhaustion that she had never before felt.

Ben had the tea ready. He had put it in a mug and was now raising her up so she could drink it.

"What is it, Kate? What's wrong?"

"Nothing."

"Kate. It's me. I love you. Tell me."

"Nothing."

He got up, reached under her pillow, pulled out her nightgown. He handed it to her.

"Go home, Ben."

"No."

He helped her walk to the bathroom. He was pacing when she came out. He guided her back to the bed, pulled the covers down so she could slip between the sheets, covered her again.

She closed her eyes, couldn't hear him anymore, opened her eyes again. He had removed his shoes, and was now preparing to ... ah, to lie on top of the covers.

"I'll stay until you fall asleep. I'll have Lily here for when you wake up in the morning."

She nodded. She fell asleep, his hand on her hip. Such a comfort.

Then suddenly he was standing next to her, bending over, kissing her.

She reached out for his hand, grabbed it. "Stay," she said hoarsely.

"I'll be right back," he said.

She could hear the car leaving. She sighed. Gone, he was gone again and who knew for how long.

She started to drift back to sleep, feeling that deep fatigue still. She wasn't ready for this, didn't have her plan in place. Lily was in danger. If Katherine was this bad this soon, Lily would end up in foster care. Because they would know she was alone, Lily was, and would not know she could take care of herself.

So she needed the plan. And obviously she couldn't count on Ben. She was alone again.

And then he was back at her side. Feeling her forehead as if to check whether she had a fever. And then he was crawling under the covers, and now shifting around so he could hold her.

"I moved the car. It's in the depot parking lot with the cars from the boaters who are out for the holiday."

And then it was morning. Ben was making breakfast. She didn't want to get up.

And what would Lily be thinking? And what would Angie be thinking? Maybe they were still asleep. Maybe Ben should go home before he was caught not being home on Christmas morning.

"Can you get up?" he was asking. "Let's go to my house and celebrate with the kids."

Katherine couldn't imagine managing it but the idea was beginning to sound good to her.

So they set about making it happen. It took Katherine a while to get ready, but it was still only 9:00 or so when they arrived at Ben's house.

She had never actually been inside the house, but in the days when she was missing Ben back when she was pregnant, she had walked by several times. Back when she pictured Ben and his wife and his kids in their little house, happy together, and she, Kate, on the outside.

Until this moment.

She was going in, and it made her happy. And one of those little girls from back then was inside, and her own little girl was, too. As sisters. Almost as sisters, except maybe Lily didn't know that yet.

Maybe Ben would tell her today. If Angie hadn't, overnight.

She herself couldn't. She was still constrained by the promise.

Ben had opened the car door and they both walked down the steps on the steep walkway down to the house. The ocean well below them—actually the sound—was covered with choppy whitecaps, and across the way was the little island they had visited. Ben unlocked the door and held it for her. Crossing that threshold caused a thrill to surge through her body.

At last, a part of her heart said to her. At last. At last.

The girls were asleep side by side in the living room. Each had a blanket and a pillow. The tree nearly filled the rest of the space. Ben had her sit on the couch, got her a colorful knit blanket, and disappeared. He returned with a plate of goodies and a pot of tea.

Then he stood over the girls and said, "Good morning, good morning, ladies. Merry Christmas, time to wake up. Merry Christmas." And so on.

Gradually the girls stretched and purred and pulled themselves from sleep. Sun was streaming in the large front window, and Katherine thought they looked like contented cats. Maybe they would or maybe they would not want to get up now.

"Merry Christmas, Daddy," said Angie.

Suddenly Katherine was alert. Did Lily know? What would she say to Ben?

"Merry Christmas, Ben," and she giggled.

"Merry Christmas, Baby," said Katherine. The girls hadn't realized she was there.

"Mommy!" said Lily. "Merry Christmas."

"Merry Christmas, Mother," said Angie, with a wink. Lily laughed at Angie's clever joke.

So Angie had not told Lily. It was all up to Ben.

The girls sat on the floor around the coffee table, eating their breakfast feast. Ben served Katherine, who found she was hungry for the first time in days. And then Ben sat down next to Katherine and said, "I have an idea. I think you'll like it."

"Now?"

"After breakfast."

After it was all cleared up, Ben asked Lily where her new photo album was. He found it next to her coat and said, "Let's see how this works." He handed it to Lily. "OK, who's the first person?"

"Me."

He handed the stack of photos to her. She went through the photos until she found herself. He handed her the stickers that would hold it on and she placed it carefully in the bordered rectangle that said, "Me."

Then she proceeded with the parents' page, taking Mom's photo out of the stack and placing it.

She looked at the photo of the house and added it to the very first page of the book, right over the title where it said, "My Family."

The next page said 'Sisters and Brothers.'

She said to Angie, "I don't have any real brothers and sisters. Can I put you here?"

Angie said 'sure' and smiled a big smile first at Lily and then at Ben, who raised his eyebrows at her, Katherine noticed.

So Lily stuck the photo of Angie in on top of one of the frames for Sisters. And then she added the photo of her and Angie on another frame for Sisters.

And then she closed the book.

"You've got some more photos here. Can't you find a place for them?"

"Oh yes, there's a friends place. I'll put Clark and Horan in the friends place, together because I think they like each other, and separately because they're both my friends."

She did it and closed the book again. Then opened and put the picture of Mom and Ben in Friends right under Clark and Horan. "You're friends with each other, too," she explained.

Then she closed it again.

Everyone sat there looking at Lily. Katherine knew why Ben was doing this. And she could tell they all wanted Lily to discover the truth when she realized it, on her own.

Finally Ben said, "I think there's one more you could do."

"Who?"

"Who do you wish you could do?"

"My dad. And I will. As soon as I find out who he is. Mom knows but she can't tell me."

"Why can't she?"

"Because she promised. Him. I think he didn't want a baby and was embarrassed, so he said, don't ever tell."

The silence lengthened. Then Katherine said, "Oh, Lily. I don't think … ."

"Wait, Kate," said Ben.

"Lily," he said. "I'm absolutely certain he loves you. And I think I saw his photo in that stack."

"You did?" she said. Then she turned to Angie and said, "Did you?"

"I think I did," said Angie.

Lily grabbed the photos and started going through them. Faster and faster. "No," she said at last. "I didn't think so."

"I saw it, I really did," said Ben.

"Here," said Lily. She threw the stack at him. She was crying. "You find him if you're so smart."

"Lily!" said Katherine.

"It's OK, Kate," he said. "I'll find it and put it upside down in the book where it says 'Father' and then Lily can turn it over when she's ready."

"I've been ready for a long time," shouted Lily.

Angie took her by the hand. "Hold on. Let's see what he does."

"But I've waited for so long, Angie. How would you feel?"

"I don't know. But let's give Daddy one more chance."

"OK, Ben, go for it," said the still upset Lily.

So Ben took the book and the stack of photos onto his lap and shuffled through the photos, and picked one out and placed it on the Father frame upside down. Then he placed the album back in front of Lily.

"For you, my darling," he said.

The album sat in front of Lily. Katherine had her hands at her throat. She appeared to have stopped breathing. Angie was bouncing up and down. Ben had his hand over his face and might have been shedding a tear or two.

And Lily? She took a deep breath. Let it out. Reached out for the photo. Said, "No, I can't do it."

And Ben said, "Yes, this is the time. You've waited long enough. It's Christmas. It's the gift you wanted. Go!"

And at go, she turned it over.

"Oh Ben," she said. "That was mean. It's you. This is your photo. I'm grown up enough to understand that we don't have his photo."

"Is that the only possibility, that you think I'm just trying to make you feel good?"

"Yes, what else?"

"Think again, Little Darling," said Ben.

So Lily thought. It was either him, or him being nice. And he was nice. But what if he was nice and it was him?

"It's ... it's ... ."

She lunged across the room and grabbed him around the neck and toppled him. "It's you! It's you?"

"Yes," he said.

"Mom, it's Ben. He's my dad. Did you know?"

"Well, yes, darling, I did."

"Angie, did you know?"

"Yes, Sister, I did. And I couldn't be happier."

Lily curled herself into Ben's lap, holding him tightly around the neck. She kissed him under the ear.

Then she said, "Oh, Mom."

Then she said again, "Oh, Mom! Do you love Ben? Because I do."

## SUNDAY DECEMBER 26, 1985

THE NEXT DAY WAS Sunday, which they also planned to spend together at Ben's house. He had asked Katherine if she and Lily would spend the night Christmas night, but she had said no.

She wondered vaguely why she had said no. All she knew is that she felt uneasy being away from home, from keeping an eye on the big house, not knowing if it had sold, not knowing if the Woman in the Window was noticing the cottage had no activity going on around it. That no one was home.

So Ben drove her and Lily home again and dropped them off. It was late. He arrived to pick them up again well before the hour when any sensible folks would have had breakfast. He had made popovers, and they were baking as he waited for them to get dressed. The sun was just peeping into his car, he had the news on, but his thoughts were all about Kate. Beloved Kate. And some wisps of concern that there was something wrong with her. Some health challenge.

After breakfast, Lily and Angie lay on Angie's bed and talked and talked. Katherine didn't know what she could be talking about for all those hours. Katherine snoozed on the couch. Ben was around when she needed him. He had agreed to take Lily and Katherine home after supper, and now, in the late afternoon, with long shadows being cast by all the houses on his street, and all the tall cedars, he said, "Dear Kate, I have a question. Simple, obvious. Will you marry me? Us?"

"Good heavens, why?" she asked.

It wasn't that it was unseemly. It was unseemly. But if they married, she would move in, and then he would find out about her cancer, and then he would be sorry he had married her, and then ... then he wouldn't want to be married anymore. And think how hard that would be on Lily.

So before he could answer, she said, 'No, I don't think so."

And he said, "Well, keep thinking and I'll keep asking. And meanwhile, do you want to spend the night?"

It was really the other way around. She would like to be married, for Lily's sake, but not spend the night. Because then he would find out about the ... you know, the problem ... and then he would be disgusted and throw her and Lily out.

It was like Aunt Agnes, who threw her out when she came into the house muddy. Or with some bit of nature to show her, a worm or a beetle.

So she must never allow any intimacies to develop between them, and so they'd better not get married. And she'd better not spend the night.

And meanwhile they needed to get home and keep an eye on things.

Still, Ben was as sweet a person as she could hope to spend time with. He fed her, then made her rest. She and he sat on the couch wrapped in each other's arms when Angie and Lily put on a little play, a very romantic little play, nothing like anything Lily had done before.

So she was not entirely happy that she couldn't say yes, and neither was Lily. Until Katherine reminded Lily of the need to see if someone had bought the big house.

So Ben reluctantly took them home in the late afternoon. Angie would be there all week and invited them to come over whenever they could. And Ben spent a lot of time at the door with Mom kissing her until she told him to come in because of the Woman in the Window, even though she didn't appear to be there.

As the sun set, Lily showed Angie her garden, her chickens, the shed and its four combination locks all lined up. Then Lily took Angie up the side street because she hadn't looked to see if the for-sale sign was still up, and it wasn't. It was gone.

"Why does that matter?" asked Angie.

"Because it means someone has bought the house, or is thinking of buying it, and that could be trouble for us. Because they won't understand why we're living in the cottage."

"Why are you?"

"So we can keep an eye on the house. And get it back someday. Like Aunt Agnes's father made her promise."

"When was that?"

"1918."

"You are keeping a promise from 1918?"

"Trying to. We haven't gotten it back yet. And we can't undo the promise because he died. We better go tell Mom the sign is down. She won't be happy."

"Let's knock on the door before we go in," said Angie.

"Why?" said Lily.

"Just let's," said Angie. And so they did. And they could hear Ben say, 'Just a minute."

And then he unlocked the door. Mom seemed to be taking a nap.

After Ben and Angie left and Lily had heated up soup, Lily remembered to tell Mom about the sign being gone.

"Oh well, let's just hope it's someone nice," Mom said. Then they talked about what a wonderful weekend they had had, and read, and went to sleep.

## MONDAY, DECEMBER 27, 1985

THE WINDOW WAS SHOWING just a bit of light when they were awakened by a commotion in the yard. People. Lots of people. Really close by. "Mom, wake up," said Lily. "There are people out there."

Lily was leaving her side, but Mom grabbed her arm and stopped her. "Don't go out there, Lily. It might not be safe."

Lily checked the lock on the door and made sure the window was completely covered, though she did peek out at a moment of quiet. No one was in sight.

"Mom, I think if I can get around to the back, I can make it unseen over to that fenced area near the depot. And once I'm there I can run to town and get some help."

"But who are they? Would the cops even stop them?"

"Maybe I can find out."

"No, I want you to stay inside here."

So Lily tried to read, all the while listening. At one point a chicken squawked, and it was only because Mom seemed to be having a bad day that she didn't disobey and go see what was happening.

She heard more squawking and then silence. The silence sounded ominous. She went to the door.

"No, Lily. I know what you heard. You're more valuable than a chicken."

"I hear a car. Maybe they're leaving."

There was more commotion outside. Yelling, the thud of heavy boots. Laughter, maybe. And then a pause and then a loud thumping on the door. "Kate! Kate! Open up. It's me, Ben."

"And me, Angie."

Lily unlocked and opened the door, and locked it behind them.

"Ben! Thank heavens. What's going on out there?" Katherine got out of bed and pulled the blanket around her

"I couldn't tell. But they're gone. For the moment. Maybe Lily can come out and tell me if she sees anything missing."

So both girls went out with Ben.

Lily ran to the chicken enclosure. The henhouse had been opened, and apparently the chickens had run out expecting their usual breakfast. But the little fence had been stomped on and Lily could see only two chickens. Then in the back of the henhouse she could see the crumbled body of Rita, her oldest and favorite hen, her best producer.

She started into the henhouse, but Ben stopped her by taking her by the arm. "No, Lily," he said.

"But what happened to her?"

"I'm guessing she was kicked. Here, let's look at the other things." Then he turned her in the other direction, away from the twisted corpse.

"Oh, Rita!" she cried out. Then she saw the damage before her.

Lily yelled, "Oh no. The garden."

It was trampled by heavy boots without regard for the paths or the planted swaths from one side to the other.

The garden was a wreck. Lily showed Angie the plantings, which had been destroyed, which might still survive. A few sprouts of baby oriental greens were all that appeared to be salvageable. Most had been ground by footwear into the heavy, wet winter soil.

The carrots and beets seemed intact. And some of the potato vines had been broken off but the potatoes themselves grew deep and would survive. Lily told Angie about each planting, which ones they would keep to eat, which ones she would sell.

"Lily, this is so impressive! Look at all the work you did!" said Ben.

"Well, some of it is still OK. Want some carrots for your supper?"

"If you'll come help me fix them."

"I'll ask Mom. Angie, want to help pull them and clean them?"

"I'll ask her about supper," said Ben. "But let's go now. The sun is shining. We can go out fishing. You'll need a warm jacket."

Angie said, "Fishing is fun. Mostly we just talk, but sometimes we catch something."

"Wow, I'd love to go. Ben, tell Mom she has to go fishing."

"OK, but I'm not sure it works that way."

Meanwhile he was hunkered down looking at the baby greens, gently righting them, putting the crushed ones aside in a pile for the chickens, Lily thought. He combed through them, thinning as he went. "There," he said. "That's all the time I have now. I think these will survive."

Lily looked at the square foot he had been working on. "It looks so much better, Ben," she said with delight.

"Dad?" he said.

"Dad," she said. But she turned awkwardly away from him.

Then Ben said, "Tell me, why does your garden stop right here?" He hadn't been trying to force her to acknowledge that.

"That's the edge of what we own."

"How do you know?"

"It's always been like that. We've always stopped there. Before I started planting veggies, my grandmother, Isabelle, had rosebushes there. She said it was to keep people out of our yard. When I ran out of room for what I wanted to grow, I dug out the rose bushes so I had more room for veggies. They were in bad shape anyway."

Katherine, now dressed and standing in the open door of the cottage, called out, "What were they doing here? Those men? Why were they here? How many were there?"

"Four, I think," said Ben. "They made a mess of everything."

"I hope they don't come back," said Katherine. "I wonder what they want."

"It could be as innocent as checking out the property—because it's for sale. Lily did say the sign was down, so they could be buyers, not just shoppers."

"But this part of the property is ours."

"Maybe they don't know that. Have you been to the county offices to see what it says about your ownership? I was hoping to take you and Lily fishing but maybe we need to go to the county offices first and check out your claim that this is yours."

"But first I have to bury Rita," she said. She had gone into the henhouse and brought Rita out, cradling her in her arms.

"OK, sweetie," said Ben. "I'll help."

"As for this being our property, it is," said Katherine. "It was part of John Steele's original property. When we had to sell the house, we got to keep the back part of the property here. We wanted the garden, but we also wanted to live where we could keep an eye on the big house. So maybe we could buy it back someday, Aunt Agnes said."

"So she took over the whole enterprise? Everything around here has the name Steele on it."

"No, not that I know of. But Aunt Agnes inherited the house, and then when they couldn't keep it up—that was a long time later, in 1950—they made an arrangement with the new owners so that we could stay here in the cottage and use the garden."

"So they legally subdivided the property?"

"I don't know. I was seven. All I know is that Agnes insisted my mom Isabelle and I keep an eye on the house so if someday the new owners didn't want it we would know and could get it back."

"That's a lot to ask."

"It's what she promised her father."

"And so you're keeping her promise now, all those years later? That's ... almost seventy years?"

"I guess so. Aunt Agnes was old, maybe ninety, when she died. I was about twenty-four or twenty-five. I remember my mother calling me home from work when Agnes was dying, and the last thing she said to us was, "Remember the Steele legacy. That house is yours. Keep an eye on it."

Ben was shaking his head. "And so you've lived in that tiny old cottage ever since?"

"Yes, I guess so. I never really had a choice. There was no one left to tell them I wouldn't. Not that I ever really thought about it. And Lily and I do fine here. It's our home."

"So that's why ... ." He didn't want to continue in the presence of his daughters, who were hanging around looking impatient about getting a move on. He was watching Katherine to see if she could figure out what he was going to say. But he saw no indication that she had.

So he helped Lily bury the chicken beside the henhouse. And when they were done, he said, "Girls, go get in the car. We'll be right there," said Ben.

"I'll stay here and keep an eye on things," said Katherine.

"Let's you and I go to the county offices if you don't want to go fishing. The girls can stay here and keep an eye on things."

"Dad!" said Angie. "Really?"

"Sure, we'll be back soon. And then we can go."

"I can't go," said Katherine. "We can't all leave at the same time."

Ben was exasperated. "OK, one thing at a time. Kate, you and I are going to town. Girls, we'll be back ASAP. As soon as we have those papers, you can show them to any buyers and they'll leave you alone. Of course, that may kill the deal for them."

"And then we'll go fishing," said Angie.

"Are you sure there weren't any papers from the sale, Kate?" said Ben.

"I don't know. It was all such a mess. I was seven and I didn't understand anything except that Aunt Agnes and my mother were upset. I think the sale took them by surprise. As if they couldn't believe it. They didn't pack up their things, and then when the time came, they just walked away. And of course I was upset too."

"Lily said your aunt did take some things from the house with them, though. And put them in the shed and called it treasure."

"Yes, I guess so. I don't remember her doing that, but she locked it up tight so I'm assuming the story is correct. The Treasury is what we always called it, but I never knew what was actually in there."

"As for papers, there were papers before we moved, lots of papers for them to sign. I remember that because they were upset, both of them. They didn't want to sign anything. Agnes thought it was all a mistake of some sort. Maybe she thought that someone was stealing her house."

"But certainly she put it on the market."

"No, I think the bank took it. Something like that. She was in her seventies and had lived in the house all her life. She and her brother William were born there, he and their dad died there. She never admitted it was someone else's house. And she made my mother Isabelle promise never to give up on it. So I know there were papers, but that's all I can say."

"OK. Probably long gone," said Ben, and Katherine nodded.

"Well, I think you and Lily had better spend the night at my house. The fact that there were four intruders together worries me a little. I can just see Lily attacking them, pounding on them to get them to leave. We'll get copies of those papers from the county and make sure their real estate agent understands your rights and explains them to potential buyers from the beginning."

"OK, I'll pack a few things."

"Just know that whoever the owner is, if they thought they owned the whole parcel all these years, they're not going to be happy. All the more reason to stay with me tonight until we see what the papers say and get it all straightened out."

Kate nodded. She already had her jacket. He kissed her. "Ben! The Woman in the Window!"

"I don't care about her. Better she should see you're not alone. Will you marry me?"

"I'll go get my overnight things," she said, then realized he might think that was her response to his proposal. He laughed.

"Me, too," said Lily, and Ben and Kate laughed.

While he was waiting, Ben went with Angie over to look at the shed, the Treasury. Angie pointed out where Lily had added tar paper to the roof.

"Look, Dad. I think someone was trying to get in," she said.

"Or maybe tear the whole shed apart," he said. "To see what's inside. That's my guess. If they think it's on the property they want to buy, they might want to see what sort of bounty comes with the house."

"Bounty?"

"Something of value that would automatically be bought with the property."

"Like treasure? Did you know they call it 'the Treasury'?"

"Yes, but why?" he asked.

Lily came up with her jacket and a bag for overnight.

Lily said, "I don't really know. I think it might be the books Agnes left in the house when she didn't move her things out. When she thought it would be hers again."

"Why books?"

"Because Mom remembers the built-in shelves in the house being filled with old books that John Steele brought from the east with him when he settled here. And when she went into the big house last week, there were no books there. Her old kitchen table and chairs were, but not a single book."

"Why don't we open the shed and find out?" he asked.

"Because Aunt Agnes said not to open it unless we had an emergency," explained Lily. "So we always thought it was something valuable we could sell if we needed the money."

"So maybe this is an emergency? Because someone wants to break into it, it seems," said Ben.

"Mom doesn't think we should open it now."

"OK, she knows best," he said. "I think it's more important for us to go to the county offices and see if we can find a copy of the paper that says that you could always use the cottage and the rest of this back property. That would put an end to people trampling your garden and trying to destroy or break into your shed."

Katherine said, "Do you need me?"

"Probably," he said. "Maybe the girls should go to the house instead of being here, in case the roughnecks come back," said Ben.

"What if they come back and break into the shed? Or the cottage?"

"That's true, that would be bad, but it would be worse if they found the two of them in their way."

Then Kate said, "I ... I wish you'd take Lily with you. I can go to your house with Angie, if she's OK with that. I agree about not being here. Until you see if that record is there."

Lily was astounded. Mom always opted to stay where she could keep an eye on the house. Ben must have persuaded her somehow.

Or maybe she was tired. Not that she was saying so, not in so many words.

"Wait, Mom. One other thing. Where are the combinations for the locks? We should take those with us so if someone does break into the house and finds them, they won't be able to get into the Treasury."

"Hmm. Maybe I should just hide them."

"They'll be safe in your purse, Kate," said Ben.

"Unless someone knows they're there."

Lily wondered if Mom meant her, but she didn't say anything.

"No one will," said Ben.

While they were waiting for Katherine, Lily noticed the woman was in the window again. "It won't take us long, Ben, right?"

"Depends. Why?"

"I don't trust the Woman in the Window."

"Who's that? Is she there now?" He thought he saw someone move away just as he looked.

"She's the owner, the one who wants to sell it. She's always watching our house. Or maybe watching me. One time she thought I was breaking into the shed and came out. I think she thought I was stealing her treasure. And another time I think she called the cops on me."

"Lily, dear girl, she won't know it, but we're not coming back until tomorrow. We're going to the county offices, then we'll drop the papers off with the real estate agent and that should put an end to worries about that woman. And then we're going fishing, aren't we?"

"Great!" said Lily.

Ben and Lily dropped Mom and Angie at Ben's house, then went to the county recorder's office. It was an interesting place. After Ben filled out a form, the man behind the counter brought them an enormous book, dusty. It had a label glued to it that said '1944-1958.' They went to a desk to look at it. Ben said he thought they should start with 1950 and look for anything with Agnes's name on it. It took only a minute to find the entry listing her sale of the house, but the cottage wasn't mentioned. Ben said this was only an index and went back to the counter to get the book that had the details of the sale in it. But even though they both read it twice, they found nothing about the use of the cottage. Then they went through the index page by page looking for other sales of 1 Main Street. When they found the sale to the current owners, it didn't mention the cottage. It took them two hours to be sure that no paper about a division of the property or use of the cottage was on file.

"So, I think that means that unless the buyer respects you and believes your story, you might not be able to stay. At least I don't know how you could prove you belong," said Ben.

"What?" Lily understood the words, but what Ben had said made no sense to her.

"Yes, except maybe that you can prove you have been there for a long time. That might be something a lawyer could argue."

"Lawyer? Aren't they expensive?" asked Lily.

"Usually, yes."

"But, Ben, we'd have to get out, right?" asked Lily.

"Right. But only when they actually purchase it."

"Can we find out when that would be?"

"Not unless they want to tell you. Or if they inform you that you have to leave. But maybe they haven't made an offer yet."

"Would they have been there this morning if they hadn't bought it?" Lily wanted to know.

"Yes, if they were thinking of making an offer, they might have wanted to see what was going on in the back of the property. I know I would have. They haven't been there before that you know of, have they?"

"No. Not that I know of. But we were away for Christmas."

It took only a minute or two to drive from the recorder's office to Ben's house. "Well, let's go fishing," he said.

When they stopped at his house, Lily ran in.

"Mom, no papers. They must be in the shed. Let's go get them!"

"Let's go fishing," said Angie.

"Maybe you can get them tomorrow," said Ben. "I'll take you home first thing in the morning."

"I've got lunch ready," said Angie. "Let's eat here and then head out."

But while they were eating, clouds rolled in and a light drizzle began to fall. Already the front walk was damp.

"Games?" suggested Angie.

Lily looked out the window. "It's cloudy everywhere," she said. "No breaks. Maybe this will turn into a real storm."

The air was chilly. Katherine was huddled on the couch. Ben got her a blanket and a pillow and suggested a nap. He rubbed her back while the girls got out the games. It was disappointing that they couldn't go fishing, but pleasantly cozy in the house, too. Ben sat on the couch at Katherine's feet and rubbed them. Lily and Angie looked at each other and tiptoed to

Angie's room. Ben fell asleep, the girls talked, the storm strengthened, Kate slept on, and in no time it was suppertime.

Kate had seen Ben had put her things in the third bedroom, his other daughter's room for when she visited. He'd put Lily's things in there, too. But Angie was suggesting Lily stay in her room on her spare bed. Ben thought that was a great idea.

After an evening of games and chatter, the girls drifted off to their room. "Good night, Angie," said Ben. She came back and kissed him.

"Good night, Daddy," she said.

"Good night, Lily," said Ben.

"Good night, Ben," she said.

Ben looked surprised. He took her by the hand into the kitchen, where there was no one else to hear them.

"Are you going to start calling me Dad any time soon?" he asked her. He was almost whispering, standing close to her, still holding her hand.

"I don't know. Are you really my dad? Or are you and Mom just trying to make me feel good because I already like you?"

"What? I never would have thought of that!"

"Or maybe Angie's in on it, too."

"You have an active imagination."

"I've wanted to find out who my dad was for a really long time. I can't believe that you just happened to show up when I was asking Mom every day who it was. Sort of like, well, Lily, here's one for you."

"My dear girl, that is so not the truth. But ask Angie. Ask her how she found out that she had another sister."

"OK." She paused. Was she ready? Yes! "Good night, Dad. Daddy." Then she gave him a tiny kiss, then she gave him a loud, cheerful kiss and threw in a hug for good measure.

"Oh, Lily, I do so love you," said Ben.

They returned to the living room, and Lily followed Angie to their room.

Then Ben took Katherine by the hand. "Don't worry about those papers, Kate. We'll find them. They're probably in the shed."

Kate nodded. She expected Ben to turn on the light for her and then disappear. But he didn't. He fussed for a while with the curtains, then turned down the bed. Then he moved the vase that contained a single rose an inch or so on the lace cloth on the bureau. Then he turned on and off the light on the desk.

"Ben, what?"

"I'm having trouble saying good night. Want to sleep in my room?"

"No thanks," Kate said. "I'm here to keep me safe from home invaders, that's all, right?"

"Well, that and also to tell me you'll marry me. And things."

"One thing at a time."

"OK, let's forget the home invaders. Will you marry me?"

"Ben Brown! After all this time? Your baby is half-grown. I'm as honest a woman as I'm ever going to be."

"What? You think that's why I'm asking you? Because you're ... well, pregnant? Well, you're not. I'm asking you because I want to be married to you. I want you to live right here in my empty little house. You and Lily."

"Well, then, the answer is simple. I can't. I have to keep an eye on John Steele's big house. Good night, Ben."

Ben stepped closer to Kate but she turned before he could kiss her. He was feeling exasperated. She was more married to that house than she would ever be to him, and he might as well get used to it.

"Good night, Kate," he said.

"Good night, Ben."

## TUESDAY, DECEMBER 28, 1985

LILY AWOKE IN THE night wondering where she was. She could hear the storm, heavy winds and rain both pounding Angie's house. In sudden terror, she realized the books in the shed were in danger.

John Steele's books, in the shed, might get wet because of the storm, but she wasn't worried about that because she knew some sort of plastic had been carefully put in place to line the shed, the Treasury. The real danger was not the storm, no. It was a buyer determined to see what was in the shed. A buyer picturing something of true value, and finding instead a thousand or so old-fashioned books. A buyer who, finding the books, would be disappointed and would toss them out into the storm to get them out of the way in case there was real treasure waiting in the shed behind them.

She needed to get the books out of the shed and hidden somewhere safe, namely through the book drop at the library.

She had asked Miss Horan if she could donate a large number of old books, and Miss Horan had said she'd ask, but so far Lily hadn't seen her at the library to get the answer.

And all Lily could think to do to save those old books was to donate them to the library. Now. Before the new buyers broke into the shed and threw them, unexpected, unwanted, into the mud. Not the treasure they'd be looking for.

And maybe that big family history book would be there, and in it, Mom's father's name.

She fell back to sleep, and a moment later Ben was waking his two daughters. It seemed the sun hadn't risen. Why so early?

"Breakfast is ready, girls. Your mom is already up, Lily. Angie, you remember your busy schedule for today. Up and at 'em."

The girls groaned, the victims of too much chitchat well past midnight.

"Thanks, Dad," said Angie. "Can you check back in five?"

"Nope, last call, Kitten," said Ben.

So the girls dragged themselves out of bed and were soon eating scrambled eggs and toast. Ben had Lily and Katherine in his car and on their way home soon thereafter. The car clock said 7:30.

Lily was thinking again about the books, glad she would be home by sunrise, the earliest she figured anyone would look at the house with a purchase in mind. The soonest she could rescue the books, too. She hoped that as soon as the locks were opened, the big book would be at hand and she would learn her grandfather's name and then be able to find him when she went to the library with her first load of donated books.

And then they might find where he was because he might still be alive!

Lily had never thought before that she might have a living grandfather. Katherine had said she never thought she might have a living father, either.

But first Lily needed to find out whether the donation committee had agreed to take the collection. Too bad Ben was taking them home so early. They went right past the library on their way home, and she could have stopped except the library didn't open for more than an hour.

They hadn't been home for long when she headed out again on the pretext of returning a few books. Mom wouldn't be ready, a fact she was counting on, but the library would be open.

The town was just waking up as she ran the familiar route from home to town, her hands in her pockets, the books she was returning in her backpack. It was cold.

She was almost at the library. The sky was leaden. It looked like snow, not that they got much snow so near to the sea. Snow was exciting. She had almost never seen it. But she hoped it wouldn't interfere with pulling the wagon.

Once inside, she took a minute to catch her breath. Miss Horan was at the front desk, waiting on a short line.

Between patrons, Miss Horan looked up and saw her hanging back from the main line. "Lily, if you have books to donate, we can take two or three. The committee will decide after the New Year if we can take more."

Lily sagged. "Thanks, Miss Horan," she said. Two or three? She'd guessed she would have ten boxes, maybe even twenty. Lots. It would take her all night to get them to the library with her wagon. Unless Angie wanted to help her drive them to the library. Did Angie drive? Did she have a car? Too bad she hadn't thought to get her help earlier when they were sitting side by side at breakfast. Less than two hours ago!

Lily thought of walking the few blocks to Angie's house—Ben's house—to ask her. She could arrange to meet Angie after dark. After dark so the Woman in the Window wouldn't see they had the shed open. Dark came so early! But it would still be several hours until they could begin. And then together they could ... what?

Move the books. To the library. Or somewhere else. Before something happened to them.

She would ask Angie now while she was so close to Angie's house, and set a time to meet. So she hiked up the hill to Ben's and Angie's house and rang the bell.

Ben came to the door.

"Lily! Is your mom OK?"

"Ben! Hi. Yes, she's fine. Is Angie here?"

"No, sorry, didn't she tell you? She went to Seattle for the day. Until tomorrow. To see a friend. Can I help you?"

Lily wondered whether to tell him what she had in mind. She would be going behind Mom's back by opening the shed. Then she would be carrying off their treasure—the books—to donate them to the library. Which didn't want them.

But it had to be tonight, because those people kept coming and sooner or later one would break into the shed.

"Ben ... ."

"Dad?"

"Are you ... sure?"

"Absolutely."

"OK, Dad, this is complicated."

"Come on in and tell me, Lily, my complicated sweetheart."

"OK, but you can't tell Mom."

"That's not a great beginning."

"I know," said Lily. "It's important, though."

"OK, tell me. I don't have to say yes."

"I want to take the books from the Treasury to the library and donate them."

"I thought they were your treasure. And I thought you didn't know if the books were in the shed. And your mom told me she thought they might be in the attic of the big house. Do you know about that?"

"She told me she didn't get into the attic when she went into the big house, so maybe the books were there. But think about it. You have a really old lady, Aunt Agnes, and a sort-of old lady, my grandmother. Are they really going to carry several hundred or a thousand books up a ladder into the attic?"

"No, I don't think so. And are you really going to carry several hundred books or maybe a thousand from your house to the library?"

Lily didn't say anything. She was embarrassed to ask him the favor she had in mind.

"Oh, I see," he said. "You were going to ask for help, and that included Angie's or my help driving the books to the library."

Lily nodded just a little. "I was going to ask Angie."

"But what were you going to do with them when you got them there?"

"Put them in the book slot."

"That's ... that's not easy."

"No."

"When?"

"Tonight."

"Tonight? Why tonight?"

"Because those people who want to buy the house are going to break into the shed to find out what they're buying, and when they find out it's just books, they'll throw them out into the mud and they'll be ruined. And these are precious old books."

"How do you know that?"

"Because my great-great-grandfather John Steele brought them all the way from the east coast, and I don't think he would have bothered if they weren't special. And Aunt Agnes always called them his treasure. I've got to get them out of there right away before they're destroyed."

"What if we did it on the weekend?"

"I'm afraid with all those people fighting over the house, waiting till the weekend will be too long."

"Oh, Lily. Of course I would help you. Though I think your mom might never forgive me. And if we moved them here, we could always move them back if we had to. But I'm not going to be here tonight. I'm ..." he said, but then hesitated.

Hesitated for a long time, obviously picking his words.

"I ... have a date," he said.

"What? I thought you wanted to get married to Mom," said Lily. She found she was crying. Why was she crying?

"I thought it was a good idea, but she said no."

"Well, I want you to get married to Mom. Can't we all talk about it?"

"Sure. But tonight I have a date. I made it a long time ago. Before ... we started getting back together. And when your mom said no to getting married, I didn't cancel it. I'm fifty. If I'm ever going to find a companion, it had better be soon."

Lily didn't understand, and she couldn't keep from crying, and she didn't know if she was crying for herself, for Mom, or for the books.

"Who is it?" Maybe if it was Clark, she wouldn't mind so much.

"No one you know."

He reached for her hand, pulled her toward him. But she resisted.

"How long is your date for?"

"The evening. Dinner, dancing, you know ... ."

"I don't know anything about dating. But OK, I'll take care of the book problem myself."

"Lily, if you can just wait till tomorrow, I can help you."

"I don't think so. Plus, there's a book in there that will tell Mom her dad's name. And maybe he's still alive. And maybe we can go live with him."

Ben was holding Lily's hand still, but she pulled away and put her hands on her hips. "Goodbye, Ben," she said, with a big emphasis on the 'Ben.'

And now Lily knew she would have to move the books herself. And it would have to be to the library, not to Ben's house, because even if he was willing, his house was up a steep hill. It would be hard enough making the many trips on the somewhat flat path to the library. Flat and half the distance.

Lily was so disappointed in Ben that she almost started crying again. It wasn't the books, it was the date. Well, both. She could barely breathe. She had found her dad and lost him again in a matter of days. Why had he even told her if he wasn't going to love her mom?

At the door, before she stepped out to find it was snowing and the walkway was already snow-covered, she said, "You shouldn't have told me. I wasn't sad that I didn't have a dad. But now I'm sad that I've lost the one I found." And then she turned and ran down the hill, sliding in the snow, falling onto the grass verge.

Ben yelled after her, "Are you OK?"

He knew she wasn't OK. Just how not-OK she was he had no idea. Should he cancel his date? She would never forgive him. That is, Cindy wouldn't, his date wouldn't. Lily would probably get over hearing about his dating. Maybe. He could tell her this would be his only date. If this was the only date.

And if this was the only date, why bother?

But he had gone to long lengths to have Angie away for this night, this one night. Cindy was a perpetually single woman with an outrageous sense of humor and an easy-going manner that gave Ben hope that when he invited her back to the house after their evening out, she would say yes.

Otherwise he could help Lily.

He wasn't used to having a kid to accommodate. His other girls had been gone for three years, except for Angie's visits during college breaks. And she'd as much as said she felt he needed taking care of or she wouldn't have come.

The interesting development, now that his relationship with Kate was out in the open, was how much Angie liked Kate. And of course she enjoyed Lily as the little sister she suddenly was.

Lily was adorable, so competent and independent, and cute in the way she came up with her own ideas for adult problems.

Kate? Kate was as always. Serious, maybe even more serious now than before. She had even protected him from public scrutiny. For years. Really, on her own, with only a few hints from him. So she had hidden herself away, and that had made it all easy for him. She had her ideas, and she stuck to them doggedly.

So he had had it easy. Until Caroline had found out. About Kate and, well, one or two others. But Lily was the only baby that had resulted.

Adorable Lily. Someone he could be proud of.

Meanwhile he could see Lily had picked herself up, looked back at him, and half-waved. Then she turned and ran down the hill. It was late morning. The sun, hidden behind snow clouds, had a few hours before it would appear briefly on the horizon, peering out from below the heavy cloud cover, then dip into the waves of the sound and leave their town chilly, also windy and snowy. As Ben turned and closed his front door and locked it, he thought an additional moment about the mission Lily was about to undertake: Save the books. By sequestering them in the library. Purloined from her ancestors and then hidden in plain sight.

Clever.

Or maybe it was because she knew Horan and was comfortable with her, with Horan and Clark both.

Maybe he should let Horan know what was about to happen. Or Clark. Clark would tell Horan, and then he wouldn't be in trouble with Lily. Or Katherine.

But why not let the child have her moment of heroism? He had a date to get ready for. He'd clean up the house, then later, get a shower. Get dressed in his new totally up-to-date shirt picked out with Angie's help just yesterday afternoon. Cologne. Wine and so on. And so on and so on.

All as he had planned it.

Yes, he had made the right decision. Cindy was ... special.

As Lily ran down the hill, it took her only seconds to realize that she had been right: That was not her dad.

Angie did seem like her sister, though. She loved spending time with Angie. They had everything in common. The more they talked, the more they found common ground to explore.

So how could that be? Angie her sister, Ben not her dad?

She arrived at block with the library and little playground, and turned east toward home. A lot of people were out hurrying places, getting their errands done before the storm. It was the time of a stormy day when people did their errands before going home. She hurried along against the flow of shoppers, thinking about Angie and how close they were becoming.

And then she knew. Angie wasn't Ben's daughter either. Neither of them was.

That was the only explanation she could come up with.

She was home in ten minutes, so later she could maybe count on seven minutes from the shed to the library.

She was chilled and hungry. And she was aware that she needed to get the combinations from Mom's purse, somehow, with Mom right there.

She was ready to go, maybe after a snack. But it was still too light out. And the streets would have far fewer pedestrians and she'd be able to move faster if she waited two or so hours.

And unlock the locks. Only once if she didn't lock them again between loads.

Because if the whole shed was full of books, only a tiny fraction would fit in the wagon and it would save time not to have to open the locks over and over.

The snow was thickening. She could see a significant opacity to the snow falling in front of streetlights, and it was accumulating. If it kept up, she would have to guard against it accumulating on top of the books and be extra careful on the slippery streets and sidewalks.

Not the best of conditions for stealing a shed full of antique books, one child's wagonload at a time.

She felt some anger rise up when she realized that if Ben were to help her, it would go so much faster, safer, more smoothly. But he had chosen not to.

Angie would have.

On the other hand, Mom wouldn't have, because she was still listening to Aunt Agnes, and Aunt Agnes was still listening to Great-Great-Grandfather John Steele, founder of this very town. The one he'd named Steeletown, as if to say, 'Don't ever forget that I'm the boss here.'

But John Steele had not foreseen everything. What would he think of the current situation, when the big house was about to be sold, and their part of the property was not considered to be separate at all, but part of the big house? But then he hadn't known about that. Aunt Agnes had had to take care of such things thirty years or more after his death.

No telling what he would have done. The whole point of John Steele and his fame was that he didn't think like other people.

So it was up to Lily as the only living descendant—well, besides Mom—to preserve the real treasure, the books he had brought from the east coast. And it had to be tonight because by tomorrow the shed could be smashed and torn down and its contents destroyed or damaged.

But first, the combinations for the four locks. They were in Mom's purse.

"You're cold," said Mom. "Here, stand by the woodstove. I'll make some soup. The snow must be accumulating."

Lily's feet were cold in her sneakers. She took them off and Mom wrapped them in a towel and sat her on her chair in front of the wood stove.

"Where'd you go this time?" Mom asked in a friendly way.

"Library," said Lily.

"No books?"

"Not today."

"Why did you go, then?"

"Just ... for fun. I was going to go do something with Angie, but I found out she wasn't home."

"Oh?" said Mom. "I wonder where they went."

"Ben was home, just not Angie. She went to Seattle. She's going to be gone till tomorrow."

"Oh. So Ben is all alone. Maybe I should take him some dinner."

"I ... I think he's going somewhere." Lily realized she could have told Mom about Ben's date, but Mom wouldn't be happy, Lily guessed. So she decided not to mention it.

They could hear that the wind had picked up. Mom looked out the window and even from where she was sitting Lily could see that snow had accumulated on the panes. Maybe it would let up soon.

Well, it wouldn't matter. She still needed to move the books tonight or by tomorrow they'd be ruined.

She ate the soup. It was barely noon, and a great deal of snow had fallen. Maybe it would discourage house buyers from coming the next morning.

But tonight it would probably slow her down, too. Which she couldn't afford if she had as many as five or six wagonloads. Or it could even be more than that.

"Well, we're not going anywhere today, are we? Let's play a game. How about Scrabble?"

So they played Scrabble, and then read for a while, and then Mom was tired so she crawled under the covers and fell asleep. Lily thought that was a good idea for her, too. She had stayed up late talking to Angie and would be up maybe all night tonight. But first she needed to find the combinations for the locks. They were in Mom's purse.

And where was that?

Its usual place was next to the breadbox, but it wasn't there. Or rarely, on top of the newest stack of library books, if she had just gotten home. But it wasn't there, either.

She started to ask her where her purse was, but Mom was asleep. From where she lay under the cozy covers, Lily looked all around but couldn't see it anywhere. And then in no time she was also asleep.

She didn't stir until she heard Mom get up.

No harm in asking her now. "Mom, where's your purse?"

"What do you need?"

"Nothing. I just don't see it anywhere. The last I saw it was in Ben's car. This morning when he drove us back."

"Oh yeah. Interesting. I think it might still be there! Oh well, he'll have to bring it back tomorrow."

"It's a vacation week for him. What if he goes away? I think I should go get it."

"It's snowing!"

"So what? Rain is worse and we go out in rain all the time. I'll just run over there and if he's there, I'll grab it and run home. I should be back in less than an hour."

"It's a mile and a half."

"So less than an hour. And then we can go get some groceries tomorrow."

"We can take cash from the breadbox."

"Right, true. Well, if you don't mind it not being here for a few days, we can get it on New Year's."

Lily was thinking of the New Year's Eve decorating of the boats. It seemed far away to her, and she hoped it would seem far away to Mom, too. Because the whole plan was about fall apart because the combinations were in the purse.

"OK, I guess you can go."

"OK, I'll be right back."

"Be safe."

She went out through the door and took off at a run, though her boots, always encumbering, were now slowing her down. She took them off and set them back beside the shed, one upside down inside the other so they wouldn't fill with snow. Then as an afterthought she turned the wagon upside down so it wouldn't fill with snow and put the boots underneath.

The snow had settled down to a steady pace, now and then accompanied by squalls of swirling wind. She was facing straight into it as she ran across town to the library, then turned south to Ben's. Climbing his hill was tricky because the sidewalk was slippery, so she walked on the grass of the lawns that lined the sidewalk. She thought she could see hints of her footprints from earlier.

She got to his street, turned left, and left at his house. There were cheery lights on in the front room, but his car, and Angie's if she were back, would be at the garage off the alley behind. 'Let her be here,' said Lily as she crossed her fingers.

She knocked loudly at the door. No answer.

It was already dark. Ben would probably be on his date, out to dinner. His car wouldn't even be here in that case.

She knocked again. Nothing.

She went around back. No cars.

There was just about no point in going home because the plan was dead without the combinations. She would just sit on the front step and wait. Mom would wonder where she was but maybe figure she had gone in. But then she had told Mom she thought Ben was going somewhere. Oh well. Mom would not be worrying yet.

So she sat on the step and watched the snow drift down and cover her sneakers. Even if he and his date came in the back, she would hear them inside or maybe see the lights change.

So this was a good place to wait. For a while. Otherwise she would have to forget moving the books and go home, and that might prove a disaster for the books.

Ben did not come home for a long time. When he finally came, Lily was cold, drowsy. He pulled up out front. All the more convenient for the date, Lily thought. Lily, her feet numb, ran awkwardly up to the driver's door and knocked before he could open it. He rolled down the window, so she said, "Mom's purse," and held out her hand.

"Back seat," he said, looking first shocked, then annoyed.

She looked in. A pretty lady sat in the passenger seat. "Thanks," said Lily.

She heard the woman say, "Who's that?" but she didn't hear the response.

Who was she? A matter of opinion.

Had Ben said, 'That's my daughter'?

Lily ran home. She had wasted an hour and a half getting a hold of the combinations. Now what? Take them out of the purse before she got to the cottage? Or leave them where Mom had put them, in case she looked?

Lily's feet were frozen, her sneakers full of snow. She took them off, emptied them out the front door, wrapped her feet in a towel. Mom set the purse next to the breadbox and got Lily's nightgown for her.

"Here, get into this and get warm," said Mom. "And eat your supper."

The cottage was cozy. Lily was sleepy. Maybe she could take a nap for an hour, until Mom was asleep, and then find the combinations and head out.

Mom made her cocoa. After a few sips Lily was overwhelmingly sleepy and lay down shivering. Seven-thirty. She set her mental alarm for ten-thirty.

As she drifted off she realized that by a few hours from now she would know for certain the books were in the shed.

Including Mom's family book with her dad's name in it. Maybe.

Or maybe it could wait till tomorrow night.

NO, it couldn't! Her eyes flew open. She would not let herself sleep through this important night. She looked at the clock, and found it was already 11:15 p.m.

She looked over at Mom. She was sound asleep.

What a relief! Lily walked through the plan mentally. Get up silently, silently open the purse, maybe take it into the bathroom so she could turn on the light, find the combinations. She had no idea what they were written on. A scrap of paper, a file card, an old deposit slip? All together or separ … .

## WEDNESDAY, DECEMBER 29, 1985

RAIN CRASHED ON THE roof. Wind whistled between the cottage and the shed. Lily wiggled herself deeper into the cozy bed. She shifted her feet toward Mom as she often did on winter nights.

No Mom.

Lily woke with a start. Gray light trickled into the room through the curtain. A blast of wind made the curtain move, a testament to the ancient and amateur framing of the window. Lily huddled under the blankets, not cold but not inspired to leave her warm nest, either.

Where was Mom?

She heard a bang, wood on wood, then the door opened.

Mom said, "The henhouse door blew open. It's OK now. Both hens are inside."

Mom was soaked.

How late was it?

Then Lily remembered her night errand. Undone.

Another bang. "I think that was the ladder falling over," said Mom.

"But it was on its side."

"This is the worst winter storm in years. I'm worried about the roof. I don't want you going out in it. A virtual river is streaming across the property from the big house through the garden to the walkway. It's making a deep gouge in the alley. I'm afraid it will undermine the foundation of the cottage if it swerves this way. It can't be built that deep."

"It's probably coming off their roof," said Lily. She pulled a blanket around her and went to the door. As soon as she unlatched it, the whole door whipped out of her hand and heavy rain blasted in. She hurried to close it.

"That flood of water is already up to the sill," said Lily. "It may come in. Unless the door stops it."

"It may come in anyway. I'm sure the cottage is basically just sitting on its foundation. Here, let's move everything we can off the floor."

"What time is it?"

"About 10:00 a.m."

"Mom! Did you see the wagon out there?"

"Not that I noticed. But you can't go out and look. We need to stay as dry as we can for as long as we can."

Lily looked at the ceiling: No leaks. The repair was holding, doing its job. Maybe it would hold on the shed, too.

Something smacked the side of the cottage. Then a second smack.

"Probably a branch or something," said Mom.

"I'm afraid it was tar paper," said Lily. "From the Treasury."

"No harm done, then."

"Not to the cottage. But what about to the books? If that roof blows off, everything will be ruined."

"I thought I told you I thought the books were probably in the attic," said Mom. Lily could tell she was irritated.

"They wouldn't have been able to get them up there. You said the only way up is a ladder."

"Well, there's nothing we can do," said Mom, clearly ready to drop the subject.

"Oh yes, there is. We can bring them in here. They're valuable, precious," said Lily. Why didn't Mom understand?

"You really believe that, don't you?"

"I do. They were an investment John Steele made. Wasn't everything he did an investment? The railroad to bring revenue to his town? His shipyard? Even the house?" Lily was thinking out loud but it made sense to her, and it was important.

"Well, I guess so. But how did you figure all that out?" asked Katherine.

"I'll tell you later. Right now we need to rescue the books. They were as important to John Steele as the house was. And maybe they're keeping their value better," said Lily.

"But how can we get them in here in this wind and rain without their being ruined? And how can we get them in here without the Woman in the Window coming out and claiming them?" asked Mom.

"It would be best if we had a car. We could load them into the car and drive away and she wouldn't know where they were, or have any proof they were ever here."

"Where would you take them?" asked Mom.

"Me? I would take them to Ben's house and put them in Angie's bedroom. She's going back to college in a week or so. I don't think she'd mind."

"Why wouldn't she?" asked Mom.

"Because we were talking about John Steele and how he did things and she's the one who said they would have been an investment just like everything else."

"But we don't have a car." Mom was picking things up, moving them here and there, wiping the counters.

"But Ben does. He has two cars. Or maybe one's Angie's."

"And he might as well live on the moon. There's no way to reach him in this storm," said Katherine.

"Well, I could," argued Lily.

"No."

"No, you're right. It's too stormy. But Clark and Horan live much closer."

"It's still too bad to go out in." Mom sounded firm, and Lily was afraid that the next thing she would say was 'no.'

"It's not quite as bad now."

"And it will be worse in a few minutes," said Mom, her voice rising.

"True. But I can do it. It's only ten minutes to their place."

"And what would you do once you got there?"

"Ask them for a ride to Ben's. Tell him to come pick you up. Give you his car. You can still drive, can't you?"

"I don't know. It's been about a year. I think I could. If it's automatic."

"So I'll wear my boots. My sneakers are still wet. OH NO, my boots are outside."

"No, I brought them in, but they are a bit wet inside."

"That doesn't matter. I know I'll get wet. But the whole business should take less than an hour. I'll survive. Mom. There's one thing you could do while I'm gone. You could unlock the locks. Sometime when it's raining really hard. So the Woman in the Window probably wouldn't be able to see you through the rain, and wouldn't come out in any case."

"Wouldn't that be taking a risk?" asked Mom.

"Yes. But it only takes a second to lock them again. Do all but one and then wait a bit and make sure the coast is clear. And then when we come with the car, we'll be ready to toss them in."

"She'll recognize Ben." Katherine sounded like she was still arguing against the plan, but she was also reaching for her coat.

"We'll have to take a chance. It's not like she has high school age kids."

The storm was raging. Small rivers would be springing up around town, and Lily realized she might have to detour. She had experience with walking around town during storms. This was, what, just five times as powerful?

"Mom, don't worry if I'm not back right away. I may have to detour."

Mom had made eggs but Lily hadn't stopped to eat them. She did now, then put on her rain slicker and a rain hat, then pulled the hood of the slicker over her head. She opened the door. It was surprisingly warm. Maybe this was a tropical storm, one that successfully pushed out the winter blizzard of last night. The snow had all melted. She put on her flip-flops. Cold meltwater ran off the roof, making the rain feel extra-warm. The flipflops were easier to run in than boots in this warm rain. "I'm ready. Bye," she said.

She leaped across the stream that now ran across the garden. She could see the torrents of rain running down the roof of the big house that fed the stream. She could see the Woman in the Window. Lily waved at her without thinking, and the woman turned away.

Lily saw two sheets of tar paper across the alley, swept there by the torrents or winds. She thought maybe she ought to stop to check out the shed roof but she could do nothing about it if it were damaged. She ran on.

No traffic was coming on the side road. No traffic was coming on the business-district road. No traffic was coming on the next or the next road.

No one was out.

She ran the remaining four blocks to Clark's and Horan's house. She banged on the door.

Clark answered, saw her, pulled her into a small foyer, peeled back her hood, ran to the kitchen for a towel, dried her red, soaked face, dried her hair where it was escaping the hat and hood, dried her hands, dried her feet.

"What are you doing, Lily? What's the matter? Why were you out in the storm?"

Lily was breathless. She sat down on the step that led from the foyer into the house.

"I need ... I need to go to Ben's house," she said.

"Is your mother all right?"

"Yes."

Horan appeared. Lily had been hoping Horan wouldn't be home because she had seemed annoyed about the books yesterday. But it couldn't be helped.

"Lily! Let's get all those wet clothes off you."

It was true. Lily's jeans were soaked all the way up to the hips.

"I can't wait, I can't wait," said Lily. "The shed roof is blowing off and the books will be ruined. And they are an investment for an emergency."

"What?" said Clark.

"I get it. I'll tell you later," said Horan. "But what does going to Ben's have to do with it? So let me guess, you came here because it's closer, and you'd like us to drive you to Ben's? Maybe I should call him first."

"I don't know if he's awake yet. He had a date last night. She might still be there."

"Hmm," said both Clark and Horan.

"Did he tell you that?" asked Clark.

"Yes, I asked him if he would drive the books to the library but he didn't want to make Mom mad and he had a date anyway."

"Why were you taking the books to the library?" asked Clark.

"I have to put them somewhere. They're about to get stolen. And rained on. Both. And I wasted a couple of hours trying to get Ben's help and then I fell asleep and didn't wake up till this morning and now it's raining and the roof I just put on the shed is ripping off in the wind."

By now Lily's jeans and socks were in the dryer and she was wrapped in a blanket, sitting on the couch.

"Lily, what if we drove you to get the books? Where were you going to put them?" asked Clark.

"Well, last night I was going to put them in the book slot at the library. Because some people are buying the big house and they think they own what's in the shed. But they don't, we do, but we can't find the paper that says so. If there is a paper. I've never seen it.

"But then the storm came up overnight, and if I take them in my wagon, they'll get soaked. And there are rivers running in all the streets and the wagon isn't big enough to make it through.

"And if I just put them in our house, in the cottage, the Woman in the Window will be able to break in and take them.

"So I thought that maybe I could put them in Angie's room. She wouldn't mind. She's nice. She's like a sister to me. Even if Ben isn't like much of a dad."

"I see," said both Clark and Horan, catching each other's eye as if to say, 'What?'

"Well, Lily, we could take you home. And get the books. Put them in the car and bring them back here and put them in the spare bedroom. How many are there?" asked Clark.

"Four by four by six," said Lily.

"Four by four by six what?" asked Clark.

"Feet."

"That's almost 100 cubic feet of books. Or 36 feet of shelf. Or maybe three to four car trunks full. At least," said Horan.

"Yes," said Lily. "Or I would need to make several trips with my wagon."

"Several trips," said the Horan and Clark as one.

"But why now?" asked Clark.

"Because lots of people are looking at the big house so they can buy it. It's a hot property, Ben said. And they want to know what's in the shed. They think they are getting the cottage where we live, and the garden, and the henhouse and the shed when they buy the big house.

"And the woman who lives in the big house thinks what's in the shed is hers. So she really wants to see what's in there, and when we unlock it, she will suddenly appear and want to take it all. I think she wants to take what's in there before any buyers see it.

"So I want to move it at night when she can't see what we're doing. She watches me all day long every day and if I go near the shed, she's right there."

"So why right now?" asked Clark again.

"Because I was going to do it last night with my wagon, because Ben had a date, and I fell asleep."

"Thank heavens you fell asleep," said Clark.

"Why?"

"You would have been caught with a wagon full of precious books when the storm rolled in," said Horan.

"True," said Lily. She was grateful someone realized the books were precious, and that it was Horan, who knew all about books.

The storm seemed to be abating somewhat, though another wave could come in at any time. If the skies did clear, it would leave the book-rescue visible to the Woman in the Window. Or buyers could show up to take advantage of the lull. So Lily said, "We should wait till after dark."

"OK, we'll take you home now, and that will give us a sense of how big the shed is, and you can show us where to pick you up again tonight."

"And do you think your mother wants to come along?" asked Horan.

"I don't know. She likes to keep an eye on the house. She leaves sometimes, though. I can ask her."

"I think what we'll do," said Clark, "is to come over at around 4:30 when it's dark, pick up you, your mom, and the first load and come back here and take a look at what you've got, find a place for them, and have supper. Then go back for the rest."

Lily was excited. She hoped Mom would be. When the locks were opened, she and Mom would know for sure that the books were in there.

Clark and Horan dropped Lily at the cottage. The storm could go either way. For the moment the rain had stopped, but the new little river between the cottage and shed was, if anything, heavier. Lily got out at the corner of the alley and the main street so the woman would not see a strange car and become suspicious. So Clark and Horan got only a quick glance at the shed, still a hundred feet down the alley from where they turned the car around.

Mom listened to Lily describe the plan she had cooked up with Clark and Horan, and it seemed to entail her going to dinner at their house and moving some books. But she didn't want to commit to go until Lily promised she could come back after the first load. The one advantage to going along was that she could see if anything in the load of old books looked familiar.

But Katherine wasn't feeling well. She didn't want Lily to know, Lily who was so excited, so full of gratitude to Clark and Horan, and for some reason rather angry with Ben, though he wasn't even part of the plan. Katherine had probably misunderstood how the plan was going to work.

And speaking of plans, today, while Lily was gone, feeling how large the lump was in her breast, and how she ached in various ways, and other afflictions she had begun to notice—but maybe it was the change in weather—she had taken up the paper called The Plan and bent over it with renewed intensity.

Part One had to do with Lily's skills, and as she reviewed what Lily needed to know, she thought that that part was in good shape. Lily was resourceful. Lily was flexible. Lily had helpers in the community, though apparently not Ben any longer.

And hadn't it always been that way with Ben? Hadn't he always waxed hot and cold, hadn't he always professed his love only to disappear for extended periods, such as for years at a time? And now, just when Katherine had let him tell Lily he was her dad, just when she had given him that privilege after avoiding, refusing to tell Lily the truth about her parentage, just when she had finally agreed, and he had been ready, he had squandered it. Somehow, though Katherine wasn't sure how.

The man couldn't be trusted. He was hot and cold, involved and avoidant, responsible beyond expectation and then shunning responsibility.

And now Lily had been caught by it. He'd apparently turned down a request for help for some sort for some no-good reason, with some lame excuse.

Yes, that sounded like Ben. The question was, would he rise to the challenge when something important was at stake, someone important. As if a child discovering her parent was anything but important. Building an exemplary reputation with Lily should be a top priority for him.

But better she find out now.

Katherine had raised her to be independent, and she was. But right now, at this critical moment, if Lily suddenly felt that she could depend on someone else, especially someone who couldn't in reality be counted on—like Ben maybe—it would leave her vulnerable. She needed to be entirely capable of standing on her own two feet, right here in sight of John Steele's house, never taking her eye off it because others would try to take it from her, and it was her birthright.

Lily already knew the rules. Stay here. Watch. And be ready when the time came to reoccupy it.

Back to The Plan. What else would Lily need to know? She already knew how to find the key helpers she might have for a bit of advice. That was enough. Anyone else and questions might be raised.

And what was the worst thing that could happen? Some snoopy official might find she was a ten-year-old living on her own and take her to some home. Like poor Susan. A foster home. And much as she didn't need that, and would hate it, it would take her away from the house, just now, at this critical moment when it appeared that someone might buy it. And if not the first mob, then one of the others.

To live in HER house, Katherine's house, promised to her in her cradle, so to speak. Promised to her mother, who had died too soon. Promised to her aunt, and her uncle before that, but he had died.

Aunt Agnes said he would have sold it for gambling debts, so perhaps Isabelle, his only child, would not have achieved her birthright. But that didn't stop her from keeping her vigil. And Katherine knew that Lily understood that and wouldn't be stopped from keeping her own vigil until it should become hers.

Katherine could feel a certain fury building up in her, not for the first time. She would never live in it again. She was dying. Well, she had shed hours and hours of tears about that, but they hadn't changed a thing.

She'd been tempted to tell Lily a few times, prepare her. But no. Not a good idea. Lily would tell someone. She would have told Ben by now. No, Lily's safety depended on no one knowing what became of her mom.

She hadn't been able to put the finishing touches on The Plan, but now she had an idea, thanks to those damn books that had taken a powerful hold on her daughter. Let her get into the shed. Let Lily find that family history in the huge volume Katherine remembered so well. Let Lily find who her grandfather was. Because then Katherine could tell Lily that Mom was going to take a trip to find him and bring him back.

And so Katherine would not be here when she died, and without a body, they couldn't declare Lily an orphan and take her away and put her in foster care and cut her out of her birthright, the house.

Yes, Lily would be fine at ten to take care of herself. She wouldn't need a mom. She knew how to do things. Far better to be alone than to be whisked away to live according to someone else's plan, in somebody else's house.

She herself had only weakened that once, with Ben, when he suggested he could get her a house for her and the baby. But she'd come to her senses and said no thanks, this was their home.

So Lily would be all right. New socks, that sort of thing, was all she'd need.

What Katherine didn't have worked out was the car. Haha. 'The get-away car,' she had written on The Plan. She would get in the car and drive, and drive and drive, and someplace along the way she would die, and no one would know who she was.

But she couldn't figure out how to get a car.

Maybe steal one! What difference would that make to her? She'd be dead before she could be arrested.

If she stole an older one, maybe it wouldn't have one of those alarms the newest cars had.

How do you steal a car? She'd need a key.

But wait, maybe someone with a horrible old wreck might be willing to sell it for cash. And take their license plate with them.

That's what she'd do. At the last minute. When she could barely stand the pain, like sometimes, but not all the time these days, when she could barely walk to the library anymore. When she could be sure that before she ran out of highway she would die driving straight east, to the east coast if necessary. Then no one would know who she was and Lily would tell everyone, because that's what she'd tell Lily, that Katherine was at her dad's someplace far away and was due back, and they'd leave the child alone while she waited.

She just didn't dare wait too long. If she died overnight in her bed, it would ruin everything.

And then she realized that she should be glad about the books, if they were in the shed. Because, what if her father's name really was listed there? What if she really could drive east and find him along the way and meet him before it was too late? Yay for Lily. Too bad she couldn't meet him, too, her grandfather!

And so despite her fatigue and pain, she agreed to go to dinner at Horan's.

Well, of course the plan as Lily had explained it couldn't be that simple, it seemed to Katherine.

And it turned out that she was right. Because they needed to open the shed first. But they had trouble with the locks, and it took so much time that they decided to go back to Horan's and have dinner.

And then as they ate, they revised the rest of the expedition: Horan and Lily would go back to the shed and get the first load and bring it back to Horan's and Clark's and spend some time together looking at what they'd found. And then they would take Katherine back home when they went for the second load.

Mom grew edgy and suspicious when Lily laid out these details. She was feeling trapped, in the wrong place, hanging out as she would be at someone else's house. Until Lily had said, "You could always walk home. At any time."

So right after supper, Clark stayed with Katherine while Lily and Horan set out on the book-rescue mission.

They were at the shed in a few minutes. They left the car out on the main road and walked in. The mud from the morning flood had washed across the grass-and-gravel alley, causing them to slip and ultimately to take a detour around the back of the shed. A streetlight from the main road one hundred feet away cast only the feeblest light.

Lily thought she was seeing a hole in the shed, near the top, and it caused her to hurry so she could find out what had happened. If anything. But it wasn't a hole. It was something living, maybe a bat, maybe a rat, furry, a bit warm and very wet. She pulled back, then laughed. It wasn't a hole and that was good.

And then the moment was upon them. Horan had a flashlight in the car, so they brought it. Lily held it in one hand, in the other the scraps of paper from Mom's purse with the combinations on them. She had to strain to see what was written. As she read out the numbers, Horan manipulated the locks. One down, two down, three down, four down.

Lily was being careful to keep the flashlight from being visible from the house, but it wasn't easy. She needed to move the tiny spot of illumination to the paper and then back to the lock. So she kept an eye out for the woman, for her sudden and unwelcome appearance at the shed. Or in the window.

She was not sure she would be able to see the woman on this dark a night. Or, of course, if the woman would be able to see her.

But so far so good, as far as she could tell.

They could feel a bubbling up of excitement. Horan had unthreaded the shafts of the locks from the loops they held together. She set them on a patch of grass, then heaved a sigh, and said to Lily, "Here we go. Books, here we come."

The door, the kind that was supposed to slide on its tracks, was reluctant, complaining with a loud screech that surely could be heard in the big house and probably over at the depot. Lily and Horan giggled together.

Time to shine the light into the shed.

It didn't go far. Something black and shiny reflected the flashlight from just inside the door. Like the shiny black material Lily had seen inside the hole in the roof back when she'd tar-papered it.

She pushed against it. It yielded, but just a bit. Should she pull it down? Push harder against it? She pictured it to be a sheet of plastic, protection against a leaking roof or wall.

She pulled on it. It resisted. She pulled more. It fell in one intact sheet.

And behind it were books. But not a shed full of books. About four stacks, about a dozen books in each stack. And lying on the wood floor, a ring of keys. And an ancient sewing machine, some tall wood objects Horan said were probably looms, two looms, the larger one wedged diagonally across the shed. And an old bicycle, the kind with one big and one small wheel.

And then as they continued to move the sheet aside—oil cloth according to Horan, not plastic—they could see a large wooden box with large tools sticking out of the top. And another box, larger, also constructed of wood, lid closed.

Lily moved toward it, but Horan said, "Better to be opened in daylight," and Lily agreed.

And then a canvas-wrapped bundle, about two feet on a side.

Too big for Mom's big book, but maybe the book and other things.

Lily was sure this bundle contained Mom's big book that might give her her father's name. And the other things in that same bundle could be equally important, thought Lily.

Lily stood guard while Horan got the car. They loaded in the books and bundle and locked the car.

Then they struggled to drag the boxes into the cottage. Then to carry in the looms, the sewing machine, the bicycle without getting them muddy. Lily imagined all these had originally been stored in the cottage, not the house, and had been moved out of the cottage only when Agnes, Isabelle, and Mom had needed to move in. These bulky items barely fit with the current arrangement of bed and table filling most of the small space. But Lily found it satisfying to put them back in the cottage, as if it were the first step in returning things to their proper order, the first step to their getting the house back. She knew she was making up her own fairy tale, but it still felt good.

She put the keys in her raincoat pocket for now. There was no clue what they might open, huge and hefty as they were.

As she was carrying the bundle, a tin box fell out. She picked it up and shook it. Just thuds. She put it back in the folds of the packet and carried the whole bundle to the car.

The shed was empty now except for the oilcloth. Horan locked it up again. Let someone think the treasure was still inside and slow themselves down trying to get at it!

They both got in the car. After churning briefly in the mud, the car lurched forward and in two minutes, they and the treasure were at Horan's house.

Mom was standing at the door in her coat. "That took quite a while," she said.

"We've got the treasure, Mom. No question it's John Steele's treasure. Wait till you see it."

"I need to get home."

"There's nothing to keep an eye on on a dark night like this, Mom."

"Your mother has been asking me if I know anyone with a car for sale," said Clark.

"Mom, a car? Why do we need a car?"

"Never mind. Just a crazy idea. I changed my mind. We don't need a car."

"Oh, OK."

Lily was eager to undo the bundle. They had left the books in the car, but why not open this one package? Like one gift on Christmas Eve?

"How can you be so certain it's John Steele's treasure, Lily?" asked Clark.

"Because I can see why he thought these things were valuable. Everything we saw was something you could use to make money if you needed to. Or wanted to. Like the sewing machine. With a sewing machine I could make things to sell at the depot in the winter when the garden is running out."

"So instead of stacks of gold, you have a way to make gold."

"Yes. Plus, maybe these were the first looms and sewing machine in this part of the world. If he hadn't brought them, maybe people would forget how to make them.

"Good thought," said Clark. "Of course, times have changed. It was still smart of him to bring them."

"Yes, in more than one way, I think, but let's open this package, OK, Mom? Your dad might be in there."

"Lily! A little privacy is in order," said Mom.

Where was her smile? No sign of it. She still had her coat on, though she had perched on the couch.

"Oh, come on, Katherine," said Horan. "We just want a little peek. Then I'll take you home."

And with that, Lily placed the bundle on Mom's lap. Mom gasped.

Lily knew why, but she wouldn't say it out loud and embarrass Mom. She was sure the bundle suddenly appearing on her lap reminded her of Aunt Agnes setting their family history on her knees so many years ago.

And, Lily had a new thought: In a way, Mom's had the weight of it there ever since.

The bundle was loosely wrapped in canvas, and then there was a layer of oilcloth inside. "It's too big for the big book," said Katherine.

Clark and Horan exchanged a glance as they stood looking on silently. Lily sat on the couch next to her mother. Katherine was taking her time.

The oilcloth, stiff, wrapped tight around the bundle, was awkward to unwrap. Lily was about to reach over and help, but she thought that Katherine needed to own the whole moment.

Finally, Katherine had peeled back all the layers. The big book was on the bottom. On top of it was a large thickness of various sizes of folded papers and some small books or notebooks. Katherine set them all aside and laid her hands on the big book.

"A big moment," she sighed. "I hope," she said, smiling, then tearing up. "It's been thirty-five years, maybe more."

Clark and Horan drew up some chairs from the dinner table. Silence descended again.

Katherine slowly opened the cover. She fingered the book plate on the inside of the cover. 'John Steele,' it read in a fancy hand.

Lily ran her finger over the signature. "Ah, it's him," she sighed. "I wonder when he wrote that?"

"Seventy years ago or more is my guess," said Katherine.

Then she closed the book again. "I almost don't dare look," she said.

Clark and Horan smiled and nodded. Lily was not being successful at sitting still, but she took her lead from them and smiled and nodded, too.

Katherine sighed again and opened the book. "I know it's right here in the front," she said.

"What is?" asked Horan.

"The family tree. John Steele and his descendants. Of course, he died, but then Aunt Agnes took over. I remember seeing the different handwriting. Here it is!"

Clark, Horan, and Lily leaned over. Katherine was fingering the names. John Steele, Agnes Steele, William Steele, Isabelle Steele. Katherine Steele.

No spouses listed. No parents listed.

"It's not here," said Katherine.

"Wait, Mom," said Lily. "These are just Steeles. Maybe there's a page where the parents and kids are together."

So Katherine turned the page. The next was blank, but after that was one showing John Steele and Susannah Rumford. And their two children 'Agnes, born October 1, 1877.' And 'William, born June 7, 1880.'

Then the next page showed William Steele and Charlotte Weatherby and 'their daughter Isabelle, born August 27, 1911.'

And also 'their son Alexander, born October 8, 1913.' And then in a different ink, more hastily written, 'died age 1 month.'

Katherine inhaled sharply. She hadn't known her mother had had a little brother. William's only son.

The others looked on and absorbed the sad little story.

Katherine hesitated, then turned the page.

'Isabelle Steele' on the top line, 'Katherine Steele, her daughter,' below her, with the right birthdate, in 1943.

No father's name.

"My father's name isn't here," she said coolly, appearing to be unconcerned.

Lily was peering at the empty line next to the word 'Father.' She looked more closely.

"Mom, look. In pencil."

Katherine looked. "It's just a smudge or something," she said.

"Let me see," said Clark and Horan at the same time.

Katherine held out the heavy book, wincing from the pain of lifting it. Clark saw. "What is it, Katherine?"

"It's nothing," said Katherine firmly, dismissively.

Lily and Horan took the big book closer to the light.

"There's definitely something there," said Horan, and Lily nodded.

"What?" whispered Katherine.

"It's definitely two names. The first name is Samuel, I think."

"Samuel? That doesn't mean anything to me. Or maybe someone called Sam?"

"Could be, but here it's 'Samuel.' Written in pencil, maybe a sharp pencil, and then erased, leaving a smudge."

"I think the second name is 'White,'" said Lily.

"Oh? Yes, I think so, too."

They returned the book to Katherine. She peered at the page and shook her head. "I don't know. Who's Samuel White?"

"And why did she erase it?" asked Lily.

"Can you see a place, a location for your birth?"

"No. Not here. But my birth certificate says I was born right here in Steeletown. And besides, I don't think Isabelle went anywhere but here."

"What about the World War Two records we were looking at? Do you remember the name of Samuel White?"

"No, but that was the story she told me. That he went to war. And died in the war maybe, but also that he was a fisherman."

Lily, sitting next to Katherine again, turned the page.

It was a page of 'Christenings' on the left and 'Marriages' on the right. Most of it was blank, but John Steele's marriage was there, written in a hand different from his. His wife's or Agnes's, Lily guessed. Then William and his wife. Then Isabelle and her husband Samuel White, of Steeletown. Married in February 1943.

Katherine sat back and cried. And cried and cried. She wondered why her mother had not told her. What had happened to Sam White? And had they really gotten married?

"Mom! Mom! We can go to the library tomorrow and see if he's in the World War Two records!"

Horan said, "Lily, I thought we were going to go get those wooden crates out of the cottage tomorrow. If we can get Ben's help."

"Oh, right. They're definitely still in danger. And I know we need Ben's help, but I'm not going," said Lily. "He's ... ." And then she stopped saying what she had in mind, which was: He's mean. He's not my dad.

Then Horan added, "And Angie will be there to help. After this weekend, she'll go back to college and won't be back for a long time."

"Angie. Right," said Lily. "OK. But Saturday we can go find my grandfather, Sam White."

"Sorry again," said Horan. "That's New Year's Day, and the library is closed again. Bad timing, eh?"

"Oh," said Lily, Clark, and Horan.

While they were all making their plans, Katherine was mulling over the information from the book. So now she knew, Katherine thought to herself. She had not experienced any sense of rightness about the name Sam White, no faint recognition from her early days. Nothing.

What had happened to him? Had they gotten divorced? Was he sitting somewhere, a lonely old man, in his 70s or 80s, in town here, or in Alaska? Or did he have a houseful of grandkids, while she, his loyal but unknowing first daughter, had never stopped thinking about him but also had never known him?

Or had he died in the war? Or disappeared off the fishing vessel he worked on? Or settled down in Alaska?

All she had that she hadn't had yesterday was a name. And a marriage date. Four months before her birth.

Was he in fact her father? Or had he been just some willing guy who made Isabelle honest when she had become obviously pregnant?

And what had Agnes thought all the while, formidable Aunt Agnes, who had lived at that time with Isabelle in the big house?

Maybe with Isabelle and Sam? Or had Isabelle moved out for a while?

Katherine continued to flip through the pages. Most were blank, but some had brief entries that were hard to read in what appeared to be an old entry, reminiscent of John Steele's hand. One had to do with building ships, another with uses of the local railroad. It's not what Katherine was looking for. Long descriptions in long sentences she had no patience for at the moment. She wanted to see if there was a page devoted to 'Divorces.'

But no. Nothing that revealed what happened after the marriage. Just her own name in the front.

John Steele's handwritten notes went on for the whole center portion of the book. Then came pages of a sort of ledger, figures, dollar signs, transactions and dates, items crossed out. Photographs of places around town that Katherine recognized. A list of public offices he'd held, if she understood his notes. Then a long list of dates and brief items, beginning in 1914 and ending in October 1918, the month he died. Maybe a hundred pages of notes.

A good project for Lily, to decipher it all. As for Katherine herself, she knew she would not have time.

The other items from the bundle would have to wait. Horan had said it was time to go. Katherine and Lily collected the items from the bundle and put them away in the spare bedroom. They agreed that nothing from the shed should remain in the cottage as soon as they could be moved, and in fact, Katherine was getting anxious to get back as soon as possible to make sure nothing happened to them overnight. Clark, Horan, and Lily went to the car for the books. They might prove interesting, but there was no time tonight to begin to look through them.

When they got back from the car, after having made several trips, Clark said, "We're not going to be able to manage another trip with those big boxes tonight. I'll call Ben and ask him to help us with them tomorrow. He's a good guy, and maybe he can bring Angie to help."

Lily wanted to say something about how much help Ben was apt to be. But then she realized no one had told Clark and Horan that he was her dad. Maybe they hadn't heard her say before that he wasn't a great dad.

Clark rode along with Horan when she drove Katherine and Lily home. Ben had said he'd be around tomorrow and could help. And he would pick up Katherine and Lily first thing in the morning.

On the way back home, Horan filled Clark in on the intruders who might raid the cottage and shed, as apparently a few had tried. Horan told Clark about the division of property that was being challenged, and that the current owner, desperate to sell, resented that the fact that the cottage was occupied appeared to be interfering with buyers wanting the property.

Clark said, "That's rough. Especially when Kate doesn't seem entirely well. I wish I knew what was going on there."

"Maybe she's depressed. It's such a dark little hut they live in! Surely she can afford better."

"Depressed? Maybe you're right. You'd think she might afford a real house. She was working till a short time ago, and you'd think the father would provide child support."

"It's all about wanting to keep an eye on the big house. Which she wouldn't be able to do elsewhere. I think that's why they're there," said Horan. "As I understand it, they have no paper that shows the property was divided. They could lose their home, and that would be enough to make me depressed."

"I don't know if that's it. I'll keep an eye on Lily and see if she keeps being OK. She's usually more than OK, a real delight in the classroom, as you can imagine."

"I'll say. She's full of ideas. Katherine's lucky. She's got a real partner in Lily," said Horan.

"I think Lily must be like her grandfather. Her what? Great-great-grandfather? John Steele, town founder. She's full of ambition, as he must have been in his day. I've heard he was ruthless, too, but I don't see anything of that in Lily. Maybe she's a bit fanatical, at least about the books. And the house. Or maybe that's Katherine, and not Lily."

As they pulled into their garage, Clark said, "I have an idea. If it still sounds good in the morning, I'll tell you all about it. After we get a good night's sleep."

By the time she got to bed, Katherine was exhausted and in serious pain. Now she had a name for her father, and what did that do for her? At least with a name she could create the story of her going to find him.

All she needed was a get-away car. It came to her over and over during the night that this lack of a car was an impediment to the whole plan.

## THURSDAY, DECEMBER 30, 1985

BEN DROVE UP ON Thursday morning and knocked on the cottage door. "Clark and Horan are coming in an hour to help load some things into both the cars. Then they have to do an errand. And I am taking you to breakfast. You can't even walk around in this cottage until all the stuff is moved out. OK?"

Katherine and Lily hesitated, and while they were looking at each other and thinking about what to do, Ben stepped in, kissed each of them lightly on the nose.

"Let's go," he said.

They had never gone out for breakfast. They climbed into the car, Lily in the front seat. "Hmm, smells like Cindy. How was your date?"

Ben choked on something.

"Fine," he said.

"Well, as you can see, it all worked out. Clark and Horan are wonderful. I had to get their help because when I got home from getting Mom's purse, I was so cold that I got under the covers to get warm and then I fell asleep and forgot to wake up in time to take the books to the library."

"Glad to hear they were able to help. But surely you understand, Lily. It's not nice to cancel a ... a prior commitment." He was caught between wanting to be sincere and convincing to Lily, and inaudible to Katherine. Just in case Lily hadn't told her. And looking in the rearview mirror, it seemed he'd gotten away with it, because Katherine seemed lost in thought, paying him no attention at all.

But Lily turned on him, fists up, raging, hissing. "I needed your help. It's still an emergency. It's wonderful to have the help of my teacher and the town librarian. They saved the day. Well, so far. But I needed my dad. I wasn't going to ask you again, but they thought you wouldn't mind helping us lift those wooden boxes. They're super-heavy. Because if we don't get them put away someplace safe, someone else will get them."

Breakfast was a silent affair. Lily pretended Ben wasn't there. Katherine was lost in thought, secretly rejoicing in Lily's spunk, whatever she had been upset about. Which might serve her well in the years to come. And Ben tried being chatty and entertaining, and ended up hurrying them along, then paying the bill, all the while looking sad.

When they got back in the car, he said, "I'm sorry." He was greeted with silence.

It took two minutes to get back to the cottage. He looked at the huge boxes taking up most of the room in the cottage.

"Let's put them in my garage," he said. "Or Clark said they could go in their spare bedroom. And then we can look at what's in them any time, no rush. Won't that be fun?"

Katherine noticed Lily wasn't giving him the time of day, doing her best to pretend he wasn't there, all the while helping by carrying individual tools to his car trunk to lighten the open-topped box. She didn't know what some of the tools were, but she wasn't in the mood to ask.

Clark and Horan had driven up, and along with Ben were able to move the heaviest of all, the closed-top box, to the car without needing to open it and carry the contents separately. Angie hadn't come with Ben, much to Lily's disappointment, but they managed to move everything anyway.

"We have something to tell you all," said Clark. "So we're having supper at our house because we all need to eat and we might as well do both things at once."

"I have something to tell you all, too," said Ben. "As long as Angie can come along, I can do it at the same time."

"Great," said Clark. "We'll need everyone's help if we're going to get all these things into your garage. I had no idea there'd be so much to deal with."

"Well, I think there's more stuff, even if it wasn't in the shed," said Lily.

Katherine, who had been busy in the cottage, had just come out and said, "Really? What? Isn't this enough?"

"I think John Steele had other ideas," said Lily. "I'll tell you tonight. Clark and Horan are going to tell us something tonight, and so is Ben, and so am I!"

The looms were hard to get into the car. Finally, Horan slid one into her backseat, but there was no room for the other. And they didn't want to leave it untended at the cottage. Katherine had seen the Woman in the Window a few times, and she had to have been aware that things were being moved around, even if she didn't know they'd come out of the shed.

But they needed Ben to help carry things into his garage at the other end, and the only reasonable combination was to leave Clark with Katherine and send Horan with her car and Ben with his car to do the drop-off. After that, one more trip would finish the job.

And what would Lily do?

"I think I'll stay and get some potatoes and carrots for supper tonight. There are still plenty."

Clark helped her by pulling carrots, carefully so they wouldn't break off, the way Lily taught her. Lily liked her teacher very much.

"How many potatoes do we need? There are six of us, three pairs."

"Let's have one potato each, plus one for the pot," said Clark.

So they dug around one of the broken potato vines with their fingers until they began to encounter the potatoes themselves. These were white ones, light pinkish brown on the outside. There were more than they needed. Clark picked out the seven that were the closest to each other in size, and Lily put the rest away in the cottage after rinsing them in the rain bucket.

She was surprised not to see the woman standing in the window or out in the yard with them, challenging them. Or potential buyers snooping around.

"Clark, I'm going to run around the block and see if the for-sale sign is still up. Can you stay here with Mom?"

"Oh, you don't need to do that, Lily. Um, Horan and I drove that way and it wasn't up."

"Oh, gee, I don't know if that's good or bad. Maybe it's bought and we'll have to move." She was quiet, subdued. "I don't want to tell Mom yet, not till we're sure."

"I think waiting is a good idea," said Clark. "Wait until you know something."

Ben and Horan arrived back in their two cars, and Ben had picked up Angie. It took them all another half hour to get the final packing up done, and as they got underway, a certain festive air seemed to capture them. They were going to have a party with good food and the best company, and almost everyone seemed to have a surprise to disclose.

Lily found herself getting caught up in the good cheer. Ben had asked her to help him carry the remaining loom, and together they struggled with the awkward shape, huge and perhaps delicate. They ended up laughing, and Lily felt her heart swell with love for her dad, a new sort of feeling, and one she liked very much. What had she been upset with him about? She remembered for a moment but then dismissed it. He was, after all, her very own father, and she loved him even though he wasn't perfect.

Katherine, catching herself beginning to worry about leaving the cottage empty and exposed, realized there wasn't much to protect anymore, so she switched gears and took up the spirit of rejoicing. She realized how happy she was with these dear friends around. She was sitting in the front seat with Ben, with Lily and Angie chattering along behind them.

"Do you have any surprises to share tonight, Angie?" asked Lily.

"Hmm, I haven't given it any thought."

"Well, if you do, I will be listening. And you can listen to mine. Because I think I have three."

"Wow, hmm, I need to think."

"Well, Daddy does, and either Clark or Horan does."

"I'll think of something."

"What about you, Mom?" Lily called out in a louder voice aimed at the front seat. "Do you have any surprises to disclose tonight at dinner?"

"I doubt it," she said. She looked out the window on her side. Tears had sprung up and she didn't want anyone to see. Because she did have a surprise, but no one must know it.

Ben wasn't fooled. He reached over and pried her hand from her tightly held arms and squeezed it. "You can tell us, my darling," he said.

She was shocked. How did he know? Well, yes, he had guessed she wasn't well. He'd mentioned it not a few times, at first to her annoyance and then in a way that left her softened and almost eager to share her burden with him.

But she must not. The Plan required ... not secrecy, no, just ignorance. His, Lily's, everyone's. Even the ignorance of the Woman in the Window. No one could know she was gone.

Except of course Lily, who would think Mom was gone to find her father. Which Lily wanted for her more than anything, having found her own dad.

Her dad who was for the most part such a comfort, and whose company she was enjoying. At the moment, at least.

And then they were at his house.

They had debated whose house they should share their dinner at, but Ben had an ulterior motive, that if they ate at his house, Katherine would be that much closer to spending the night. With Lily, of course.

And Angie backed him up.

So they convened in the living room while many hands made light work of the finishing touches for the supper. The six of them fit perfectly at Ben's dining table, and then after the meal was finished, Ben and Clark fit perfectly in front of the sink and dishwasher and soon had things tidied up.

Angie served a gooey dessert she'd made, and in no time they were sitting around in the living room full of excitement and anticipation.

Ben took charge. He intended to say his huge news quickly, then turn the floor over to whoever wanted it and resume his place next to Katherine.

"Welcome, friends. I want to catch everyone up on our big news. Lily, please come up here with me."

Lily bounced to his side and took his offered hand. She had figured out what was coming. She felt a little embarrassed for a brief moment but ended up beaming at him. And he at her.

"Clark, Horan, I want you to meet my beloved daughter Lily Brown Steele."

And then he kissed her on the forehead.

Angie clapped, Katherine joined her, and Lily jumped up and down.

Clark and Horan looked at each other and after a lengthy pause, nodded to each other. Lily wondered if they'd figured it out, or it was just making sense to them.

"Katherine," said Horan. "You've ... you've kept this to yourself all these years? Or have I just been out of the loop?"

Lily said, "Daddy didn't want anybody to know, so Mom didn't tell."

"Lily!" said Katherine. "Let's not talk about that!"

Ben looked at Angie. She was shaking her head. He was on his own.

Here he was with his best friends, whom he had expected to rejoice with him, and a certain downside seemed to accompany the announcement. He hadn't thought about it, but Horan, at least, seemed to imply that his behavior had been questionable.

"I believe Lily has an announcement," said Clark.

Ben was relieved to be out of the spotlight, though he suspected it would return. Kate was looking down at her hands. Maybe she would explain later that it had all been for the best. It had, hadn't it? All's well that ends well? Certainly she had seemed fine with the way things were evolving toward a happy conclusion, though it had taken ten years. Ten years. Hmm, maybe he could have sought out his daughter before this. But it hadn't come to him. The idea simply hadn't come to him.

Meanwhile Lily was talking about what she and her helpers had found. He realized it when he heard her say, "... not enough books."

There were not enough books?

She went on. "I saw on the drawing of the house"—here she held up the huge, yellowed sheet, Ben belatedly helping her by holding up the other side —"that there's a back stairwell that goes directly to the attic." Here she pointed with her finger. They could see the stairwell rise up from a hallway opposite the kitchen, then continue on to another level. It seemed maybe a window or door to the outside marked the second story level, but on a different hallway, maybe one the family would not have used. Then the stairwell turned 90 degrees and continued to the attic.

"Mom didn't know about it. I think Aunt Agnes carried as many books up there as she could in the days before they moved out, and then put the rest of them in some vehicle and moved them to the shed.

"And then when they all moved into the cottage, they moved the things stored in the cottage, the looms, sewing machine, and so on, to the shed before locking it.

"And I think most of the books are still up there in the attic. I just wish I could see if that's true. If it's not, they'll be somewhere else. I just hope they're not in the basement. Mom says it's damp and moldy down there."

Everyone was nodding. Lily had talked about bits and pieces of her theory of where the books were for days, so only a few of the details were a surprise.

"But that's not all."

At this point she reached into her jeans pocket and took out the key ring. "I think there's more treasure in other places. I think these keys are the real treasure, the reason Aunt Agnes called the shed 'the Treasury.'"

"What do those keys open, Lily?" asked Clark.

"I don't know yet. But I know where to look."

"Where?" everyone said.

"You can't tell," said Lily. "If I tell you, you have to keep it a secret."

"OK," everyone agreed.

"I think they open doors around town of places that were owned by John Steele back in 1900 or whenever. In various buildings he owned. Or the buildings themselves."

"You mean places that haven't been opened all this time?"

"I don't know, but I'm going to find out. I just haven't had time yet."

"Not on your own, you're not," said Ben. "It might not be safe."

She turned on him with squinty eyes, her face all drawn up tight. "You don't get to tell me what to do all of a sudden," she said.

And then he realized he hadn't been forgiven for failing to help her when she needed him. Being her dad was more complicated than he'd realized. He needed backup. He turned to Katherine.

Katherine was nodding. "She's quite capable of making good decisions," she said.

But, Katherine realized, at the same time, these keys were a whole new factor she had to contemplate in creating the Plan, and time was short. And she had no idea what to think, or where to begin. She just knew that Lily was naïve and trusting and could get herself into situations she knew nothing about.

But Lily was still speaking. "I already found another treasure, and I'm sure one of these keys will unlock it. But I don't need it. Yet. It's well-hidden, not in any danger.

"What is it?" asked Angie.

"A piece of railroad equipment," said Lily. Maybe she shouldn't have said that, but she had the keys and only she knew where it was, so it was probably safe for the moment.

Not that she could figure out why anyone would want it, or exactly what it did. But she had plans to find out.

"Lily!"

"What, Mom?"

"Please be careful."

Then she picked up the packet again and took out the little tin. "And I have some old, old seeds from my grandmother. I'm going to see if I can make them grow. But not until spring. If we still have the garden then. But I'm scared that we won't be able to live there anymore, me and Mom. And then I'll have to throw them away or find someone who would treasure them as much as Grandma Isabelle. Because they must have been valuable to her or she wouldn't have saved them."

"The end."

Everyone applauded.

"Well, then," said Clark. "That's a perfect introduction to our announcement. Ours because it was Horan's idea and she helped me with it. Ready? I've bought a new home."

"What's the matter with your other house? I love it," said Lily.

"Oh, I do, too. And I love my friends Horan and Edna, and I'll keep living there. But I bought a house that I knew would be a good investment. Something I can fix up and enjoy well into the future. Something special and lovely and full of potential. Something that feeds the imagination. Something with a grander perspective than the little house we live in.

"Granted our little house is perfectly located so we can walk to work, all three of us, one to the town library, only blocks away, one to my school, and one to the high school. We bought that house together for just that reason, and it's quite perfect for the three of us.

"But I have a good imagination, you see, and I can see the potential of this other house for all sorts of grand things. So I bought it. Today. I sign tomorrow. It needs a lot of work, but as I said, I can imagine it the way it will be as the work gets done, bit by bit."

"Can we see it?" asked Lily. "It sounds exciting!"

"Yes, I think we have a photo of it right in the other room."

"Here at my house?" asked Ben.

"I think so. In Angie's room is my guess."

Then Clark went over to Angie, sitting as she was on the couch next to Lily, and whispered to her. Angie's face changed to enthusiastic understanding, and she leapt up and ran to her room, returning with Lily's photo album.

"Clark says it's in here," said Angie, handing the album to Lily.

Lily took it, wondering. She had found places for all the photos Angie had taken, and there was nothing loose that could be Clark's new house.

"Nothing here," she said. She felt that she was going through the same embarrassing episode of trying to find her father, all over again. She shoved the album back at Angie and crossed her arms.

"Here," said Clark, taking the album. "Lily, I'm not making fun of you. There is a house in this album and that is the house I bought today."

"Yes, there is a house in the album, but it's the big house my mom was born in."

The room was silent.

"OH!" said Lily. "I get it." There was a long pause. "OH NO," yelled Lily. "You can't have that house. That's Mom's house for someday."

"How about next week? Is that someday enough? Because I don't want my new house to be vacant. I'll need someone to live in it, starting next week. If you don't mind some workers around from time to time doing repairs and painting."

Katherine had been listening. She had caught on about the photo in the album before Lily had, that the house Clark had bought was in fact the big house that was 'hers'—not that it ever was really going to be hers. And she was lost in thought about how now it was lost for real, so she had missed the suggestion that she and Lily might live in it. And then she had caught on that Clark had bought it so it would be their house. And now she was realizing that her dream was about to come true, and just as she realized she could live in it after all, it all came crashing down because by next week she would be both gone and dead.

And she had to absorb that and hide it. And Ben was watching her.

Ben had caught on quickly. Now all he needed was for Katherine to agree to marry him. She realized he would figure that out right away.

He could see at once that the whole problem of Katherine keeping an eye on the house and being married, both, were solved by living in the big house; also not trying to live as a couple, with Lily, all in one room.

But Clark had more to say. "I don't know yet that the sale will go through. I have a few things to take care of before it's certain. I'll know in the next few days."

Angie, seeing the turmoil from the house announcement, stood up and motioned for Ben to sit down. He took his place beside Katherine, who seemed lost in thought.

Angie said, "My announcement is simple. I have a new sister and I love her very much. And I'm looking forward to decorating the boat with her tomorrow. And then it's back to college with me. And after spending many hours talking to my dear new sister, I've decided on my major. When I came home I didn't know what it would be. But now I know. It's business. Maybe that way we can take her wonderful and ambitious ideas—you have no idea how outrageous and ambitious they are—and combine them with the business expertise I'll have by then and have a lot of success and fun together. The End."

Lily ran up to her and hugged her, stuck her tongue out at her dad, gave her mom a quick hug, and shook Clark's and Horan's hands and said, "That was a brilliant investment, Clark. Good idea, Horan. On behalf of my mother and me, we accept your kind offer. As long as I get to check out the attic and see if the books are there."

Everyone laughed. "Yes," said Clark. "Next week. I think you must have the key to the attic on that ring, because the door that corresponds to the attic stairwell on the map is locked. Good old Aunt Agnes! Putting the books there and the key elsewhere—in the Treasury—was brilliant. Those books must really be something."

The party was over. Angie put out the gooey dessert so anyone could have seconds, but they passed it by. "All the more for us tomorrow," said Angie to Lily. "You are spending the night, aren't you? Both of you?"

"Yes," said Lily.

"Yes," said Ben.

Katherine, showing little joy, shrugged. "I guess," she said.

Ben kissed her, then went to the door with the departing Clark and Horan. "We'll see you at the boat. In the morning."

He shut the door, turning back to Katherine. "You can have my bed," said Ben. "I'll sleep out here on the couch. Or on Arabelle's bed. You look tired tonight."

"I guess I am. Good night."

"Marry me!" he said.

"No, it's too late."

"I don't mean tonight."

"I know."

## FRIDAY, DECEMBER 31, 1985 – NEW YEAR'S EVE

HAVING PREPARED BREAKFAST AND all they would need for the boat-decorating party, Ben woke Lily and Katherine at 8:30. The day was sunny. He hurried them along until they were ready for a day on the water.

Ben's moorage was all the way across town, too far to walk. He had bags full of what looked like decorative materials riding along with them in the cargo area of the station wagon. He stopped by to pick up Clark and Horan but they decided to drive themselves.

"Where's Angie?" asked Lily. She was riding in the front seat, while Katherine sat behind Ben, his arrangement, whatever his message might have been. Lily was feeling suspicious of him and his motives and his ways of doing things and anything else she could think of. And she thought the seat she was sitting in smelled of perfume, as in Cindy's perfume, and it was reminding her how mad she was at the guy who called himself her dad.

The trouble was, he was fun. The day decorating the boat, and then sailing in the parade, and even getting judged, and hearing applause from shore, sounded exciting.

But then, where was Angie? She was part of what made it fun.

"She's already down at the docks. She drove her car down this morning. Early. Six a.m. She loves being on the boat."

"I can't wait," said Lily. She said it so he'd know she wasn't mad anymore, but she also meant it. She hoped Mom would enjoy it and not feel like she had to go home right away.

Katherine had not been excited about the day, not in the least, and if it was a good day for decorating boats, it was probably a good day for house buyers to show up. Clark had bought it, yes, but had also expressed some uncertainly. Something about signing papers to be certain. So Katherine probably didn't need to worry about the house anymore, didn't need to worry about failing to keep it safe, here at this eleventh hour of life. It was safe. Probably.

Good. Because she had heard the only word that could distract her from keeping an eye on the big house, and that was 'car.' As in, Angie had a car.

"When is Angie going back to college, Ben?" she asked.

"She flies out on Sunday. So soon. It's been so quick."

"Oh. Sad."

"I'm so glad you like her."

Katherine was listening with a mind not so much on Angie's plans as on the realization that Angie would be leaving her car behind. Angie would fly to college. The car wouldn't be needed, wouldn't be missed if she stole it. Though of course stealing it would be rude. Illegal, too, though she didn't really care about that at this point. She almost laughed out loud when she thought she would get off easy because she would be a first offender.

Lily ran down the ramp and greeted Angie with enthusiasm. Ben had asked her to carry several of the bags he'd brought, but they didn't slow her down. For the boat, he'd said, and she'd agreed to help carry them. When Angie saw her being agreeable to Ben, she patted Lily on the back. "Let's have fun!" she said.

Lily ran back to Ben and took the remaining bags. "Have fun," she said to Ben and Katherine and gave them both a kiss.

And as Katherine and Ben walked slowly down to the boat, such a lovely boat with cabin and overhead lounge, Katherine started to think once again that she really needed to be back at the house, but then wavered. It was a gorgeous day, warmish for December, a perfect day for ... she almost said buying and selling houses. Ha! The house was sold. And she didn't need to worry about the shed being broken into. Let them pick the locks. There was nothing left inside, according to Lily.

Ben took some cushions from a storage locker and made a comfortable place for Katherine, and after making a few adjustments on obscure boat parts, sat down next to her. Lily, working on something with Angie, turned and waved to one or both of them with a grin.

So Katherine, who had been ready to sass Ben on Lily's behalf, saw that she had at least for the moment forgiven him. She relaxed and held his hand and put her mind to figuring out how to ask him for Angie's car. She couldn't let Lily know or she'd be full of questions. And she didn't know Angie well enough just to ask her. And she didn't want to wait till Angie was gone late Sunday afternoon, just a few hours before she, Katherine, needed to use the car, because what if he said no? She would have no time to find another car, and she couldn't afford to delay.

The decorating was fun to watch. But she didn't want him to know it. A part of her wanted him to feel some guilt for his neglect over the years, though she could see that sometimes she had misinterpreted his actions. But still, if she was to get the use of the car, shouldn't she make him feel that he owed her something?

Or would it be better if he did it as a favor because he loved her? But she couldn't count on that. Could she?

It was delightful to see the two girls working side by side, sometimes building something, sometimes with their heads together. His daughters both. What if ... ? But no, there would never have been a way for them to grow up under one roof, sisters from the beginning.

He got up from time to time, apparently to check on whether they needed his help, but they always sent him back to Katherine.

"Not needed," he said.

"Not like the old days, I suppose," said Katherine. "When your daughters needed you to help decorate?"

"It's a fact they don't need me. But even more, they like to see us together. That's what's happening. Maybe we should both go help, but they might be just as happy if we sat here and kissed."

Lily would have liked doing this before. The fact was—as she knew perfectly well—that she had always protected him by avoiding him, in all ways making Lily unavailable for activities such as this. Such as anything at all, including letting him see her. And her him. By nobly staying invisible.

And look what Lily had missed out on! He'd ended up divorced anyway, so what had she been protecting him from?

"Ben, Lily would have loved this when she was little!"

He looked at her. He nodded slowly. "I should have tried harder," he said.

"Yes," she said.

He turned to her with torment in his eyes. She knew it was her turn to accept some of the guilt. Because—she had to admit it—he had tried.

And she had kept him out. She had kept Lily from being part of his family, having sisters.

And now she could see that a little forgiveness and even acceptance of her own guilt might open ... she was going to say open the way to get Angie's car, but instead her heart felt something new. She'd find a way to get Angie's car. But first she wanted to make it truly right with Ben.

On an impulse she stood and maneuvered herself between his knees as he sat on that cushion he'd brought out to make sitting on the boat more comfortable. She took him by the head, holding him tight against her. "I'm sorry, Ben," she said. "I ... I ... I have been selfish."

He looked up at her. Tears were streaming down her face. She had so little time left. She had squandered all these years with Lily, when Lily could have had a home, a family. His home, his family. Maybe even his wife would have loved her. She, Kate, wouldn't have been part of it, but Lily would have loved these things. Instead, she had been selfish.

"Lily's a great little person because of you, Kate," he said. "We can't go back, but from here on we can be a real little family."

"It's too late," she sobbed.

"It's never too late," he said. "Let's enjoy today as the beginning of our new life as a family."

"The beginning and the ..." She had almost said, '... end,' but he mustn't have a clue of that. So she said, "... surprises." As in, 'The beginning and the surprises of our new life as a family.'

Because that would certainly be true.

All lovely. But right now what she needed more than anything was Angie's car.

When Lily looked over, she wasn't sure whether Mom and Ben were happy with each other, or sad for some reason. Ben had gotten up, Mom was sitting there with her hands between her knees, looking like her mind was far away.

She came over and kissed Katherine and rubbed her back, and Katherine knew she had upset her.

"I know he's not perfect, Mom. But he is my dad."

"Sorry, Lily. I thought you were mad at him."

"I was. But it's over. And speaking of dads, don't forget we're going to go find your dad, Sam White, next week."

Katherine knew that wouldn't turn out to be true, to be possible, but as the festive spirit built up on the small boat, and on other boats nearby, with seafaring friends calling back and forth as the decorations and clever use of craft supplies transformed the boats, especially Ben's boat, into a floating piece of art, Katherine felt more and more free of the burdens of past mistakes.

It didn't hurt that Clark and Horan, who had just arrived, were full of joy. A transformation had happened to them, too, apparently due to Clark's having bought the big house. Good for them, Katherine rehearsed to herself. She had many years of ownership, or you could call it 'imagined ownership' to overcome before she'd be ready to rejoice with and for them. One less worry, one more disappointment.

But at the moment, disappointment mixed with an amazing amount of cheer.

As for Angie, she had been full of good cheer since they'd arrived. She'd already been at work since early, and, as Ben bragged, was the one who had designed the whole concept.

The mood of celebration of the past and future had fully captured Lily, so Ben, clearly keeping an eye on her, relaxed, and they all began to feel as they had on Christmas Eve, like a family.

And when Katherine reflected that this would be her last new year, that her tombstone (if any) would read 1943-1986, she thought it was the best ending for herself that she could imagine.

But what was up with Clark and Horan? It was almost as if they had just found out they were going to have a baby, Katherine thought. Such giddiness! And neither of them was even going to live in the house.

Katherine had been reminded of those first few minutes when she realized she was going to have a baby. Maybe elation and great joy as Clark and Horan were exhibiting was not really her experience. More embarrassment and desperation. And some joy and exhilaration. She had been 32. The clock had been ticking. Ben had, well, he had seduced her. He had charmed her. He had made himself irresistible. He had even leveled with her that he was married, rather too late in the proceedings for her to care. And then she was going to have a baby, a sweet baby of her own. Mixed feelings, that's what she had had.

Because, well, she'd wanted a baby, she was going to have a baby, and where else would she have gotten one? And Ben was so smart and handsome.

And there, at this moment wrapping colored ribbon around a railing, was the result, the love of her life and the vehicle that would carry forward the Steele legacy. Lily, her flower.

Katherine needed to make a mental note to warn Lily away from unworthy strangers as the years went by, no matter their charm.

And now, Lily might be able to hold onto the house, and ultimately pass on what John Steele himself had chosen for their legacy. Clark would install Katherine and Lily there, and then when it was time to disappear—Monday it had better be, she thought, just three days away—she would drive away, leaving word for Lily that Mom was going to go find her father.

The trouble was, they wouldn't be able to go to the library in the meantime. But though she would be lacking the key information she needed to tell Lily where her father, Lily's grandfather, had gone, if such a thing were to be found at the library, she couldn't wait any longer. Time was short. So she wouldn't have this Sam White's address. But maybe she could tell

Lily she had an inkling of it, in the papers from the shed, and that she was rushing to bring him back. And be sure not to tell anyone.

Not even Ben. Or maybe she shouldn't say that. It might make Lily suspicious, or even give her the idea of telling him.

And once she was gone, Lily would have the house to herself to do her exploring and arranging, and she would be happy. She would have her garden, even, more than either of them had dared to hope for, if the house were sold. And she would have her kind teacher, Miss Clark, and her librarian friend, Miss Horan, and all would be well. And Ben, when he wasn't too busy.

Katherine felt edgy again. Because much as Lily seemed to be like John Steele in so many ways, maybe she would also inherit her father's flightiness. Because while John Steele was dedicated to his railroads and fancy houses and shipyards, Ben Brown liked women. He really did. Because he had liked her. That was just the way he was, and if he had come around again, she would have taken him into her life again.

But that would not do for Lily. Lily, if it turned out she liked men as Ben liked women, would not have a happy life. One man was enough. Let her find one worthy man who could support her and love her and cherish her.

Katherine would have to write Lily a note about that. Maybe to be opened on her 15$^{th}$ birthday. Or 16$^{th}$. Not that Lily would ever need support, come to think of it, not with her independence and clever ways of earning.

A shadow fell on her. The sun had coursed its way off to the southwest, and Ben was standing between her and it, so that when she looked up, she had to shield her eyes. He reached down and kissed her on the lips. "I love you, Katherine. We make good babies."

He had thrilled her again.

"Want a tour of the boat?" he said, a play of innocence about his eyes, in his easy smile. But he was up to something, she suspected. Well, so was she. Because she had her plan.

So she said yes, and he showed her around. Topside up a steep ladder, main deck where the girls were working, and down some stairs to the stateroom below. He held her hand as she stepped carefully down the steep and narrow stairs. He closed the hatch over as she looked about. In the center of the area belowdecks was a table and seating. They moved past them into a narrow hallway and went down a few more steps to a door. "The head," said Ben. Another door, straight ahead, blocked the area toward the bow, but Ben opened it and pulled her gently into that space. It was a sleeping area.

And in a split second she revised her plan to something better, cleverer.

He kissed her while sliding the door over, and she kissed him back with at least equal fervor. She met his every subtle invitation with a positive response. She gave into her every impulse. He pulled her to the double-wide berth, and she moved easily with him and without resistance lay beside him. Only when he wanted to bare her chest did she stop him.

But she willingly accepted his other offers of engagement, one lingering escalation at a time. She could hear Lily just above, talking to Angie. Like an angel, an unknowing angel, Lily was standing guard over them while they deepened their relationship once again. Then Ben said, "But no baby this time," and made a move toward safety. But Katherine stopped him, mystifying him (or maybe worrying him, who knew which) and raising his passion to a level beyond anything he had known. Ever. With anyone.

They clung to each other in waves of increasing love.

And then, after a bit of lingering closeness, she whispered, "Ben, could I borrow Angie's car next week, after she goes back to school?"

"Sure," he said, before falling asleep.

Clark and Horan had left again, saying they'd be right back. Ben could see them walking back down the ramp to the boat dock as the sun approached the western horizon. They had bags of take-out food of all varieties. "You're hungry, and we're celebrating. Let's take a food break."

"What's up?" asked a drowsy Ben, emerging from below.

"We signed for the house. We'll talk about it later. The decorations look great. Is that a little lighthouse? Does the light actually work?"

And so on. Lily and Angie gave Clark and Horan a quick tour of the decorations, and the girls explained how they'd managed this, how they'd struggled with that. Then they sat around with plates of food on their laps. Katherine hadn't reappeared. Ben responded to curious looks with a shrug of the shoulders. He rearranged the girls so he could sit between them and put an arm around each of them, gave each of them a squeeze.

He kept the buckets of food circulating and listened to the girls talk about their project and wondered if Kate were going to reappear.

Lily saw her first. "Mom!" said Lily. "Come eat. It's fried fish sandwiches." She made her mother a place on her other side. Katherine was emerging from below. She crossed the small space, stepping over extended legs, and gave Ben a lingering kiss on the lips.

"Mom, wow," said Lily, and giggled.

She moved over so Mom could sit next to Ben. Mom snuggled her face down under Ben's ear and rested her head on his shoulder. Lily heard her say, "Mmmm, you smell good."

Lily was thinking how much she liked having both a mom and a dad and how interesting it was, the way they kissed and snuggled.

Then Ben said, "Here, Kate, eat," and handed her a fish sandwich. But she wasn't hungry.

And when Mom stood up again, Lily thought she didn't look good. "Mom, are you OK?" she asked.

Katherine said, "I think I need to go home."

Several chorused, "Oh no, don't go," but both Clark and Horan were looking at her with concern.

"I'll take you, Katherine," said Horan. "Remember, everyone, I am not going out on the boat anyway. I'm done with being on this tippy bucket as it is. I'll happily take Katherine home."

"Well, I hope you can watch the parade as it goes by and clap for us," said Lily.

"Sorry you have to leave, Kate," said Ben. He had stood to steady Katherine as she stepped off the boat, handing her to Horan on the dock. Then he reached over and kissed her on the forehead and said, "I'll miss you."

"You have Lily," she said

"Wouldn't miss the parade, you all. You've done a great job with the decorations," said Horan.

Katherine and Horan walked slowly down the dock to the parking lot. Horan had taken Katherine's arm in a seemingly friendly gesture. Her support appeared casual, but from the boat Lily could see that Katherine was leaning on Horan. Something was wrong with Mom and maybe she liked Horan enough to talk to her about it.

When Katherine and Horan got to the car, Horan said, "I want to stop by my house a moment to get something. I won't be a minute."

Once inside, Horan hurried to add some of the smaller items from the canvas bundle to a bag, then went back to add a nightgown and toothbrush in case she needed to stay over with Katherine. If Katherine was sick, Horan could always send Lily to spend the night with Angie.

Because Lily might have no idea her mother was having a rough time physically. Yes, Lily had told Clark she thought her mother was sick. But how much had the little girl taken in the changes that Horan was sure had grown worse since Christmas?

The sun had set and the light was rapidly disappearing from the sky as Horan locked her door, hurrying to get Katherine home. She'd drop her off behind the cottage, then go back to the street to park. No need to feed the fantasies of the woman on this, her last night in the big pink house.

By the time Horan got back, Katherine had the cottage door unlocked and the light on. Such a dim light, such a cold, dark space in which to live. And Katherine had lived here for how long? How miserable. And right in sight of her 'real' home, as she apparently saw it, the well-known Victorian her grandfather—some sort of grandfather—had built.

Couldn't she have found a better place for herself and her daughter before this?

"So, before Lily was born, were you here all by yourself?"

"Oh no, my mother was here. My mother died when Lily was four."

"It looks like a tight fit."

"It would have been if she hadn't died. Lily was getting too big to sleep in the same bed with us."

"Didn't you want to find something else by then?"

"I couldn't. Any more than I can now, even if Clark bought the house. Unless we can prove we have rights to this end of the property."

"She's not going to give you any trouble about your rights to the cottage, I wouldn't think."

"You never know. The owners over the years have given us a bad time."

"The county will have a recording of your rights."

"They don't. We looked. But Lily knows she needs to protect it ..." and then as an afterthought, "... in case I can't."

Horan didn't say anything. She had her own thoughts, but the realization that Katherine had devoted her life to protecting the right to live in this dark, tiny cottage disturbed her. All those trips they'd made to the library, two and three times a week, had probably been to give them a bright, cheerful place to be, and some joy.

Though truth be told, Lily was a joyous child most of the time. Except when she was thwarted in some outrageous plan, such as donating hundreds of books to the library, and through the book slot at that. Telling her no had not made Horan happy, but she hadn't expected the outrage Lily had expressed.

And if she'd known all that she knew now, the answer would still have had to be no. Except now they knew there were only about fifty books, not a thousand.

She wondered vaguely what John Steele or his assigns, that Aunt Agnes for example, had done with the rest of the books. She knew Lily's theory, but there was no proof, just the romantic notions of a ten-year-old. And she didn't want to trouble Katherine about those right now. If she was coming down with something, Katherine didn't need to worry about old books.

Katherine had boiled water and made tea. The two women sat at the table and Horan emptied the bag she had brought: a few small notebooks, old-looking, some folded large sheets of heavy paper, a couple of pencils.

The heavy paper needed special care as they unfolded it. Horan helped clear the table and Katherine laid a towel on it before the papers were set down. "Just in case," she said.

Horan nodded. Even a tiny bit of food could damage this find, whatever it might be. She guessed the top item was a map.

When they got the thick sheets fully unfolded, and gently constrained from refolding by laying books on the corners, they could see it was a house plan, without a doubt the house plan for the big house: 1 Main Street, Steeletown, was written in the lower right corner. This was the sheet Lily had showed off last night and put back in the packet, then asked Horan to keep the whole stack safe.

With delight, Katherine pointed out the rooms to Horan. Here was her room, a tiny space between Aunt Agnes's at the front—she was sure she was right about that—and Isabelle's master bedroom to the rear. Perhaps, Katherine thought to herself, the very room where Isabelle had entertained her father, either for a single night—perhaps his last night before being redeployed, if one of those stories about Sam White were true—or for the duration of her marriage, perhaps likewise to Sam White if one page of the big book were true.

Maybe she should look for divorce papers. Well, it was too late for that. For anything.

But seeing her mother's bedroom certainly gave her a sense for the first time that her mother had been a real person. How odd to think at this late date that she had had years and years of real life of her own before Katherine was born.

On her own in a way, but always with Aunt Agnes, apparently. And just how deaf had Aunt Agnes been? Blind would have helped, too.

Ben had managed to spend his four nights with her because Isabelle had been 'out.' Katherine never knew where she went on those occasions, but she was used to it. And a good thing she did spend the night elsewhere so often. Because where else would they have gone, Kate and Ben? Certainly not to Ben's house. Yes, his wife had been away, but Angie and Arabelle were home alone. Weren't they? And Angie no older than seven, Arabelle several years younger? How had Ben managed to be with her those four nights in a row, the same four nights his wife was away? The same four nights, if not more, that Isabelle was away? She'd never know.

What she did know was that it was a good thing, however disreputable, that Isabelle was away so often, because from it she had Lily, and Lily was her treasure. Forget the shed. Lily was the real treasure.

Her mind had drifted, and in the silence Horan had traced various rooms with a finger. As Katherine's musings returned to the paper before her, she realized there were parts of the drawing she didn't understand. She could see all four stories laid out, attic and basement included. She could see that back stairwell Lily had mentioned. She had no memory at all of such a thing. Exploring would be fun, even if just on paper, but time was short. They would need to go to the end of town, to the pier, to watch the procession, which was bound to start soon given how dark it was.

She could easily see Lily having fun on her own exploring mysterious spaces of that sort, after Katherine was gone. It gave Katherine both a pang of sorrow and great comfort that Lily would not miss her, she'd be so busy exploring, reading, gardening, doing a good job on her homework ... and who knew what other passions she'd develop as the years went by.

Given the thoughts she'd just been having about Ben, about her own father (Sam White or otherwise), the idea that Lily would be occupied with 'passions' was not the image she wanted. 'Let's just call them projects,' she thought.

Time to go. Even now Horan had stood to put on her coat. The night was mostly clear, and chilly. Katherine got her warm coat and together they walked out into the night. Katherine was feeling better, enjoying the cold air and the light breeze, feeling alive, feeling that her life was more and more in order, enjoying the recent success of getting herself a car and all the ... what? Yes! Pleasure that had been part of the promise that she could have it.

But as she and Horan walked along together, Katherine was also feeling that time was short. She hoped to be upright until Lily's school started up again, not even three days away. Three days? Could she pull off all she had to do and still be in good enough shape to drive at least as far as the next state? To leave Lily some appropriate parting words in writing? To create some deceptive clues to carry with her so the car could not be traced back to Ben, to Lily?

And within those three days would be New Year's, tomorrow, spent at Ben's. Then Sunday when Angie would leave. And then school on Monday. And if all went well, by the time the beloved daughter got home Monday afternoon, the ailing mother and the borrowed car would be gone.

Lily would think Mom had gone to bring her father back, because Katherine would say so, would mention a distant destination, would provide a timetable for when to expect them to return, sufficiently far in the future that Lily would have time to settle in and learn whatever new ropes she needed to survive on her own. And then to keep living on her own when Mom didn't return.

Maybe she'd even go so far as to make up a bed for Sam White, father and grandfather, in the cottage, Katherine thought. Things like that that would lend an air of realism.

It all depended on her energy.

She would have liked to spend days looking at the house plans, remembering how things had been, thinking of what she would do to improve it when it was hers again. Well, Lily could have that fun in her quiet evenings at home after Katherine was gone.

And probably Lily would find ways to correlate windows and eaves and stories she knew so well from the outside with the house plan and enjoy it even more than Katherine would. Even more than Katherine would have.

They were almost at the pier, and Katherine was feeling yet more buoyant. Her plan was developing. Empty spots were filling themselves in.

"There they are," said Horan. "The procession is starting."

"How will we ever know which one is Ben's?" asked Katherine.

"Oh, I think we'll know," said Horan with a big smile.

What had Katherine missed? She'd paid no attention to the decorations they'd all been working on all day.

The weather, so unpredictable this time of year, had held so far. The first boat, by tradition an ancient tug kept for this purpose plus a few ceremonial launches from the boat yard each year, was recognizable because its entire shape, from high bow to smokestacks, was outlined in Christmas lights.

It had announced its arrival at the pier with three toots of its horn. Loud cheers went up, and a few firecrackers exploded.

Katherine hadn't realized the whole town would be gathered on the pier. She clung to Horan's arm.

The boats were spaced a minute or two apart. Katherine asked Horan when to expect theirs, but Horan just shook her head.

Horan was trying to move forward in the crowd. "I love this parade," she said. "Every year Clark goes out with some friends on Ben's boat. And every year they come up with something more creative than the last. I can't wait to see this year's all lighted up."

A dozen boats had gone by now, to cheers and applause. They motored past in a line, perhaps a quarter mile out into the harbor, in the strait that would take them past the headland at the north end of town. Then they would turn around before they reached the far-east end of town and make a second pass. "That way we can see both sides of each boat," said Horan.

They waited a long time. There was a break in the procession. Someone's timing had been bad or perhaps there'd been a breakdown. And then all at once the crowd let out a loud 'oooooo.' Katherine couldn't see the next boat, but Horan said, "There it is." Katherine couldn't tell if the crowd was pleased or something was amiss.

And then there it was. The whole of Ben's boat above the deck was built into a model of the old pink Victorian on Main Street. It was pink, it had all the right windows, it had all the elaborate eaves, the porch.

"See the garden?" said Horan.

Katherine hadn't seen it. But there, over the place where they'd been sitting to have their fish sandwiches, was now a flat area, half grass and half garden, with a few small buildings in all the right places.

And flood lights were focused in such a way that the crowd could see it all.

The crowd knew it for what it was and cheered.

Katherine felt a pang. Her house!

"I hope they took pictures," Horan said. "Maybe the library can make an exhibit of all the decorated boats."

Katherine wanted to say, "Maybe they can make an exhibit of my house." But then she was afraid that it would become even more sought after, that Lily might have to defend it and her right to live there, however that might all work. Katherine realized she was still picturing life as it was and hadn't really accepted a different future, such as the one in which Clark had bought the big house.

The last of the boats went past. Ben's boat had been near the end, and then the parade concluded with a modern-looking sailboat from the local boatyard. Katherine was surprised to see the large sign on its side: J. S. Steele Boats. And then under it: For Sale.

Even now, the first boats were making their second pass, and in a matter of half an hour the whole parade had dispersed, the boats going back to their home piers and docks.

The cheers went on for a good while. They could hear them even as they walked away from the pier, even as they approached Horan's car parked around the corner from the cottage.

Horan said, "I'll go get Lily now. Or I can stay the night with you, and we'll see if Ben brings her home. Or keeps her."

Katherine's fatigue was growing by the minute.

"Though I have to warn you that it usually takes them a long time to disassemble the decorations, and the harbor has a rule that all the materials have to be cleaned up by 6:00 a.m."

"Oh," said Katherine.

"So how about we go in the car down to the docks where Ben's boat is, or soon will be, and congratulate them and tell them 'good job' and arrange with Ben and Angie for Lily to spend the night. Or if you're too tired, I can. And then I'll come back and keep you company overnight."

"I don't need you to do that. I'll just go to bed. If you don't mind going out to the docks to tell Lily to spend the night at Ben's, I'll send along her things."

"OK, don't forget we have dinner at Ben's at 2:00 p.m. tomorrow. Do you want me to pick you up?"

"No, I'm sure I can manage."

And so Katherine had the cottage to herself. As they had driven down the road beside the big house, she could see that the for-sale sign was gone. Of course it was. Clark had bought the house, or was still buying it. But for herself, nothing had really changed, nor ever would. She needed to sleep. She told herself firmly that the house was safe, the shed was safe, the garden was safe, and she could sleep as long and as deeply as she wished. It was, in fact, her fate to sleep without rising. But first she needed to save some time to prepare things for Lily. Tomorrow morning might be the only time when she could do that.

## SATURDAY, JANUARY 1, 1986 – NEW YEAR'S DAY

AND SO THE REMAINING days were spent. Of course no one came to claim the shed or cottage. Katherine was climbing the hill to Ben's the next day, on New Year's Day, after a full morning of contriving deceit in the form of diversionary clues for anyone who stumbled on her body along the route she had chosen, and hiding them so Lily wouldn't see them. But the uphill climb was exhausting. Then who should happen to drive by but Clark and Horan on their way to the dinner, and Katherine was able to luxuriate in the soft upholstery of their backseat for the final half mile.

Ben greeted Katherine with a lingering kiss and caresses of an unseemly nature except no one could see them in his foyer. "Marry me," he said.

Katherine ignored him. She wanted to say, 'Yes, except I can't.' But that was too complicated. And she knew it would be simpler just to say no.

Then she remembered about the car and turned back to him, and he kissed her again. She wanted to ask him for the car keys for Monday, but she didn't want Lily to know anything about it.

So when Ben said, "Do you want to trade places with Lily tonight? You can sleep here with me, and she can sleep at home?" Katherine said yes.

It would give her a chance to get the car keys and so on without Lily being aware of anything except that her mother was having a sleepover with her father.

But Angie had another idea. "Lily can stay, too. Aren't you guys going to the library tomorrow? It's closer this way."

And so even though they later remembered the library would be closed for the whole holiday weekend, it was arranged.

Katherine went into Ben's bedroom, the first time she had been in there. She enjoyed the thought of tossing her things on his bed, as she might do if she were indeed at home. Just this once, she thought with a deep sense of irony.

"Will you marry me?"

She didn't know he'd come in behind her. "Yes," she said.

"When?"

"A week from today, next Saturday," she said.

She wasn't deceiving him. She would marry him then. If only she could.

She knew she'd made other plans. But there was a will to live that kept exerting itself, providing its own plan, and according to that unrealistic, unreal plan, she said, 'a week from Saturday,' and meant it.

"I'll tell the girls!" he exulted.

"No, let's keep it a secret. For a few more days." Both her life paths were OK with that.

"OK, but I think Angie would want to hear it in person. And she leaves on Sunday, tomorrow."

"OK, we'll tell them tomorrow." What harm would it do? They could rejoice, if that's what would be in their hearts to do, for a day. And then Katherine would be gone.

The problem was, she felt now she would die before Saturday, but Ben didn't know anything about that. So it would be OK with her to be gone for good on Monday, but he would feel she had lied to him in promising to marry him the next Saturday, and she wasn't lying to him. It was just that other reality expressing itself. She couldn't help it. Life would not let her buy into that plan of death, so Life told its own story, and in that story she would marry Ben on Saturday. She got it.

Ben had left Clark in the kitchen to serve dinner so he could follow Kate into the bedroom. He had to ask her again. His sense of his own existence demanded that she say yes, and it was so strong, had been so powerful since the boat, since they had found their way to the front berth on the boat and united heart and soul, that he could not imagine that she might say no, but just in case he had to make sure and hear it again.

He had had a potholder in hand when he'd asked her on their way into the living room, and then she had agreed to spend the night and made her way toward the bedroom, and he had tossed the potholder to Clark and said please serve dinner, we will be right there.

And then he had followed Kate. His Kate. The love of his life, the one against whom all others were found wanting.

And this time she had said yes. She had kissed him and he thought she had whispered, "God forgive me, yes."

Whatever that meant, yes was all he wanted to hear.

Then he went to the table, then he went back to the bedroom and found Kate bemused and looking out the front window. "It has begun," she said, and smiled and let him pull her along to the table.

She was in a different world. She was in a world of the living, of Life Itself. She wouldn't die. She would play out her plan, of course. And things would happen according to the plan. But Life Itself would go on.

She hoped Ben and Lily would realize that when appearances might lead them to other conclusions. Horan and Clark, too. Life Itself would go on.

As it always had and always would. She could see that plainly now.

She watched the proceedings at the table with great fondness, though she ate next to nothing. Why eat? Life Itself would sustain her. She found she was amused that they all felt the need to take bite after bite, again and again.

"Kate, eat something," said Ben. "It's delicious."

Kate ate something.

Tomorrow Lily would not be able to go to the library and find Katherine's father. So far she had only a name. Lily would hold onto him, whoever he was, or had been, for her whole life. Just as firmly as she would hold onto the house. Lily didn't put one above the other, maybe didn't have that firm attachment to John Steele that Katherine had. Maybe that was the problem with knowing one's father, as Lily did. She knew for herself the difference between real and wished-for.

Overnight Saturday Katherine curled herself around Ben but found she couldn't sleep that way, so they spent the night as if Life Itself insisted on their being aware of each other, touching each other, finding little cold spots and warming them, finding little sore spots and rubbing them until they eased, finding little lonely spots and caressing them. Katherine felt she had had no moments of sleep in between, but awoke refreshed.

## SUNDAY, JANUARY 2, 1986

LIFE ITSELF WAS STILL having its way with her. She wasn't tired, she wasn't hungry, she didn't need to go home, she paid no heed to Lily and the way she sassed Ben, treating him as a ten-year-old treats her dad, treating Angie as she would a sister.

Yes, Life Itself was having its way with both of them, with her and Lily. They paid no mind whatever to each other.

Katherine found she liked it. Life Itself was freeing, easy, lovely, light, had its own plan, held Katherine by the hand and eased her along the way.

The four of them had a quick breakfast of bagels and cream cheese. Lily wanted to know what happened to Sam White, but the library was closed. "Someday I'll find him," she told Katherine in a most sincere way.

"For all I know, he neither lived nor died," Katherine said. "My mother used him to make me. That's all."

Lily didn't like the way her mother was acting. She was uneasy that she had spent the night in Ben's bed. She had heard them giggling and thrashing about until dawn. She was tired and grumpy and wanted to go home, but then Ben suggested they go out fishing.

"We have enough time before Angie goes to the airport. I'll drop you home on our way to the airport shuttle. Grab something warm and we'll be on our way."

Angie, all packed for the flight, made sandwiches. It took them an hour to get the boat ready for fishing. A brisk breeze was blowing, and the water as far as they could see in either direction was choppy. Ben maneuvered the boat out beyond the little island Katherine and Lily had visited because it was in just the right place to block the wind.

They could feel the calm as soon as they got around to the north of the little island.

Ben and Angie got down to work setting up the fishing equipment. Katherine said she didn't need to fish, but Ben handed her a rod anyway, then helped her into a cozy spot at the stern, right next to him. The two girls already had their hooks in the water at the bow and were clearly enjoying each other's company. Before Ben sat down, he went back up to the bow.

"All set?" he said. "Lily, Little Love, Angie knows more about fishing than I do. You're in good hands. See you later."

"OK, Ben," said Lily, then corrected herself to say, "OK, Dad." And smiled at him.

"I think Daddy's in good hands, too," said Angie. "Take a look."

Lily turned around just in time to see Katherine holding Ben around the neck with her head on his shoulder.

"Mom looks tired," said Lily.

"She can always go below and take a nap," said Angie with a wink.

"Then maybe he'll come up here and fish with us," said Lily.

"Hmm, I sort of doubt it," said Angie.

"Oh, OK," said Lily. "But it would be fun."

"Do you want to know how I found out he was your father?" asked Angie.

"Sure. And when. I know it was before I found out," said Lily.

"Yes, but not by much. He didn't know your mom hadn't told you until the other day."

"She promised she wouldn't. I think he knew that."

"Probably. But a lot of time people don't keep their promises. Anyway, did you know that my mom was married to Daddy when ... when Kate got pregnant with you?"

"No. Well, I guess so? I don't know. I thought you had to be married to have babies."

"It's certainly the best way," said Angie. "He told me they fell in love, though, even though he was already married to my mother."

"I wonder how that happened," said Lily.

"I don't really know."

"Maybe they'll tell us," said Lily.

"Maybe. Or maybe it's private."

"Private? Oh," said Lily. "I just know it was here in town. Because Mom's never gone anywhere else."

"Maybe they met at a party. Anyway, they liked each other and then they fell in love and then they had you."

"So you can have a baby even if you're not married? As long as you fall in love? I see," said Lily. "But how did you find out? About me?"

"It was the day before Christmas Eve, and Daddy and I were shopping for the gifts we gave everyone around the tree, and he suggested I could give you that photo album. Then on the way home Daddy said that that would be the perfect way to let you know he was your father. And I was shocked. I think he forgot I didn't know. Then he saw my face and said, 'Well, you needed to find out sometime.'

"So then we talked a lot about him and my mom and their divorce—which was later—and how even with the baby he never got to be with your mom, and how much he loved her for all those years since they made you, and then how he saw you at volleyball and didn't know it was his daughter but he suspected when he heard your name, and then he went to your birthday party and realized the dates were right. Well, and because once he saw your mom, he knew of course. And then he realized he was really happy."

"Oh, Angie. I'm a little confused. But I'm glad he's happy. And I'm happy, too, to know who my father is. Do you think if they get married they'll have another baby? That would be fun."

"I don't know. Maybe they're too old. Old people don't have babies."

"So it's a good thing for me that they met each other because I don't think I would want Mom to have met someone else. Then I would have had a different dad."

"I don't think that would have happened," said Angie.

"I think they really do love each other, and I know Ben wants to get married to Mom. But I think we might have to live in your house. Or else your dad would have to live with us, and we don't have much room."

"Let's wait and see," said Angie. "Have you had any nibbles on your hook?"

And so they talked about other things, and Angie thought she might tell her dad that Lily had a few points of confusion when it came to making babies.

"I always wanted a sister, Angie. So I'm glad Dad had other children."

Lily was thinking it through. She had her life and memories and Angie, her sister, had a whole different set of memories. A different home. Different moms. But so close, right in the same part of the same town, that they might have seen each other, maybe several times, and not known they were sisters. It seemed weirder and weirder.

"Angie, do you mind that your dad had another family not very far away?"

Angie, usually cheerful, was quiet for a long time. "Lily, I am happy you are my sister. I did find out a couple of years ago that Daddy loved someone who wasn't my mom, and that was hard. Can you imagine how that would be?"

"No! If Ben loved somebody else, it would make Mom unhappy."

"Right, and my mom was unhappy, very unhappy, that my dad loved somebody else. He told her that. I remember. I said, 'Why can't you just love Mom instead of someone else,' and he said, 'I can't help it. I love her. But don't worry. She doesn't love me.'"

"Who was that that he loved who didn't love him back?"

"Your mom."

Lily said, "I don't believe that."

"Well, he said it. You can ask him sometime. To me it seemed unfair. I wanted him to love my mother and he didn't, and he wanted this other woman to love him, and she didn't. I think it's like your big house. Your family had to get out, but no one moved in."

Lily got up. "Here," she said, handing the fishing pole to Angie. "I've got to talk to Mom." She had to step over various lines and hooks and boat things, and she was in a hurry and tripped and nearly fell, but in a matter of half a minute she was on her way through the hatch and to the stairs that led to the stateroom. Mom and Ben weren't there. She saw the door ahead, and crooked her fingers into the small handle and pulled it open.

Mom and Ben were all tangled up and seemingly connected with each other, partly dressed and partly naked.

Angie was right behind Lily. She took her by the hand and pulled her up the stairs to the deck. Lily sat where Angie put her. Angie gathered up the fishing gear, taking care to put it away properly, not only her own but all of it.

Lily still hadn't said a word but was sitting looking at nothing at all with her mouth a bit open and droopy.

Angie didn't know for sure what Lily had seen, and it really wasn't up to her to do any explaining, she knew that. And she could hear murmuring below. She expected her father to emerge soon and put it all to rights. But meanwhile, Lily might need more than she, Angie, was giving her.

Finally, when no one emerged from below, Angie said, "Lily, listen. It's one way grown-ups have of loving each other."

Lily said, "Mom told me. Sort of. But I didn't know it was like that."

"No, I suppose not," said Angie. "But it's what people who love each other like to do. It's a way of getting close."

"They like it?"

"Yes."

"I'm glad I'm not married."

"You're ten."

They could hear steps approaching, Ben emerging from below. He reached over and gave Angie a brief hug, then took Lily by the hand, sat down, and had her sit on his knee. He kissed her forehead, and said, "I love your mom, Lily. I have for years. That's what men and women who love each other do to feel close to each other."

"Angie told me."

Ben looked at Angie and raised his eyebrows. "And your mom? She said she told you."

"Sort of."

"I think you should knock before you come into a closed room, Lily."

"I think you should get married, Ben, to my mom."

"You are right."

"And I don't ever want to get married because ... ."

"I know. But when the time comes, you will want to get close to the person you love, and that's the best way."

Katherine had not yet climbed out from below. Ben looked down the stairs and could see her sitting in the stateroom, her face in her hands. "Come on up, Katherine," he said. "Lily is OK."

"It's OK, Mom," said Lily. "But you should get married. And just so you know, I'm never getting married. And I'm sorry I didn't knock first. And I think you should lock your door."

The sun was getting low in the sky. Time to put away the boat and get in the car. "I have soup and homemade bread for our supper," said Ben. "Thanks to Angie's help. Let's get ourselves home and warmed up, then make an early night of it."

"But aren't Clark and Horan coming for dessert? Because they had something to tell us? I want to hear before I go back to college," said Angie.

They had arrived home. "Right. I'd forgotten. And we also have something to tell everyone. Are you sure you're all packed?"

"I'm going to go check one last time."

Lily went with Angie but came back within minutes. "Angie says she can't think and talk at the same time. I think she means she can't think when I'm talking."

Ben smiled. "Maybe so," he said.

Katherine didn't say anything. Lily had expected her to say she had to go home, but she didn't. She seemed to be lost in thought, sprawled out on a living room chair, looking out the picture window. There was nothing to see out there but other houses with their lights on, and dark sky, with clouds covering the moon.

So Lily had nothing to do.

She wandered around her dad's unfamiliar living room. He had taken the tree down. Supper was over, Clark and Horan hadn't arrived. She drifted toward Ben, who was reading the paper. She stared at him, then stuck out her tongue, but he didn't notice. So she flicked the paper, then flicked Ben's nose when he put the paper down.

"What, Lily?"

"I don't have anything to do."

"What do you want to do?"

"Sit on your lap."

"You're pretty big to sit on my lap," said Ben.

"You would let Mom sit on your lap if she asked you," said Lily.

"True. But that's different."

"How's it different?"

Ben said, "Kate. Change of plans. Let's share our secret, or this girl's going to end up spanked for the first time in her life."

"I dare you," said Lily.

Ben smiled. "Kate. The time has come."

Kate said, "Oh OK. Lily, can you get Angie?"

"No," said Lily.

"OK, no Angie," said Ben. "And unless Clark and Horan show up quickly, it will be no one but the three of us.

Katherine suddenly realized that a point of no return was upon her. It was the last moment when she could reasonably pull back and say no.

Tomorrow she would be gone. Let them have their moment.

But right now she was feeling excessively grounded. Life Itself had begun to elude her. Lily was being a brat as never before. Ben was doing what he probably always did on a Sunday evening after supper, reading the paper. This was how things were, apparently, at home with Ben. And Lily didn't like it.

Oh well. Lily wouldn't be here. She would be in the cottage. Or conceivably in the big house, though that whole notion seemed ephemeral, Clark's words nothing but wisps in Katherine's mind. It was easier to picture Lily with her books, with her garden, with her keeping an eye on the big house. She, Kate, would not be here with Ben. The marriage wouldn't happen. Lily would not be here in this house with her dad reading the paper. Lily would be contentedly playing out her existence as an independent-minded ten-year-old, enjoying herself as always.

So this strange girl who looked like her daughter Lily would not have reason to pop up and misbehave again. Next Sunday, Ben would be able to read his paper and have no need to think about Lily. He would have read Katherine's letter of apology and the excuse of going to find her World War Two Missing In Action father. Aka the guy who had planted the seed that had led to her birth, existence, and now death, and who otherwise didn't exist. Except as part of The Plan, the excuse for her leaving.

Tomorrow.

Suddenly she had to go home. She had things to do. Get this little step out of the way, then get on with The Plan. Save Lily from foster care, let her grow up on her own. It all started tomorrow.

And then as Ben had them sit down, Clark and Horan appeared, rang the bell, came in, shucked their coats, rubbed their cold hands together, and smiled enormous smiles. They were excited, full of cheer.

Conversation happened for a while, did you catch any fish, too bad, worth a try, and so on.

And then Ben was done with waiting. "OK, enough," he said. "Katherine?"

"We're getting married. On Saturday."

She knew she'd said it in a rather flat voice. Where was Life Itself when she need a boost?

No one said anything.

"One p.m. All invited," said Ben. "Now Angie needs to go to the airport and Lily and Kate have to go home. Thank you all for coming."

He stood and moved them toward the door. Horan offered a ride but Mom said no. Lily said, "Dad, if Mom doesn't marry you, I will," and everyone laughed. Katherine thought she didn't look as though she was kidding.

Kate took Ben aside and whispered, "I need the keys before I go. Don't let Lily see."

"Why not?" he asked.

"Just don't. Come on, Lily, get your coat on. We've got to get home."

As Katherine moved toward the door, as Angie was dragging a suitcase out of the hallway to the bedrooms, Clark cornered Ben. He had just slipped the keys to Angie's car to Katherine, so Clark saw something happen but she didn't know what.

When she had him cornered, she said, "We also have something to share. It will take one minute. Everyone, listen. We just signed the papers on the pink house. I've bought it. I take occupancy this Tuesday. I was hoping for sooner, but that's how it worked out. I hope Lily and Katherine can move in that afternoon."

"Wow, Mom! Did you hear that? Thanks, Clark. It will take us only a couple of hours to move. This is so perfect."

"It is, isn't it," said Ben. "How amazing of you, Clark and Horan."

"It was all Clark, believe me," said Horan. "But I will help you move."

"Not necessary," said Katherine snippishly. "Lily is strong."

All clustered in the front hall as they were, everyone was conscious of Katherine's lack of excitement, or even of engagement. It was almost as if she hadn't heard that the big house was to be owned by friends. Safe from strangers and developers. No one knew what to say, except Ben. While taking the suitcase from Angie, he said, "Kate, how wonderful! An answer to generations of dreams!"

"Good for Clark," said Katherine in a flat voice. And then in a whisper Ben heard her say, "I failed."

Angie gave hugs all around and headed out the back toward the cars. Ben closed the door behind Clark and Horan, who went to the car, and Katherine and Lily, who having decided not to go with Ben, began their walk home.

From the time they left Ben's and began their walk through town to their house, Katherine found herself looking at everything as if for the last time. Well, it was for the last time, face it, except for tomorrow's necessary last-minute errands. Ben would be at school so she'd just said her final goodbye to him. Grumpily. Without a kiss. Oh well. She couldn't very well make a big fuss out of saying goodbye for no apparent cause. Better this way.

Then tomorrow she would walk back to Ben's to get Angie's car and she would be on her way. And as soon as she acknowledged that simple fact, she lightened up. Life Itself began to flow through her again. This was it. When she drove away sometime during the day, it would be as if she were entering a dark tunnel, and she would drive and drive until the tunnel entered oblivion. She would not stop except for gas. It had truly begun.

She reckoned she wasn't really going to die tomorrow. Maybe Tuesday or Wednesday. She could sense it coming. She felt she had just enough steam to get through the rest of her list and then get the car and drive far enough away that no one would know she was from here. If she could make it to the other side of the state, or to Montana or North Dakota or somewhere like that, no one would think of looking for her way back in the islands of Puget Sound, nearly at the Pacific Ocean.

So she was glad to have three days or so of life left. That's how long the black tunnel appeared to be from the perspective of this moment.

Ben would be at work when she walked to his house and got the car. She would bring it back to the cottage, keep it out of sight, carry the few things she needed in shopping bags, nothing to cause snooping eyes to take alarm. And she would start driving.

She had chosen the most northerly route, State Route 20. It would not be the most obvious route to take on her journey east. She had found it on a map at the library and taken the most cursory notes about how to get there. Essentially, it came down to driving east, and east and east and east. Because State Route 20 came right into Steeletown, and if she got on it and never got off, she would end up all the way across the state and beyond, and she would probably never be found.

Except, she realized—quite all at once, in a panic—that if she left the registration papers in the car, the cops could trace the car back to Ben. The car was probably in Ben's name. The license plates would also cause them to look him up. If they found the car.

And then they'd know the body was hers and then they would know Lily was alone, and right away they would put her in foster care.

Why hadn't she thought of that before? After all this time?

What other impediments hadn't she thought of?

When they were nearly home, at the little path between the shed and the cottage, all looked well. No signs of potential buyers trampling in the mud. No locks tampered with. The hens were squawking, looking for feed. Katherine hadn't thought to feed them last night, but Lily would take care of it.

So she was left to think about license plates and whether stealing a car wouldn't be a better plan.

Then she had it. She would go to the first large parking lot, steal a car, and leave Angie's in its place. Except that she didn't know how to start a car without a key.

No no no, the whole plan could not fail on this one problem!

She was feeling desperate. And she couldn't do anything until tomorrow or Lily would find out.

Unless … .

"Lily, I think I need to go find my dad. He's older now. We need to get him and bring him back here and take care of him. Like my Mom and I did for my Aunt Agnes."

"Cool, let's do it! How will you find him?"

"Go to Spokane, ask around. Too bad you have school."

"Yeah, I don't want to miss school."

"Maybe I'll go while you're in school. There's not another vacation for a couple of months."

"Too bad we didn't find out sooner. How would you get there?"

"Maybe Ben would let me use Angie's car while she's back at college."

"Good idea. When would you go?"

"Soon. He's not likely to live forever."

"Sounds great!"

"Can you take care of yourself?"

"Sure, for a few days."

Katherine's thinking had shifted. If she could make it to some distant town, ditch the car, and then walk until she died, it would be just as good as driving until she died. Better, because the car could be traced, but she couldn't, not if she was on foot.

The best thing for Lily would be for her to disappear, but it didn't matter how she disappeared.

She did all the usual evening things, buoyant, cheerful, hopeful. 'Of all times to be hopeful,' she said to herself.

## MONDAY, JANUARY 3, 1986

LILY WAS EQUALLY CHEERFUL the next morning. She loved school, she loved Miss Clark, she was ready to leave extra-early.

But Mom was strangely huggy this morning. "You have your key, right? In case I don't make it back from the ... library when you get home?"

Lily showed her.

"I'm going to go get some groceries this morning. Is there anything special you want?"

"Do we have enough butter?"

"I'll check. What else?"

Lily was finally on her way. Miss Clark was standing in the classroom door. Lily was tempted to give her a hug, but knew better. This was her teacher Miss Clark, not her special friend Clark, almost family.

Lily had been planning to check out the garden when she got home, and found herself thinking about it at school. Miss Clark was teaching them multiplication, and she got the idea that if she multiplied twenty carrots by fifty cents each she could make ... um ... ten dollars!

So far it wasn't raining, and she'd been so busy that she hadn't done anything with the veggies for days. She'd see if Mom wanted to go over to the little island this Saturday so she could sell that many carrots and maybe some potatoes, whatever they could carry. She didn't know if she could take the little wagon on the ferry without paying extra.

If the wagon wouldn't work, she'd have to use her backpack. But she wouldn't be able to take as much. And how many carrots were left, anyway? She often sold twenty or thirty.

Thirty would be fifteen dollars!

As soon as school was out, she hurried home. The garden needed her.

When she arrived, Mom wasn't there and the door was locked. There were bags of groceries on the floor, so Lily put them away: Tuna, peanut butter, flour, butter. Poor Mom, so many heavy things to carry!

And where was Mom? There was no note telling Lily to meet her at the library or someplace else.

Lily went out to the garden. The carrots all had tall, healthy-looking tops and no signs of having been trampled. She counted sixty of them, enough for several trips to the market, and even more worthwhile if she could also take potatoes, too. She thought she would dig one plant to see how many potatoes had grown deep in the soil from it.

Then she and Mom could have potatoes for dinner these next several nights. She used a trowel and carefully dug around the roots descending from the stem. She didn't reach the spuds themselves until she had dug down more than a foot, and then there they were, all growing close together. She yanked the plant out and started removing the potatoes from the loose soil around the plant. Some were huge, most about average, and of course some very tiny ones that would never develop.

She cleaned them and set them on the footpath: Twelve large potatoes, a total (not counting the very small ones) of twenty-five or so. A good harvest from one plant.

And, she counted twenty intact plants and maybe another ten that had been broken off by heavy boots, but the potatoes would still be fine deep below the surface as they were. Thirty times twenty-five was … . Enough to feed them all winter and still have some to sell.

The newly planted greens were ruined, though. Some tiny seedlings, the size of grains of rice, were growing, but she couldn't tell if they would turn out to be oriental greens. She might have to wait to sell greens to the Chinese restaurants until next year.

Lost as she was in planning future gardens, she did not see the policeman walk up behind her.

She gasped in surprise, then said, "Hi."

"Are you Lily Steele?"

"Yes."

A woman in regular clothes appeared behind the cop.

"Where is your mother?"

"I think she's at the library. She wasn't here when I got home from school."

"What are you doing here?"

"I live here."

"Where?"

At this point Lily wasn't sure she should answer any more questions. Hadn't Mom always told her that the less people knew, the better? She hoped she hadn't said too much already.

"Where do you live?"

"I need to talk to my ... ." Here she wasn't sure if she should say mom or dad or parents, so she didn't say anything.

"What are you doing in this garden?"

"Growing food. Potatoes and carrots right now, and a few squash are left, too."

"Who told you you could be here? Did you get permission from the property owners?"

Lily said, "This is our property."

"That doesn't appear to be the case," said the cop. "You're going to have to come with us."

"I can't. I have to do my homework. I've got a busy schedule this afternoon."

"Unless you can produce a parent, you are an abandoned child and you will be taken into custody by children's services," said the cop.

"My dad is probably still at school."

"Your dad is at school? Doing what?"

"He works there," said Lily.

But here Lily knew she wasn't supposed to disclose that Ben was her father. She could ruin everything for him if people found out. That's what Mom had told her. She wasn't sure how it worked, but she did know her mother hadn't told people Ben was her dad, no one but Clark and Horan.

"OK, we'll call him so you can tell him you'll be at Child Protective Services. What's his number?"

"I don't know."

"Which school?"

Lily resolved not to say another word. But she had to find out something.

"Who said I was abandoned?"

"Can't say."

"The woman standing in that window up there?" said Lily, pointing.

"Yes," said the woman.

"Why does she think that?"

"Saw a woman pull up in a car, run into that shed there and run off with a couple of bags, and drive off."

Lily was struck dumb. Not Mom, because they didn't have a car. But who else? Had they been broken into and she hadn't even noticed?

"Hold on," she said.

"You can't leave," said the cop.

"I want to see if we had a break-in," said Lily.

But when the cop and the woman followed her, she stopped. Where was her key? Inside, in her backpack.

She didn't want to open the door for them, or have them follow her inside. Wasn't there some law that would keep them out?

The woman was gone from the window. Lily looked at the window longer than she needed to to distract the cop, to make him think she was looking at something important up there.

Then she bolted.

She ran out to the alley and then down the alley into the deep grass beyond, to the place where the stream had cut a deep bed under the chain link fence. The chain link fence that surrounded the blackberry patch, where she had gotten stuck before.

If she could get under the fence, they would not be able to get her out. Unless of course they figured out how to get into the fenced-in area by way of the depot and past all the blackberry bushes.

But as she got closer to the stream, the adults close behind her, she didn't know if she'd have time to get under the fence. Should she wiggle under head-first, or foot-first?

She realized if she went head-first, she could get her face badly scratched, and that her feet were protected by boots. So when she got to the stream, she flopped down into it on her belly and started backing up. She had to push with her hands, and couldn't make progress with her feet except to hook her toes over some large stone or sink her toes into the mud and pull.

She found some stones for her hands to help her push, to protect her hands a bit. Her fingers were frozen. She kept reaching for mud with her toes to get some traction. But she was making only a little progress.

The cop reached for her outstretched arms. She pulled them to her sides and tried pushing from there. She tried to rotate her body so she could get her head and shoulders under the cross piece at the bottom of the fence. She had one shoulder under when the cop grabbed her other shoulder, hooked his fingers into her armpit, and pulled.

Lily resisted. She stretched her legs out behind her, grabbing whatever would give her a hold with the toes of her boots. One hole in the mud allowed her to pull back several more inches, but her face ended up in the storm-fed stream. She banged her front teeth on a rock and scraped her chin along the gravel of the stream.

She had managed to get her head under the cross piece of the fence. But she was stuck, her face deep in the center of the stream.

When she couldn't hold her breath any longer she had to push with all her might with her toes. She burst out of the fenced area, got her head above water, took a deep breath, coughed and coughed again, and felt herself being lifted up by the cop.

Lily knew she really needed help now. But who would help her? She couldn't get Ben involved, but what about Miss Clark?

"I'll tell you where my mom is," she said in a draggy voice. She intended to sound defeated. She thought it might pay for them to think she'd given up, so she threw in a few tears for effect. She wasn't sad so much as mad. Plus she was cold and her hands were bleeding and aching from the cold water.

Reluctantly she got into the squad car. The woman sat next to her in the back seat. Lily directed them to Miss Clark's house. Lily hoped that Miss Clark was home by now. And she hoped she would understand the words Lily would say, the words Lily was carefully working out as they drove the three minutes to Clark's house.

The woman and the cop got out. The cop said, "Show us." They walked up the front walk. Lily hoped Miss Clark was watching, and catching on that something was wrong. Lily had her little speech all prepared.

Maybe Miss Clark could fool them into thinking she was Lily's mom, but where was her real mom? Maybe she was at the library, or even here having a quick visit with Clark. Why hadn't she thought of that? That would be perfect.

They rang the bell. The door opened, and before Miss Clark could say anything, Lily threw herself at her and said, "Mommy!"

"You're her mother?"

"Who's asking?" said Miss Clark.

The cop and the CPS woman ran through the complaint. Miss Clark said, "That's where we have our garden. We have permission from the woman who lives in the big pink house out front. Lily, look at you, all dirty from the garden! Right into the shower with you. And take off your boots here before you track in all that mud," said Miss Clark in a motherly sort of way.

"Kids," said Miss Clark. "Do you have any? I feel like I have about twenty-five."

"Do you have any ID?" asked the CPS person.

"Do you have a warrant?" asked Miss Clark.

Soon Clark was able to close the door with Lily safely in the house with her. Then over cocoa Lily told her all that had transpired in the garden and her attempted escape, and that Mom was missing, gone to find her father.

"I thought you didn't find your grandfather," said Miss Clark.

"I didn't. But I think she did. She thinks he lives in Spokane or Great Falls or someplace like that."

"They're far far apart, Lily, and it's a long trip. And besides, how did she drive? You don't have a car."

"I have no idea."

"Maybe she's just at the library. Or the store."

"She did go to the store. The groceries are at the house."

"And no notes, no messages?"

"None that I saw. And I did look, because if she goes somewhere, she tells me."

"I'll call Horan and see if she's seen her."

Lily could tell Clark was talking on the phone but not what she was saying. And then Clark was back shaking her head. "She hasn't been at the library all day," said Clark.

"OK, I'd better go home. I've got my homework to do, and I'll make some supper, and probably by then Mom will be home."

"Lily, right now this has got to be your home. I just told a cop I'm your mother. If they come back, you need to be here. Let's go in my car and get your backpack and whatever else you need, clothes for school for the next couple of days ... ." At this Lily must have looked shocked, because Clark added, "... just in case."

So they did the errand. Lily was surprised not to see Mom at home. She took her bookbag and clothes out to Clark's car, but then went back in to look around for a note.

She found a few envelopes with her name on them under the bread box. And she saw that the usual stack of money was much shorter. She took some money in case she needed it. And she saw a large stack of papers that looked like the ones from the shed the other day, though she didn't know how Mom had gotten them. She put all these in a paper bag to keep with her, turned off the light, locked the door, locked the chickens in, and got back in the car with Clark.

The sun was setting. And no sign of Mom.

So Mom was probably off looking for her father, Sam White. Lily didn't blame her, but she hadn't expected her to go so soon. She wondered if she had been to the library this morning when Horan was in her office and had learned something new. Lily could see she'd have to go look at the World War Two records again and see what Mom might have learned. Or maybe it was in these papers she had brought with her, though they looked old, not like some new jottings from a library visit as recent as earlier today.

Lily had wanted to tell Mom that when she found her father, she couldn't expect him to be perfect. But he would be worth finding, a part of her. Just like Ben. Ben had made Lily angry more than once. But she also loved him and was grateful for him, and felt protective of him.

Lily did her homework at Clark's dining room table. She had given Clark the two biggest potatoes from the garden so she could use them for supper. She was anxious for supper to be over and Ben to come and Clark and Horan to tell their surprise. But she also was keeping an ear open for Mom. Lily had left a note and if Mom did have a car somehow, she could even drive to the Ruths' house. Or of course walk as usual.

So when Lily did hear a car, she jumped up from the table. But it was only Ben.

Ben, who walked in and announced Angie's car was gone and asked if Katherine had taken it.

Only Ben, but he did give Lily a hug, and then asked where Mom was, and did she know about the car? Then Lily told them about the cop and the lady who tried to take her, and how Clark had understood something was wrong and had protected Lily and sent the cops on their way. Then Lily told Ben about Mom finding her dad, and as she told him she began to feel sad. Before she was done, she had fallen into his surprised arms, sobbing.

"What, Sweetie? I thought you just said you were expecting her to go. Though she didn't say anything to me. It does seem odd."

"She talked about it when we got home last night, but I thought it was more like she would like to go someday. I didn't think we had enough information about him. Just a name. Sam White. And it might not even have said White, just something beginning with W."

"Sam White? My dad's best friend was Sam White. He was from here, from right here in Steeletown."

"What?"

"Yes. They went to high school together. And then they went to war, but not together. During the war my dad was a POW, and I don't remember what happened to Sam White. Just that he was injured, came home for a while, and was redeployed. He had gone into the Coast Guard and had an accident at sea, I think. Information about it is in the library. I did a report on the soldiers and sailors from S-Town for a report in school. I still have it somewhere.

"But that still doesn't make him your mom's father. We'll have to look closer at the details, like the dates when he was home."

Lily grabbed him around the neck and kissed him and asked, "Did my grandpa Brown come home from the war?"

"He did. He was captured late in the war and let go at the end of the war. But he would never talk about it."

"Is he still alive?"

"No, he died three years ago. Not here, though. He died at a VA hospital in Seattle."

"I'm so sorry I never met him."

Then Lily was quiet, lost in thought. She wanted Mom to come back, and she wished she knew that Mom was safe. When was the last time she had driven? Would she run into one of those winter storms that everyone talked about?

"Daddy, do they have bad weather on State Route 20?"

"Why State Route 20?"

"Mom said."

"She told you she was leaving?"

"Sort of. Someday, I thought. But maybe now."

"That's a rough road in the winter. It goes through the mountains. Why did she choose that?"

"I don't know. But can we go see if she broke down or had an accident or something?"

Ben and the Ruths had question after question for Lily, and after a couple of hours, with Lily looking droopy, they debated where she should sleep. Edna was still away so they tucked her in her bed, all three of them kissing her goodnight, and then talked among themselves for several more hours. What was Katherine up to?

No one could make sense of it and it was late. They would look for clues in the papers Lily brought tomorrow, and meanwhile Katherine would probably show up. As Clark and Horan escorted Ben to the door, he said, "I think Lily is right. We should go find her. I don't know how we would, but like Lily, I'm afraid she's going to run into trouble on the road."

"Can't you alert the state police?"

"Good idea, but I think we need try to find her ourselves, too. Leave no stone unturned. I've heard the cops don't go chasing after runaway adults without a good reason."

"Can you get time off?"

So a plan was hatched. Ben couldn't get away until after school on Wednesday, Tuesday being the awards ceremony for the seniors who were graduating early. He and Lily would need to pack for a few days. Horan said she would be off all day Wednesday and would put together winter travel items like blankets and food for the expedition.

By then Katherine would have had about two days' head start.

Katherine had made herself some tuna sandwiches, also egg salad. And she had hot tea to drink, to start with. When she really wanted it, when dark set in, when she was beginning to feel chilled, the tea was tepid. She'd also had to stop to pee by the roadside a couple of times. So by dark she was barely to the Mount Baker turn-off from State Route 20.

She hadn't gone far at all, and she was exhausted.

She'd thought about driving up the Mount Baker highway, and then heading out on foot until the end, but then it would be obvious that the car and the body were related to each other. So she drove on.

She drove on until she was drowsy. A nap was in order. Not a long one. Just a quick refresher so she could keep going. If she could find a good place to stop.

It was cold and rainy, and then as the elevation increased it became snowy. Huge flat flakes hit first, then tiny particles pinged against her windshield. If she stopped now, the car might become buried, hard to get out because of bad road conditions. Or because no sign of the car might remain.

So not a good time to stop. She could overcome the drowsiness. Just think. Think about the big house, her visit to it pretending to be a cleaning woman, the later discovery from the papers Lily had found that there was a back stairwell. It had been a long time, but where might that back stairwell come out on the second story? She couldn't visualize where. Maybe the stairs went straight to the attic? Maybe to maid's quarters up there, ones that reasonably would have no need to be exited and entered from the family bedroom area?

And if the stairs went to the attic, then the books she remembered filling the shelves could have been carried up bit by bit using those back stairs. Similar to Lily's suggestion, but of course she hadn't known about those stairs. In Lily's view, Agnes would have carried them up there. But what about the little attic she'd had to climb up to with a ladder? She'd have to look when she went back home.

She wasn't going back home.

Suddenly it was the most reasonable explanation for the books, though. And hadn't Clark said she had signed the papers? And then hadn't she mentioned that the stairwell was locked?

But just in case, she needed to get word to Lily. In case she didn't put two and two together.

She needed to leave a note. She'd do it when she stopped, after she was out of the snow, when she was drowsy again.

She wasn't drowsy now. She was full of adrenaline, anxious to find out if the books were in the attic. She wouldn't need a ladder now that she knew about the secret stairwell.

The little space that she had had to climb to as a child to get the Christmas ornaments was not nearly as big as that house's attic was likely to be. It was a place apart, she could plainly see now. Hadn't it had plumbing, electrical conduits, various pieces of equipment?

It also might have her Shirley-Doll. She could just about see herself climbing the ladder to get the Christmas lights, and then putting her precious dolly on the edge of the opening so she could gather the tangle of lights. And there she might have remained, forgotten. Mom needed to let Lily know that, too. Lily might love Shirley-Doll just like her mother, if she were there, if Lily ever went up there.

The snow wasn't falling here. She seemed to be descending, at least for the moment. She wasn't used to snow. It rarely fell at home in Steeletown. Lily in her ten years had probably seen it only a handful of times close up, and maybe never this much accumulation. She had of course seen that ancient volcano Mount Baker in the distance, at least partly snow-covered year-round, a familiar sight to all residents of Steeletown.

Such a remarkable place John Steele had picked out for their family! Where the mountains met the fertile valleys, the ones that had become farmland. And the farmland met the sea! Where else did that happen?

Katherine had no idea. She had never been anywhere.

But she had heard visitors talk about the beauty of their area, its uniqueness, its ability to grow food, its benign climate, if you didn't mind rain. Though not as much rainfall as Seattle, not by half. One got used to it.

And now she could add snow—driving in snow—to her experience.

It had certainly slowed her down, the snow had. She felt as though she would slide right off the road if she drove at anything like normal speed, and when the snow was falling heavily it ruined the visibility.

She wasn't ready to slide off the road, not yet! Yes, sliding off the road and the car disappearing into some stream would suit her purposes, but not yet! The end was days away. It wasn't time.

The Plan! She had been so absorbed that she hadn't thought about her plan. So how was Lily doing now that she had realized her mother was missing? She would know Katherine had gone looking for her father. All that Lily knew was that he might be in Spokane. And had Katherine mentioned Great Falls to her, too? She knew that Katherine, if she found him, would bring him back so they could care for him, a thought she could hold onto indefinitely.

Lily would understand. She had found her own father, and that had made her happy. Well, not always. Lily was capable of being angry with him. Aunt

Agnes had made Katherine angry more than once, too, though Isabelle—Mom—had warned her sternly not to let on how angry she was.

That was hard.

Finding her own father would be a delight. She had never really believed it was possible until Lily had found Ben.

But it was a ruse. She'd almost forgotten finding him was a ruse, an excuse for driving away so she could die and no one would know Lily was alone, including Lily.

And Lily could stay in their little cottage until she was grown up and keep an eye on the big house. No! She had been invited to stay in the big house. And probably she would. Why not? But she couldn't picture it, Katherine couldn't. Already the Plan was different. She had had one idea for months now, and her mind kept going back to it.

Had Aunt Agnes signed papers that allowed them to stay there? She had said so, hadn't she? Were they wrapped up in the canvas? What would happen to Lily if she wasn't allowed to stay? What would stop a new owner from building a fence to keep her out? Or tearing down the cottage?

Well, if it was Clark who bought it, if that had worked out, then probably no problem.

How would Lily keep an eye on the big house then?

Where would she live?

Where would her home be?

These were old questions! Stop worrying about old issues, she admonished herself. She kept slipping into old thinking. The idea that Lily might live in the big house had no place in her thinking. A little girl couldn't manage a house of that size!

Katherine had planned to leave Lily all sorts of notes about what to do. But she could never cover all she needed to know. Good thing she was such a sensible child. In the end, she had left no notes except for an older Lily. Labeled for Lily on her twelfth birthday. Lily on her sixteenth birthday. And a few others.

And good thing she had not taken time to leave a lot of notes. Everything had changed. It was confusing to think about how much had changed.

Katherine was cold, and now seriously drowsy. And there seemed to be no break in the guardrails that ran beside the single-lane road. Winding, climbing steeply, dropping off suddenly, utterly dark, no other cars—but now at least no snow. The snow had fallen here earlier, though.

A single set of tire tracks through the snow showed someone was not far ahead.

She tried driving in those tracks to keep her mind busy while she kept an eye open for a pull-out. The breaks came so quickly that she had already missed one, and now it was guardrails again.

She hadn't counted on it being so dark. No streetlights. No towns.

She found that while lost in thought she had accelerated so that she barely made it around the next curve without running off the road.

It would not do for her to run off the road and be found in the car. The entire Plan would fail, and Lily would end up in foster care, trying to make a home of someone else's house.

What was it Lily had said? Something like, 'home is where you are, Mom.'

And that meant she would never find a home.

'That means having the big house has nothing to do with having a home, Mom,' whispered the ever-sensible Lily.

## TUESDAY, JANUARY 4, 1986

DAWN WAS BEGINNING TO show itself. Katherine had successfully driven through Monday night. Gradually the dark gave way to gray, then to clear skies ahead. She was descending from the mountains to the plains below. She could see a town ahead, or a few streetlights maybe. Or a gas station. She would pull off there, whatever it was, to let herself sleep for a few minutes.

It was a gas station. She filled up. It needed only half a tank. She pulled out of sight around the building, moved some things around on the back seat and covered herself with blankets. It was uncomfortable. She should have brought a pillow. And she didn't have Lily next to her to keep her warm.

She ached, she was exhausted, but if she died right here in the car, all would be lost.

Sleep began to descend. Lily would be missing her. 'Where are you, Mom? Come home.'

Yes, it would be like Lily to say that. But didn't she see, she couldn't have Mom anymore? Mom was dying. Better you be on your own, Sweet Girl. Wasn't that what Ben had called her?

'Come home,' she heard again. 'As long as we're together, Mom.'

'Not possible, Lily,' Katherine's mind insisted.

'Sure it is, turn the car around and come back to me.'

'But I am dying.'

'Don't leave me by myself, Mom.'

'But you need to keep your eye on the big house so you can live there someday.'

'Tomorrow. I'll live there tomorrow.'

'Do you promise?'

'Yes.'

'Oh good, I'll sleep now.'

'Sleep now, Mom, and then turn the car around and come home.'

'I can't, I'm dying.'

'Not yet, you have time, come home, we'll take care of you.'

'Who is we?'

'Daddy and I will.'

And then as she faded into the oblivion of sleep, she heard them both say, 'We love you.'

Katherine, hurting, sank deeper into oblivion, dreamless sleep taking over. It snowed. The car was covered, her tracks were covered. The snow continued, a wind sprang up out of the mountains and blew more snow, buried her in white. She slept on.

A faint voice whispered: 'Time to go home. It's time, it's time, it's time.'

She let herself sink deeper into the soft white snow. It was time. 'Yes, it's time.' She drifted, settled. It was so cold, so peaceful, so still.

Peace was good, comfortable, a place without problems, white, soft, cozy, a sameness, trackless, pure, simple, easy, still.

BUT NO.

She pulled herself upward, opened her eyes. She was still in the car. She must not give up until she was far away from the car, full of IDs as it was.

'Come home, Mom. It's time.'

And then a new message from Lily: 'We're coming to you. We're coming to you. Come home, come home, come home, turn around, come home. We're looking for you. Where are you? Come home.'

Katherine woke fully. She felt rested. She got herself some crackers and peanut butter, found the water bottle half-frozen, took a few sips.

She had no way to get the snow off the windshield except to use her bare hands. They hurt from the cold. Maybe the rest would blow off as she drove. Lily! She needed to find Lily. To say goodbye to Lily. To lie down with Lily and get warm again.

She was so cold.

She drove on, up a hill, down the hill.

The driving was helping blow the snow from the windows, so she drove faster. She needed to be able to see out.

A day with no traffic, snow on the ground everywhere, clear skies for now. When she sped into an intersection where State Route 20 met a small country road, she braked, slid past, spun the wheel, sideslipped into a wide arc, skidded sideways, backward, sideways, gained traction, faced the side road, turned to go on using her chosen route, then ... a decision: should she go on? It would be so easy to stop right here. Or take this pretty little side road with its fluffy snow and no tire tracks and where might it lead? She needed oblivion but she would leave tracks.

No, stick with the Plan. And straight ahead was the sign for State Route 20. She took it. For now. She took it because that was The Plan. She would take it while she thought. She would take it at least to the next intersection.

Somewhere she would stop and get out and walk. Where there was no snow to tattle on her.

Ben was on her mind. She hadn't left him a note about the wedding, that it had been the truth when she'd said yes. She had meant yes.

For such a long time she had daydreamed about being married to Ben. That he would get divorced and marry her, at the same time admiring him for not getting divorced. How sweet it would be to wake up, the two of them, and plan what to do today with their sweet baby Lily. How awkward for him, not to be able to live in his nice house anymore. Well, because his ex would probably still want to live there. And he would of course live with Kate and the baby .... No, that wasn't right. With Kate and the baby and her mother Isabelle.

Needing to live in the cottage had definitely been a complicating factor. But necessary.

He was married to Caroline. Katherine was married to the house. Ha! Put that way, it sounded idiotic. She felt a spark of rage.

Did she love him or not?

He had gotten divorced. But she hadn't, in a way.

Is that why she had been avoiding him, because he would be asking her to choose? Between him and the house?

'Death was the only way to avoid that choice,' whispered her mind. 'That's why you chose it.'

She drove on. The day was turning out to be sunny. For now. But she could see dark clouds ahead. No matter.

She was drowsy. And she had to pee. Braking, she drifted down an icy hill. A river, not frozen, ran under the road at the bottom.

A pull-out. Good. She pumped the brakes. The car skidded. She eased off the brakes. It continued down the hill sideways, headed for the pull-out. More or less. She might hit the guardrail, though. She accelerated slightly. The car gripped the road and sailed across the river. She had missed the pull-out. She put on the brake, came to a stop in the road, got out and peed.

She was tired, achy. The tell-tale snow surrounded the car.

Too bad Lily couldn't live with Ben in the big house. If Clark really had bought it. If Clark really let her live there.

But no one would let Ben have Lily. There was no legal connection. No one knew officially that he was her dad. He might say so all he wanted, but would the State hand a ten-year-old girl to a man just because he said he was her father?

She was back in the car, had trouble accelerating on the ice, found herself sliding toward a ditch by the side of the road. Slammed on the brakes, spun so she was facing backwards.

She banged her head in frustration. Why was it so hard to disappear?

A car swerved to get past her. It was headed up the hill she had just slid down. She was in danger, sitting as she was straddling the center strip of State Route 20. Well, she was the danger. It wouldn't do to be killed here. She put the car in gear.

Up above the road where the driver had just disappeared she could see the snowy silhouette of Mt Baker. She had not made much progress. Mt Baker, visible from Steeletown, visible from here. She had not gotten far. Farther than ever before but not far.

Even now Lily might be telling Ben that her mother had planned on using State Route 20 to go find her father, far away as he was. She could see Ben pointing out Mt Baker to Lily and saying, 'State Route 20 goes past Mt Baker.'

Lily could ... live with Ben!

Lily could live with Ben. They could learn to get along.

Lily could live with Ben! She needn't live alone!

Could she do that? No, not at the moment. Only if ... .

Only if Ben was known to be her father. Legally.

And only Katherine could make that right.

She had to go home. Now. Before it was too late.

Before she could no longer make it official, that Ben was Lily's father.

'It's time,' said the voice in her head. 'Pull over, you are so tired, sleep your deep sleep, it's time to go.'

A pull-out was just ahead. She would pull over and sleep. She began to brake early, gently. She drifted into the pull-out, stopped gently. She got into the backseat and took a sip of water. Covered herself. Sank into sleep. Slept long and deep.

The sky was dark when she woke. She turned awkwardly, painfully, and drifted back toward sleep. Lily could live with Ben.

Perfect.

Except no one knew he was her father. Except Lily. And Clark and Horan, and of course Katherine herself. But no one official of any sort.

She sat up, her mind on high alert.

It was too late.

It had been time, and then she had slept, and now it was too late.

The birth certificate was incomplete.

Too late!

She lay down, huddled under her blanket. It was what? Tuesday? Maybe Tuesday night.

She'd thought she might die on Tuesday. Or possibly Wednesday.

She must get out and walk. Disappear. Then Lily would not be put in foster care.

'Or,' said her inner voice, 'you could go home and sign the birth certificate so Lily will have a real father to take care of her as she grows up. So she won't be lonely. So the cops won't get her.'

'Good idea,' said Katherine to herself. But she was drowsy. Her thinking was fuzzy.

'Go now,' said the voice in her head.

'But The Plan!'

'Ben is not in The Plan. Give Ben a chance. He loves you. And he is her father. A father is a worthy thing.'

'I don't know about fathers. And I'm so tired.'

'Think of Lily. Didn't she call you home? She needs you. And she needs her father for when you're gone. Go home. Make it your new plan.'

Katherine could feel herself drifting deeper, deeper, not exactly asleep but close.

'Home, Katherine. Time to go home. It's the new plan.'

'In just a minute.'

'NOW.'

Katherine sat up, fully awake. Where exactly was she? She had to get home. Lily needed her. She hadn't left any instructions for Lily! Lily was only ten.

And Ben hadn't put his name on the birth certificate, and neither had she put his name there.

## WEDNESDAY, JANUARY 5, 1986

SHE STARTED UP THE car. The night was black, no traffic. She turned out and headed back up State Route 20. She could barely see the way. She drove back toward the mountain, which loomed up so high, black on black creating a starless blank so black that it seemed it would block her way.

Her two thoughts repeated became a sort of mantra to her: Go home. Add Ben.

She drove on through the sunrise, the sun bright in her rearview mirror. Heavy clouds piling up from the warm, damp air blown in from the distant Pacific lay before her ready to block her way. The mountain was even now elevating and chilling that ocean air and turning it to snow, so it was with snow and a driving headwind and cold that she climbed back into the mountains.

The mountains—the Cascades, the North Cascades the sign said—loomed above her, and above them the skies were gray. 'Gray because it's snowing up there,' she realized.

She remembered weather reports from the past that said such things as 'worst storm in a century' and maybe this was one of those. Because what could be more formidable? She entered the zone of obscurity a few minutes later. It felt like being buried.

But she drove on toward home, even though the world was invisible. And she was invisible.

But she didn't feel alone. In her mind's eye, or maybe it was in her heart, she could see Ben and Lily coming to find her.

It was Wednesday. Clark called the Principal's Office and demanded to speak to Mr. Brown himself, even though the secretary said he was in a meeting.

"Ben, listen," she said. "I'm going with you and Lily. You might need my help."

"Thanks," was all he said for a moment. Then, clearing his throat, he said, "We're leaving right at 3. We need as much daylight as we can get."

"And that is how Ben and I, and of course Lily, brought Katherine home," Clark told Horan later.

"I got everything ready. We were able to leave right at 3 o'clock."

They drove east on State Route 20. From the time they turned onto State Route 20, right in downtown Steeletown, they could see the worsening conditions up over the mountains.

"Here we go," said Ben. "Everyone keep your eye out for cars pulled over or off the road. I don't see how she could have made it through this."

"And you don't want to hit a deer," said Clark.

Lily could see the squall line up ahead, up high in the mountains. At least that's what they called it in the ocean. On their side they still had sunshine, coming as it was from the west. But straight ahead of them, all was gray, growing whiter.

"Complete white-out conditions, it looks like," said Ben.

No traffic came from the mountains. No one was out driving. The sun was setting behind them by the time they reached the Mount Baker turnoff. Soon the dark of the winter evening would mean that even if they passed a car, they wouldn't be able to see it.

All three of them strained to see anything in the dark, in the white-out conditions just ahead. They would be in the snow themselves in another minute.

"There!" yelled Lily. "Here comes a car! Is that Angie's car?"

Ben slowed to a crawl. At a distance they could see a car descending slowly down the steep hill from the obscuring gray and white roiling mass still visible in the last of the sunlight at that high altitude.

The car was swerving. Ice on the road. Snow from last night at that elevation must have melted in the day's sun and refrozen.

The car had begun to spin, but only slowly. It looked like it might be able to stop as it began to cross the center line, but no, it kept coming, accelerating.

The spin tightened as the car spiraled down the hill.

Ben pulled all the way to the left to get out of its way. The car, pointing uphill for the moment, drifted rapidly backward down the uphill lane, facing uphill, bulleting downhill, spinning again, now facing the far guardrail where Ben had taken refuge, just missing broadsiding them. Lily could see the front grill as it swung past her. She thought it would take off the door handle, but then it veered toward the opposite guardrail. And accelerated. A crash would stop her, but at what speed? With what damage? At what cost?

Maybe at the cost of her life.

Lily held her breath. Dad and Clark, in the front seat, were yelling. Clark had Dad by the arm, Daddy had the steering wheel in his grip. Out the backdoor window Lily could see Angie's car, across the highway, continue to slide downhill backwards, accelerating as the hill's steepness increased, spinning slowly. In moments it would be beyond the guardrail.

Ben could see Katherine bowed over the steering wheel, not looking at the road, not moving at all.

The car with the unresponsive Katherine had now sped up so that if it drifted beyond the extent of the guardrail it would almost certainly end up in the roadside ditch. Ben spun the wheel. His car made a half-circle and drove as fast as he dared down the hill until he was well beyond Katherine's car. Rain mixed with snow had begun to coat the windshield and his visibility was becoming more and more limited despite his windshield wipers.

He had a plan, if he could see, but he had just a moment to make it work or Katherine might slam into the passengers' side of the car, risking both Clark and Lily. He braked. Should he try it?

Katherine's car was still accelerating toward the guardrail or maybe the ditch. He spun around again so he was facing uphill, positioned his car behind Angie's, flipped into reverse, and kept his foot on the brake as long as he dared. Then with only feet to spare, he took his foot off the brake. Angie's car drifted into his and together they moved more slowly down the hill until Ben braked them to a stop. He put his car in Park and ran to Katherine's door, pounding on it.

"Open the door," he yelled.

She roused herself dreamily, slowly. He repeated himself and she reached for the handle, fumbled a bit, then opened the door. He reached in a flipped the gear lever to Park.

Then he caught her as she slipped sideways out the door.

Lily and Clark had run up.

"Mom! Mom! Mommy!" yelled Lily. "It's time to go home!"

Clark drove Angie's car back to Ben's house. Ben asked Lily if she thought they should take Mom straight to the doctor, but Lily said no. Instead they took her to Ben's and put her in Ben's bed, and Lily crawled in with her and held her.

Katherine was cold, sleepy, not interested in talking. She clung to Lily.

Ben came in.

She said, "Tell Lily I'm home."

"I'm right here, Mom," said Lily.

Then Katherine said, "I need to sign. Sign now. Today."

"Sign what, Mom?" But Katherine didn't explain. She might have been asleep.

Ben made hot soup and Katherine had some and went back to sleep.

Lily came out after Katherine was asleep.

"Now what?" Ben asked her.

"Wait and see, I guess," said Lily.

So they waited. When night came, Wednesday night, Lily slept with Katherine again.

## THURSDAY, JANUARY 6, 1986

WHEN THURSDAY CAME, KATHERINE was ready for some hot oatmeal for breakfast. Ben had gone to the high school but had said call him if Lily or Katherine needed him. They were at Ben's house, and Lily had stayed home from school to take care of Mom.

"Tell your dad I need to sign. Today."

"Sign what?"

But she just shook her head. "Just tell him," she said.

Then Katherine told Lily she should go to school, so Lily did. Miss Clark was surprised to see her.

"I think you and Horan should come over to Ben's tonight. I think Mom would love to hear you really did buy the house."

"Is she really OK?"

Lily hesitated. "I don't think so."

"What's the matter?"

"I don't know. But she is weak and she sleeps a lot."

"Exhausted, I'd think."

"Maybe," said Lily.

So they all planned to gather on Thursday night. Ben had been home from the high school for only an hour. He found Katherine asleep in his bed. He felt her forehead. Was she sick? Lily came in and told him Mom said he had to sign something, she didn't know what. Katherine stirred.

"The birth papers, Ben. I have to add your name to Lily's birth papers. I have to go to the county offices and do that right now."

"Maybe tomorrow," said Ben. "There's no rush."

"Please, Ben. Now."

"Clark and Horan are coming. Let's do it tomorrow."

Katherine sighed. "Tomorrow, then."

The guests were expected at any moment. Ben helped Katherine move into the living room so she could lie on the couch. Lily and Ben sat on the floor next to her. Clark and Horan told her that they had bought the big house, the old owners had left, and now Lily would always be able to have her chickens and garden. As many chickens as she wanted.

"And live in the cottage? So she can keep an eye on the house?" asked Katherine. Her voice was breathy, halting.

"Good heavens, no," said Clark. She looked at Horan, who nodded.

"We have a perfectly good house already that we share with Edna. Aren't you and Lily going to live in the big house? Aren't you getting married to Ben on Saturday and all three of you can live there? Because I already told Ben I'd rent it to him."

Katherine looked at Ben. "Yes!" he said. "Remember, you said yes, you would marry me on Saturday! Do you still want to?"

Lily held her breath. Mom wasn't saying anything. Lily wanted to hear her verify it all over again. It was the first she'd heard of all of them living in the big house as a family, and it was exactly what Aunt Agnes had said, and it all depended on Mom saying yes to Ben.

And then while she was waiting for Mom to say yes, she remembered about Sam White. "Mom, Ben knows who Sam White was. He was from here."

Mom covered her face. Ben hunkered at her side and held her. "What is it, Kate?"

"So little time," said Katherine.

"What do you mean?

"I have to leave."

"You can't go anywhere. You're not recovered from your car trip. And where were you going, anyway? And why?"

Once they began, the questions poured in from all sides.

"Shh, everyone," said Horan.

"Ben," said Katherine. She held his head so she could whisper in his ear and no one else could hear.

"Ben, I'm dying. I thought I'd be dead by today. If I'm still alive on Saturday I would very much like to marry you. And put your name on Lily's birth certificate. I'd like to spend Saturday night with you, here or maybe in the big house. I hope very much to make it to Sunday. I think you need to tell everyone. We have a lot to make right in the next couple of days."

Everyone was surprised that Ben had suddenly collapsed in tears and assumed she had said no.

"Mom, marry him! Please," said Lily.

Katherine smiled at her, though she had tears in her eyes. "Yes, Baby. I will marry your father. On Saturday."

Then what was wrong with Ben?

He stood. He was unsettled. His voice was wavering. He was saying happy things, but as he went on he became less and less stable.

"First, Kate and I are getting married on Saturday."

"Yay," cheered Lily.

"Second, Kate and I would like to spend Saturday night in the big house."

"A honeymoon!" yelled Lily.

"And while we're at the courthouse getting married, I'm going to sign Lily's birth certificate."

"Oh!" said Lily.

"And then"—here he paused and looked at Katherine and she nodded slightly—"we will have a special gathering here at my house on Sunday night."

"A reception!" said Lily.

"A kind of reception," said Ben.

And then he told them all they needed to know and they gathered themselves around Katherine until she needed to go to bed.

## FRIDAY, JANUARY 7, 1986

Clark insisted that Lily should stay home from school. Ben said he could be home in time for lunch. Lily got the papers that she'd brought from the cottage and Katherine pointed things out to her and told her her theory about the attic.

They could see the attic on the house plan and the long staircase that ascended to it. And then they could see the little separate utility room that Katherine had accessed with the tall and scary ladder. Two separate spaces, the large attic locked, the small one open to anyone who might dare to climb up to it.

Katherine thought it was the kind of deception that Aunt Agnes might set up. Let only those with the keenness to figure it out have access to the true attic.

If Katherine was right, Lily's keyring would give access—the only access—to the real attic. Which meant that the Woman in the Window would never have been up there.

And oh, how Katherine wanted to see it for herself.

And, well, here she was. She was still alive. She and Lily could go and find out for themselves.

Lily had been lying next to her, turning away to cry, turning back to hold her, feigning cheerfulness.

Katherine said, "Let's go find that attic!"

"MOM! Mom, really? Can you?"

"Well, it would be easier if you could drive. And by now Ben has probably hidden Angie's keys. I'm not sure I could walk all the way down there. But I could try."

"No, Mom. You really aren't strong enough, and tomorrow is such a big and important day. But we could ask Daddy when he comes home for lunch."

So after he made lunch, Ben called Clark and asked her where the keys to the big house were. She sent him to the library to get Horan's housekeys to their house so he could let himself in at Clark's and get the keys to the big house. Then he put his daughter and his fiancée into his car. Lily had her backpack with her with the keyring and house plan drawings.

Ben had been having a rough day. Well, that was such an understatement that it upset him just thinking about it. Katherine was dying. She had assured him that it was the truth, and that this extra day was unexpected and sweet to her. When they got to the big house, the new house, the old and now new house, Katherine slid out of the passenger seat and stood at the gate and then bent over double. He ran to her side.

"What is it? Here, I'll help you back into the car."

"No, Ben. No. I'm just so ... happy. I'm going home!"

He wasn't sure how she meant it, but Lily was saying, "OK, let's go, Mom," as she swung open the gate.

Ben used the key from Clark's house, and they entered to a cold emptiness. The stairwell rose before them, but it was of no interest now. Katherine led the way, with Ben holding her tightly, kissing her from time to time. They were moving too slowly for Lily, who bounced on ahead. She turned left at the back of the house. "This way, Mom?"

"Yes, it's got to be."

When Ben and Katherine arrived, Lily was fumbling in her backpack for the keyring. Katherine was seeing it up close for the first time. It had about eight hefty keys on it, the old-fashioned steel kind that you'd expect to use to open some government building, or maybe a factory.

"I think it's one of these two little ones, Mom," said Lily. Katherine hadn't seen those, but Lily tried one and the lock began to turn.

Ben thought he might step forward to give her a hand, but Katherine pulled him back.

Lily wiggled it back and forth, and then all at once it yielded with a screech.

The stairwell was brightly lighted from a window at the top. No wide space was visible from where they stood. Lily started up, but Katherine said to wait, something wasn't right. Where was the attic?

"Oh, no problem, Mom," said Lily. "That's only the second-floor level. There's another set of stairs. It goes that way," she said, pointing toward the front of the house.

Lily was running up the steep stairs. "Careful," yelled her parents.

"Ready?" Ben asked Katherine. "Or are they too steep?"

"We've come this far, Ben, so much farther than I'd truly ever hoped for. I can't not try."

"OK, we can stop as often as you'd like."

From a distance they could hear a young voice say, "Oh, wow!"

So Katherine set her foot on the first step, and every few steps she could hear Lily saying, "Mom, Daddy, you've got to see this!"

When Katherine got to the window, she looked down on the tiny cottage, the henhouse, the shed, the garden. She looked out at the town, the harbor, the depot. By standing to one side she could see the library and its little park. And just south of there, the high school. And much closer, Lily's elementary school. If she had time, she would put a comfortable chair in this window and her stack of books and embrace all Steeletown, today's Steeletown and all her Steeletown memories.

"Hurry, Mom," said Lily. "I mean, if you ... can."

"Coming, Lily."

It was slow but she and Ben made it together to the attic. As she drew herself up the last few stairs and could see above the attic floor, a thousand books greeted her with a familiar and ancient smell. Skylights lit the room. A vast space stretched out in every direction. Dormers with windows provided niches on three sides, and in the front a vast window opened to the harbor and the island beyond. Taller as it was than most of the surrounding buildings, they could see for miles, probably as far as the mountains of Canada. And Mount Baker with its brilliant white cap framed their view in the middle distance.

Inside were walls interrupted by doors, some tiny, some tall and thin. "Look at this, Mom," said Lily, as she disappeared into one of the tall doors, her voice becoming muffled. "A passageway. I don't know yet where it goes. But I think it has a little set of stairs." When she came back, she said, "It's a rooftop place for chairs. And it has a metal thing that turns."

"For a telescope," said Ben.

"I know where the telescope is, Dad," said Lily, opening one of the small doors. "I just found it a minute ago."

"I hope there's a wall up there so you can't fall off," said Mom.

"You mean you were never up there?" asked Lily.

"Not up there and not up here," said Katherine.

Lily was running from space to space, from little door to little door, but Katherine said, "Ben," and began to sink.

"Lily, time to go," he said, as he struggled to hold Kate from falling all the way to the floor.

"Here, open the car," he said, tossing Lily the keys.

He guided Katherine down the stairs, then down the other stairs. She had insisted on taking another moment to look out over the town, but after a brief moment he urged her along, down and then out the front door. Lily ran back in to lock the stairwell, then locked the front door behind them and jumped into the car. Mom was lying in the back seat. Lily thought she was having trouble breathing.

At home they got her into bed, and she slept restlessly through supper and into the evening. Lily slept in Angie's bed and Ben slept next to Katherine or perhaps he didn't sleep at all.

## SATURDAY, JANUARY 8, 1986

THE SMALL GROUP GATHERED at the courthouse. A judge, a friend, met them and had them sign some papers. Then Clark, Horan, Edna, Lily, Angie, Ben, and Katherine stood in a circle. Katherine, supported by Ben, stepped into the middle of the circle, and the judge, Ben's friend Dennis, joined them there. Then all the others stepped forward and laid their hands on a convenient shoulder or arm of either Ben or Katherine, or both in the case of Lily. The few vows were made.

And then the judge took out another paper or two, and Katherine, after receiving a kiss from Ben, entered his name on the line that said Father for the child now named Lily Isabelle Brown Steele.

Lily and Katherine had talked about what her name would be and this was Lily's choice. Ben was hearing it at the signing for the first time, though, and Lily couldn't tell how he felt about it.

Dennis shook the hands of the Mother and Father and then the Child whose birthname was being amended. And he kissed the child and her mother. Then he turned to the father and said, "Well, Ben, what can I say. About time?"

Afterwards. Clark served lunch to Lily and Horan while Katherine and Ben made themselves comfortable at the big house. In Aunt Agnes's bedroom, where Aunt Agnes's bed was still in place. The events at the courthouse were all Katherine could manage. She had slowly climbed the long flight of stairs, Ben supporting her step after step. She now lay on the old familiar quilt on Agnes's bed. Ben removed her shoes and rubbed her feet.

"I think this is where it will happen, Ben. Very soon. Hold me."

The northern sky, all that Agnes's window looked out on, was gray. Only a few blocks away was the busy harbor John Steele had built, a terminal between land and sea for the transportation of goods to and from far-away places.

Katherine thought she was in the right place for her journey ahead, at home here with Aunt Agnes. But it would be too hard to explain to Ben.

Little light penetrated. The room was dim, somber. Ben held Kate as she had requested, but she was restless.

"Make love to me, Ben. This is our one and only wedding night. I've hoped for it for ten—more like eleven—years."

He rearranged things, helped her into her nightgown. Horan had been here before them with chrysanthemums, those fall flowers reminding them of the shortening of days. She had been cleaning, freshening, making all comfortable for Katherine. Ben helped Kate settle into the ancient bed with its fresh sheets and new pillows, then sat beside her.

"I'll be back in a few minutes. I need to get my things. But I thought before I go I would tell you about Sam White. Lily said ... ."

"Yes, we may have found him on my birth certificate. But it was hard to read. What did Lily tell you?"

"She mentioned the name to me, and I told her I knew a Sam White. He was my father's best friend in high school, right here in Steeletown. My dad went to college, Sam worked on a fishing boat. And then they got drafted. The war ... it was hard on everyone. I remember my father being gone. We thought he wasn't coming back. And Sam got wounded and was sent home to recover. He was in the Coast Guard. Then he was sent back and was part of the rescue at Guadalcanal. A real hero. But I don't know where he is now. There's a plaque with his name on it at that little park near the library. Did you ever see that?

"I must have," sighed Katherine. "I wonder if it's him."

"Probably, don't you think? Maybe Lily and I can find him."

He kissed her. "Do you realize you and I probably grew up together right here in town?"

"But I'm younger, a different school. High school at different times. I don't remember you until ... later."

He kissed her again, got his things, crawled in beside her, held her.

They spent the rest of the afternoon making love, and then he held her while she slept. They made love again in the night, and in the morning she was gone.

## SUNDAY, JANUARY 9, 1986

ON SUNDAY NIGHT THEY had their little gathering at Ben's house and told stories about Katherine. It was almost as if she was right there with them. Almost. But when they looked around, each of them, they couldn't seem to see her. She was always in the other room.

Lily thought she would like to spend her first night in the big house in her mom's old room. Ben suggested they go down to the house for a bit, but then spend the night at his place. "I know you want to be close to her, Lily, and so do I. But she spent much more time here. We'll be moved in soon enough."

So she and Ben stood at the window of the big house and looked down on the little cottage, her garden, her chickens, her shed that had held real treasure after all.

"She didn't want you to go to a foster home, Lily. That's why she wanted to disappear before she died, so no one knew you were alone. She forgot you had me."

"I got you just in time. And Angie. And Clark and Horan. But what I think she forgot is that I need her. There's no one else who's my mom. And there never will be. But ... ."

"But what?"

Lily didn't explain what. It was a new thought. Instead she said, "I want to get up in that little attic." She was pointing at the ceiling. She could clearly see the outline of the frame and its inset that Mom had had to push open to deal with the Christmas lights.

"OK, someday we'll do that," said Ben.

"No, it can't wait till someday, Daddy. I have to get something for Mom. Before it's too late."

"We'll need a ladder. Are you sure it can't wait?"

"It can't. I promise. And I have a ladder." She pointed to it out the window. It was leaning on its side against the cottage where she had left it after the big storm.

So they went together and carried the ladder. Ben thought that he'd just go along with Lily at this time of loss. They hosed off the mud and dried it, and carried it up the long stairwell. Ben had to lift it over the banister until it was resting on the second story floor, and together they opened it into its 'A' shape.

Lily looked up. She could probably reach the inset from the next-to-top rung. How had Mom ever pushed the inset out of the way when she was only seven, or maybe younger? Poor little girl!

Lily started up the ladder, and after stepping on the second rung, she looked down. She could see over the banister all the way down to the first floor. Ben inched his way over so he was between the ladder and the banister where he could break her fall should she lose her balance.

She held onto the ladder and went up two more rungs, then reached over her head and pushed the inset out of the way. Ben handed her his flashlight.

This was no attic, just a tiny space with some plumbing and electrical equipment. A little cupboard, maybe. The Christmas lights. And YES, Katherine's Shirley-Doll.

Lily felt unstable on the ladder. As soon as she had the doll in hand, she stepped down, stretching to pull the wood inset back into position. She handed the doll to Ben, and carefully stepped down the remaining rungs.

"For Mom," she said. "Her name is Shirley. She's been missing for thirty-five years. I'm going to give her to Mom to keep with her while she ... sleeps."

Ben hugged Lily and they cried a bit together. Then Lily said, "I have an idea, Daddy. It's OK to say no."

"What is it, dear girl? I'll do it if I can."

"Marry Clark."

"Marry Clark?"

"Yes. We need her. And this house is big. And I need help in the garden. And I need a mom."

"Well, now."

"I'm sure she likes you. And I know you like her. You could always ask her."

"Well, that's true. Are you sure?"

"Yes. I don't mind sharing you."

"OK then! Let's think about it for a while. And meanwhile let's get back to my house. For just a few more days. We'll lock up tight here and this old house of your mom's will take care of itself this once."

## WEDNESDAY, JANUARY 12, 1986

A FEW DAYS LATER, they gathered in the cemetery around the large pillar that said 'John Steele, Railroad Man, Founder of Steeletown, 1902' and 'Hannah, his wife.' Small headstones surrounded the large granite monument: 'Agnes Steele'; 'William Steele' and 'Millie, his wife'; 'Isabelle Steele,' 'Alexander Steele.' And now a new resting place for 'Katherine Steele, daughter of Isabelle.'

Lily planted lily bulbs around Katherine's stone, and then added a few at the foot of John Steele's monument. "I'm here, Great-Great-Grandfather, ready to get to work. Thank you for the big book and all your messages of what I should do."

"It should say 'Katherine Steele Brown,' Daddy, shouldn't it?"

"Well, do you want to be called Lily Brown?"

Lily thought for several minutes. "No, Daddy. I love you. But I have been a Steele all my life. I'm the last of the Steeles. When I was little, Mom's mom Isabelle told me to keep an eye on the Steele legacy, and I think I can do that best as a Steele."

"You'll be in the house. It will be easy to keep an eye on it that way."

"Yes, but from Aunt Agnes's room—yours and Mom's room—you can see the boatyards, the tracks, and beyond those, warehouses. It's all the Steele legacy, all my responsibility. I'd like to have that room for myself. You can sleep in the big bedroom. When I walk into those offices, I need to be a Steele."

Lily seemed to be lost in thought. "But I wish I could be a Brown, too."

"You are a Brown. You just didn't know it. I'm sorry I made your mom keep it a secret. I'm proud of you."

"I was hoping you and Mom would have another baby. My own baby sister."

They held each other tight again, and Ben kissed Lily's head. "That would have been beautiful."

Another pause. "Daddy! You know ... you and ... ." She paused.

"What?"

"Clark. We talked about it already. You and Clark. What if you did marry Clark? You could have a baby. You're not too old, are you? Angie said when you're old you can't have a baby."

"No, uh, I'm not too old. And I don't think Clark is too old, either. But Lily, I love your mom. And I always will."

"But Mom died. And I need a mom, and you need a wife. And you like Clark, right? And I know she likes you."

"I do like Clark. And she likes me. We're friends. But that doesn't mean she'd want to be married to me."

"To us."

"Right, to us."

"I think she wants to. Let's ask her."

"Really?"

"You and Clark could stay in that big bedroom together. There's room for both of you. And I could stay in the front room so I can keep an eye on things. And if there's a baby, she can stay in the little room where Mom slept when she was a little kid."

There was a long pause, and Lily grew impatient. "Let's ask her," she said insistently.

"I don't know."

"What don't you know? Let's do it."

Ben gave the matter some thought, maybe one or two more minutes of thought. Through his head went images of just the two of them in that old pink Victorian. And learning to live together, just the two of them, day by day. Lily was used to having her mom there all the time. They even slept in the same bed. Lily was right. She needed a mom. And Ben needed her to have a mom.

"Yes, we'll ask Clark. Do you think we should do it now, or wait?"

"I think we should do it now. Maybe you should ask her on a date. You don't need me."

"Oh, I think I do need you. Because she will be marrying both of us."

"Now?" said Lily. She still had tears in her eyes but she was also grinning.

"OK. I'm a little nervous, but I think I'm ready."

The attendees were wandering away from the new hillside grave in little groups or one by one. No one was surprised that Ben Brown and his newly discovered daughter Lily Steele were spending a bit more time there, touchingly standing in each other's arms.

So then it was a little surprising when young Lily seemed to spring from his arms and run like a frisky puppy across the grassy lawn until she reached the last few visitors.

"Clark!" she said.

Clark, Edna, and Horan had been walking together. Horan and Edna went on, but Clark turned back to see what was what. One never knew with Lily.

"Clark, Clark, Daddy and I need to talk to you a minute. We have an idea. Daddy said you can always say no. I'm not sure I agree with him. I mean, I hope you don't say no."

By now Ben had caught up with Lily. Clark gave him a hug. "I'm so sorry, Ben, Lily. I'll do what I can to help, Lily, you know I will."

Lily jumped up and down, then gave Clark a hug.

"We need to ask her first," said Ben.

"Not me, right? You?"

"Yes, me," said Ben.

Clark looked over her shoulder to see if Horan and Edna were waiting for her. And in fact they had moved on but then had turned around to see what was happening.

"Is this not a good time?" asked Ben.

"Daddy, now!"

"OK."

And then he took them all by surprise by getting down on his knee. "Clark, Ruth, will you marry me? Us?"

"Ben Brown, whatever are you thinking?"

"It was actually Lily's idea. She knows I like you. And she's convinced you like me. And she loves us both. And I thought it was a splendid idea."

"So soon, Ben?"

"I think so. But it IS soon, so soon." He gave Lily a hug. She was looking at him.

Then she pulled him down to her so she could whisper in his ear. "Mom doesn't mind, Daddy. She just wanted me to be taken care of. And you can't do that by yourself. We need Clark."

Then Lily moved over to Clark and gave her a hug around the waist. "Daddy and I need you," Lily told her, looking up to her face, waiting.

Clark looked at Ben. He gave her a light kiss on the cheek, and before he could move away again, she kissed him on the mouth, just for a moment.

"Well, at least I know where we could live," said Clark. "I have a house ... ."
"YAY!" yelled Lily. "I get the front bedroom!"

While you're waiting for Lily's next Pink Victorian adventure (coming soon), we invite you to enjoy Maggie Awake: A Starting Over Women's Fiction Story, Book 1 of the *Always Maggie Series*. On Amazon. Click the link or use this: **https://amzn.to/3yLOy11**.

WE SEND OUT NEWS, new releases, articles, posts, and other matter of interest. Use this link to join.

# Please Leave a Review

## Please Leave a Review

https://bookhip.com/GFSWWH

Readers: If you'd like to leave a review, Amazon and Goodreads have easy-to-use places for your thoughts.

Thank you! Peg

## About Author Peg Lewis

Peg Lewis, traveler, linguist, great grandmother, took advantage of the stay-home days of the COVID era to get going on her writing career. Better late than never. Having brought up 6 children, raised goats and ducks, lived in distant places (Switzerland, Spain, China, New Zealand) and driven to all 49 road-accessible states (and 2 of the islands of the State of Hawaii) and all 9 Canadian provinces plus Yukon Territory, with children and boxes of books and their musical instruments and pets, having organized and gone on book tour with her author/scientist husband John S. Lewis (and their children) to 22 campuses, having spent weeks on end camping in their travel trailer, visiting family or national parks, she is ready to get it on paper. Her women's fiction captures the complications and fulfillment of family and other relationships, the trade-offs of impulsivity and routine, the side-by-side challenges of joy and sorrow, and the elixir of clever problem-solving. She is the author of a dozen books that bring all these elements together in unexpected ways. You'll enjoy her rich characters and settings and the trouble and joy that result.

### Books by Peg Lewis

The House of Steele series of women's fiction, featuring life in the Pacific Northwest

- Legacy of the Pink Victorian
- Shadow of the Pink Victorian (2022)

The *Always Maggie* series of women's fiction, featuring life in the Pacific Northwest and Alaska

- *Maggie Awake: A Starting Over Women's Fiction Story* (Book 1 of *Always Maggie*)
- *Maggie Alone: A Small-Town Story of Old Love* (Book 2 of *Always Maggie*)
- *Maggie At Last* (Book 3 of *Always Maggie*)
- *Maggie At The Wheel* (Book 4 of *Always Maggie*) (2022)

The *Song Dog* series of New Adult and Women's fiction, featuring music camp in the mountains and desert

- *Rainforest Rhapsody*
- *A Rainy Night in G Minor*
- *A Moonlit Night on Six Strings*
- *The Song Dog Sings a Sad Song* (2022)
- plus a music camp extra, *Annie and the Music Camp Challenge*

Made in the USA
Middletown, DE
22 January 2022